A WHITE WOLF REDISCOVERY TRIO

# T H R E E   I N   S P A C E

THE VOYAGE OF THE SPACE BEAGLE
BY A. E. VAN VOGT

GALAXIES
BY BARRY N. MALZBERG

THE ENEMY STARS
BY POUL ANDERSON

FOREWORD BY ARTHUR C. CLARKE

JACK DANN, PAMELA SARGENT, GEORGE ZEBROWSKI SERIES EDITORS

WHITE WOLF PUBLISHING
735 PARK NORTH BOULEVARD, SUITE 128
CLARKSTON, GA 30021
WWW.WHITE-WOLF.COM

BOREALIS

WHITE WOLF PUBLISHING

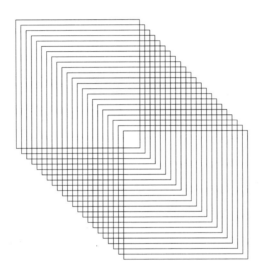

# CONTENTS

## ABOUT THIS SERIES:

The word "rediscovery" is almost a contradiction; you can only discover something once. But we all know what it means: people have forgotten and need to be reminded. Also, there are new readers, for whom discovery is still a possibility, even if the book was published a long time ago and forgotten. A book you haven't read is just as good as a new one published this year. The literature of science fiction has grown so incredibly rich and varied in this century that any group of reprints will inevitably fall short of what could be done to keep important works in print. White Wolf has undertaken to set this right, to the best of its resources. Future White Wolf Rediscovery Trios will feature other themes. If you have suggestions, please make your views known by writing to the editors, and by supporting the series.

JACK DANN

PAMELA SARGENT

GEORGE ZEBROWSKI

SERIES EDITORS

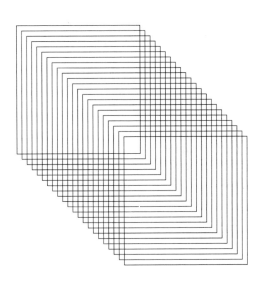

# FOREWORD

BY ARTHUR C. CLARKE

It has been said (I believe by Ted Sturgeon) that the Golden Age of Science Fiction is around 15. This locates me fairly accurately at the birth of *Astounding Stories*, and I have just been browsing through Mike Ashley's invaluable *The Complete Index to Astounding/Analog* to see what titles still ring a bell after more than sixty years.

A surprising number: how many, I wonder, of today's readers ever heard of Ray Cummings' "Beyond the Vanishing Point," "Phantoms of Reality," "Brigands of the Moon," and "Jetta of the Lowlands;" S.P. Meek's "Cold Light" and "Beyond the Heaviside Layer;" Charles W. Diffin's "The Power and the Glory" and "The Finding of Haldgren;" Arthur J. Burk's "Earth, the Marauder;" Murray Leinster's "The Fifth Dimension Catapult;" Paul Ernst's "World Behind the Moon" and "The Raid on the Termites;" Edmond Hamilton's "The Sargasso of Space;" Robert Wilson's "Out Round Rigel"...pardon me while I wipe away a manly tear and misquote Wordsworth: "Sweet in that dawn it was to be alive, But to be an S.F. fan was very heaven."

And though I have not looked at any of these tales for more than half a century, I am quite sure that many of them merit rereading—if only for historic interest, and as a reminder of the astonishing scientific progress we have been privileged to see in a single lifetime. "Beyond the Heaviside Layer"—I still recall a thrill that title once gave me! When I was a boy, such a locale seemed as remote and mysterious as Mars, or the other side of the Moon. Yet today, as I write these words, there are a dozen astronauts up there, probably complaining to NASA that the zero-gee toilet is giving problems once again.

I therefore welcome this new series, and the efforts of Jack Dann, Pamela Sargent and George Zebrowski to recover works that have been unjustly forgotten. I doubt if they comprise even 10% of the canon (Sturgeon again: "It's said that 90% of science fiction is crud—but then so is 90% of everything"). Well—would you believe 5% of noncrud?

The writers in these Trios have contributed disproportionately to that worthwhile 5%, and I am happy to see that most of them are still with us. And so, incredibly, is the writer whose 1930s tales epitomise the best of the era, and who is still going strong—Jack Williamson (born 1908). Perhaps today's retired Professor of English may be embarrassed if I remind him of his early works and of course much of their science is hopelessly dated—but across the decades I am still moved by the poignant ending of "The Moon

Era." It is indeed amazing how many ideas that are now tools of the trade originated with Jack—"terraforming" (he coined the very word), "ceetee" (contraterrene matter, created for the first time in late 1995 in the CERN Low Energy Antiproton Ring), parallel universes...and, perhaps most far-sighted of all, the danger that might be posed by benevolent robots whose prime directive was to serve Man. (Not, as in Damon Knight's little classic, broiled or fried.)

Yet, when one considers that several science fiction (not to mention fantasy) novels are published *every day*, can such excavations from the genre's Early Bronze Age be justified? I hope so: to quote from my sadly missed friend Isaac Asimov's Foreword to this series' precursor: "Naturally, the revival of these classics will benefit the publisher, the editors, and the writers, but almost by the way. The real beneficiaries will be the readers, among whom the older are likely to taste again delicacies they had all but forgotten, while the younger will encounter delights of whose existence they were unaware."

Hear, hear...


Arthur C. Clarke
Columbo, Sri Lanka
1996 January 14

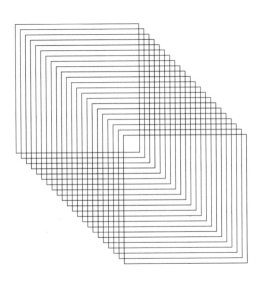

INTRODUCED BY GEORGE ZEBROWSKI

# THE VOYAGE OF THE SPACE BEAGLE

BY A. E. VAN VOGT

# INTRODUCTION

Space travel is the great archetypal theme of science fiction—and the one by which the general public identifies science fiction writing.

It is still sometimes referred to as "space stuff, huh?"

Some time ago it was "that *Buck Rogers* stuff."

I've often wondered why it wasn't called "that *Flash Gordon* stuff."

Today it's "that *Star Trek* stuff" or "that *Star Wars* stuff."

But long before the starship *Enterprise* went out on its five-years' missions (in 1966) to explore our galaxy, L. Sprague de Camp, A. E. van Vogt, Eric Frank Russell and others had sent out starships to see what there was interesting and dramatic to be found out in the galaxy. Edward E. Smith's *Skylark of Space* sent a starship beyond our solar system when we thought that our galaxy might be the whole universe, and the faint smudges of Andromeda and other galaxies were mere nebulae, not vast systems of stars among countless others. Smith's novel was written from 1915 to 1920, and serialized in 1928 in *Amazing Stories*, and it freed the imagination of science fiction writers from the confines of the solar system.

The *Star Trek* television series and motion pictures have as their pedigree the little recognized universe of print science fiction. Edward E. Smith, known as "Doc" by his generations of fans, has been called the "father of the Star Wars films." L. Sprague de Camp popularized the term "E. T." during the Forties. And *Close Encounters of the Third Kind* is a film that has all the look and feel of Chad Oliver's alien contact novels of the Fifties. One cannot help but smile at the film makers who so jealously guard their trademarks of terms and backgrounds, which they think are new with them, but which they have both knowingly and unknowingly picked up from written SF, second and third hand. The profit motive has a lot to answer for to the creative human heart and mind, which makes new things out of love and interest, and literally gives them away, since the balance of most writers' careers comes out having cost more than they earn.

To complete *Star Trek*'s pedigree one needs only to see the 1956 movie *Forbidden Planet*, which Gene Roddenberry himself publicly recognized as his immediate inspiration. To read about A. E. van Vogt's starship *Beagle* today is impossible without seeing *Star Trek* images in one's head. This particular novel is also the recognized inspiration for the film *Alien* and its sequels. But to truly appreciate van Vogt's starship and the work of this newly, belatedly celebrated Nebula Award Grand Master of science fiction, one must consider a few points of subtle history:

What is first forgotten about a writer's career is the order of events— the sequence in which the first impressions of his work were formed. Critical opinion sets up a toll booth, usually late in the game, and charges for the privilege of reading the writer, at least among those readers who can be intimidated. But it can do so only if you believe critics are needed and willingly put on their special glasses. Thus is destroyed the original experience of reading for yourself, of reading a writer for the first time without preconceptions—before one can say, "Who knew he was going to become so-and-so."

The one phenomenon that the tollkeepers of taste rarely discuss is the *experience* of reading a particular writer. It is not considered anything interesting in a critical theory. Most critical theories are make-work systems, set up by the untalented to give them a sense of participation with the talented. Reading and accepting the act as self-sufficient does not seem to be enough.

One wonders: What was the fourteen-year-old Jacques Derrida pleasuring his reading potential with that would make him develop deconstructionism in later years? Graham Greene and many others in their later years confessed to a great love of Robert Louis Stevenson and H. Rider Haggard. Vladimir Nabokov loved H. G. Wells, and even the great composer Gustav Mahler was seen slipping into cheap Viennese theaters to see popular operettas.

A memorable experience is uncritical, and it is a failure of critical theory that later repudiates the irreducible simple fact of the memorable experience. This is not to say that one day we may not have a truthful theory of literature. It is to say that human writings are multifarious and not easily caught in the net of theory. Something always escapes. Deconstructionism tells the truth about fiction, by insisting that fiction is a human construction, that it is by its very nature artifice and a prisoner of its social, political, and even biological origins; but so what? Telling the truth behind fiction is not enough. Something resists and escapes—and it is the need for narrative as a human explanation of why a character got to be himself; the need for the suspension of disbelief toward what is only superficially false, in favor of the profoundly meaningful. "The truth is no excuse," a writing teacher once said to a student who told him that every word of his story was true. "The truth in and of itself does not make for a good piece of fiction." The same may be said for the central "truth" of deconstructionist theories—that the most interesting and revealing element of fiction is the "lies," and that it is this artifice that deserves our attention rather than the suspension of disbelief. The "truth" of deconstructionist theories is no excuse. At best, it is of peripheral interest to the main effect.

In one of the other novels in this volume, Barry Malzberg, an admirer of van Vogt's work, seems to be writing a deconstruction of "believable science fiction." But reviewers noted that despite the author's protestations to the reader in the novel of how impossible it is to write "real science fiction," *Galaxies* nevertheless achieves a sense of reality about a time centuries from now that is overwhelming. Was Malzberg trying to write a post-modern SF novel that got away from him? Or was he satirizing deconstructionist post-modernism by demonstrating how traditional narrative fiction manages to resist and succeed in upholding the suspension of disbelief despite all obstacles? Malzberg artfully has it both ways.

Science fiction escapes all theories of literature. People with no knowledge of the field feel confident in passing judgment. And they might just as well be blindly groping an elephant as preparation for a textbook on zoology.

The work of A. E. van Vogt has happily resisted the theorists, because it is memorably vivid, suspenseful, filled with eye-opening imagery that exudes a steel-blue strangeness, at once in love with the stylized surfaces of technology but reminding us that barbarians are in control of the toys. His best works were the magazine stories of the 1940s, collected into book form in the Fifties and Sixties: *The Weapons Shop of Isher* (1951) and its sequel, *The Weapons Makers* (1952); *Empire of the Atom* (1957) and its sequel, *The Wizard of Linn* (1962). The well known *Slan* (1951) and the first two Null-A novels—*The World of Null-A* (1948) and *The Players of Null-A* (1956)—present dreamlike enjoyments and beauties to be found nowhere else. *The Mixed Men* (1952) is vividly beautiful. The novella "Recruiting Station," also known in book form as *Masters of Time* (1950) and *Earth's Last Fortress* (1960), will twist your mind with its hallucinatory images and ideas.

Yet until this last year, this author who helped make SF publishing in the 1950s a success was all but forgotten. His neglect may have begun with Damon Knight's critical analysis of *The World of Null-A* in the Fifties, which may have been literally correct but pointless, given van Vogt's literary goals. Van Vogt's influence can be clearly seen in Alfred Bester's first two novels, *The Demolished Man* (1953) and *The Stars My Destination* (1956); in the early works of Philip K. Dick, most notably in *Solar Lottery* (1955) and *The World Jones Made* (1956); in the works of Charles L. Harness, most clearly in *The Paradox Men* (1953); in Kurt Vonnegut's *The Sirens of Titan* (1959); and now that I can look back across two decades as a writer, in my own *The Omega Point Trilogy* (1983). Van Vogt's footprints march across many a writer's works. He is one of the last living masters of SF's Golden Age of the 1940s, yet he never won a Hugo award and no Nebula award. In 1996 he received the Grand Master Nebula Award, given by SFWA for a lifetime of achievement; and was a finalist for two Retrospective Hugo Awards in the novel and novelette categories; but most of his books are still nearly unavailable.

※

There is more rationality in van Vogt's work than his narrative technique of dream logic suggests. This is something of a heretical proposition today, even among van Vogt's fans; but it is not difficult to point to examples that support it. The one fact to remember about van Vogt's fiction is that the dream-logic technique is consciously applied, but it yields much more than reason knows. Some of this "yield" seems not to follow rationally, but it has the virtue of creating a space around the characters and events that leaves room for discovery, for the sense of the ambiguous and unknowable, a sea of truth greater than we can ever navigate or encompass. Nothing could be closer to the skeptical rationality of science, to the view that all we really do know are our models of reality, constructions made of language and mathematics.

*The Voyage of the Space Beagle* (1950) consists of four episodes that were gathered into book form after their magazine appearances in the 1940s. The starship *Beagle* (named after Darwin's ship of the same name), a very large, *extremely* fast starship, goes out to explore the galaxy, and even other galaxies. It is much, much faster than the *Enterprise*, a mobile community of explorers, as is the *Enterprise* of the second television series. In one episode of the novel there is even a discussion of extending the voyage by another five years, suggesting *Star Trek*'s "five-year missions." There is a form of timekeeping called "Star Time." And here is some dialogue with the chief engineer:

> His voice, when he responded to Morton, sounded aghast. He said, "I could sweep the ship...I won't go into details. But uncontrolled energization would kill every living thing aboard."
> "You could feed more energy to those walls, couldn't you, Mr. Pennons?"
> "No-o!" The ship's engineer sounded reluctant. "The walls couldn't stand it. They'd melt."

No one today can read this book and not think of *Star Trek* or the movie *Alien*.

There are a few background elements in van Vogt's book that merit some discussion. One is the science of Nexialism, as represented by Elliott

Grosvenor, the ship's only Nexialist. He is what I would call "the anti-specialist's specialist," whose work is what today is called "Integrative Studies." One cannot help but think of Jonathan Swift's flying island in *Gulliver's Travels*, where the specialists engage in what seems to be pointless experimentation. Elliott Grosvenor is determined to widen the vision and understanding of the *Beagle's* specialists, and it is his constant ability to "step back" from a problem and apply a variety of databases that saves the day. Nexialism is a wonderfully rational construction. Van Vogt links it to computer modelling and analysis, and this makes his book prophetic.

The other element that plays a supporting role in the novel is its theory of history, derived from Arnold Toynbee's *A Study of History*. Attempts are made by Grosvenor and others to "place" cultures on their curve of upswing and decline, including the culture that sent out the *Beagle*, and to try to predict their behavior—and that of the ship's social microcosm!

Both of these intellectual constructions provide a thoughtful, visionary counterpoint to the main action of the story—the confrontations with alien unknowns, all of which are spectacular and unforgettable.

I did not expect to enjoy rereading this book as much as I did; and I did not expect to have this much to say. The effects of received preconceptions strike deep. Which is to say that this book was for me a true "rediscovery"—and that will make it a discovery for new readers.

George Zebrowski
Delmar, NY
February 1997

# THE VOYAGE OF THE SPACE BEAGLE

BY A. E. VAN VOGT

TO FORD MCCORMACK

On and on Coeurl prowled. The black, moonless, almost starless night yielded reluctantly before a grim reddish dawn that crept up from his left. It was a vague light that gave no sense of approaching warmth. It slowly revealed a nightmare landscape.

Jagged black rock and a black, lifeless plain took form around him. A pale red sun peered above the grotesque horizon. Fingers of light probed among the shadows. And still there was no sign of the family of id creatures that he had been trailing now for nearly a hundred days.

He stopped finally, chilled by the reality. His great forelegs twitched with a shuddering movement that arched every razor-sharp claw. The thick tentacles that grew from his shoulders undulated tautly. He twisted his great cat head from side to side, while the hair like tendrils that formed each ear vibrated frantically, testing every vagrant breeze, every throb in the ether.

There was no response. He felt no swift tingling along his intricate nervous system. There was no suggestion anywhere of the presence of the id creatures, his only source of food on this desolate planet. Hopelessly, Coeurl crouched, an enormous catlike figure silhouetted against the dim, reddish skyline, like a distorted etching of a black tiger in a shadow world. What dismayed him was the fact that he had lost touch. He possessed sensory equipment that could normally detect organic id miles away. He recognized that he was no longer normal. His overnight failure to maintain contact indicated a physical breakdown. This was the deadly sickness he had heard about. Seven times in the past century he had found coeurls, too weak to move, their otherwise immortal bodies emaciated and doomed for lack of food. Eagerly, then, he had smashed their unresisting bodies, and taken what little id was still keeping them alive.

Coeurl shivered with excitement, remembering those meals. Then he snarled audibly, a defiant sound that quavered on the air, echoed and re-echoed among the rocks, and shuddered back along his nerves. It was an instinctive expression of his will to live.

And then, abruptly, he stiffened.

High above the distant horizon he saw a tiny glowing spot. It came nearer. It grew rapidly, enormously, into a metal ball. It became a vast, round ship. The great globe, shining like polished silver, hissed by above Coeurl, slowing visibly. It receded over a black line of hills to the right, hovered almost motionless for a second, then sank down out of sight.

Coeurl exploded from his startled immobility. With tigerish speed, he raced down among the rocks. His round, black eyes burned with agonized desire. His ear tendrils, despite their diminished powers, vibrated a message of id in such quantities that his body felt sick with the pangs of his hunger.

The distant sun, pinkish now, was high in the purple and black sky when he crept up behind a mass of rock and gazed from its shadows at the ruins of the city that sprawled below him. The silvery ship, in spite of its size, looked small against the great spread of the deserted, crumbling city. Yet about the ship was a leashed aliveness, a dynamic quiescence that, after a moment, made it stand out, dominating the foreground. It rested in a cradle made by its own weight in the rocky, resisting plain which began abruptly at the outskirts of the dead metropolis.

Coeurl gazed at the two-legged beings who had come from inside the ship. They stood in little groups near the bottom of an escalator that had been lowered from a brilliantly lighted opening a hundred feet above the ground. His throat thickened with the immediacy of his need. His brain grew dark with the impulse to charge out and smash these flimsy-looking creatures whose bodies emitted the id vibrations.

Mists of memory stopped that impulse when it was still only electricity surging through his muscles. It was a memory of the distant past of his own race, of machines that could destroy, of energies potent beyond all the powers of his own body. The remembrance poisoned the reservoirs of his strength. He had time to see that the beings wore something over their real bodies, a shimmering transparent material that glittered and flashed in the rays of the sun.

Cunning came, understanding of the presence of these creatures. This, Coeurl reasoned for the first time, was a scientific expedition from another star. Scientists would investigate, and not destroy. Scientists would refrain from killing him if he did not attack. Scientists in their way were fools.

Bold with his hunger, he emerged into the open. He saw the creatures become aware of him. They turned and stared. The three nearest him moved slowly back toward larger groups. One individual, the smallest of his group, detached a dull metal rod from a sheath at his side, and held it casually in one hand.

Coeurl was alarmed by the action, but he loped on. It was too late to turn back.

Elliott Grosvenor remained where he was, well in the rear, near the gangplank. He was becoming accustomed to being in the background. As the only Nexialist aboard the *Space Beagle*, he had been ignored for months by specialists who did not clearly understand what a Nexialist was, and who cared very little anyway. Grosvenor had plans to rectify that. So far, the opportunity to do so had not occurred.

The communicator in the headpiece of his space suit came abruptly to life. A man laughed softly, and then said, "Personally, I'm taking no chances with anything as large as that."

As the other spoke, Grosvenor recognized the voice of Gregory

Kent, head of the chemistry department. A small man physically, Kent had a big personality. He had numerous friends and supporters aboard the ship, and had already announced his candidacy for the directorship of the expedition in the forthcoming election. Of all the men facing the approaching monster, Kent was the only one who had drawn a weapon. He stood now, fingering the spindly metalite instrument.

Another voice sounded. The tone was deeper and more relaxed. Grosvenor recognized it as belonging to Hal Morton, Director of the expedition. Morton said, "That's one of the reasons why you're on this trip, Kent—because you leave very little to chance."

It was a friendly comment. It ignored the fact that Kent had already set himself up as Morton's opponent for the directorship. Of course, it could have been designed as a bit of incidental political virtuosity to put over to the more naïve listeners the notion that Morton felt no ill will towards his rival. Grosvenor did not doubt that the Director was capable of such subtlety. He had sized up Morton as a shrewd, reasonably honest, and very intelligent man, who handled most situations with automatic skill.

Grosvenor saw that Morton was moving forward, placing himself a little in advance of the others. His strong body bulked the transparent metalite suit. From that position, the Director watched the catlike beast approach them across the black rock plain. The comments of other departmental heads pattered through the communicator into Grosvenor's ears.

"I'd hate to meet that baby on a dark night in an alley."

"Don't be silly. This is obviously an intelligent creature. Probably a member of the ruling race."

"Its physical development," said a voice, which Grosvenor recognized as that of Siedel, the psychologist, "suggests an animal-like adaptation to its environment. On the other hand, its coming to us like this is not the act of an animal but of an intelligent being who is aware of our intelligence. You will notice how stiff its movements are. That denotes caution, and consciousness of our weapons. I'd like to get a good look at the end of those shoulder tentacles. If they taper into handlike appendages or suction cups, we could start assuming that it's a descendant of the inhabitants of this city." He paused, then finished, "It would be a great help if we could establish communication with it. Offhand, though, I'd say that it has degenerated into a primitive state."

Coeurl stopped when he was still ten feet from the nearest beings. The need for id threatened to overwhelm him. His brain drifted to that ferocious edge of chaos, where it cost him a terrible effort to hold back. He felt as if his body were bathed in molten liquid. His vision kept blurring.

Most of the men walked closer to him. Coeurl saw that they were frankly and curiously examining him. Their lips moved inside the transparent helmets they wore. Their form of intercommunication— he assumed that was what he sensed—came to him on a frequency that was well within his ability to receive. The messages were meaningless. In an effort to appear friendly, he broadcast his name from his ear tendrils, at the same time pointing at himself with one curving tentacle.

A voice Grosvenor didn't recognize drawled, "I got a sort of static in my radio when he wiggled those hairs, Morton. Do you think—"

"It's possible," the leader answered the unfinished question. "That means a job for you, Gourlay. If it speaks by means of radio waves, we might be able to create some sort of language code for him."

Morton's use of the man's name identified the other. Gourlay, chief of communications. Grosvenor, who was recording the conversation, was pleased. The coming of the beast might enable him to obtain recordings of the voices of all the rest of the important men aboard the ship. He had been trying to do that from the beginning.

"Ah," said Siedel, the psychologist, "the tentacles end in suction cups. Provided the nervous system is complex enough, he could with training operate any machine."

Director Morton said, "I think we'd better go inside and have lunch. Afterwards, we'll have to get busy. I'd like a study made of the scientific development of this race, and particularly I want to know what wrecked it. On Earth, in the early days before there was a galactic civilization, one culture after another reached its peak and then crumbled. A new one always sprang up in its dust. Why didn't that happen here? Each department will be assigned its special field of investigation."

"What about pussy?" somebody said. "I think he wants to come in with us."

Morton chuckled, then said seriously, "I wish there were some way we could take it in with us, without forcibly capturing it. Kent, what do you think?"

The little chemist shook his head decisively. "This atmosphere has a higher chlorine than oxygen content, though actually not much of either. Our oxygen would be dynamite to his lungs."

It was clear to Grosvenor that the catlike being had not considered that danger. He watched the monster follow the first two men up the escalator and through the great door.

The men glanced back towards Morton, who waved a hand at them and said, "Open the second lock and let him get a whiff of the oxygen. That'll cure him."

A moment later the Director's amazed voice was loud on the communicator. "Well, I'll be damned! He doesn't notice the difference! That means he hasn't any lungs, or else the chlorine is not what his lungs use. You bet he can go in! Smith, here's a treasure house for a biologist—harmless enough if we're careful. What a metabolism!"

Smith was a tall, thin, bony man with a long, mournful face. His voice, unusually forceful for his appearance, sounded in Grosvenor's communicator. "In the various exploring trips I've been on, I've seen only two higher forms of life. Those dependent on chlorine, and those who need oxygen—the two elements that support combustion. I've heard vague reports of a fluorine-breathing life form, but I've yet to see an example. I'd almost stake my reputation that no complicated organism could ever adapt itself to the actual utilization of both gases. Morton, we mustn't let this creature get away if we can help it."

Director Morton laughed, then said soberly, "He seems anxious enough to stay."

He had been riding up the escalator on one side of the gangplank. Now he moved into the air lock with Coeurl and the two men. Grosvenor hurried forward, but he was only one of a dozen men who also entered the large space. The great door swung shut, and air began to hiss in. Everybody stood well clear of the catlike monster. Grosvenor watched the beast with a growing sense of uneasiness.

Several thoughts occurred to him. He wished he could communicate them to Morton. He should have been able to. The rule aboard these expeditionary ships was that all heads of departments should have easy access to the director. As head of the Nexial department—though he was the only one in it—that should have applied to him also. The communicator of his space suit should have been fitted so that he could talk to Morton as did the heads of the other departments. But all he had was a general receiver. That gave him the privilege of listening in to the great men when they were doing field work. If he wanted to talk to anyone, or if he were in danger, he could throw a switch that would open a channel to a central operator.

Grosvenor did not question the general value of the system. There were just under one thousand men aboard, and it was obvious that all of them could not talk to Morton whenever they pleased.

The inner door of the lock was opening. Grosvenor pushed his way out with the others. In a few minutes they were all standing at the bottom of a series of elevators that led up to the living quarters. There was a brief discussion between Morton and Smith. Finally, Morton said, "We'll send him up alone if he'll go."

Coeurl offered no objection until he heard the door of the elevator clang shut behind him, and the closed cage shot upward. He whirled with a snarl. Instantly, his reason twisted into chaos. He pounced at the door. The metal bent under his plunge, and the desperate pain maddened him. Now he was all trapped animal. He smashed at the metal with his paws. He tore the tough welded panels loose with his thick tentacles. The machinery screeched in protest. There were jerks as the magnetic power pulled the cage along in spite of projecting pieces of metal scraping against the outside walls. Finally, the elevator reached its destination and stopped. Coeurl snatched off the rest of the door and hurtled into the corridor. He waited there until the men came up with drawn weapons.

Morton said, "We're fools. We should have shown him how it works. He thought we'd double-crossed him, or something."

He motioned to the monster. Grosvenor saw the savage glow fade from the beast's coal-black eyes as Morton opened and closed the door of a nearby elevator several times. It was Coeurl who ended the lesson. He trotted into a large room that led off from the corridor.

He lay down on the carpeted floor and fought down the electric tautness of his nerves and muscles. He was furious at the fright he had shown. It seemed to him that he had lost the advantage of appearing a mild and placid individual. His strength must have startled and dismayed them.

It meant greater danger in the task he must accomplish: to seize this ship. On the planet from which these beings had come, there would be unlimited id.

**2**

With unwinking eyes, Coeurl watched two men clear away loose rubble from the metal doorway of a huge, old building. The human beings had eaten lunch, had again donned their space units, and now he could see them, singly and in groups, wherever he looked. Coeurl assumed that they were still investigating the dead city.

His own interest was entirely in food. His body ached with the hunger of his cells for id. The craving put a quiver in his muscles, and his mind burned with the desire to be off after the men who had gone deeper into the city. One of them had gone alone.

During the lunch period, the human beings had offered him a variety of their own food, all valueless to him. They apparently did not realize that he must eat living creatures. Id was not merely a substance but a configuration of a substance, and it could be obtained only from tissues that still palpitated with the flow of life.

The minutes went by. And still Coeurl restrained himself. Still he lay there watching, aware that the men knew he watched. They floated a metal machine from the ship to the rock mass that blocked the great door of the building. His fierce stare noted all their movements. Even as he shivered with the intensity of his hunger, he saw how they operated the machinery, and how simple it was.

He knew what to expect finally when the flame ate incandescently at the hard rock. In spite of his preknowledge, he deliberately jumped and snarled as if in fear.

From a small patrol ship, Grosvenor observed the action. It was a role he had assigned himself, watching Coeurl. He had nothing else to do. No one seemed to feel the need of assistance from the one Nexialist aboard the *Space Beagle*.

As he watched, the door below Coeurl was cleared. Director Morton and another man came over together. They went inside, and disappeared from view. Presently their voices came through Grosvenor's communicator. The man with Morton spoke first.

"It's a shambles. There must have been a war. You can catch the drift of this machinery. It's secondary stuff. What I'd like to know is, how was it controlled and applied?"

Morton said, "I don't quite understand what you mean."

"Simple," said the other. "So far, I've seen nothing but tools. Almost every machine, whether it's a tool or a weapon, is equipped with a transformer for receiving energy, altering its form, and applying it. Where are the power plants? I hope their libraries will give us a clue. What could have happened to make a civilization crash like this?"

Another voice broke through the communicators. "This is Siedel. I heard your question, Mr. Pennons. There are at least two reasons why a territory becomes uninhabited. One is lack of food. The other is war."

Grosvenor was glad that Siedel had used the other's name. It was another voice identified for his collection. Pennons was chief ship's engineer.

Pennons said, "Look, my psychological friend, their science should have enabled them to solve their food problem, for a small population at least. And, failing that, why didn't they develop space travel and go elsewhere for their food?"

"Ask Gunlie Lester." It was Director Morton. "I heard him expounding a theory before we landed."

The astronomer answered the first call. "I've still got to verify all my facts. But one of them, you'll agree, is significant by itself. This desolate world is the only planet revolving around that miserable sun.

There's nothing else. No moon. Not even a planetoid. And the nearest star system is nine hundred light-years away. So tremendous would have been the problem of the ruling race of this world that in one jump they would have had to solve not only interplanetary but interstellar space flight. Consider for comparison how slow our own development was. First, we reached the moon. The planets followed. Each success led to the next, and after many years the first long journey was made to a nearby star. Last of all, man invented the anti-accelerator drive which permitted galactic travel. With all this in mind, I maintain it would be impossible for any race to create an interstellar drive without previous experience."

Other comments were made, but Grosvenor did not listen. He had glanced towards where he had last seen the big cat. It was not in sight. He cursed under his breath for having let himself be distracted. Grosvenor swung his small craft over the whole area in a hasty search. But there was too much confusion, too much rubble, too many buildings. Everywhere he looked there were obstacles to his vision. He landed and questioned several hardworking technicians. Most recalled having seen the cat "about twenty minutes ago." Dissatisfied, Grosvenor climbed back into his lifeboat and flew out over the city.

A short while before, Coeurl had moved swiftly, seeking concealment wherever he found it. From group to group he sped, a nervous dynamo of energy, jumpy and sick from his hunger. A little car rolled up, stopped in front of him, and a formidable camera whirred as it took a picture of him. Over on a mound of rock, a gigantic drilling machine was just going into operation. Coeurl's mind became a blur of images of things he watched with half-attention. His body ached to be off after the man who had gone alone into the city.

Suddenly, he could stand it no longer. A green foam misted his mouth. For the moment, it seemed, no one was looking at him. He darted behind a rocky embankment and began to run in earnest. He floated along with great, gliding leaps. Everything but his purpose was forgotten, as if his brain had been wiped clean by some magic, memory-erasing brush. He followed deserted streets, taking short cuts through gaping holes in time-weakened walls and through long corridors of moldering buildings. Then he slowed to a crouching lope as his ear tendrils caught the id vibrations.

Finally, he stopped and peered from a scatter of fallen rock. A two-legged being was standing at what must once have been a window, directing the beams of his flashlight into the gloomy interior. The flashlight clicked off. The man, a heavy-set, powerful individual, walked off swiftly, turning his head alertly this way and that. Coeurl didn't like that alertness. It meant lightning reaction to danger. It presaged trouble.

Coeurl waited until the human being had disappeared around a corner, then he padded into the open, faster than a man could walk. His plan was clearly made. Like a wraith he slipped down a side street and past a long block of buildings. He turned the first corner at great speed, leaped across an open space, and then, with dragging belly, crept into the half-darkness between the building and a huge chunk of debris. The street ahead was a channel between two unbroken hills of loose rubble. It ended in a narrow bottleneck, which had its outlet just below Coeurl.

In the final moment he must have been too eager. As the human being started to pass by below, Coeurl was startled by a tiny shower of rocks that streamed down from where he crouched. The man looked up with a jerk of his head. His face changed, twisted, distorted. He snatched at his weapon.

Coeurl reached out and struck a single crushing blow at the shimmering, transparent headpiece of the space suit. There was a sound of tearing metal and a gushing of blood. The man doubled up as if part of him had been telescoped. For a moment his bones and legs and muscles combined almost miraculously to keep him standing. Then he crumpled with a metallic jangling of his space armor.

In a convulsive movement, Coeurl leaped down upon his victim. He was already generating a field that prevented the id from being released into the blood. Swiftly, he smashed the metal and the body within it. Bones cracked. Flesh spattered. He plunged his mouth into the warm body and let the lacework of tiny suction cups strain the id out of the cells. He had been at this ecstatic task about three minutes when a shadow clicked across his eyes. He looked up with a start, and saw that a small ship was approaching from the direction of the lowering sun. For one instant, Coeurl froze, then he glided into the shelter of a great pile of debris.

When he looked again, the small vessel was floating lazily off to the left. But it was already circling, and he saw that it might come back toward him. Almost maddened by the interruption of his feeding, Coeurl nevertheless deserted his kill and headed back towards the space ship. He ran like an animal fleeing danger, and slowed only when he saw the first group of workers. Cautiously, he approached them. They were all busy, and so he was able to slip up near them.

In his search for Coeurl, Grosvenor grew progressively dissatisfied. The city was too large. There were more ruins, more places of concealment than he had first thought. He headed back finally to the big ship. And he was considerably relieved when he found the beast comfortably sprawled on a rock sunning himself. Carefully, Grosvenor stopped his ship at a vantage height behind the animal. He was still there twenty minutes later when the chilling announcement came over the communicator that a group of men who were exploring the city had stumbled over the smashed body of Dr. Jarvey of the chemistry department.

Grosvenor took down the directions given, and then headed for the scene of the death. Almost immediately, he discovered that Morton was not coming to look at the body. He heard the Director's solemn voice on the communicator. "Bring the remains to the ship."

Jarvey's friends were present, looking sober and tense in their space suits. Grosvenor stared down at the horror of tattered flesh and blood-sprayed metal and felt a tightening in his throat. He heard Kent say, "He would go alone, damn him!"

The chief chemist's voice was husky. Grosvenor recalled having heard that Kent and his principal assistant, Jarvey, were very good friends. Somebody else must have spoken on the private band of the chemistry department, for Kent said, "Yes, we'll have to have an autopsy." The words reminded Grosvenor that he would miss most of what was going on unless he could tune in. Hastily, he touched the man nearest him and said, "Mind if I listen in to the chemistry band through you?"

"Go ahead."

Grosvenor kept his fingers lightly on the other's arm. He heard a man say in a shuddering tone, "The worst part of it is, it looks like a senseless murder. His body is spread out like so much jelly, but it seems to be all there."

Smith, the biologist, broke in on the general wave. His long face looked gloomier than ever. "The killer attacked Jarvey, possibly with the intention of eating him, and then discovered that his flesh was alien and inedible. Just like our big cat. Wouldn't eat anything set before him—" His voice trailed into thoughtful silence. He went on finally, slowly, "Say, what about that creature? He's big enough and strong enough to have done this with his own little paws."

Director Morton, who must have been listening, interrupted. "That's a thought that has probably already occurred to a lot of us. After all, he's the only living thing we've seen. But, naturally, we can't execute him just on suspicion."

"Besides," said one of the men, "he was never out of my sight."

Before Grosvenor could speak, the voice of Siedel, the psychologist, came over the general wave, "Morton, I've been talking by touch to a number of the men, and I get the following reaction: Their first feeling is that the beast was never out of their sight. And yet, when pinned down, they admit that maybe he was for a few minutes. I, also, had the impression that he was always around. But, thinking back over it, I find gaps. There were moments, probably long minutes, when he was completely out of sight."

Grosvenor sighed, and deliberately remained silent now. His point had been made by somebody else.

It was Kent who broke the silence. He said in a fierce voice, "I say, take no chances. Kill the brute on suspicion before he does any more damage."

Morton said, "Korita, are you around?"

"Right here at the body, Director."

"Korita, you've been wandering around with Cranessy and Van Horne. Do you think pussy is a descendant of the dominant race of this planet?"

Grosvenor located the archeologist standing slightly behind Smith and partly surrounded by colleagues from his department.

The tall Japanese said slowly, almost respectfully, "Director Morton, there is a mystery here. Take a look, all of you, at that majestic skyline. Notice the architectural outline. In spite of the megalopolis which they created, these people were close to the soil. The buildings are not merely ornamented. They are ornamental in themselves. Here is the equivalent of the Doric column, the Egyptian pyramid, and the Gothic cathedral, growing out of the ground, earnest, big with destiny. If this lonely, desolate world can be regarded as a mother earth, then the land had a warm, a spiritual place in the hearts of the inhabitants. The effect is emphasized by the winding streets. Their machines prove they were mathematicians, but they were artists first. And so they did not create the geometrically designed cities of the ultra-sophisticated world metropolis. There is a genuine artistic abandon, a deep, joyous emotion written in the curving and unmathematical arrangements of houses, buildings, and avenues; a sense of intensity, of divine belief in an inner certainty. This is not a decadent, hoary-with-age civilization but a young and vigorous culture, confident, strong with purpose. There it ended. Abruptly, as if at this point the culture had its Battle of Tours and began to collapse like the ancient Mohammedan civilization. Or as if in one leap it spanned centuries of adjustment and entered the period of contending states.

"However, there is no record of a culture anywhere in the universe making such an abrupt jump. It is always a slow development. And the first step is a merciless questioning of all that was once held sacred. Inner certainties cease to exist. Previously unquestioned convictions dissolve before the ruthless probings of scientific and analytical minds. The skeptic becomes the highest type of human being. I say that this culture ended suddenly in its most flourishing age. The sociological effects of such a catastrophe would be an end of morality, a reversion to bestial criminality unleavened by a sense of ideal. There would be a callous indifference to death. If this—if pussy is a descendant of such a race, then he will be a cunning creature, a thief in the night, a cold-blooded murderer who would cut his own brother's throat for gain."

"That's enough!" It was Kent, his voice curt. "Director, I'm willing to act as executioner."

Smith interrupted sharply. "I object. Listen, Morton, you're not going to kill that cat yet, even if he is guilty. He's a biological treasure house."

Kent and Smith were glaring angrily at each other. Smith said slowly, "My dear Kent, I appreciate the fact that in the chemistry department they would like to put pussy into retorts and make chemical compounds out of his blood and his flesh. But I regret to inform you that you're getting ahead of yourself. In the biology department we want the living body, not the dead one. I have a feeling the physics department would like to have a look at him, also, while he's still alive. So I'm afraid you're last on the list. Adjust yourself to that thought, please. You may see him a year from now, certainly not sooner."

Kent said thickly, "I'm not looking at this from the scientific point of view."

"You should be, now that Jarvey is dead and nothing can be done for him."

"I'm a human being before I'm a scientist," Kent said in a harsh voice.

"You would destroy a valuable specimen for emotional reasons?"

"I would destroy this creature because he is an unknown danger. We cannot take the risk of having another human being killed."

It was Morton who interrupted the argument. He said thoughtfully, "Korita, I'm inclined to accept your theory as a working basis. But one question. Is it possible that his culture is a later one on this planet than ours is in the galactic-wide system we have colonized?"

"It is definitely possible," said Korita. "His could be the middle of the tenth civilization of his world; while ours, as far as we've been able to discover, is the end of the eighth sprung from Earth. Each of his ten will, of course, have been builded on the ruins of the one before it."

"In that case, pussy would not know anything about the skepticism that made us suspect him as a criminal and a murderer?"

"No, it would be literally magic to him."

Morton's grim laugh sounded on the communicator. He said, "You get your wish, Smith. We'll let pussy live. And if there are any fatalities, now that we know him, it will be due to carelessness. There's a possibility, of course, that we're wrong. Like Siedel, I also have the impression that the creature was always around. We may be doing him an injustice. There may be other dangerous creatures on this planet." He broke off. "Kent, what are your plans for Jarvey's body?"

The chief chemist said in a bitter voice, "There'll be no immediate funeral. The damned cat wanted something from the body. It looks to be all there, but something must be missing. I'm going to find out what, and pin this murder on that beast, so you'll have to believe it beyond the shadow of a doubt."

Back on the ship, Elliott Grosvenor headed for his own department. The sign on the door read, "SCIENCE OF NEXIALISM." Beyond it were five rooms measuring altogether forty by eighty feet of floor space. Most of the machines and instruments that the Nexial Foundation had asked the government for had been installed. As a result, space was rather cramped. Once through the outer door, he was alone in his private preserve.

Grosvenor seated himself at his work desk and started his brief to Director Morton. He analyzed the possible physical structure of the catlike inhabitant of this cold and desolate planet. He pointed out that so virile a monster should not be regarded merely as a "biological treasure house." The phrase was dangerous in that it might make people forget that the beast would have its own drives and needs based on a nonhuman metabolism. "We have enough evidence now," he dictated into the recorder, "to make what we Nexialists call a Statement of Direction."

It took him several hours to complete the Statement. He carried the wire to the stenography section and put in a requisition for an immediate transcription. As head of a department, he got prompt service. Two hours later, he delivered the brief to Morton's office. An undersecretary gave him a receipt for it. Grosvenor ate a late dinner in the commissary, convinced that he had done what was possible to him. Afterwards, he inquired of the waiter where the cat was. The waiter wasn't sure, but he believed the beast was up in the general library.

For an hour, Grosvenor sat in the library watching Coeurl. During that time, the creature lay stretched out on the thick carpet, never once moving his position. At the end of the hour, one of the doors swung open, and two men came in carrying a large bowl. Following close behind them was Kent. The chemist's eyes were feverish. He paused in the middle of the room, and said in a weary yet harsh voice, "I want you all to watch this!"

Though his words included everyone in the room, he actually faced a group of top scientists who sat in a special reserved section. Grosvenor stood up and had a look at what was in the bowl carried by the two men. It contained a brownish concoction.

Smith, the biologist, also climbed to his feet. "Wait a minute, Kent. Any other time I wouldn't question your actions. But you look ill. You're overwrought. Have you got Morton's permission for this experiment?"

Kent turned slowly. And Grosvenor, who had seated himself again, saw that Smith's words had conveyed only a part of the picture. There were dark circles under the chief chemist's eyes. And his cheeks seemed sunken. He said, "I invited him to come up here. He refused to participate. His attitude is that if this being does willingly what I want, no harm will be done."

Smith said, "What have you got there? What's in that bowl?"

"I've identified the missing element," Kent said. "It's potassium. There was only about two-thirds or three-quarters of the normal amount of potassium left in Jarvey's body. You know how potassium is held by the body cells in connection with a large protein molecule, the combination providing the basis for the electrical charge of the cell. It's fundamental to life. Usually, after death the cells release their potassium into the bloodstream, making it poisonous. I proved that some potassium is missing from Jarvey's cells but that it did not go into the blood. I'm not sure of the full significance of that, but I intend to find out."

"What about the bowl of food?" somebody interrupted. Men were putting away magazines and books, looking up with interest.

"It's got living cells with potassium in suspension. We can do that artificially, you know. Maybe that's why he rejected our food at lunch time. The potassium was not in a usable form for him. My idea is he'll get the scent, or whatever he uses instead of scent—"

"I think he gets the vibrations of things," Gourlay interjected with a drawl. "Sometimes when he wiggles those tendrils, my instruments register a distinct and very powerful wave of static. And then, again, there's no reaction. My guess is he moves on to a point higher or lower on the wave scale. He seems to control the vibrations at will. I'm assuming the actual motion of the tendrils does not in itself generate these frequencies."

Kent waited with obvious impatience for Gourlay to finish, then he went on. "All right, so it's vibrations that he senses. We can decide what his reaction to this vibration proves when he starts reacting." He concluded in a mollifying tone, "What do you think, Smith?"

"There are three things wrong with your plan," the biologist replied. "In the first place, you seem to assume that he is only animal. You seem to have forgotten he may be surfeited after having fed on Jarvey—if he did. And you seem to think he will not be suspicious. But have the bowl set down. His reaction may tell us something."

Kent's experiment was reasonably valid, despite the emotion behind it. The creature had already shown that he could respond violently when suddenly stimulated. His reaction to being locked up in the elevator could not be dismissed as unimportant. So Grosvenor analyzed.

Coeurl stared with unblinking black eyes as the two men set the bowl before him. They retreated quickly, and Kent stepped forward. Coeurl recognized him as the one who had held the weapon that morning. He watched the two-legged being for a moment, then gave his attention to the bowl. His ear tendrils identified the thrilling emanation of id from the contents. It was faint, so faint as to have been unnoticeable until he concentrated on it. And it was held in suspension in a manner that was almost useless to him. But the vibration was strong enough to point at the reason for this incident. With a snarl, Coeurl rose to his feet. He caught the bowl with the suction cups at the end of one looping tentacle, and emptied its contents into the face of Kent, who shrank back with a yell.

Explosively, Coeurl flung the bowl aside and snapped a hawser-thick tentacle around the cursing man's waist. He didn't bother with the gun that hung from Kent's belt. It was only a vibration gun, he sensed—atomic powered, but not an atomic disintegrator. He tossed the squirming Kent into a corner, and then realized with a hiss of dismay that he should have disarmed the man. Now he would have to reveal his defensive powers.

Kent furiously wiped the gruel from his face with one hand, and with his other hand reached for his weapon. The muzzle snapped up, and the white beam of the tracer light flashed at Coeurl's massive head. Ear tendrils hummed as they automatically canceled out the energy. Round, black eyes narrowed as he caught the movement of men reaching for their vibrators.

From near the door, Grosvenor said sharply, "Stop! We'll all regret it if we act hysterically."

Kent clicked off his weapon and half turned to send a puzzled glance at Grosvenor. Coeurl crouched down, glowering at this man who had forced him to reveal his ability to control energies outside his body. There was nothing to do now but wait alertly for repercussions.

Kent looked again at Grosvenor. This time his eyes narrowed. "What the hell do you mean by giving orders?"

Grosvenor made no reply. His part of the incident was finished. He had recognized an emotional crisis, and he had spoken the necessary words in the right tone of peremptory command. The fact that those who had obeyed him now questioned his authority to give the command was unimportant. The crisis was over.

What he had done had no relation to the guilt or innocence of Coeurl. Whatever the eventual result of his interference, any decision made about the creature must be made by the recognized authorities, not by one man.

"Kent," said Siedel coldly, "I don't believe you actually lost control of yourself there. You deliberately tried to kill pussy, knowing that the Director has ordered him kept alive. I have a good mind to report you, and to insist that you suffer the penalties. You know what they are. Loss of authority in your department, ineligibility for any of the dozen elective offices."

There was a stirring and a murmur in a group of men whom Grosvenor recognized as Kent supporters. One of them said, "No, no, don't be foolish, Siedel." Another was more cynical. "Don't forget there are witnesses for Kent as well as against him."

Kent stared grimly at the circle of faces. "Korita was right when he said ours was a highly civilized age. It's positively decadent." He went on passionately. "My God, isn't there a man here who can see the horror of the situation? Jarvey dead only a few hours, and this creature, whom we all know to be guilty, lying here unchained, planning his next murder. And the victim is probably here in this room. What kind of men are we? Are we fools, cynics, or ghouls? Or is it that our civilization is so steeped in reason that we can contemplate even a murderer sympathetically?" He fixed his brooding eyes on Coeurl. "Morton was right. That's no animal. That's a devil from the deepest hell of this forgotten planet."

"Don't go melodramatic on us," Siedel said. "Your analysis is psychologically unstable. We're not ghouls or cynics. We're simply scientists, and pussy here is going to be studied. Now that we suspect him, we doubt his ability to corner any of us. One against a thousand hasn't a chance." He glanced around. "Since Morton isn't here, I'll put this to a vote here and now. Do I speak for all of us?"

"Not for me, Siedel." It was Smith who spoke. As the psychologist stared in astonishment, Smith continued. "In the excitement and momentary confusion, no one seems to have noticed that when Kent fired his vibration gun, the beam hit this creature squarely on his cat head, and didn't hurt him!"

Siedel's amazed glance went from Smith to Coeurl, and back again to Smith. "Are you certain it hit him? As you say, it all happened so swiftly—when pussy wasn't hurt I simply assumed that Kent had missed him."

"I was pretty sure it hit him in the face," Smith said. "A vibration gun, of course, can't even kill a man quickly, but it can injure him. Pussy is showing no sign of injury; he's not even trembling. I don't say that's conclusive, but in view of our doubts—"

Siedel was briefly distracted. "Perhaps his skin is a good insulation against heat and energy."

"Perhaps. But in view of our uncertainty, I think Morton should be requested to order him locked in a cage."

While Siedel frowned doubtfully, Kent spoke up. "Now you're talking sense, Smith."

Siedel said swiftly, "Then you would be satisfied, Kent, if we put him in the cage?"

Kent considered, then said reluctantly, "Yes. If four inches of micro-steel can't hold him, we'd better give him the ship."

Grosvenor, who had remained in the background, said nothing. He had discussed the problems of imprisoning Coeurl in his brief to Morton, and found the cage inadequate, principally because of its lock mechanism.

Siedel walked to a wall communicator, talked in a low voice to someone, and then returned. "The Director says if we can get him into the cage without violence, it's fine with him. Otherwise, just lock him up in any room that he's in. What do you think?"

"The cage!" A score of voices spoke in unison.

Grosvenor waited for a moment of silence, then said, "Put him outside for the night. He'll stay around."

Most of the men ignored him. Kent glanced at him and said sourly, "You don't seem to be able to make up your mind, do you? One moment you save his life, the next you recognize him as dangerous."

"He saved his own life," said Grosvenor shortly.

Kent turned away, shrugging. "We'll put him in the cage. That's where a murderer ought to be."

Siedel said, "Now that we've made up our minds, how are we going to do this?"

Grosvenor said, "You definitely want him in the cage?" He didn't expect an answer to that, and he didn't get one. He walked forward and touched the end of the nearest of Coeurl's tentacles.

It shrank away from him slightly, but Grosvenor was determined. He grasped the tentacle again firmly, and indicated the door. The animal hesitated a moment longer, and then started silently across the room.

Grosvenor called, "There's got to be exact timing here. Get set!"

A minute later Coeurl trotted docilely after Grosvenor through another door. He found himself in a square metal room, with a second door on the opposite wall. The man went through that. As Coeurl started to follow, the door slid shut in his face. Simultaneously, there was a metallic clang behind him. He whirled, and saw that the first door was shut also. He felt the flow of power as an electric lock clicked into place. His lips parted in a grimace of hate as he realized the intent of the trap, but he gave no other outward indication. He was aware of the difference between his earlier reaction to a small enclosure and his present one. For hundreds of years he had been intent on food, and food only. Now a thousand memories of the past were reawakening in his brain. There were powers in his body that he had long since ceased using. In remembering them, his mind automatically fitted their possibilities to his present situation.

He sat back presently on the thick, lithe haunches into which his body tapered. With his ear tendrils he examined the energy content of his surroundings. Finally he lay down, his eyes glowing with contempt. The fools!

It was about an hour later when he heard the man—Smith— fumbling with some mechanism on top of the cage. Coeurl leaped to his feet, startled. His first feeling was that he had misjudged these men, and that he was to be killed out of hand. He had counted on being given time, and on being able to do what he planned.

The danger confused him. And when he suddenly sensed radiation far below the level of visibility, he stimulated his entire nervous system against possible peril. Several seconds went by before he realized what was happening. Somebody was taking pictures of the inside of his body.

After a while, the man went away. For a time, then, there were noises of men doing things far away. These died away gradually. Coeurl was patient as he waited for the silence to envelop the ship. In the long ago, before they had achieved relative immortality, coeurls also had slept at night. Watching some of the men dozing in the library, he had remembered the habit.

There was one sound that did not fade away. Long after the great ship was generally silent, he could hear the two pairs of feet. They paced rhythmically past his cell, receded to some remote distance, and then came back. The trouble was, the guards were not together. First one pair of footsteps walked past. Then, about thirty feet behind, came the second pair.

Coeurl let them come by several times. Each time he estimated how long it took them. Finally, he was satisfied. Once again he waited for them to make their round. This time, the moment they were past, he switched his senses from concentration on human-made vibrations to a vastly higher range. The pulsating violence of the atomic pile in the engine room stammered its soft story to his nervous system. The electric dynamos hummed their muffled song of pure power. He felt the whisper of that flow through the wires in the walls of his cage, and through the electric lock of his door. He forced his quivering body into straining immobility, while he tried to tune in on that sibilant tempest of energy. Abruptly, his ear tendrils vibrated in harmony.

There was a sharp click of metal on metal. With a gentle touch of one tentacle, Coeurl pushed open the door. Then he was out in the corridor. For a moment he felt a return of contempt, a glow of superiority, as he thought of the stupid creatures who dared to match their wits against a coeurl. And in that moment he suddenly remembered that there were a few other coeurls on this planet. It was a strange and unexpected thought. For he had hated them and had fought them ruthlessly. Now he saw that vanishing small group as his kind. If they were given a chance to multiply, no one—least of all these men—would be able to stand against them.

Thinking of that possibility, he felt weighted down by his limitations, his need for other coeurls, his aloneness—one against a thousand, with the galaxy at stake. The starry universe itself beckoned his rapacious, vaulting ambition. If he failed, there would never be a second chance. In a foodless world he could not hope to solve the secret of space travel. Even the builders had not freed themselves from their planet.

He padded along through a large salon and into the adjoining corridor. There he came to the first bedroom door. It was electrically locked, but he opened it noiselessly. He pounced inside and smashed the throat of the sleeping man in the bed. The lifeless head rolled crazily. The body twitched once. The id emanations from it almost overwhelmed him, but he forced himself to go on.

Seven bedrooms; seven dead men. Then, silently, he returned to the cage and locked the door behind him. His timing was beautifully precise. Presently, the guards came along, peered through the audioscope, and went on their way. Coeurl emerged for his second foray, and within minutes had invaded four more bedrooms. Then he came to a dormitory with twenty-four men sleeping in it. He had been killing swiftly, aware of the exact moment when he must again return to the cage. The opportunity to destroy a whole roomful of men confused him. For more than a thousand years he had slain all the living forms he could capture. Even in the beginning, that had yielded him no more than one id creature a week. And so he had never felt the necessity for restraint. He went through that room like the great cat he was, silent but deadly, and emerged from the sensuous joy of the kill only when every man in the dormitory was dead.

Instantly, he realized he had overstayed his time. The tremendousness of the blunder made him cringe. For he had planned a night of murder, each wave of deaths timed exactly so that he would be able to return to his prison and be there when the guards glanced in at him, as they had done on every round. That hope of seizing this monster ship during one sleep period was now jeopardized.

Coeurl caught at the vanishing remnants of his reason. Frantically, careless now of accidental sounds, he raced through the salon. He came out into the cage corridor, tense, half expecting to be met by energy blasts too powerful for him to handle.

The two guards were together, standing side by side. It was obvious that they had just discovered the open door. They looked up simultaneously, briefly paralyzed by the nightmare of claws and tentacles, the ferocious cat head and hate-filled eyes. Far too late, one of the men reached for his blaster. But the other was physically frozen by the doom he could not avoid. He uttered a shriek, a shrill cry of horror. The eerie sound floated along the corridors, activating sensitive wall communicators, awakening a shipload of men. The sound ended in a frightful gurgle as Coeurl flung the two corpses with one irresistible motion the full length of that long corridor. He didn't want the dead bodies found near the cage. That was his one hope.

Shaken to the depths, conscious of his terrible mistake, unable to think coherently, he plunged into the prison. The door clicked softly shut behind him. Power flowed once more through the electric lock. He crouched down on the floor, simulating sleep, as he heard the rush of many feet and caught the sound of excited voices. He knew when someone actuated the cage audioscope and looked in at him. The crisis would come when the other bodies were discovered.

Slowly, he stiffened himself for the greatest struggle of his life.

4

"Siever gone!" Grosvenor heard Morton say. The Director's voice sounded numb. "What are we going to do without Siever? And Breckenridge! And Coulter and—horrible!"

The corridor was packed with men. Grosvenor, who had come some distance, stood at the tail end of one overflow. Twice he tried to jostle through, but he was effectively jostled back by men who did not even glance around to identify him. They blocked his passage impersonally. Grosvenor gave up the futile effort, and realized that Morton was about to speak again. The Director looked out grimly over the throng. His heavy chin seemed more prominent than usual. He said, "If anybody's got so much as a germ of an idea, bring it out!"

"Space madness!"

The suggestion irritated Grosvenor. It was a meaningless phrase, still current after all these years of space travel. The fact that men had gone insane in space from loneliness, fear, and tension did not make a special sickness of it. There were certain emotional dangers on a long voyage like this—they were among the reasons why he had been put aboard—but insanity from loneliness was not likely to be one of them.

Morton was hesitating. It seemed clear that he also regarded the remark as valueless. But it was not a moment to argue subtle points. These men were tense and afraid. They wanted action and reassurance and the feeling that adequate countermeasures were being taken. At such moments, directors of expeditions, commanders-in-chief, and others in authority had been known to lose permanently the confidence of their followers. It seemed to Grosvenor that those possibilities were in Morton's mind when he spoke again, so careful were his words.

The Director said, "We've thought of that. Dr. Eggert and his assistants will examine everybody, of course. Right now, he's looking at the bodies."

A thunderous baritone bellowed almost in Grosvenor's ear. "Here I am, Morton. Tell these people to make way for me!"

Grosvenor turned and recognized Dr. Eggert. Men were already crowding aside for him. Eggert plunged forward. Without hesitation, Grosvenor pushed after him. As he had expected, each individual took it for granted that he was with the doctor. As they came up near Morton, Dr. Eggert said, "I heard you, Director, and I can tell you right now the space-madness theory won't fit. The throats of these men were smashed by something with the strength of ten human beings. The victims never had a chance to cry out."

Eggert paused, then asked slowly, "What about our big cat, Morton?"

The Director shook his head. "Pussy is in his cage, Doctor, pacing back and forth. I'd like to ask the opinion of the experts on him. Can we suspect him? That cage was built to hold beasts four or five times as large as he is. It seems hard to believe that he can be guilty, unless there's a new science here, beyond anything we can imagine."

Smith said grimly, "Morton, we have all the evidence we need. I hate to say this; you know that I'd rather keep the cat alive. But I used the telefluor camera on him, and tried to take some pictures. They were all blanks. Remember what Gourlay said. This creature can apparently receive and send vibrations of any wave length. The way he dominated the power of Kent's gun is adequate proof for us—after what has happened—that he has a special ability to interfere with energy."

A man groaned. "What in the name of all the hells have we got here? Why, if he can control that energy and send it out on any wave length, there's nothing to stop him killing all of us."

"Which proves," said Morton, "that he isn't invincible, or he would have done it long ago."

In a deliberate fashion, he walked over to the mechanism that controlled the cage.

"You're not going to open the door!" Kent gasped, and reached for his blaster.

"No, but if I pull this switch, electricity will flow through the floor and electrocute whatever is inside. We had that built into all our specimen cages as a precaution."

He unlocked the special electrocution switch and jerked the switch itself hard over. For a moment the power was full on. Then blue fire flashed from the metal, and a bank of fuses above Morton's head went black. Morton reached up, took one of them out of its socket, and frowned down at it.

"That's funny," he said. "Those fuses shouldn't have blown!" He shook his head. "Well, we can't even look inside the cage now. That wrecked the audio, also."

Smith said, "If he could interfere with the electric lock enough to open the door, then he very likely probed every possible danger and was ready to interfere when you threw the switch."

"At least it proves he's vulnerable to our energies," Morton said grimly. "Because he had to render them harmless. The important thing is, we've got him behind four inches of the toughest of metals. At the worst, we can open the door and turn a semiportable blaster on him. But, first, I think we'll try to feed electricity in there through the telefluor power cable."

A sound from inside the cage interrupted his words. A heavy body crashed against a wall. That was followed by a sustained thudding, as if many small objects were collapsing to the floor. Grosvenor mentally compared it to a small landslide.

"He knows what we're trying to do," Smith said to Morton. "And I'll bet it's a very sick pussy in there. What a fool he was to go back in the cage, and does he realize it!"

The tension was relaxing. Men were smiling nervously. There was even a ripple of humorless laughter at the picture Smith had drawn of the monster's discomfiture. Grosvenor was puzzled. He didn't like the sounds he had heard. Hearing was the most deceptive of senses. It was impossible to identify what had happened or was happening in the cage.

"What I'd like to know," said Pennons, the chief engineer, "is why did the telefluor-meter dial jump and waver at full power when pussy made that noise? It's right here under my nose, and I've been trying to guess what happened."

There was silence both within and without the cage. Abruptly, there was a stir in the doorway behind Smith. Captain Leeth and two officers in their military uniforms stepped into the corridor.

The commander, a wiry man of fifty, said, "I think I'd better take charge here. There seems to be some conflict between the scientists as to whether or not this monster should be killed—is that right?"

Morton shook his head. "The conflict is over. We all feel now he should be executed."

Captain Leeth nodded. "That was the order I was about to give. I believe the security of the ship is threatened, and that's my province." He raised his voice. "Make room here! Get back!"

It took several minutes to ease the pressure in the corridor. Grosvenor was glad when it was done. If the creature had come out while those in the foreground were unable to move back quickly, he'd have been able to destroy or injure many men. That danger wasn't completely over, but it was alleviated.

Somebody said, "That's funny! The ship seemed to move just then!"

Grosvenor had felt it, also, as if for an instant the drive had been tested. The big ship trembled as it settled back from that moment of straining.

Captain Leeth said sharply, "Pennons, who's down in the engine room?"

The chief engineer was pale. "My assistant and his helpers. I don't see how they—"

There was a jerk. The big ship careened, and threatened to fall on its side. Grosvenor was flung with cruel violence to the floor. He lay stunned, and then in alarm fought back to consciousness. Other men were sprawled all around him. Some of them were groaning in pain.

Director Morton yelled something, an order Grosvenor didn't hear. Then Captain Leeth was struggling to his feet. He was cursing. Grosvenor heard him say savagely, "Who the devil started those engines!"

The frightful acceleration continued. It was at least five, possibly six gravities. Having assessed its tremendous force as being within his capabilities, Grosvenor climbed agonizedly to his feet. He fumbled with the nearest wall communicator, and punched the engine-room number, not really expecting that it would work. Behind him, a man let out a bass bellow. Grosvenor turned in surprise. Director Morton was peering over his shoulder. The big man called out, "It's pussy! He's in the engine room. And we're heading out into space."

Even as Morton spoke, the screen went black. And still the pressure of acceleration continued. Grosvenor staggered through the door into the salon, and across the great room into a second corridor. There was, he remembered, a space-suit storeroom there. As he approached it, he saw that Captain Leeth was ahead of him and was in the act of fumbling his body into a suit. As Grosvenor came up, the commander closed up the suit and manipulated its anti-acceleration unit.

Quickly he turned to help Grosvenor. A minute later, Grosvenor sighed with relief as he reduced the gravity of his suit to one G. There were two of them now; and other men were stumbling up. It took only a few minutes to exhaust the supply of space suits in that storeroom. They went down to the next floor and brought up suits from there. But now dozens of crew members were available for the job. Captain Leeth had already disappeared; and Grosvenor, guessing the next step to be taken, hurried back to the cage where the big cat had been imprisoned. He found a score of scientists assembled at the door, which had apparently just been opened.

Grosvenor pressed forward and peered over the shoulders of those who were ahead of him. There was a gaping hole in the rear wall of the cage. The hole was big enough for five men to have squeezed through at one time. The metal looked bent, and had numerous jagged edges. The hole opened onto another corridor.

"I'll swear," whispered Pennons through the unclosed headpiece of his space suit, "that it's impossible. The ten-ton hammer of the machine shop couldn't more than dent four inches of micro-steel with one blow. And we heard only one. It would take at least a minute for the atomic disintegrator to do the job, but the whole area would be poisonously radioactive for several weeks at least. Morton, this is a super-being!"

The Director made no reply. Grosvenor saw that Smith was examining the break in the wall. The biologist glanced up. "If only Breckenridge weren't dead. We need a metallurgist to explain this. Look!"

He touched the broken edge of the metal. A piece crumbled between his fingers and slithered away in a fine shower of dust to the floor. Grosvenor pushed his way in.

"I know something of metallurgy," he said.

Several men automatically made way for him. And presently he was standing beside Smith. The biologist frowned at him. "One of Breck's assistants?" he asked pointedly.

Grosvenor pretended not to hear. He bent down and ran the fingers of his space suit through the pile of metallic debris on the floor. He straightened quickly. "No miracle here," he said. "As you know, such cages as this are made in electromagnetic molds, and we use a fine metallic powder for the job. The creature used his special powers to interfere with the forces holding the metal together. That would account for the drain on the telefluor power cable that Mr. Pennons noticed. The thing used the electric energy, with his body as a transforming engine, broke down the wall, ran along the corridor, and so down into the engine room."

He was surprised that he was allowed to complete the hurried analysis. But it seemed clear that he had been accepted as an assistant of the dead Breckenridge. It was a natural error in so big a ship, where men had not yet had time to identify all the lower-rank technicians.

"In the meantime, Director," Kent said quietly, "we are faced with a super-being in control of the ship, completely dominating the engine room and its almost unlimited power, and in possession of the main section of the machine shops."

It was a simple statement of the situation. And Grosvenor felt its impact upon the other men. Their anxiety showed on their faces.

A ship's officer spoke up. "Mr. Kent is wrong," he said. "The thing doesn't dominate the engine room completely. We've still got the control bridge, and that gives us first control of all the machines. You gentlemen, being supernumeraries, may not know the mechanical setup we have. Undoubtedly, the creature could eventually disconnect us, but right now we could cut off all the switches in the engine room."

"For God's sake!" said a man, "why didn't you just shut off the power instead of putting a thousand men into space suits?"

The officer was precise. "Captain Leeth believes we are safer within the force fields of our space suits. It is probable that the creature has never before been subjected to five or six gravities of acceleration. It would be unwise to give up that and other advantages in panicky moves."

"What other advantages have we got?"

Morton spoke up. "I can answer that. We know things about him. And right now I'm going to suggest to Captain Leeth that we make a test." He turned to the officer. "Will you ask the commander to authorize a little experiment I want to make?"

"I think you'd better ask him yourself, sir. You can reach him by communicator. He's up on the bridge."

Morton came back in a few minutes. "Pennons," he said, "since you're a ship's officer and head man in the engine room, Captain Leeth wants you to take charge of this test."

It seemed to Grosvenor that there was a hint of irritation in Morton's tone. Evidently, the commander of the ship had been in earnest when he had said that he was taking charge. It was the old story of partially divided commands. The dividing line had been defined as precisely as possible, but obviously the authorities could not predict all contingencies. In the final issue, much depended on the personality of the individuals. Until now, the ship's officers and crew, all military people, had meticulously carried out their ship duties, subordinating themselves to the purpose of the tremendous voyage. Nevertheless, past experience on other ships had proved to the government that for some reason military men did not have a high opinion of scientists. In moments such as this, the hidden hostility showed itself. Actually, there was no reason why Morton should not be in charge of his own experimental attack.

Pennons said, "Director, there isn't time for you to explain the details to me. You give the orders! If I disagree with any of them, we'll talk it over."

It was a graceful surrender of prerogative. But then Pennons, as chief engineer, was a full-fledged scientific man in his own right.

Morton wasted no time. "Mr. Pennons," he said crisply, "detail five technicians to each of the four approaches to the engine room. I'm going to lead one group. Kent, you take number two. Smith, number three. And Mr. Pennons, of course, number four. We'll use mobile heaters and blast through the big doors. They're all shut, I noticed. He's locked himself in.

"Selenski, you go up to the control bridge and shut off everything except the drive engines. Gear them to the master switch, and cut them all off at the same time. One thing, though. Leave the acceleration on full blast. No anti-acceleration must be applied to the ship. Understand!"

"Yes, sir!" The pilot saluted, and started along the corridor.

Morton called after him, "Report to me through the communicators if any of the machines start to run again!"

The men selected to assist the leaders were all members of the fighting crew. Grosvenor, with several others, waited to watch the action from a distance of about two hundred feet. He felt an empty sense of waiting for disaster as the mobile projectors were brought up and the protective screens arranged. He appreciated the forcefulness and the purpose of the attack that was about to be made. He could even imagine that it might be successful. But it would be a hit-or-miss success, not actually predictable. The affair was being handled on the basis of an old, old system of organizing men and their knowledge. Most irritating was the fact that he could only stand by and be negatively critical.

Morton's voice came over the general communicator. "As I've said, this is largely a test attack. It's based on the presumption that he hasn't been in the engine room long enough to do anything. That gives us an opportunity to conquer him now, before he's had time to prepare against us. But aside from the possibility that we can destroy him immediately, I have a theory. My idea is this: Those doors are built to withstand powerful explosions, and it will take fifteen minutes at least for the heaters to burn them down. During that period, the creature will have no power. Selenski is about to shut it off. The drive, of course, will be on, but that's atomic explosion. My guess is he can't touch stuff like that. In a few minutes you'll see what I mean—I hope."

His voice went up in pitch as he called, "Ready, Selenski?"

"Ready."

"Then cut the master switch!"

The corridor—the whole ship, Grosvenor knew—was abruptly plunged into darkness. He clicked on the light of his space suit. One by one, the other men did the same. In the reflections from the beams, their faces looked pale and tense.

"Blast!" Morton's command was clear and sharp in the communicator.

The mobile units throbbed. The heat that sprayed out of them, though not atomic, was atomic generated. It poured upon the hard metal of the door. Grosvenor could see the first molten drops let go of the metal and begin to flow. Other drops followed until a dozen streams moved reluctantly out of the path of the energy. The transparent screen began to mist, and presently it was harder to see what was happening to the door. And then, through the misted screen, the door began to shine with the light of its own hotness. The fire had a hellish look to it. It sparkled with a gemlike brightness as the heat of the mobile units ate at the metal with slow fury.

Time went by. At last Morton's voice came, a husky sound. "Selenski!"

"Nothing yet, Director."

Morton half whispered, "But he must be doing something. He can't just be waiting in there like a cornered rat. Selenski!"

"Nothing, Director."

Seven minutes, then ten, then twelve went by.

"Director!" It was Selenski's voice, taut. "He's got the electric dynamo running."

Grosvenor drew a deep breath. And then Kent's voice sounded on the communicator. "Morton, we can't get any deeper. Is this what you expected?"

Grosvenor saw Morton peering through the screen at the door. It seemed to him, even from the distance, that the metal was not as white-hot as it had been. The door grew visibly redder, and then faded to a dark, cool color.

Morton was sighing. "That's all for now. Leave the crew men to guard each corridor! Keep the heaters in place! Department heads come up to the control bridge!"

The test, Grosvenor realized, was over.

**5**

To the guard at the entrance of the control bridge, Grosvenor handed his credentials. The man examined them doubtfully.

"I guess it's all right," he said finally. "But so far I haven't admitted anyone in here who's under forty. How did you rate?"

Grosvenor grinned. "I got in on the ground floor of a new science."

The guard looked again at the card, and then said as he handed it back, "Nexialism? What's that?"

"Applied whole-ism," said Grosvenor, and stepped across the threshold.

When he glanced back a moment later, he saw that the man was gazing after him blankly. Grosvenor smiled, and then put the incident out of his mind. It was the first time he had been on the bridge. He gazed around him with curious eyes, impressed and fascinated. In spite of its compactness, the control board was a massive structure. It was built in a series of great curving tiers. Each arc of metal was two hundred feet long, and a full sweep of steps led steeply from one tier to the next. The instruments could be manipulated from the floor, or, more swiftly, from a jointed control chair that hung from the ceiling at the end of a power-driven, upside-down crane structure.

The lowest level of the room was an auditorium with about a hundred comfortable chairs. They were big enough to hold men wearing space suits, and nearly two dozen men so dressed were already sitting in them. Grosvenor settled himself unobtrusively. A minute later, Morton and Captain Leeth entered from the captain's private office, which opened from the bridge. The commander sat down. Morton began without preamble.

"We know that of all the machines in the engine room, the most important to the monster was the electric dynamo. He must have worked in a frenzy of terror to get it started before we penetrated the doors. Any comments on that?"

Pennons said, "I'd like to have somebody describe to me just what he did to make those doors impregnable."

Grosvenor said, "There is a known electronic process by which metals can be temporarily hardened to an enormous degree, but I've never heard of it being done without several tons of special equipment, which doesn't exist on this ship."

Kent turned to look at him. He said impatiently, "What's the good of knowing how he did it? If we can't break through those doors with our atomic disintegrators, that's the end. He can do as he pleases with this ship."

Morton was shaking his head. "We'll have to do some planning, and that's what we're here for." He raised his voice. "Selenski!"

The pilot leaned down from the control chair. His sudden appearance surprised Grosvenor. He hadn't noticed the man in the chair. "What is it, sir?" Selenski asked.

"Start all the engines!"

Selenski swung his control seat skillfully toward the master switch. Gingerly, he eased the great lever into position. There was a jerk that shook the ship, an audible humming sound, and then for several seconds a shuddering of the floor. The ship steadied, the machines settled down to their work, and the humming faded into a vague vibration.

Presently, Morton said, "I'm going to ask various experts to give their suggestions for fighting pussy. What we need here is a consultation between many different specialized fields and, however interesting theoretical possibilities might be, what we want is the practical approach."

And that, Grosvenor decided ruefully, effectively disposed of Elliott Grosvenor, Nexialist. It shouldn't have. What Morton wanted was integration of many sciences, which was what Nexialism was for. He guessed, however, that he would not be one of the experts whose practical advice Morton would be interested in. His guess was correct.

It was two hours later when the Director said in a distracted tone, "I think we'd better take half an hour now to eat and rest. This is the big push we're coming to. We'll need everything we've got."

Grosvenor headed for his own department. He was not interested in food or rest. At thirty-one, he could afford to dispense with an occasional meal or a night of sleep. It seemed to him he had half an hour in which to solve the problem of what should be done with the monster that had taken control of the ship.

The trouble with what the scientists had agreed on was that it was not thorough enough. A number of specialists had polled their knowledge on a fairly superficial level. Each had briefly outlined his ideas to people who were not trained to grasp the wealth of association behind each notion. And so the attack plan lacked unity.

It made Grosvenor uneasy to realize that he, a young man of thirty-one, was probably the only person aboard with the training to see the weaknesses in the plan. For the first time since coming aboard six months before, he had a sharp appreciation of what a tremendous change had taken place in him at the Nexial Foundation. It was not too much to say that all previous educational systems were outdated. Grosvenor took no personal credit for the training he had received. He had created none of it. But as a graduate of the Foundation, as a person who had been put aboard the *Space Beagle* for a specific purpose, he had no alternative but to decide on a definite solution, and then use every available means to convince those in authority.

The trouble was he needed more information. He went after it in the quickest possible fashion. He called up various departments on the communicator.

Mostly, he talked to subordinates. Each time he introduced himself as a department head, and the effect of that was considerable. Junior scientists accepted his identification of himself and were usually very helpful, though not always. There was the type of individual who said, "I'll have to get authority from my superiors." One department head—Smith—talked to him personally, and gave him all the information he wanted. Another was polite and asked him to call again after the cat was destroyed. Grosvenor contacted the chemistry department last and asked for Kent, taking it for granted—and hoping—that he would not get through. He was all ready to say to the subordinate, "Then you can give me the information I want." To his annoyance and amazement, he was connected with Kent at once.

The chemist chief listened to him with ill-concealed impatience, and abruptly cut him off. "You can obtain the information from here through the usual channels. However, the discoveries made on the cat's planet will not be available for some months. We have to check and countercheck all our findings."

Grosvenor persisted. "Mr. Kent, I ask you most earnestly to authorize the immediate release of information regarding the quantitative analysis of the cat-planet atmosphere. It may have an important bearing on the plan decided upon at the meeting. It would be too involved at the moment to explain fully, but I assure you—"

Kent cut him off. "Look, my boy," and there was a sneer in his tone, "the time is past for academic discussion. You don't seem to understand that we're in deadly danger. If anything goes wrong, you and I and the others will be physically attacked. It won't be an exercise in intellectual gymnastics. And now, please don't bother me again for ten years."

There was a click as Kent broke the connection. Grosvenor sat for several seconds, flushing at the insult. Presently, he smiled ruefully, and then made his final calls. His high-probability chart contained, among other things, check marks in the proper printed spaces showing the amount of volcanic dust in the atmosphere of the planet, the life history of various plant forms as indicated by preliminary studies of their seeds, the type of digestive tracts animals would have to have to eat the particular plants examined and, by extrapolation, what would be the probable ranges of structure and types of the animals who lived off the animals who ate such plants.

Grosvenor worked rapidly, and since he merely put marks on an already printed chart, it was not long before he had his graph. It was an intricate affair. It would not be easy to explain it to someone who was not already familiar with Nexialism. But for him it made a fairly sharp picture. In the emergency it pointed at possibilities and solutions that could not be ignored. So it seemed to Grosvenor.

Under the heading of "General Recommendations," he wrote, "Any solution adopted should include safety valve."

With four copies of the chart, he headed for the mathematics department. There were guards, which was unusual and an obvious protection against the cat. When they refused to let him see Morton, Grosvenor demanded to see one of the Director's secretaries. A young man emerged finally from another room, politely examined his chart, and said that he would "try to bring it to Director Morton's attention."

Grosvenor said in a grim tone, "I've been told that kind of thing before. If Director Morton does not see that chart, I shall ask for a Board of Inquiry. There's something damn funny going on here in connection with the reports I make to the Director's office, and there's going to be trouble if there's any more of it."

The secretary was five years older than Grosvenor. He was cool and basically hostile. He bowed, and said with a faintly satirical smile, "The Director is a very busy man. Many departments compete for his attention. Some of them have long histories of achievement, and a prestige that gives them precedence over younger sciences and—" he hesitated—"scientists." He shrugged. "But I shall ask him if he wishes to examine the chart."

Grosvenor said, "Ask him to read the 'Recommendations.' There isn't time for any more."

The secretary said, "I'll bring it to his attention."

Grosvenor headed for Captain Leeth's quarters. The commander received him and listened to what he had to say. Then he examined the chart. Finally, he shook his head.

"The military," he said in a formal tone, "has a slightly different approach to these matters. We are prepared to take calculated risks to realize specific goals. Your notion that it would be wiser in the final issue to let this creature escape is quite contrary to my own attitude. Here is an intelligent being that has taken hostile action against an armed ship. That is an intolerable situation. It is my belief that he embarked on such an action knowing the consequences." He smiled a tight-lipped smile. "The consequences are death."

It struck Grosvenor that the end result might well be death for people who had inflexible ways of dealing with unusual danger. He parted his lips to protest that he did not intend that the cat should escape. Before he could speak, Captain Leeth climbed to his feet. "I'll have to ask you to go now," he said. He spoke to an officer. "Show Mr. Grosvenor the way out."

Grosvenor said bitterly, "I know the way out."

Alone in the corridor, he glanced at his watch. It was five minutes to attack time.

Disconsolately, he headed for the bridge. Most of the others were already present as Grosvenor found a seat. A minute later, Director Morton came in with Captain Leeth. And the meeting was called to order.

Nervous and visibly tense, Morton paced back and forth before his audience. His usually sleek hair was rumpled. The slight pallor of his strong face emphasized rather than detracted from the outthrust aggressiveness of his jaw. He stopped walking abruptly. His deep voice was crisp to the point of sharpness as he said, "To make sure that our plans are fully coordinated, I'm going to ask each expert in turn to outline his part in the overpowering of this creature. Mr. Pennons first!"

Pennons stood up. He was not a big man, yet he looked big, perhaps because of his air of authority. Like the others, his training was specialized, but because of the nature of his field he needed Nexialism far less than anyone else in the room. This man knew engines, and the history of engines. According to his file record—which Grosvenor had examined—he had studied machine development on a hundred planets. There was probably nothing fundamental that he didn't know about practical engineering. He could have spoken a thousand hours and still only have touched upon his subject.

He said, "We've set up a relay in the control room here which will start and stop every engine rhythmically. The trip lever will work a hundred times a second. And the effect will be to create vibrations of many kinds. There is just a possibility that one or more of the machines will shatter, on the same principle as soldiers crossing a bridge in step—you've heard that old story, no doubt—but in my opinion there is no real danger of a break from that cause. Our main purpose is simply to interfere with the interference of the creature, and smash through the doors!"

"Gourlay next!" said Morton.

Gourlay climbed lazily to his feet. He looked sleepy, as if he were somewhat bored by the proceedings. Grosvenor suspected that he liked people to think him lackadaisical. His title was chief communications engineer, and his file record chronicled a sustained attempt to acquire knowledge in his chosen field. If his degrees were any evidence, then he had an orthodox educational background second to none. When he finally spoke, he drawled in his unhurried fashion. Grosvenor noticed that his very deliberateness had a soothing effect on the men. Anxious faces relaxed. Bodies leaned back more restfully.

Gourlay said, "We've rigged up vibration screens that work on the principle of reflection. Once inside, we'll use them so that most of the stuff he can send will be reflected right back at him. In addition, we've got plenty of spare electric energy that we'll just feed him from mobile copper cups. There must be a limit to his capacity for handling power with those insulated nerves of his."

"Selenski!" called Morton.

The chief pilot was standing by the time Grosvenor's gaze flicked over to him. It was so swiftly done that he seemed to have anticipated Morton's call. Grosvenor studied him, fascinated. Selenski was a lean-bodied, lean-faced man with startlingly vivid blue eyes. He looked physically strong and capable. According to his file record, he was not a man of great learning. He made up for it in steadiness of nerve, in lightning response to stimuli, and in a capacity for sustained clocklike performance.

He said, "The impression I've received of the plan is that it must be cumulative. Just when the creature thinks that he can't stand any more, another thing happens to add to his trouble and confusion. When the uproar's at its height, I cut in the anti-acceleration. The Director thinks with Gunlie Lester that this creature will know nothing about anti-acceleration. It's a development of the science of interstellar flight and wouldn't have been likely to come about in any other way. We think when the creature feels the first effects of the anti-acceleration—you all remember the caved-in sensation you had the first time it happened to you—it won't know what to think or do." He sat down.

Morton said, "Korita next!"

"I can only offer you encouragement," said the archeologist, "on the basis of my theory that the monster has all the characteristics of the criminal of the early ages of any civilization. Smith has suggested that his knowledge of science is puzzling. In his opinion, this could mean that we are dealing with an actual inhabitant, and not the descendant of the inhabitants, of the dead city we visited. This would ascribe a virtual immortality to our enemy, a possibility which is partly borne out by his ability to breathe both oxygen and chlorine—or neither. But his immortality in itself would not matter. He comes from a certain age in his civilization; and he has sunk so low that his ideas are mostly memories of that age. In spite of his ability to control energy, he lost his head in the elevator when he first entered the ship. By becoming emotional when Kent offered him food, he placed himself in such a position that he was forced to reveal his special powers against a vibration gun. He bungled the mass murders a few hours ago. As you can see, his record is one of the low cunning of the primitive, egotistical mind, which has little or no understanding of its own body processes in the scientific sense, and scarcely any conception of the vast organization with which it is confronted.

"He is like the ancient German soldier who felt superior to the elderly Roman scholar as an individual, yet the latter was part of a mighty civilization of which the German of that day stood in awe. We have, then, a primitive, and that primitive is now far out in space, completely outside of his natural habitat. I say, let's go in and win."

Morton stood up. There was a twisted smile on his heavy face. He said, "According to my previous plan, that pep talk by Korita was to be the preliminary to our attack. However, during the past hour I have received a document from a young man who is aboard this ship representing a science about which I know very little. The fact that he is aboard at all requires that I give weight to his opinions. In his conviction that he had the solution to this problem, he visited not only my quarters but also those of Captain Leeth. The commander and I have accordingly agreed that Mr. Grosvenor will be allowed a few minutes to describe his solution and to convince us that he knows what he is talking about."

Grosvenor stood up shakily. He began, "At the Nexial Foundation we teach that behind all the grosser aspects of any science there is an intricate tie-up with other sciences. That is an old notion, of course, but there is a difference between giving lip service to an idea and applying it in practice. At the Foundation we have developed techniques for applying it. In my department I have some of the most remarkable educational machines you have ever seen. I can't describe them now, but I can tell you how a person trained by those machines and techniques would solve the problem of the cat.

"First, the suggestions so far made have been on a superficial level. They are satisfactory so far as they go. They do not go far enough. Right now, we have enough facts to make a fairly clear-cut picture of pussy's background. I will enumerate them. About eighteen hundred years ago, the hardy plants of this planet suddenly began to receive less sunlight in certain wave lengths. This was due to the appearance of great quantities of volcanic dust in the atmosphere. Result: Almost overnight, most of the plants died. Yesterday, one of our exploring lifeboats flying around within a hundred miles of the dead city detected several living creatures about the size of a terrestrial deer but apparently more intelligent. They were so wary they couldn't be captured. They had to be destroyed; and Mr. Smith's department made a partial analysis. The dead bodies contained potassium in much the same chemical-electrical arrangement as is found in human beings. No other animals were seen. Possibility: This could be at least one of the potassium sources of the cat. In the stomachs of the dead animals the biologists found parts of the plants in various stages of being digested. That seems to be the cycle: vegetation, herbivore, predator. It seems probable that when the plant was destroyed, the animal whose food it was must have died in proportionate numbers. Overnight, pussy's own food supply was wiped out."

Grosvenor sent a quick glance over his audience. With one exception everyone present was watching him intently. The exception was Kent. The chief chemist sat with an irritated expression on his face. His attention seemed to be elsewhere.

The Nexialist continued swiftly. "There are many examples in the galaxy of the complete dependency of given life forms on a single type of food. But we have met no other example of the intelligent life form of a planet being so exclusive about diet. It does not seem to have occurred to these creatures to farm their food and, of course, the food of their food. An incredible lack of foresight, you'll admit. So incredible, indeed, that any explanation which does not take that factor into account would, *ipso facto*, be unsatisfactory."

Grosvenor paused again, but only for breath. He did not look directly at anyone present. It was impossible to give his evidence for what he was about to say. It would take weeks for each department head to check the facts that involved his particular science. All he could do was give the end conclusion, something which he had not dared to do in his probability chart or in his conversation with Captain Leeth. He finished hurriedly. "The facts are inescapable. Pussy is not one of the builders of that city, nor is he a descendant of the builders. He and his kind were animals experimented on by the builders.

"What happened to the builders? We can only guess. Perhaps they exterminated themselves in an atomic war eighteen hundred years ago. The almost-leveled city, the sudden appearance of volcanic-like dust in the atmosphere in such quantities as to obscure the sun for thousands of years, are significant. Emotional man almost succeeded in doing the same thing, so we must not judge this vanished race too harshly. But where does this lead us?"

Once more, Grosvenor took a deep breath and went on quickly. "If he had been a builder, we would by now have had evidence of his full powers and would know precisely what we are up against. Since he is not, we are at the moment dealing with a beast who can have no clear understanding of his powers. Cornered, or even if pressed too hard, he may discover within himself a capacity not yet apparent to him for destroying human beings and controlling machines. We must give him an opportunity to escape. Once outside this ship, he will be at our mercy. That's all, and thank you for listening to me."

Morton glanced around the room. "Well, gentlemen, what do you think?"

Kent said sourly, "I never heard such a story in my life. Possibilities.

Probabilities. Fantasies. If this is Nexialism, it will have to be presented much better than that before I'll be interested."

Smith said gloomily, "I don't see how we could accept such an explanation without having pussy's body for examination."

Chief physicist von Grossen said, "I doubt if even an examination would definitely prove him a beast who has been experimented upon. Mr. Grosvenor's analysis is distinctly controversial, and will remain so."

Korita said, "Further exploration of the city might uncover evidence of Mr. Grosvenor's theory." He spoke cautiously. "It would not completely disprove the cyclic theory, since such an experimental intelligence would tend to reflect the attitudes and beliefs of those who taught him."

Chief engineer Pennons said, "One of our lifeboats is in the machine shop right now. It is partly dismantled and occupies the only permanent repair cradle available below. To get a usable lifeboat in to him would require as much effort as the all-out attack we are planning. Of course, if the attack should fail, we might consider sacrificing a lifeboat, though I still don't see how he would get it out of the ship. We have no air locks down there."

Morton turned to Grosvenor. "What is your answer to that?"

Grosvenor said, "There is an air lock at the end of the corridor adjoining the engine room. We must give him access to it."

Captain Leeth stood up. "As I told Mr. Grosvenor when he came to see me, the military mind has a bolder attitude in these matters. We expect casualties. Mr. Pennons expressed my opinion. If our attack fails, we will consider other measures. Thank you, Mr. Grosvenor, for your analysis. But now, let's get to work!"

It was a command. The exodus began immediately.

In the blazing brilliance of the gigantic machine shop, Coeurl labored. Most of his memories were back, the skills he had been taught by the builders, his ability to adjust to new machines and new situations. He had found the lifeboat resting in a cradle. It had been partly dismantled.

Coeurl slaved to repair it. The importance of escaping grew on him. Here was access to his own planet and to other coeurls. With the skills he could teach them, they would be irresistible. This way, victory would be certain. In a sense, then, he felt as if he had made up his mind. Yet he was reluctant to leave the ship. He was not convinced that he was in danger. After examining the power sources of the machine shop, and thinking back over what had occurred, it seemed to him that these two-legged beings didn't have the equipment to overcome him.

The conflict raged on inside him even as he worked. It was not until he paused to survey the craft that he realized how tremendous a repair job he had done. All that remained was to load up the tools and instruments he wanted to take along. And then—would he leave, or fight? He grew anxious as he heard the approach of the men. He felt the sudden change in the tempestlike thunder of the engines, a rhythmical off-and-on hum, shriller in tone, sharper, more nerve-racking than the deep-throated, steady throb that had preceded it. The pattern had an unnerving quality. Coeurl fought to adjust to it and, by dint of concentrating, his body was on the point of succeeding when a new factor interfered. The flame of powerful mobile projectors started its hideous roaring against the massive engine-room doors. Instantly, his problem was whether to fight the projectors or counter the rhythm. He couldn't, he quickly discovered, do both.

He began to concentrate on escape. Every muscle of his powerful body was strained as he carried great loads of tools, machines, and instruments, and dumped them into any available space inside the lifeboat. He paused in the doorway at last for the penultimate act of his departure. He knew the doors were going down. Half a dozen projectors concentrating on one point of each door were irresistibly, though slowly, eating away the remaining inches. Coeurl hesitated, then withdrew all energy resistance from them. Intently, he concentrated on the outer wall of the big ship, toward which the blunt nose of the forty-foot lifeboat was pointing. His body cringed from the surge of electricity that flowed from the dynamos. His ear tendrils vibrated that terrific power straight at the wall. He felt on fire. His whole body ached. He guessed that he was dangerously close to the limit of his capacity for handling energy.

In spite of his effort, nothing happened. The wall did not yield. It was hard, that metal, and strong beyond anything he had ever known. It held its shape. Its molecules were monatomic but their arrangement was unusual—the effect of close packing was achieved without the usual concomitant of great density.

He heard one of the engine-room doors crash inward. Men shouted. Projectors rolled forward, their power unchecked now. Coeurl heard the floor of the engine room hiss in protest as those blasts of heat burned the metal. Closer came that tremendous, threatening sound. In a minute the men would be burning through the flimsy doors that separated the engine room from the machine shop.

During that minute, Coeurl won his victory. He felt the change in the resisting alloy. The entire wall lost its bitterly held cohesion. It looked the same, but there was no doubt. The flow of energy through his body became easy. He continued to concentrate it for several seconds longer, then he was satisfied. With a snarl of triumph, he leaped into his small craft and manipulated the lever that closed the door behind him.

One of his tentacles embraced the power drive with almost sensuous tenderness. There was a forward surge of his machine as he launched it straight at the thick outer wall. The nose of the craft touched, and the wall dissolved in a glittering shower of dust. He felt tiny jerks of retardation as the weight of the metallic powder that had to be pushed out of the way momentarily slowed the small ship. But it broke through and shot irresistibly off into space.

Seconds went by. Then Coeurl noticed that he had departed from the big vessel at right angles to its course. He was still so close that he could see the jagged hole through which he had escaped. Men in armor stood silhouetted against the brightness behind them. Both they and the ship grew noticeably smaller. Then the men were gone, and there was only the ship with its blaze of a thousand blurring portholes.

Coeurl was turning away from it now, rapidly. He curved a full ninety degrees by his instrument board, and then set the controls for top acceleration. Thus within little more than a minute after his escape, he was heading back in the direction from which the big vessel had been coming all these hours.

Behind him, the gigantic globe shrank rapidly, became too small for individual portholes to be visible. Almost straight ahead, Coeurl saw a tiny, dim ball of light—his own sun, he realized. There, with other coeurls, he could build an interstellar space ship and travel to stars with inhabited planets. Because it was so important, he felt suddenly frightened. He had turned away from the rear viewing plates. Now he glanced into them again. The globe was still there, a tiny dot of light in the immense blackness of space. Suddenly, it twinkled and was gone.

For a moment, he had the startled impression that, just before it disappeared, it had moved. But he could see nothing. He wondered uneasily if they had shut off all their lights and were following him in the darkness. It seemed clear that he would not be safe until he actually landed.

Worried and uncertain, he gave his attention again to the forward viewing plates. Almost immediately, he had a sharp sense of dismay. The dim sun toward which he was heading was not growing larger. *It was visibly smaller.* It became a pin point in the dark distance. It vanished.

Fear swept through Coeurl like a cold wind. For minutes he peered tensely into the space ahead, hoping frantically that his one landmark would become visible again. But only the remote stars glimmered there, unwinking points against a velvet background of unfathomable distance.

But wait! One of the points was growing larger. With every muscle taut, Coeurl watched the point become a dot. It grew into a round ball of light and kept on expanding. Bigger, bigger, it became. Suddenly it shimmered, and there before him, lights glaring from every porthole, was the great globe of the space ship—the very ship which a few minutes before he had watched vanish behind him.

Something happened to Coeurl in that moment. His mind was spinning like a flywheel, faster and faster. It flew apart into a million aching fragments. His eyes almost started from their sockets as, like a maddened animal, he raged in his small quarters. His tentacles clutched at precious instruments and flung them in a fury of frustration. His paws smashed at the very walls of his ship. Finally, in a brief flash of sanity, he knew that he couldn't face the inevitable fire of disintegrators that would now be directed against him from a safe distance.

It was a simple thing to create the violent cell disorganization that freed every droplet of id from his vital organs.

One last snarl of defiance twisted his lips. His tentacles weaved blindly. And then, suddenly weary beyond all his strength to combat, he sank down. Death came quietly after so many, many hours of violence.

Captain Leeth took no chances. When the firing ceased and it was possible to approach what was left of the lifeboat, the searchers found small masses of fused metal, and only here and there remnants of what had been Coeurl's body.

"Poor pussy!" said Morton. "I wonder what he thought when he saw us appear ahead of him, after his own sun disappeared. Understanding nothing of anti-accelerators, he didn't know that we could stop short in space, whereas it would take him more than three hours. He would seem to be heading in the direction of his own planet, but actually he'd be drawing farther and farther away from it. He couldn't possibly have guessed that, when we stopped, he flashed past us, and that then all we had to do was follow him and put on our little act of being his sun until we were close enough to destroy him. The whole cosmos must have seemed topsy-turvy to him."

Grosvenor listened to the account with mixed emotions. The entire incident was rapidly blurring, losing shape, dissolving into darkness. The moment-by-moment details would never again be recalled by an individual exactly as they had occurred. The danger they had been in already seemed remote.

"Never mind the sympathy!" Grosvenor heard Kent say. "We've got a job—to kill every cat on that miserable world."

Korita murmured softly, "That should be simple. They are but primitives. We have merely to settle down, and they will come to us, cunningly expecting to delude us." He half turned to Grosvenor. "I still believe that will be true," he said in a friendly tone, "even if our young friend's 'beast' theory turned out to be correct. What do you think, Mr. Grosvenor?"

"I'd go even a little further," Grosvenor said. "As a historian, you will undoubtedly agree that no known attempt at total extermination has ever proved successful. Don't forget that pussy's attack on us was based on a desperate need for food; the resources of this planet apparently can't support this breed much longer. Pussy's brethren know nothing about us, and therefore are not a menace. So why not just let them die of starvation?"

**7**

LECTURE AND DISCUSSION

NEXIALISM IS THE SCIENCE OF JOINING IN AN ORDERLY FASHION THE KNOWLEDGE OF ONE FIELD OF LEARNING WITH THAT OF OTHER FIELDS. IT PROVIDES TECHNIQUES FOR SPEEDING UP THE PROCESSES OF ABSORBING KNOWLEDGE AND OF USING EFFECTIVELY WHAT HAS BEEN LEARNED. YOU ARE CORDIALLY INVITED TO ATTEND.

LECTURER, ELLIOTT GROSVENOR
PLACE, NEXIAL DEPARTMENT
TIME, 1550, 9/7/1 *

Grosvenor hung the notice on the already well-covered bulletin board. Then he stepped back to survey his handiwork. The announcement competed with eight other lectures, three motion pictures, four educational films, nine discussion groups, and several

* THE SHIP OPERATED ON WHAT WAS CALLED STAR TIME, BASED ON A HUNDRED-MINUTE HOUR AND A TWENTY-HOUR DAY. THE WEEK HAD TEN DAYS, WITH A THIRTY-DAY MONTH AND A THREE-HUNDRED-AND-SIXTY-DAY YEAR. THE DAYS WERE NUMBERED, NOT NAMED, AND THE CALENDAR WAS RECKONED FROM THE MOMENT OF TAKE-OFF.

sporting events. In addition, there would be individuals who remained in their quarters to read, the spontaneous gatherings of friends, the half-dozen bars and commissaries, each of which could expect its full quota of customers.

Nevertheless, he was confident his would be read. Unlike the others, it was not just a sheet of paper. It was a gadget about a centimeter in thickness. The print was a silhouette focused on the surface from inside. A paper-thin chromatic wheel, made of light-battery material, turned magnetically and provided the varicolored light source. The letters changed color singly and in groups. Because the frequency of the emitted light was subtly, magnetically, altered from moment to moment, the pattern of color was never repeated.

The notice stood out from its drab surroundings like a neon sign. It would be seen, all right.

Grosvenor headed for the dining salon. As he entered, a man at the door thrust a card into his hand. Grosvenor glanced at it curiously.

### KENT FOR DIRECTOR

> MR. KENT IS HEAD OF THE LARGEST DEPARTMENT ON OUR SHIP. HE IS NOTED FOR HIS COOPERATION WITH OTHER DEPARTMENTS. GREGORY KENT IS A SCIENTIST WITH A HEART, WHO UNDERSTANDS THE PROBLEMS OF OTHER SCIENTISTS. REMEMBER, YOUR SHIP, IN ADDITION TO ITS MILITARY COMPLEMENT OF 180 OFFICERS AND MEN, CARRIES 804 SCIENTISTS HEADED BY AN ADMINISTRATION HASTILY ELECTED BY A SMALL MINORITY BEFORE THE TAKE-OFF. THIS SITUATION MUST BE RECTIFIED. WE ARE ENTITLED TO DEMOCRATIC REPRESENTATION.

### ELECTION MEETING, 9/7/1
### 1500 HOURS
### ELECT KENT DIRECTOR

Grosvenor slipped the card into his pocket and went into the brilliantly lighted room. It seemed to him that tense individuals like Kent seldom considered the long-run effects of their efforts to divide a group of men into hostile camps. Fully fifty per cent of interstellar expeditions in the previous two hundred years had not returned. The reasons could only be deduced from what had happened aboard ships that did come back. The record was of dissension among the members of the expedition, bitter disputes, disagreement as to objectives, and the formation of splinter groups. These latter increased in number almost in direct proportion to the length of the journey.

Elections were a recent innovation in such expeditions. Permission to hold them had been given because men were reluctant to be bound irrevocably to the will of appointed leaders. But a ship was not a nation in miniature. Once on the way, it could not replace casualties. Faced with catastrophe, its human resources were limited.

Frowning over the potentialities, annoyed that the time of the political meeting coincided with his own lecture, Grosvenor headed for his table. The dining room was crowded. He found his companions for the week already eating. There were three of them, junior scientists from different departments.

As he sat down, one of the men said cheerfully, "Well, what defenseless woman's character shall we assassinate today?"

Grosvenor laughed good-naturedly, but he knew that the remark was only partly intended as humor. Conversation among the younger men tended towards a certain sameness. Talk leaned heavily on women and sex. In this all-masculine expedition, the problem of sex had been chemically solved by the inclusion of specific drugs in the general diet. That took away the physical need, but it was emotionally unsatisfying.

No one answered the question. Carl Dennison, a junior chemist, scowled at the speaker, then turned to Grosvenor. "How're you going to vote, Grove?"

"On the secret ballot," said Grosvenor. "Now, let's get back to the blonde Allison was telling us about this morning—"

Dennison persisted. "You'll vote for Kent, won't you?"

Grosvenor grinned. "Haven't given it a thought. Election is still a couple of months away. What's wrong with Morton?"

"He's practically a government-appointed man."

"So am I. So are you."

"He's only a mathematician, not a scientist in the true sense of the word."

"That's a new one on me," Grosvenor said. "I've been laboring for years under the delusion that mathematicians were scientists."

"That's just it. Because of the superficial resemblance, it *is* a delusion." Dennison was clearly trying to put over some private conception of his own. He was an earnest, heavy-set individual, and he leaned forward now as if he had already made his point. "Scientists have to stick together. Just imagine, here's an entire shipload of us, and what do they put over us?—a man who deals in abstractions. That's no training for handling practical problems."

"Funny, I thought he was doing rather well in smoothing out the problems of us workingmen."

"We can smooth out our own problems." Dennison sounded irritated.

Grosvenor had been punching buttons. Now his food began to slide up from the vertical conveyor at the center of the table. He sniffed. "Ah, roast sawdust, straight from the chemistry department. It smells delicious. The question is, has the same amount of effort been lavished to make the sawdust from the brushwood of the cat planet as nourishing as the sawdust we brought?" He held up his hand. "Don't answer. I don't wish to be disillusioned about the integrity of Mr. Kent's department, even though I don't like his behavior. You see, I asked him for some of the cooperation they mention on the card, and he told me to call back in ten years. I guess he forgot about the election. Besides, he's got a nerve scheduling a political meeting on the same night that I'm giving a lecture." He began to eat.

"No lecture is as important as this rally. We're going to discuss matters of policy that will affect everybody on the ship, including you." Dennison's face was flushed, his voice harsh. "Look, Grove, you can't possibly have anything against a man you don't even know very well. Kent is the kind of person who won't forget his friends."

"I'll wager he also has special treatment for those he dislikes," said Grosvenor. He shrugged impatiently. "Carl, to me Kent represents all that is destructive in our present civilization. According to Korita's theory of cyclic history, we're in the 'winter' stage of our culture. I'm going to ask him to explain that more fully one of these days, but I'll wager Kent's caricature of a democratic campaign is an example of the worst aspects of such a period."

He would have liked to add that this was exactly what he was aboard to prevent, but that, of course, was out of the question. It was just such discord as this that had brought disaster to so many previous expeditions. As a result, unknown to the men, all vessels had become proving grounds for sociological experiments: Nexialists, elections, split command—these and innumerable small changes were being tried out in the hope that man's expansion into space could somehow be made less costly.

There was a sneer on Dennison's face. He said, "Listen to the young philosopher!" He added flatly, "Vote for Kent if you know what's good for you!"

Grosvenor restrained his irritation. "What'll he do—cut off my share of the sawdust? Maybe I'll run for the directorship myself. Get the votes of all the men thirty-five and under. After all, we outnumber the oldsters three or four to one. Democracy demands that we have representation on a proportional basis."

Dennison seemed to have recovered himself. He said, "You're making a grave error, Grosvenor. You'll find out."

The rest of the meal was eaten in silence.

At five minutes before 1550 hours the following evening, Grosvenor began to feel that his lecture notice had drawn a blank. It baffled him. He could understand that Kent might conceivably forbid his followers to attend lectures given by men who had indicated that they would not support him. But even if the chief chemist controlled a majority of the voters, that still left several hundred individuals who had not been influenced. Grosvenor couldn't help remembering what a Nexial-trained government executive had said to him on the eve of departure.

"It won't be easy, this job you've taken aboard the *Beagle*. Nexialism is a tremendous new approach to learning and association. The older men will fight it instinctively. The young men, if they have already been educated by ordinary methods, will automatically be hostile to anything which suggests that their newly acquired techniques are out of date. You yourself have still to use in practice what you learned in theory, although in your case that very transition is part of your training. Just remember that a man who is right often enough gets a hearing in a crisis."

At 1610, Grosvenor visited the bulletin boards in two of the lounges and in the central corridor, and changed the time of his lecture to 1700 hours. At 1700 o'clock, he made it 1750 hours, and then still later altered it to 1800 hours. "They'll be coming out," he told himself. "The political meeting can't last forever, and the other lectures are two-hour affairs at most." At five minutes to 1800 hours, he heard the footsteps of two men come slowly along the corridor. There was silence as they paused opposite his open doorway, then a voice said, "This is the place, all right."

They laughed, for no apparent reason. A moment later, two young men entered. Grosvenor hesitated, then nodded friendly greeting. From the first day of the voyage, he had set himself the task of identifying the individuals aboard the ship, their voices, their faces, their names—as much about them as he could discover. With so many men to investigate, the job was not yet completed. But he remembered these two. They were both from the chemistry department.

He watched them warily as they wandered around looking at the display of training devices. They seemed to be secretly amused. They settled finally in two of the chairs, and one of them said with subtly exaggerated politeness, "When does the lecture begin, Mr. Grosvenor?"

Grosvenor looked at his watch. "In about five minutes," he said.

During that interval, eight men came in. It stimulated Grosvenor considerably after his bad start, particularly since one of the men was Donald McCann, head of the geology department. Even the fact that four of his listeners were from the chemistry department did not disturb him.

Pleased, he launched into his lecture on the conditioned reflex, and its development since the days of Pavlov into a cornerstone of the science of Nexialism.

Afterwards, McCann came up and talked to him. He said, "I noticed that part of the technique is the so-called sleep machine, which educates you while you sleep." He chuckled. "I remember one of my old professors pointing out that you could learn all that is known about science in just under a thousand years. You didn't admit that limitation."

Grosvenor was aware of the other's gray eyes watching him with a kindly twinkle. He smiled. "That limitation," he said, "was partly a product of the old method of using the machine without preliminary training. Today, the Nexial Foundation uses hypnosis and psychotherapy to break initial resistance. For instance, when I was tested, I was told that normally for me the sleep machine could only be turned on for five minutes every two hours."

"A very low tolerance," said McCann. "Mine was three minutes every half hour."

"But you accepted that," said Grosvenor pointedly. "Right?"

"What did you do?"

Grosvenor smiled. "I didn't do anything. I was conditioned by various methods until I could sleep soundly for eight hours while the machine ran steadily. Several other techniques supplemented the process."

The geologist ignored the final sentence. "Eight solid hours!" he said in astonishment.

"Solid," agreed Grosvenor.

The older man seemed to consider that. "Still," he said finally, "that only reduces the figure by a factor of about three. Even without conditioning, there are many people who can take five minutes out of every quarter hour of a sleep period without waking."

Grosvenor replied slowly, studying the other's face for reaction. "But the information has to be repeated many times." He realized from the staggered expression on McCann's face that the point had been made. He went on quickly. "Surely, sir, you've had the experience of seeing or hearing something—once—and never forgetting it. And yet at other times what seems to be an equally profound impression fades away to a point where you cannot recall it accurately even when it is mentioned. There are reasons for that. The Nexial Foundation found out what they were."

McCann said nothing. His lips were pursed. Over his shoulder, Grosvenor noticed that the four men from the chemistry department were gathered in a group near the corridor door. They were talking together in low tones. He gave them only a glance, and then said to the geologist, "There were times in the beginning when I thought the pressure would be too much for me. You understand, I'm not talking only about the sleep machine. In actual quantity of training, that was just about ten per cent of the total."

McCann was shaking his head. "Those figures almost overwhelm me. I suppose you get your largest percentage figure from those little films where each picture stays on but a fraction of a second."

Grosvenor nodded. "We used the tachistoscopic films about three hours a day, but they constituted some forty-five per cent of the training. The secret is speed and repetition."

"An entire science at one sitting!" McCann exclaimed. "That's what you call learning-as-a-whole."

"That's one facet of it. We learned with every sense, through our fingers, our ears, our eyes, and even from smell and taste."

Once more McCann stood frowning. Grosvenor saw that the young chemists were trooping out of the room at last. From the corridor came the sound of low laughter. It seemed to startle McCann out of his brown study. The geologist thrust out his hand and said, "How about coming up to my department one of these days. Perhaps we can work out a method of coordinating your integrative knowledge with our field work. We can try it out when we land on another planet."

As Grosvenor walked along the corridor to his own bedroom, he whistled under his breath. He'd won his first victory, and the feeling was pleasant.

The next morning, as Grosvenor approached his department, he saw with astonishment that the door was open. A bright swath of light cut out from it across the more dimly illuminated corridor. He hurried forward, and stopped short in the doorway.

In his first glance, he saw seven chemist technicians, including two who had attended his lecture. Machinery had been moved into the room. There were a number of large vats, a series of heating units, and an entire system of pipes for supplying chemicals to the vats.

Grosvenor's mind leaped back to the way the chemist technicians had acted at his lecture. He moved through the doorway, tense with the possibilities and sick with the thought of what might have been done to his own equipment. He used this outer room for general purposes. It normally contained some machinery, but it was primarily designed to channel the output from the other rooms for purposes of group instruction. The remaining four rooms contained his special equipment.

Through the open door that led into his film and sound-recording

studio, Grosvenor saw that it also had been taken over. The shock of
that held him silent. Ignoring the men, he went through the outer
room and into each of the four special sections in turn. Three had
been occupied by the invading chemists. That included, in addition
to the film studio, the laboratory and the toolroom. The fourth
section, with its technique devices, and an adjoining storeroom were
not completely unscathed. Into them had been shoved and piled the
movable machinery and furniture from the other rooms. A door led
from the fourth section to a smaller corridor. Grosvenor presumed
grimly that it was henceforth to be his entrance to the department.

And still he held in his anger, weighing the potentialities of the
situation. He would be expected to protest to Morton. Somehow,
Kent would try to turn that to his own advantage in the election.
Grosvenor couldn't see just how it would benefit the chemist in his
campaign. But Kent evidently thought it would.

Slowly, Grosvenor returned to the outer room—his auditorium. He
noticed for the first time that the vats were food-making machines.
Clever. It would look as if the space were being put to good use,
something which, it could be argued, had not been true before. The
shrewdness of it challenged his own ingenuity.

There seemed little doubt as to why it had happened. Kent disliked
him. In setting himself verbally against Kent's election—a fact which
must have been reported—he had intensified that dislike. But the
chief chemist's vindictive reaction, if handled in the proper manner,
might be used against him.

It seemed to Grosvenor that he must see to it that Kent definitely
did not benefit from his invasion.

He walked over to one of the men and said, "Will you pass the word
along that I welcome this opportunity to further the education of the
staff of the chemistry department, and that I hope no one will object
to learning while he works."

He moved off without waiting for a reply. When he glanced back,
the man was staring after him. Grosvenor suppressed a smile. He felt
quite cheerful as he entered the technique room. Now, at last, he was
confronted by a situation in which he could employ some of the
training methods he had available.

Because of the way his movable cabinets and other equipment had been jumbled into a comparatively small space, it took him a little time to find the hypnotic gas he wanted. He spent nearly half an hour fitting a baffler to the spout, so that the compressed matter inside wouldn't hiss as it poured out. When that was done, Grosvenor carried the container into the outer room. He unlocked a wall cabinet that had a grated door, placed the container inside, and released the gas. Quickly, he locked the door again.

A faint odor of perfume mingled with the chemical smell from the vat.

Whistling softly, Grosvenor started across the room. He was stopped by the straw boss, one of the men who had attended his lecture the previous night.

"What the hell do you think you're doing?"

Grosvenor said mildly, "You'll hardly notice it in a minute. It's part of my educational program for your staff."

"Who asked you for an educational program?"

"Why, Mr. Malden," said Grosvenor in simulated astonishment. "What else would you be doing in my department?" He broke off with a laugh. "I'm just kidding you. It's a deodorant. I don't want this place smelled up."

He moved off without waiting for a reply, and then stood to one side watching the men for reactions to the gas. There were fifteen individuals all together. He could expect five wholly favorable reactions and five partially favorable. There were ways of telling how a person had been affected.

After several minutes of careful observation, Grosvenor walked forward, paused beside one of the men, and said in a low but firm voice, "Come to the washroom in five minutes, and I'll give you something. Now forget about it!"

He retreated to the doorway that connected the outer room with the film studio. As he turned, he saw Malden go over and speak to the man. The technician shook his head in evident surprise.

The straw boss's voice held a note of astounded anger. "What do you mean, he didn't speak to you? I saw him."

The technician got angry. "I didn't hear a thing. I ought to know."

If the argument continued, Grosvenor neither heard it nor saw it. From the corner of his eye, he noticed that one of the younger men in the next room was showing signs of sufficient response. He walked over to the man in the same casual way, and spoke the same words that he had to the first subject—with one difference: He made the time fifteen minutes instead of five.

In all, six men responded to the degree Grosvenor considered essential to his plan. Of the remaining nine individuals, three—including Malden—showed a milder reaction. Grosvenor left the latter group alone. At this stage, he needed virtual certainties. Later, he could try a different pattern for the others.

Grosvenor was waiting when the first subject of his experiment entered the washroom. He smiled at the man, and said, "Ever seen one of these?" He held out the tiny ear crystal, with its flanges for fastening it inside the ear.

The man accepted the little instrument, looked at it, then shook his head in puzzlement. "What is it?" he asked.

Grosvenor commanded, "Turn this way, and I'll fit it into your ear." As the other obeyed without question, Grosvenor went on firmly. "You'll notice, I'm sure, that the part facing outside is flesh colored. In other words, it can be seen only on close examination. If anyone does notice it, you can say it's a hearing aid."

He completed the fitting and stepped back. "After a minute or so, you won't even know it's there. You won't feel it."

The technician seemed interested. "I can hardly feel it now. What does it do?"

"It's a radio," Grosvenor explained. He went on slowly, emphasizing each word. "But you will never consciously hear what it says. The words come through, and go directly into your unconscious. You can hear what other people say to you. You can carry on conversations. In fact, you'll just go about your normal business unaware that anything unusual is going on. You'll forget all about it."

"Well, imagine that!" said the technician.

He went out, shaking his head. A few minutes later, the second man came in; and then, each in turn, the remaining four who had shown deep trance response. Grosvenor fitted them all with duplicates of the nearly invisible ear radio.

Humming tunelessly, he brought out another hypnotic gas, put it into a suitable container, and substituted it for the one in the cabinet.

This time, the straw boss and four other men responded profoundly. Of the rest, two showed a slight reaction, one—who had previously been slightly affected—seemed to come out of his state completely, and one man gave no sign at all.

Grosvenor decided to be satisfied with eleven out of fifteen deep-trance subjects. Kent was going to be unpleasantly surprised at the number of chemical geniuses that turned up in his department.

Nevertheless, this was far from final victory. That was probably not obtainable except by a somewhat more direct attack on Kent himself.

Swiftly, Grosvenor made a tape recording for an experimental broadcast to the ear radios. He left it running steadily while he wandered among the men and observed how they were reacting. Four individuals seemed to be worried about something. Grosvenor went up to one, who was shaking his head frequently.

"What's the matter?" he asked.

The man laughed unhappily. "I keep hearing a voice. Silly."

"Loud?" It was not exactly the question a solicitous inquirer might normally be expected to ask, but Grosvenor was intent.

"No, it's far away. It keeps going away, and then—"

"It'll fade," said Grosvenor soothingly. "You know how the mind can be overstimulated. I'll wager it's going away right now, just from having someone talk to you and distract your attention."

The man cocked his head to one side, as if he were listening. He shook his head wonderingly. "It *is* gone." He straightened, and sighed with relief. "Had me worried for a while there."

Of the other three men, two were reassured with comparative ease. But the remaining individual, even with additional suggestion, continued to hear the voice. Grosvenor finally took him aside, and, under the pretense of examining his ear, removed the tiny radio. The man probably needed more training.

Grosvenor talked briefly with the other subjects. Then, satisfied, he returned to the technique room and set up a series of records to play three minutes out of every fifteen. In the outer room again, he glanced around and saw that all was well. He decided that he could safely leave the men to their work. He went out into the corridor and headed for the elevators.

A few minutes later, he entered the mathematics department and asked to see Morton. To his surprise, he was admitted at once.

He found Morton sitting comfortably behind a big desk. The mathematician indicated a chair, and Grosvenor sat down.

It was the first time he had been in Morton's office, and he gazed around curiously. The room was large and had a viewplate occupying one whole wall. At the moment, the plate was focused on space at such an angle that the great wheeled galaxy, of which Sol was but one tiny dust mote, was visible from rim to rim. It was still near enough for innumerable individual stars to be seen, and far enough away for the misty grandeur of it to be at the peak of brilliance.

Also in the field of vision were several of the star clusters which, though outside the galaxy proper, spun with it through space. The sight of them reminded Grosvenor that the *Space Beagle* was at the moment passing through one of the smaller clusters.

The initial greeting being over, he asked, "Any decision yet as to whether we're going to stop at one of the suns of this cluster?"

Morton nodded. "The decision seems to be against. I agree with that. We're heading for another galaxy, and we'll be away from Earth long enough as it is."

The Director leaned forward to pick up a paper from his desk, then sank back in his chair. He said abruptly, "I hear you've been invaded."

Grosvenor smiled wryly. He could imagine the satisfaction some of the members of the expedition would gain from the incident. He had made the ship's company just aware enough of his presence to cause them to feel uneasy about what Nexialism might be able to do. Such individuals—and many of them were not yet Kent supporters—would be opposed to the Director's interfering in the affair.

Knowing that, he had nevertheless come to find out if Morton understood the necessities of the situation. Tersely, Grosvenor described what had happened. He finished by saying, "Mr. Morton, I want you to order Kent to cease his encroachment." He had no desire for such an order to be issued, but he wanted to see if Morton also realized the danger.

The Director shook his head, and said mildly, "After all, you do have a large space for one man. Why not share with another department?"

The answer was too noncommittal. Grosvenor had no recourse but to press on. He said firmly, "Am I to understand that it is possible for the head of any department aboard this ship to take over space in another department without permission from any authority?"

Morton did not reply immediately. There was a wry smile on his face. He toyed with a pencil as he said, finally, "I have an idea you misunderstand my position aboard the *Beagle*. Before making a decision involving a department head, I must consult with other department heads." He gazed at the ceiling. "Let us suppose that I placed this matter on the agenda, and then it was decided that Kent could have that part of your department he has already taken over. The status, being affirmed, would thereafter be permanent." He finished in a deliberate tone. "It occurred to me that you might not care to have that limitation placed upon you at this stage." His smile broadened.

Grosvenor, his purpose accomplished, smiled back. "I am very happy to have your support in this matter. I can count on you, then, not to let Kent place the matter on the agenda?"

If Morton was surprised by the swift reversal of attitude, he gave no sign. "The agenda," he said with satisfaction, "is one thing I do have considerable control over. My office prepares it. I present it. The department heads can vote to place Kent's request on the agenda for a subsequent meeting, but not for any that is in progress."

"I gather," said Grosvenor, "that Mr. Kent has already made application to take over four rooms of my department."

Morton nodded. He put down the paper he had been holding and picked up a chronometer. He studied it thoughtfully. "The next meeting takes place in two days. Thereafter, every week unless I postpone them. I think"—he sounded as if he were musing aloud—"I should have no difficulty canceling the one scheduled for twelve days hence." He put down the chronometer and stood up briskly. "That will give you twenty-two days to defend yourself."

Grosvenor climbed slowly to his feet. He decided not to comment on the time limit. At the moment, it seemed to be far more than adequate, but it might sound egotistical if he said so. Long before the time was up, he would either regain control of his department, or his defeat would be established.

Aloud, he said, "There's another point I've been wanting to bring up. I feel I should be entitled to communicate directly with the other department heads when I am wearing a space suit."

Morton smiled. "I am sure that is merely an oversight. The matter will be rectified."

They shook hands and separated. As he headed back to the Nexial department, it seemed to Grosvenor that, in an extremely indirect manner, Nexialism was gaining ground.

As he entered the outer room, Grosvenor was surprised to see that Siedel was standing off to one side watching the chemists at work. The psychologist saw him and came over, shaking his head.

"Young man," he said, "isn't this a little unethical?"

Grosvenor guessed with a sinking sensation that Siedel had analyzed what he had done to the men. He kept that awareness out of his voice as he said quickly, "Absolutely unethical, sir. I feel exactly as you would feel if your department were taken over in flagrant disregard of legal rights."

He thought, Why is he here? Has Kent asked him to investigate?

Siedel stroked his jaw. He was a heavily built man with bright, black eyes. "That isn't what I meant," he said slowly. "But I see that you feel justified."

Grosvenor changed his tactics. "Are you referring to the method of instruction I am using on these men?"

He felt no qualms of conscience. Whatever the reason this man was here, the opportunity had to be turned to his own advantage, if possible. His hope was to set up a conflict in the psychologist's mind, to make him neutral in this fight between Kent and himself.

Siedel said, with a thinly sardonic edge to his words, "I am. At the request of Mr. Kent, I have examined those members of his staff whom he thought were acting in an abnormal fashion. It is now my duty to report my diagnosis to Mr. Kent."

"Why?" said Grosvenor. He went on earnestly. "Mr. Siedel, my department has been invaded by a man who dislikes me because I have openly stated that I will not vote for him. Since he acted in defiance of the laws of this ship, I have every right to defend myself as best I can. I beg you, therefore, to remain neutral in this purely private quarrel."

Siedel was frowning. "You don't understand," he said. "I am here as a psychologist. I regard your use of hypnosis without the permission of the subject as completely unethical. I am surprised that you expect me to associate myself with such an act."

Grosvenor said, "I assure you that my code of ethics is just as scrupulous as your own. While I have hypnotized these men without their permission, I have carefully refrained from taking advantage of it to harm or embarrass them in the slightest degree. Under the circumstances, I cannot see that you should feel obliged to take Kent's side."

Siedel frowned. "This is a quarrel between you and Kent—is that right?"

Grosvenor said, "Substantially." He could guess what was coming.

"And yet," said Siedel, "it is not Kent you have hypnotized, but a group of innocent bystanders."

Grosvenor remembered how the four chemist technicians had acted at his lecture. Some of them at least were not quite innocent. He said, "I'm not going to argue with you about that. I could say that, from the beginning of time, the unthinking majority has paid the price of obeying without question the commands of leaders whose motivations they didn't trouble themselves to inquire into. But rather than go into that, I'd like to ask one question."

"Yes?"

"Did you enter the technique room?"

Siedel nodded, but said nothing.

"You saw the records?" Grosvenor persisted.

"Yes."

"You noticed what they dealt with?"

"Information on chemistry."

"That's all I'm giving them," said Grosvenor. "That's all I intend to give them. I regard my department as an educational center. People who force themselves in here receive an education whether they like it or not."

"I confess," said Siedel, "I don't see how that will help you get rid of them. However, I shall be happy to tell Mr. Kent what you are doing. He shouldn't have any objection to his men learning more chemistry."

Grosvenor did not answer. He had his own opinion as to how much Kent would like having a group of his underlings know, as they shortly would, as much as he did about his own specialty.

He watched gloomily as Siedel disappeared into the corridor. The man would undoubtedly give Kent a full report, which meant a new plan would have to be worked out. Standing there, Grosvenor decided that it was too soon for drastic defense measures. It was hard to be certain that any sustained, positive action would not produce on board the ship the very situation he was supposed to prevent. Despite his own reservations about cyclic history, it was well to remember that civilizations did seem to be born, grow older, and die of old age. Before he did anything more, he'd better have a talk with Korita and find out what pitfalls he might inadvertently be heading towards.

He located the Japanese scientist at Library B, which was on the far side of the ship, on the same floor as the Nexial department. Korita was leaving as he came up, and Grosvenor fell in step beside him. Without preamble, he outlined his problem.

Korita did not reply immediately. They walked the length of the corridor before the tall historian spoke, doubtfully. "My friend," he said, "I'm sure you realize the difficulty of solving specific problems on the basis of generalizations, which is virtually all that the theory of cyclic history has to offer."

"Still," Grosvenor said, "a few analogies might be very useful to me. From what I've read on this subject, I gather we're in the late, or 'winter,' period of our own civilization. In other words, right now we are making the mistakes that lead to decay. I have a few ideas about that, but I'd like more."

Korita shrugged. "I'll try to put it briefly." He was silent for a while, then said, "The outstanding common denominator of the 'winter' periods of civilizations is the growing comprehension on the part of millions of individuals of how things work. People become impatient with superstitious or supernatural explanations of what goes on in their minds and bodies, and in the world around them. With the gradual accumulation of knowledge, even the simplest minds for the first time 'see through' and consciously reject the claims of a minority to hereditary superiority. And the grim battle for equality is on."

Korita paused for a moment, then continued. "It is this widespread struggle for personal aggrandizement that constitutes the most significant parallel between all the 'winter' periods in the civilizations of recorded history. For better or worse, the fight usually takes place within the framework of a legal system that tends to protect the entrenched minority. The late-comer to the field, not understanding his motivations, plunges blindly into the battle for power. The result is a veritable melee of undisciplined intelligence. In their resentment and lust, men follow leaders as confused as themselves. Repeatedly, the resulting disorder has led by well-defined steps to the final static fellahin state.

"Sooner or later, one group gains the ascendancy. Once in office, the leaders restore 'order' in so savage a bloodletting that the millions are cowed. Swiftly, the power group begins to restrict activities. The licensing systems and other regulative measures necessary to any organized society become tools of suppression and monopoly. It becomes difficult, then impossible, for the individual to engage in new enterprise. And so we progress by swift stages to the familiar caste system of ancient India, and to other, less well-known but equally inflexible societies, such as that of Rome after about A.D. 300. The individual is born into his station in life and cannot rise above it…. There, does that brief summary help you?"

Grosvenor said slowly, "As I've already said, I'm trying to solve the problem Mr. Kent has presented me without falling into the egotistical errors of the late civilization man you have described. I want to know if I can reasonably hope to defend myself against him without aggravating the hostilities that already exist aboard the *Beagle*."

Korita smiled wryly. "It will be a unique victory if you succeed. Historically, on a mass basis, the problem has never been solved. Well, good luck, young man!"

At that moment, it happened.

9

They had paused at the "glass" room on Grosvenor's floor. It wasn't glass, and it wasn't, by strict definition, a room. It was an alcove of an outer wall corridor, and the "glass" was an enormous curving plate made from a crystallized form of one of the resistance metals. It was so limpidly transparent as to give the illusion that nothing at all was there.

Beyond was the vacuum and darkness of space.

Grosvenor had just noticed absently that the ship was almost through the small star cluster it had been traversing. Only a few of the five thousand-odd suns of the system were still visible. He parted his lips to say, "I'd like to talk with you again, Mr. Korita, when you have time."

He didn't say it. A slightly blurred double image of a woman wearing a feathered hat was taking form in the glass directly in front of him. The image flickered and shimmered. Grosvenor felt an abnormal tensing of the muscles of his eyes. For a moment, his mind went blank. That was followed rapidly by sounds, flashes of light, a sharp sensation of pain. Hypnotic hallucinations! The awareness was like an electric shock.

The recognition saved him. His own conditioning enabled him instantly to reject the mechanical suggestion of the light pattern. He whirled and shouted into the nearest communicator, "Don't look at the images! They're hypnotic. We're being attacked!"

As he turned away, he stumbled over Korita's unconscious body. He stopped and knelt.

"Korita!" he said in a piercing tone, "you *can* hear me?"

"Yes."

"Only *my* instructions influence you. Understand?"

"Yes."

"You're beginning to relax, to forget. Your mind is calm. The effect of the images is fading. Now it's gone. Gone completely. Do you understand? Gone completely."

"I understand."

"They cannot affect you again. In fact, every time you see an image, you're reminded of some pleasant scene from home. Is that clear?"

"Very."

"Now you're beginning to wake up. I'm going to count to three. When I say 'three,' you're wide awake. One…two…three—wake up!"

Korita opened his eyes. "What happened?" he asked in a puzzled tone.

Grosvenor explained swiftly, and then said, "But now, quick, come along! The light pattern keeps pulling at my eyes in spite of my countersuggestion."

He hurried the bewildered archeologist along the corridor toward the Nexial department. At the first corner, they came to a human body lying on the door.

Grosvenor kicked the man, not too lightly. He wanted a shock response. "Do you hear me?" he demanded.

The man stirred. "Yes."

"Then listen. The light images have no further effect on you. Now get up. You're wide awake."

The man climbed to his feet and lunged at him, swinging wildly. Grosvenor ducked, and his assailant staggered past him blindly.

Grosvenor ordered him to halt, but he kept on going without a backward glance. Grosvenor grabbed Korita's arm. "I seem to have got to him too late."

Korita shook his head dazedly. His eyes turned toward the wall, and it was clear from his next words that Grosvenor's suggestion had not taken full effect, or else was already being undermined. "But what are they?" he asked.

"Don't look at them!"

It was incredibly hard not to. Grosvenor had to keep blinking to break the pattern of light flashes that came at his eyes from other images on the walls. At first it seemed to him that the images were everywhere. Then he noticed that the womanish shapes—some oddly double, some single—occupied transparent or translucent wall sections. There were hundreds of such reflecting wall areas, but at least it was a limitation.

They saw more men. The victims lay at uneven intervals along the corridors. Twice they came upon conscious men. One stood in their path with unseeing eyes, and did not move or turn as Grosvenor and Korita hurried by. The other man let out a yell, grabbed his vibrator, and fired it. The tracer beam flashed on the wall beside Grosvenor. And then he had tackled the other and knocked him down. The man—a Kent supporter—glared at him malignantly. "You damned spy!" he said harshly. "We'll get you yet."

Grosvenor didn't pause to discover the reason for the man's astounding behavior. But he grew tense as he guided Korita to the door of the Nexial department. If one chemist could so quickly be stimulated to open hatred of him, then what about the fifteen who had taken over his rooms?

To his relief, they were all unconscious. Hurriedly, he secured two pairs of dark glasses, one for Korita and one for himself, then turned a barrage of flashing lights against the walls, the ceilings, and the floors. Instantly, the images were eclipsed by the strong light.

Grosvenor headed for his technique room and there broadcast commands intended to free those he had hypnotized. Through the open door, he watched two unconscious bodies for response. After five minutes, there was still no sign that they were paying any attention. He guessed that the hypnotic patterns of the attacker had bypassed, or even taken advantage of, the conditioned state of their minds, nullifying any words he might use. The possibility was that they might awaken spontaneously after a while and turn on him.

With Korita's help, he dragged them into the washroom, and then locked the door. One fact was already evident. This was mechanical-visual hypnosis of such power that he had saved himself only by prompt action. But what had happened was not limited to vision. The image had tried to control him by stimulating his brain through his eyes. He was up to date on most of the work that men had done in that field. And so he knew—though the attackers apparently did not—that control by an alien of a human nervous system was not possible except with an encephalo-adjuster or its equivalent.

He could only guess, from what had almost happened to him, that the other men had been precipitated into deep trance sleeps, or else they were confused by hallucinations and were not responsible for their actions.

His job was to get to the control room and turn on the ship's energy screen. No matter where the attack was coming from—whether from another ship or actually from a planet—that should effectively cut off any carrier beams the enemy might be sending.

With frantic fingers, Grosvenor worked to set up a mobile unit of lights. He needed something that would interfere with the images on his way to the control room. He was making the final connection when he felt an unmistakable sensation—a slight giddy feeling—that passed almost instantly. It was a feeling that usually occurred during a considerable change of course, a result of readjustment of the anti-accelerators.

Had the course actually been changed? It was something he'd have to check—later.

He said to Korita, "I intend to make an experiment. Please remain here."

Grosvenor carried his arrangement of lights to a nearby corridor, and placed it in the rear compartment of a power-driven loading vehicle. Then he climbed on and headed for the elevators.

He guessed that, altogether, ten minutes had gone by since he had first seen the image.

He took the turn into the elevator corridor at twenty-five miles an hour, which was fast for these comparatively narrow spaces. In the alcove opposite the elevators, two men were wrestling each other with a life-and-death concentration. They paid no attention to Grosvenor but swayed and strained and cursed. The sound of their breathing was loud. Their single-minded hatred of each other was not affected by Grosvenor's arrangement of lights. Whatever world of hallucination they were in, it had taken profoundly.

Grosvenor whirled his machine into the nearest elevator and started down. He was beginning to let himself hope that he might find the control room deserted.

The hope died as he came to the main corridor. It swarmed with men. Barricades had been flung up, and there was an unmistakable odor of ozone. Vibrators fumed and fussed. Grosvenor peered cautiously out of the elevator, trying to size up the situation. It was visibly bad. The two approaches to the control room were blocked by scores of overturned loading mules. Behind them crouched men in military uniform. Grosvenor caught a glimpse of Captain Leeth among the defenders and, on the far side, he saw Director Morton behind the barricade of one of the attacking groups.

That clarified the picture. Suppressed hostility had been stimulated by the images. The scientists were fighting the military, whom they had always unconsciously hated. The military, in turn, was suddenly freed to vent its contempt and fury upon the despised scientists.

It was, Grosvenor knew, not a true picture of their feeling for each other. The human mind normally balanced innumerable opposing impulses so that the average individual might live his life span without letting one feeling gain important ascendance over the others. That intricate balance had now been upset. The result threatened disaster to an entire expedition of human beings, and promised victory to an enemy whose purpose could only be conjectured.

Whatever the reason, the way to the control room was blocked. Reluctantly, Grosvenor retreated again to his own department.

Korita met him at the door. "Look!" he said. He motioned to a wall-communicator plate, which was tuned to the finely balanced steering devices in the fore part of the *Space Beagle*. The sending plate there was focused directly along a series of hairline sights. The arrangement looked more intricate than it was. Grosvenor brought his eyes to the sights and saw that the ship was describing a slow curve which, at its climax, would bring it to bear directly on a bright, white star. A servomechanism had been set up to make periodic adjustments that would hold it on its course.

"Could the enemy do that?" Korita asked.

Grosvenor shook his head, more puzzled than alarmed. He shifted the viewer over to the bank of supplementary instruments. According to the star's spectral type, magnitude, and luminosity, it was just over four light-years distant. The ship's speed was up to a light-year every five hours. Since it was still accelerating, that would increase on a calculable curve. He estimated roughly that the vessel would reach the vicinity of the sun in approximately eleven hours.

With a jerky movement, Grosvenor shut off the communicator. He stood there, shocked but not incredulous. Destruction *could* be the purpose of the deluded person who had altered the ship's course. If so, there were just ten hours in which to prevent catastrophe.

Even at that moment, when he had no clear plan, it seemed to Grosvenor that only an attack on the enemy, using hypnotic techniques, would effectively do the job. Meanwhile…

He stood up decisively. It was time for a second attempt to get into the control room.

He needed something that would directly stimulate brain cells. There were several devices that could do that. Most of them were usable for medical purposes only. The exception was the encephalo-adjuster, an instrument that could be used to transmit impulses from one mind to another.

Even with Korita's help, it took Grosvenor several minutes to set up one of his adjusters. Testing it consumed still more time; and, because it was such a delicate machine, he had to fasten it to his loading vehicle with a cushion of springs around it. All together, the preparation required thirty-seven minutes.

He had a brief, though rather sharp, argument then with the archeologist, who wanted to accompany him. In the end, however, Korita agreed to remain behind and guard their base of operations.

Carrying the encephalo-adjuster made it necessary for him to keep down the speed of his vehicle as he headed for the control room. The enforced slowdown irked him, but it also gave him an opportunity to observe the changes that had taken place since the first moment of attack.

He saw only an occasional unconscious body. Grosvenor guessed that most of the men who had fallen into deep trance sleeps had awakened spontaneously. Such awakenings were common hypnotic phenomena. Now they were responding to other stimuli on the same chance basis. Unfortunately—although it also was to be expected—that seemed to mean that long-suppressed impulses controlled their actions.

And so men who, under normal circumstances, merely disliked each other mildly had, in an instant, had their dislike change to murderous hatred.

The deadly factor was that they would be unaware of the change. For the mind *could* be tangled without the individual's knowing it. It could be tangled by bad environmental association, or by the attack that was now being made against a shipload of men. In either case, each person carried on as if his new beliefs were as soundly based as his old ones.

Grosvenor opened the elevator door on the control room level, and then drew back hastily. A heat projector was pouring flame along the corridor. The metal walls burned with a harsh, sizzling sound. Within his narrow field of vision, three men lay dead. As he waited, there was a thunderous explosion. Instantly, the flames stopped. A blue smoke hazed the air, and there was a sense of suffocating heat. Within seconds, both the haze and the heat were gone. It was obvious that at least the ventilating system was still working.

He peered out cautiously. At first sight, the corridor seemed deserted. Then he saw Morton, half hidden in a protective alcove less than a score of feet away. At almost the same moment, the Director saw him and beckoned him over. Grosvenor hesitated, then realized he had to take the risk. He pushed his vehicle through the elevator doorway and darted across the intervening apace. The Director greeted him eagerly as he came up.

"You're just the man I want to see," he said. "We've got to get control of the ship away from Captain Leeth before Kent and his group organize their attack."

Morton's gaze was calm and intelligent. He had the look of a man fighting for the right. Nor did it seem to occur to him that an explanation for his statement was required. The Director went on. "We'll need your help particularly against Kent. They're bringing up some chemical stuff I've never seen before. So far, our fans have blown it right back at them, but they're setting up fans of their own. Our big problem is, will we have time to defeat Leeth before Kent can bring his forces to bear?"

Time was also Grosvenor's problem. Unobtrusively, he brought his right hand up to his left wrist and touched the activating relay that controlled the directional-sending plates of the adjuster. He pointed the plates at Morton as he said, "I've got a plan, sir. I think it might be effective against the enemy."

He stopped. Morton was looking down. The Director said, "You've brought along an adjuster, and it's on. What do you expect from that?"

Grosvenor's first tense reaction yielded to a need for a suitable answer. He had hoped that Morton would not be too familiar with adjusters. With that hope blasted, he could still try to use the instrument, though without the initial advantage of surprise. He said in a voice that was taut in spite of himself, "That's it. It's this machine I want to use."

Morton hesitated, then said, "I gather from the thoughts coming into my mind that you're broadcasting—" He stopped. Interest quickened his face. "Say," he said presently, "that's good. If you can put over the notion that we're being attacked by aliens—"

He broke off. His lips pursed. His eyes narrowed with calculation. He said, "Captain Leeth has twice tried to make a deal with me. Now we'll pretend to agree, and you go over with your machine. We'll attack the moment you signal us." He explained with dignity. "You understand, I would not consider dealing with either Kent or Captain Leeth except as a means to victory. You appreciate that, I hope?"

Grosvenor found Captain Leeth in the control room. The commander greeted him with stiff-backed friendliness. "This fight among the scientists," he said earnestly, "has placed the military in an awkward position. We've got to defend the control room and the engine room and so perform our minimum duty to the expedition as a whole." He shook his head gravely. "It's out of the question, of course, that either of them be allowed to win. In the final issue, we of the military are prepared to sacrifice ourselves to prevent the victory of either group."

The explanation startled Grosvenor out of his own purpose. He had been wondering if Captain Leeth was responsible for aiming the ship directly at a sun. Here was at least partial confirmation. The commander's motivation seemed to be that victory for any group but the military was unthinkable. With that beginning, it was probably only a tiny step to the concept that the whole expedition must be sacrificed.

Casually, Grosvenor pointed the directional sender of the adjuster at Captain Leeth.

Brain waves, minute pulsations transmitted from axon to dendrite, from dendrite to axon, always following a previously established path depending on past associations—it was a process that operated endlessly among the ninety million neuron cells of a human brain. Each cell was in its own state of electrocolloidal balance, an intricate interplay of tension and impulse. Only gradually, over the years, had machines been developed that could detect with some degree of accuracy the meaning of the energy flow inside the brain.

The earliest encephalo-adjuster was an indirect descendant of the famous electroencephalograph. But its function was the reverse of that first device. It manufactured artificial brain waves of any desired pattern. Using it, a skillful operator could stimulate any part of the brain, and so cause thoughts, emotions, and dreams, and bring up memories from the individual's past. It was not in itself a controlling instrument. The subject maintained his own ego. However, it could transmit the mind impulses of one person to a second person. Since the impulses varied according to the sender's thoughts, the recipient was stimulated in a highly flexible fashion.

Unaware of the presence of the adjuster, Captain Leeth did not realize that his thoughts were no longer quite his own. He said, "The attack being made on the ship by the images makes the quarrel of the scientists traitorous and unforgivable." He paused, then said thoughtfully, "Here's my plan."

The plan involved heat projectors, muscle-straining acceleration, and partial extermination of both groups of scientists. Captain Leeth failed even to mention the aliens, nor did it seem to occur to him that he was describing his intentions to an emissary of what he regarded as the enemy. He finished by saying, "Where your services will be important, Mr. Grosvenor, is in the science department. As a Nexialist, with a coordinative knowledge of many sciences, you can play a decisive role against the other scientists..."

Weary and disheartened, Grosvenor gave up. The chaos was too great for one man to overcome. Everywhere he looked were armed men. Altogether, he had seen a score or more dead bodies. And at any moment the uneasy truce between Captain Leeth and Director Morton would end in a burst of projector fire. Even now he could hear the roaring of the fans where Morton was holding off Kent's attack.

He sighed as he turned back to the captain. "I'll need some equipment from my own department," he said. "Can you pass me through to the rear elevators? I can be back here in five minutes."

As he guided his machine into the back door of his department a few minutes later, it seemed to Grosvenor that there was no longer any doubt about what he must do. What had seemed a farfetched idea when he first thought of it was now the only plan he had left.

He must attack the aliens through their myriad images, and with their own hypnotic weapons.

**10**

Grosvenor was aware of Korita watching him as he made his preparations. The archeologist came over and looked at the array of electrical instruments he was attaching to the encephalo-adjuster, but he asked no questions. He seemed to be fully recovered from his experience.

Grosvenor kept wiping the perspiration from his face. And yet it was not warm. The room temperature stood at normal. By the time his preliminary work was done, he realized that he had to stop to analyze his anxiety. He just didn't, he decided finally, know enough about the enemy.

It was not sufficient that he had a theory about how they were operating. The great mystery was an enemy who had curiously womanlike bodies and faces, some partly doubled, some single. He needed a reasonable philosophic basis for action. He needed that balance for his plan which only knowledge could give him.

He turned to Korita, and asked, "In terms of cyclic history, what stage of culture could these beings be in?"

The archeologist sat down in a chair, pursed his lips, and said, "Tell me your plan."

The Japanese grew pale as Grosvenor described it. He said finally, almost irrelevantly, "How is it you were able to save me, and not the others?"

"I got to you right away. The human nervous system learns by repetition. For you, their light pattern hadn't repeated as often as for the others."

"Is there any way we could have avoided this disaster?" he asked grimly.

Grosvenor smiled a wan smile. "Nexial training could have done it, since that includes hypnotic conditioning. There's only one sure protection against hypnosis, and that is to be trained in it in exactly the right way."

He broke off. "Mr. Korita, please answer my question. Cyclic history?"

A thin, wet line of moisture formed on the archeologist's brow. "My friend," he said, "surely you can't expect a generalization at this stage. What do we know about these beings?"

Grosvenor groaned inwardly. He recognized the need for discussion, but vital time was passing. He said indecisively, "Beings who can use hypnosis over a distance, as these can, would probably be able to stimulate each other's minds, and so would have naturally the kind of telepathy that human beings can obtain only through the encephalo-adjuster."

He leaned forward, abruptly excited. "Korita, what effect would the ability to read minds without artificial aids have on a culture?"

The archeologist was sitting up. "Why, of course," he said. "You have the answer. Mind reading would stultify the development of any race, and therefore this one is in the fellahin stage."

His eyes were bright as he stared at the puzzled Grosvenor. "Don't you see? The ability to read another's mind would make you feel that you know about him. On that basis, a system of absolute certainties would develop. How could you doubt when you know? Such beings would flash through the early periods of their culture, and arrive at the fellah period in the swiftest possible time."

Alertly, while Grosvenor sat frowning, he described how various civilizations of Earth and galactic history had exhausted themselves, and then stagnated into fellahdom. Fellah people resented newness and change. They were not particularly cruel as a group, but because of their poverty they all too frequently developed an indifference toward the suffering of individuals.

When Korita had finished, Grosvenor said, "Perhaps their resentment of change is responsible for the attack on the ship?"

The archeologist was cautious. "Perhaps."

There was silence. It seemed to Grosvenor that he had to act as if Korita's total analysis was correct. He had no other hypothesis. With such a theory as a starting point, he could try to obtain verification from one of the images.

A glance at the chronometer tensed him. He had less than seven hours to save the ship.

Hastily, he focused a beam of light through the encephalo-adjuster. With quick movements, he set a screen in front of the light, so that a small area of glass was thrown into shadow except for the intermittent light that played on it from the adjuster.

Instantly, an image appeared. It was one of the partially doubled ones, and because of the encephalo-adjuster, he was able to study it in safety. That first clear look astounded him. It was only vaguely humanoid. And yet it was understandable how his mind had leaped to the woman identification earlier. Its overlapping double face was crowned with a neat bun of golden feathers. But its head, though now unmistakably birdlike, did have a human appearance. There were no feathers on its face, which was covered with a lacework of what seemed to be veins. The human appearance resulted from the way those markings had formed into groups, to give the effect of cheeks and nose.

The second pair of eyes and the second mouth were in each case nearly two inches above the first. They almost made a second head, which was literally growing out of the first. There was also a second pair of shoulders, with a doubled pair of short arms that ended in beautifully delicate, amazingly long hands and fingers—and the overall effect was still feminine. Grosvenor found himself thinking that the arms and fingers of the two bodies would be likely to separate first. The second body would then be able to help support its weight.

Parthenogenesis, Grosvenor thought. Reproduction without sex. The growth of a bud from a parent body, and the final separation from the parent into a new individual.

The image in the wall before him showed vestigial wings. Tufts of feathers were visible at the "wrists." It wore a bright-blue tunic over an astonishingly straight and superficially humanlike body. If there were other vestiges of a feathery past, they were hidden by the clothing. What was clear was that this bird didn't, and couldn't, fly under its own power.

Korita spoke first, in a helpless tone. "How are you going to let it know you're willing to be hypnotized in exchange for information?"

Grosvenor did not answer in words. He stood up and tentatively drew a picture of the image and of himself on a blackboard. Forty-seven minutes and scores of drawings later, the bird image suddenly faded from the wall, and a city scene appeared in its place.

It was not a large community, and his first view of it was from a high vantage point. He had an impression of very tall, very narrow buildings, clustered so close together that all the lower reaches must be lost in gloom for most of each day. Grosvenor wondered, in passing, if that might possibly reflect nocturnal habits in some primeval past. His mind leaped on. He ignored individual buildings in his desire to obtain a whole picture. Above everything else, he wanted to find out the extent of their machine culture, how they communicated, and if this was the city from which the attack on the ship was being launched.

He could see no machines, no aircraft, no cars. Nor was there anything corresponding to the interstellar-communication equipment used by human beings, which, on Earth, required stations spaced over many square miles of land. It seemed likely, therefore, that the origin of the attack was nothing like that.

Even as he made his negative discovery, the view changed. He was no longer on a hill but in a building near the center of the city. Whatever was taking that perfect color picture moved forward, and he looked down over the edge. His primary concern was with the whole scene. Yet he found himself wondering how they were showing it to him. The transition from one scene to another had been accomplished in the twinkling of an eye. Less than a minute had passed since his blackboard illustration had finally made known his desire for information.

That thought, like the others, was a flashing one. Even as he had it, he was gazing avidly down the side of the building. The space separating it from the nearby structures seemed no more than ten feet. But now he saw something that had not been visible from the hillside. The buildings were connected on every level by walks only inches wide. Along these moved the pedestrian traffic of the bird city.

Directly below Grosvenor two individuals strode towards each other along the same narrow walk. They seemed unconcerned by the fact that it was a hundred feet or more to the ground. They passed casually, easily. Each swung his outside leg wide around the other, caught the walk, bent his inside leg wide out, and then they were by, without having broken pace. There were other people on other levels going through the same intricate maneuvers in the same nonchalant manner. Watching them, Grosvenor guessed that their bones were thin and hollow, and that they were lightly built.

The scene changed again, and then again. It moved from one section of the street to another. He saw, it seemed to him, every possible variation of the reproductive condition. Some were so far advanced that the legs and arms and most of the body were free. Others were as he had already seen them. In every instance, the parent seemed unaffected by the weight of the new body.

Grosvenor was trying to get a glimpse inside one of the dim interiors of a building when the picture began to fade from the wall. In a moment, the city had disappeared completely. In its place grew the double image. The image fingers pointed at the encephalo-adjuster. Its motion was unmistakable. It had fulfilled its part of the bargain. It was time for him to fulfill his.

It was naïve of it to expect that he would do so. The trouble was, he had to. He had no alternative but to carry out his obligation.

"I am calm and relaxed," said Grosvenor's recorded voice. "My thoughts are clear. What I see is not necessarily related to what I am looking at. What I hear may be meaningless to the interpretive centers of my brain. But I have seen their city as they think it is. Whether what I actually see and hear makes sense or nonsense, I remain calm, relaxed, and at ease..."

Grosvenor listened carefully to the words, and then turned to Korita. "That's it," he said simply.

The time might come, of course, when he would not consciously hear the message. But it would be there. Its patterns would impress ever more firmly on his mind. Still listening, he examined the adjuster for the last time. It was all as he wanted it.

To Korita, he explained, "I'm setting the automatic cutoff for five hours. If you pull this switch"—he indicated a red lever—"you can break me free before then. But only do so in an emergency."

"How do you define emergency?"

"If we're attacked here." Grosvenor hesitated. He would have liked a series of breaks. But what he was about to do was not merely a scientific experiment. It was a life-and-death gamble. Ready for action, he put his hand on the control dial. And there he paused.

For this was the moment. Within a few seconds, the group mind of countless individual bird folk would be in possession of parts of his nervous system. They would undoubtedly try to control him as they were controlling the other men on the ship.

He was fairly positive that he would be up against a group of minds working together. He had seen no machines, not even a wheeled vehicle, that most primitive of mechanical devices. For a short time, he had taken it for granted that they were using television-type cameras. Now he guessed that he had seen the city through the eyes of individuals. With these beings, telepathy was a sensory process as sharp as vision itself. The enmassed mind power of millions of bird people could hurdle light-years of distance. They didn't need machines.

He couldn't hope to foresee the result of his attempt to become a part of their collective mind.

Still listening to the recorder, Grosvenor manipulated the dial of the encephalo-adjuster and slightly modified the rhythm of his own thoughts. It had to be slight. Even if he had wanted to, he could not offer the aliens complete attunement. In those rhythmic pulsations lay every variation of sanity, unsanity, and insanity. He had to restrict his reception to waves that would register "sane" on a psychologist's graph.

The adjuster superimposed them on a beam of light which in turn shone directly on the image. If the individual behind the image was affected by the pattern in the light, it hadn't shown it yet. Grosvenor did not expect overt evidence, and so he was not disappointed. He was convinced that the result would become apparent only in the changes that occurred in the patterns they were directing at him. And that, he was sure, he would have to experience with his own nervous system.

It was hard for him to concentrate on the image, but he persisted. The encephalo-adjuster began to interfere markedly with his vision. And still he stared steadily at the image.

"I am calm and relaxed. My thoughts are clear…"

One instant the words were loud in his ears. The next, they were gone. And in their stead was a roaring sound as of distant thunder.

The noise faded slowly. It became a steady throbbing like the murmur in a large sea shell. Grosvenor was aware of a faint light. It was far away and had the hazy dimness of a lamp seen through thick fog.

"I'm still in control," he assured himself. "I'm getting sense impressions through its nervous system. It's getting impressions through mine."

He could wait. He could sit here and wait until the darkness cleared, until his brain started to make some kind of interpretation of the sense phenomena that were being telegraphed from that other nervous system. He could sit here and—

He stopped. Sit! he thought. Was that what *it* was doing? He poised, intent and alert. He heard a distant voice say, "Whether what I actually see and hear makes sense or nonsense, I remain calm..."

His nose began to itch. He thought, They don't have noses; at least I didn't see any. Therefore, it's either my own nose, or a random stimulation. He started to reach up to scratch it, and felt a sharp pain in his stomach. He would have doubled up with the hurt of it if he had been able. He couldn't. He couldn't scratch his nose. He couldn't put his hands on his abdomen.

He realized then that the itch and the pain stimuli did not derive from his own body. Nor did they necessarily have any corresponding meaning in the other's nervous system. Two highly developed life forms were sending signals to each other—he hoped that he was sending signals to it also—which neither could interpret. His advantage was that he had expected it. The alien, if it was fellah, and if Korita's theory was valid, hadn't and couldn't. Understanding that, *he* could hope for adjustment. *It* could only become more confused.

The itch went away. The pain in his stomach became a feeling of satiation, as if he had eaten too much. A hot needle stabbed at his spine, digging at each vertebra. Halfway down, the needle turned to ice, and the ice melted and ran in a freezing stream down his back. Something—a hand? a piece of metal? a pair of tongs?—snatched at a bundle of muscles in his arm, and almost tore them out by the roots. His mind shrieked with pain messages. He almost lost consciousness.

Grosvenor was a badly shaken man when that sensation faded into nothingness. These were all illusions. No such things were happening anywhere, not in his body, not in that of the bird being. His brain was receiving a pattern of impulses through his eyes, and was misinterpreting them. In such a relationship, pleasure could become pain, any stimulus could produce any feeling. He hadn't counted on the misinterpretations being so violent.

He forgot that as his lips were caressed by something soft and squishy. A voice said, "I am loved—" Grosvenor rejected the meaning. No, not "loved." It was, he believed, his own brain again trying to interpret sense phenomena from a nervous system that was experiencing a reaction different from any comparable human emotion. Consciously, he substituted the words, "I am stimulated by—" and then let the feeling run its course. In the end, he still didn't know what it was that he had felt. The stimulation was not unpleasant. His taste buds were titillated by a sense of sweetness. His eyes watered, a relaxing process. A picture of a flower came into his mind. It was a lovely, red, Earth carnation and thus could have no connection with the flora of the Riim world.

Riim! he thought. His mind poised in tense fascination. Had that come to him across the gulf of space? In some irrational way, the name seemed to fit. Yet no matter what came through, a doubt would remain in his mind. He could not be sure.

The final series of sensations had all been pleasant. Nevertheless, he waited anxiously for the next manifestation. The light remained dim and hazy. Then once more his eyes seemed to water. His feet suddenly itched intensely. The sensation passed, leaving him unaccountably hot and weighted by a suffocating lack of air.

"False!" he told himself. "Nothing like this is happening."

The stimulations ceased. Again there was only the steady throbbing sound, and the all-pervasive blur of light. It began to worry him. It was possible that his method was right and that, given time, he would eventually be able to exercise some control over a member, or a group of members, of the enemy. But time was what he could not spare. Every passing second brought him a colossal distance nearer personal destruction. Out there here (for an instant he was confused)—in space, one of the biggest and costliest ships ever built by men was devouring the miles at a velocity that had almost no meaning.

He knew which parts of his brain were being stimulated. He could hear a noise only when sensitive areas at the side of the cortex received sensations. The brain surface above the ear, when titillated, produced dreams and old memories. In the same way, every part of the human brain had long ago been mapped. The exact location of stimulation areas differed slightly for each individual, but the general structure, among humans, was always the same.

The normal human eye was a fairly objective mechanism. The lens focused a real image on the retina. To judge by the pictures of their city, as transmitted by the Riim folk, they, also, possessed objectively accurate eyes. If he could coordinate his visual centers with their eyes, he would receive dependable pictures.

More minutes went by. He thought, in sudden despair, Is it possible that I'm going to sit here the full five hours without ever making a useful contact? For the first time, he questioned his good sense in committing himself so completely to this situation. When he tried to move his hand over to the control lever of the encephalo-adjuster, nothing seemed to happen. A number of vagrant sensations came, among them the unmistakable odor of burning rubber.

For the third time, his eyes watered. And then, sharp and clear, a picture came. It flashed off as swiftly as it had flashed on. But to Grosvenor, who had been trained by advanced tachistoscopic techniques, the afterimage remained as vivid in his mind as if he had had a leisurely look.

It seemed as if he were in one of the tall, narrow buildings. The interior was dimly lighted by the reflections from the sunlight that came through the open doors. There were no windows. Instead of floors, the residence was fitted with catwalks. A few bird people were sitting on these walks. The walls were lined with doors, indicating the existence of cabinets and storage areas.

The visualization both excited and disturbed him. Suppose he did establish a relationship with this creature whereby he was affected by its nervous system, and it by his. Suppose he reached the point where he could hear with its ears, see with its eyes, and feel to some degree what it felt. These were sensory impressions only.

Could he hope to bridge the gap and induce motor responses in the creature's muscles? Would he be able to force it to walk, turn its head, move its arms, and, generally, make it act as his body? The attack on the ship was being made by a group working together, thinking together, feeling together. By gaining control of one member of such a group, could he exercise some control over all?

His momentary vision must have come through the eyes of one individual. What he had experienced so far did not suggest any kind of group contact. He was like a man imprisoned in a dark room, with a hole in the wall in front of him covered with layers of translucent material. Through this filtered a vague light. Occasionally, images penetrated the blur, and he had glimpses of the outside world. He could be fairly certain that the pictures were accurate. But that did not apply to the sounds that came through another hole on a side wall, or the sensations that came to him through still other holes in the ceiling and floor.

Human beings could hear frequencies up to twenty thousand vibrations a second. That was where some races started to hear. Under hypnosis, men could be conditioned to laugh uproariously when they were being tortured, and shriek with pain when tickled. Stimulation that meant pain to one life form could mean nothing at all to another.

Mentally, Grosvenor let the tensions seep out of him. There was nothing for him to do but to relax and wait.

He waited.

It occurred to him presently that there might be a connection between his own thoughts and the sensations he received. That picture of the inside of the building—what had he thought just before it came? Principally, he recalled, he had visualized the structure of the eye.

The connection was so obvious that his mind trembled with excitement. There was another thing, also. Until now, he had concentrated on the notion of seeing and feeling with the nervous system of the individual. Yet the realization of his hopes depended on his establishing contact with, and control of, the group of minds that had attacked the ship.

He saw his problem, suddenly, as one that would require control of his own brain. Certain areas would have to be virtually blacked out, kept at minimum-performance levels. Others must be made extremely sensitive, so that all incoming sensations found it easier to seek expression through them. As a highly trained autohypnotic subject, he could accomplish both objectives by suggestion.

Vision came first, of course. Then muscular control of the individual through whom the group was working against him.

Flashes of colored light interrupted his concentration. Grosvenor regarded them as evidence of the effectiveness of his suggestions. And he knew that he was on the right track when his vision cleared suddenly, and stayed clear.

The scene was the same. His control still sat on one of the roosts inside one of the tall buildings. Hoping fervently that the vision was not going to fade, Grosvenor began to concentrate on moving the Riim's muscles.

The trouble was that the ultimate explanation of why a movement could occur at all was obscure. His visualization could not possibly include in detail the millions of cell responses involved in the raising of one finger. He thought now in terms of a whole limb. Nothing happened. Shocked but determined, Grosvenor tried symbol hypnosis, using a single cue word to cover the entire complex process.

Slowly, one of the attenuated arms came up. Another cue, and his control stood up cautiously. Then he made it turn its head. The act of looking reminded the bird being that that drawer and that cabinet and that closet were "mine." The memory barely touched the conscious level. The creature knew its own possessions and accepted the fact without concern.

Grosvenor had a hard time fighting down his excitement. With tense patience, he had the bird being get up from a sitting position, raise its arms, lower them, and walk back and forth along the roost. Finally, he made it sit down again.

He must have been keyed up, his brain responsive to the slightest suggestion, because he had barely started to concentrate again when his whole being was flooded by a message that seemed to affect every level of his thought and feeling. More or less automatically, Grosvenor translated the anguished thoughts into familiar verbalisms.

"The cells are calling, calling. The cells are afraid. Oh, the cells know pain! There is darkness in the Riim world. Withdraw from the being—far from Riim...Shadows, darkness, turmoil...The cells must reject him...But they cannot. They were right to try to be friendly to the being who came out of the great dark, since they did not know he was an enemy...The night deepens. All cells withdraw...But they cannot..."

Grosvenor thought blankly, Friendly!

It fitted, also. He could see how, in a nightmarish fashion, everything that had happened so far could be explained as easily one way as the other. Dismayed, he realized the seriousness of the situation. If the catastrophe that had already occurred aboard the ship were the result of a misguided and ignorant attempt at friendly communication, then what damage might they not be able to do if they were hostile?

His problem was greater than theirs. If he broke his connection with them, they would be free. Now that could mean an attack. By avoiding him, they might actually attempt destruction of the *Space Beagle*.

He had no recourse but to continue what he had planned, in the hope that something would happen that he could turn to his favor.

He concentrated first on what seemed the most logical intermediate stage: the transfer of control to another alien. The choice, in the case of these beings, was obvious.

"I am loved!" he told himself, deliberately producing the sensation that had confused him earlier. "I am loved by my parent body, from which I am growing to wholeness. I share my parent's thoughts, but already I see with my own eyes, and know that I am one of the group—"

The transition came suddenly, as Grosvenor had expected it might. He moved the smaller, duplicate fingers. He arched the fragile shoulders. Then he oriented himself again to the parent Riim. The experiment was so completely satisfactory that he felt ready for the bigger jump that would take him into association with the nervous system of a more distant alien.

And that, also, proved to be a matter of stimulating the proper brain centers. Grosvenor came to awareness standing in a wilderness of brush and hill. Directly in front of him was a narrow stream. Beyond it, an orange sun rode low in a dark purple sky that was spotted with fleecy clouds. Grosvenor made his new control turn completely around. He saw that a small roost building nestled among the trees farther along the stream. It was the only habitation in sight. He walked over to it and looked inside. In the dim interior he made out several roosts, one with two birds sitting on it. Both sat with eyes closed.

It was quite possible, he decided, that they were participating in the group assault on the *Space Beagle*.

From there, by a variation of the stimulus, he transferred his control to an individual on a part of the planet where it was night. The transition this time was even faster. He was in a lightless city, with ghostly buildings and catwalks. Swiftly, Grosvenor moved on to association with other nervous systems. He had no clear idea why the rapport was established with one Riim, and not with another who fitted the same general requirement. It could be that the stimulation affected some individuals slightly faster than it affected others. It was even possible that they were descendants or body relatives of his original parent control. When he had been associated with more than two dozen Riim all over the planet, it seemed to Grosvenor that he had a good overall impression.

It was a world of brick and stone and wood, and of a neurological community relationship that would probably never be surpassed. And so a race had bypassed the entire machine age of man, with its penetration of the secrets of matter and energy. Now, he felt, he could safely take the next-to-the-last step of his counterattack.

He concentrated on a pattern which would characterize one of the beings who had projected an image to the *Space Beagle*. He had then a sense of a small but noticeable lapse of time. And then...

He was looking forth from one of the images, seeing the ship through an image.

His first concern was with how the battle was progressing. But he had to restrain his will to know, because coming aboard was only part of his necessary pre-conditioning. He wanted to affect a group of perhaps millions of individuals. He had to affect them so powerfully that they would have to withdraw from the *Space Beagle* and have no choice but to stay away from it.

He had proved that he could receive their thoughts and that they could receive his. His association with one nervous system after another would not have been possible unless that were so. And so now he was ready. He projected his thoughts into the darkness. "You live in a universe; and within you, you form pictures of the universe as it seems to you. And of that universe you know nothing and can know nothing except for the pictures. But the pictures within you of the universe are not the universe..."

How could you influence another's mind? By changing his assumptions. How could you alter another's actions? By changing his basic beliefs, his emotional certainties.

Carefully, Grosvenor went on, "And the pictures within you do not show all about the universe, for there are many things which you cannot know directly, not having senses to know. Within the universe there is an order. And if the order of the pictures within you is not as the order of the universe, then you are deceived..."

In the history of life, few thinking beings had done anything illogical—within their frame of reference. If the frame was falsely based, if the assumptions were untrue to reality, then the individual's automatic logic could lead him to disastrous conclusions.

The assumptions had to be changed. Grosvenor changed them, deliberately, coolly, honestly. His own basic hypothesis behind what he was doing was that the Riim had no defense. These were the first new ideas they had had in countless generations. He did not doubt that the impact would be colossal. This was a fellah civilization, rooted in certainties that had never before been challenged. There was ample historical evidence that a tiny intruder could influence decisively the future of entire fellahin races.

Huge old India had crumbled before a few thousand Englishmen. Similarly, all the fellah peoples of ancient Earth were taken over with ease, and did not revive until the core of their inflexible attitudes was forever shattered by the dawning realization that there was more to life than they had been taught under their rigid systems.

The Riim were peculiarly vulnerable. Their method of communication, unique and wonderful though it was, made it possible to influence them all in a single intensive operation. Over and over Grosvenor repeated his message, adding each time one instruction that had to do with the ship. The instruction was: "Change the pattern you are using against those on the ship, and then withdraw it. Change the pattern, so that they can relax and sleep…then withdraw it…. Your friendly action caused the ship great harm. We are friendly to you also, but your method of expressing friendship hurt us."

He had only a vague notion as to how long he actually poured his commands into that tremendous neural circuit. He guessed about two hours. Whatever the time involved, it ended as the relay switch on the encephalo-adjuster automatically broke the connection between himself and the image in the wall of his department.

Abruptly, he was aware of the familiar surroundings. He glanced at where the image had been. It was gone. He sent a quick look toward Korita. The archeologist was crumpled in his chair fast asleep.

Grosvenor sat up jerkily, remembering the instruction he had given—to relax and sleep. This was the result. All over the ship, men would be sleeping.

Pausing only to awaken Korita, Grosvenor headed out into the corridor. As he raced along, he saw that unconscious men lay everywhere but that the walls were bright and clear. Not once on his journey to the control room did he see an image.

Inside the control room, he stepped gingerly over the sleeping form of Captain Leeth, who lay on the floor near the control panel. With a sigh of relief, he threw the switch that energized the outer screen of the ship.

Seconds later, Elliott Grosvenor was in the control chair, altering the course of the *Space Beagle*.

Before leaving the control room, he put a time lock on the steering gear and set it for ten hours. Thus protected against the possibility that one of the men might wake up in a suicidal mood, he hurried out to the corridor and began to give medical aid to injured men.

His patients were, without exception, unconscious, and so he had to guess at their condition. He played safe. Where labored respiration indicated shock, he gave blood plasma. He injected specific drugs for pain whenever he saw dangerous-looking wounds, and he applied fast-healing salves for burns and cuts. Seven times—with Korita's help now—he lifted dead men onto loading mules and rushed them to resuscitation chambers. Four revived. Even after that there were thirty-two dead men who, after an examination, Grosvenor did not so much as attempt to revive.

They were still tending the injured when a geology technician near by woke up, yawned lazily—and then groaned in dismay. Grosvenor guessed that a flood of memory had come, but he watched warily as the man climbed to his feet and came over. The technician glanced in puzzlement from Korita to Grosvenor; finally he said, "May I help?"

Soon a dozen men were helping, with a strained concentration and an occasional word that showed awareness of the temporary insanity that had caused such a nightmare of death and destruction.

Grosvenor was not aware that Captain Leeth and Director Morton had arrived until he saw them talking to Korita. Presently, Korita walked off, and the two leaders came over to Grosvenor and invited him to a meeting in the control room. Silently, Morton clapped him on the back. Grosvenor had been wondering if they would remember. Spontaneous amnesia was a common hypnotic phenomenon. Without their own recollections, it would be extremely hard to explain convincingly what had happened.

He was relieved when Captain Leeth said, "Mr. Grosvenor, in looking back over the disaster, Mr. Morton and I were both struck by the attempt you made to make us aware that we were the victims of an outside attack. Mr. Korita has now told us what he saw of your actions. I want you to tell the departmental executives in the control room exactly what took place."

It required over an hour to give an orderly account. When Grosvenor had finished, a man said, "Am I to understand that this was actually an attempt at friendly communications?"

Grosvenor nodded. "I'm afraid it was."

"You mean we can't go over there and bomb hell out of them?" he said harshly.

"It would serve no useful purpose." Grosvenor spoke steadily. "We could drop in on them and make a more direct contact."

Captain Leeth said quickly, "It would take too long. We've got distance to cover." He added in a sour voice, "It seems to be a particularly drab civilization."

Grosvenor hesitated. Before he could speak, Director Morton said quickly, "What have you to say to that, Mr. Grosvenor?"

Grosvenor said, "I assume the commander is referring to the lack of mechanical aids. But living organisms can have satisfactions that do not require machines: food and drink, association with friends and loved ones. I suggest these bird folk find emotional release in their community thinking and in their method of propagation. Time was when man had little more, yet he called it civilization; and there were great men in those days as well as now."

"Still," said physicist von Grossen shrewdly, "you did not hesitate to upset their mode of life."

Grosvenor was cool. "It is unwise for birds—or men—to live too specialized an existence. I broke down their resistance to new ideas, something which I have not yet been able to do aboard this ship."

Several men laughed wryly, and the meeting began to break up. Afterwards, Grosvenor saw Morton speak to Yemens, the only man present from the chemistry department. The chemist—second only to Kent now—frowned, and shook his head several times. Finally, he spoke at some length, and he and Morton shook hands.

Morton came over to Grosvenor, and said in a low tone, "The chemistry department will move its equipment out of your rooms within twenty-four hours, on condition that no further reference is made to the incident. Mr. Yemens—"

Grosvenor said quickly, "What does Kent think of this?"

Morton hesitated. "He got a whiff of gas," he said finally, "and will be on his back in bed for several months."

"But," said Grosvenor, "that will take us past the date of the election."

Once more Morton hesitated, then said, "Yes, it will. It means I win the election without opposition, since no one but Kent filed against me."

Grosvenor was silent, thinking of the potentialities. It was good to know that Morton would continue in office. But what about all the discontented men who had supported Kent?

Before he could speak, Morton went on. "I want to ask this as a personal favor, Mr. Grosvenor. I persuaded Mr. Yemens that it would be unwise to continue Kent's attack on you. For the sake of peace, I'd like you to keep silent. Make no attempt to exploit your victory. Admit freely that it was a result of the accident, if you are asked, but do not bring up the matter yourself. Will you promise me?"

Grosvenor promised, then said hesitantly, "I wonder if I could make a suggestion."

"By all means."

"Why not name Kent your alternative?"

Morton studied him with narrowed eyes. He seemed nonplused. He said finally, "That's a suggestion I wouldn't have expected from you. I'm not, personally, very anxious to boost Kent's morale."

"Not Kent's," said Grosvenor.

This time Morton was silent. In the end, he said slowly, "I suppose it would release tension." But he still seemed reluctant.

Grosvenor said, "Your opinion of Kent himself seems to parallel my own."

Morton laughed grimly. "There are several dozen men aboard whom I would rather see director, but for the sake of peace, I'll follow your suggestion."

They parted, Grosvenor with feelings more mixed than he had indicated. It was an unsatisfactory conclusion to Kent's attack. Grosvenor had the feeling that, in getting the chemistry department out of his rooms, he had won a skirmish and not a battle. Nevertheless, from his own point of view, it was the best solution to what might have been a bitterly fought engagement.

Ixtl sprawled unmoving in the boundless night. Time paced slowly toward the eternity, and space was fathomlessly black. Across the immensity, vague patches of light gleamed coldly at him. Each, he knew, was a galaxy of blazing stars, shrunk by incredible distance to shining swirls of mist. Life was out there, spawning on the myriad planets that wheeled endlessly around their parent suns. In the same way, life had once crawled out of the primeval mud of ancient Glor, before a cosmic explosion destroyed his own mighty race and flung his body out into the intergalactic deeps.

He lived; that was his personal catastrophe. Having survived the cataclysm, his almost unkillable body maintained itself in a gradually weakening state on the light energy that permeated all space and time. His brain pulsed on and on in the same old, old cycle of thought—thinking: one chance in decillions that he would ever again find himself in a galactic system. And then an even more infinitesimal chance that he fall on a planet and find a precious guul.

A billion billion times that thought had pounded to its unvarying conclusion. It was a part of him now. It was like an endless picture unrolling before his mind's eye. Together with those remote wisps of shiningness out there in that gulf of blackness, it made up the world in which he had his existence. He had almost forgotten the far-flung field of sensitivity his body maintained. In past ages that field had been truly vast, but now that his powers were waning, no signals came to him beyond the range of a few light-years.

He expected nothing, and so the first stimulus from the ship scarcely more than touched him. Energy, hardness—matter! The vague sense perception fumbled into his dulled brain. It brought a living pain, like a disused muscle briefly, agonizingly, forced into action.

The pain went away. The thought faded. His brain slid back into its sleep of ages. He lived again in the old world of hopelessness and shining light splotches in a black space. The very idea of energy and matter became a dream that receded. A remote corner of his mind, somehow more alert, watched it go, watched the shadows of forgetfulness reach out with their enveloping folds of mist, striving to engulf the dim consciousness that had flashed into such an anguish of ephemeral existence.

And then once more, stronger, sharper, the message flashed from a remote frontier of his field. His elongated body convulsed in senseless movement. His four arms lashed out, his four legs jackknifed with blind, unreasoning strength. That was his muscular reaction.

His dazed, staring eyes refocused. His stultified vision was galvanized into life. The part of his nervous system that controlled the field took its first unbalancing action. In a flash of tremendous effort, he withdrew it from the billions of cubic miles from which no signals had come, and concentrated its forces in an attempt to pinpoint the area of greatest stimulation.

Even as he fought to locate it, it moved a vast distance. For the first time, then, he thought of it as a ship flying from one galaxy to another. He had a moment of awful fear that it would move beyond where he could sense it, and that he would lose contact forever before he could do anything.

He let the field spread out slightly, and felt the shock of impact as once more he received the unmistakable excitation of alien matter and energy. This time he clung to it. What had been his field became a beam of all the energy his weakened body could concentrate.

Along that tightly held beam, he drew tremendous bolts of power from the ship. There was more energy—by many millions of times—than he could handle. He had to deflect it from himself, had to discharge it into the darkness and the distance. But, like some monstrous leech, he reached out four, five, ten light-years, and drained that great ship of its drive power.

After countless eons of eking out his existence on fragile darts of light energy, he did not even dare to try to handle the colossal power. The vastness of space absorbed the flow as if it had never been. What he did let himself receive shocked the life back into his body. With a savage intensity, he realized the extent of the opportunity. Frantically, he adjusted his atomic structure and drove himself along the beam.

In the far distance, the ship—its drive off but its momentum carrying it forward—coasted past him and began to draw farther away. It receded an entire light-year, then two, and then three. In a black despair, Ixtl realized it was going to escape in spite of all his efforts. And then...

The ship stopped. In mid-flight. One instant, it was coasting along at a velocity of many light-years a day. The next, it was poised in space, all its forward momentum inhibited and transformed. It was still a tremendous distance away, but it was no longer receding.

Ixtl could guess what had happened. Those aboard the vessel had become aware of his interference and were deliberately stopping to find out what had happened, and what had caused it. Their method of instantaneous deceleration suggested a very advanced science, though he could not decide just what technique of anti-acceleration they had used. There were several possibilities. He himself intended to stop by converting his gross velocity into electronic action within his body. Very little energy would be lost in the process. The electrons in each atom would speed up slightly—so slightly—and thus the macroscopic speed would be transformed to movement on the microscopic level.

It was on that level that he suddenly sensed the ship was near.

A number of things happened then, following each other too swiftly for thought. The ship put up an impenetrable energy screen. The concentration of so much energy set off the automatic relays he had established in his body. That stopped him a fraction of a microsecond before he had intended to. In terms of distance, that came to just over thirty miles.

He could see the ship as a point of light in the blackness ahead. Its screen was still up, which meant, in all probability, that those inside could not detect him and that he could no longer hope to get to the ship itself. He assumed that delicate instruments aboard had sensed his approach, identified him as a projectile, and raised the screen as a defense.

Ixtl flashed to within yards of the almost invisible barrier. And there, separated from the realization of his hopes, he gazed hungrily at the ship. It was less than fifty yards away, a round, dark-bodied metal monster, studded with row on row of glaring lights, like diamonds. The space ship floated in the velvet-black darkness, glowing like an immense jewel, quiescent but alive, enormously, vitally alive. It brought nostalgic and vivid suggestion of a thousand far-flung planets and of an indomitable, boisterous life that had reached for the stars, and grasped them. And—in spite of present frustration—it brought hope.

Till this instant there had been so many physical things to do that he had only dimly comprehended what it might mean to him if he could get aboard. His mind, grooved through the uncounted ages to ultimate despair, soared up insanely. His legs and arms glistened like tongues of living fire as they writhed and twisted in the light that blazed from the portholes. His mouth, a gash in his caricature of a human head, slavered a white frost that floated away in little frozen globules. His hope grew so big that the thought of it kept dissolving in his mind, and his vision blurred. Through that blur, he saw a thick vein of light form a circular bulge in the metallic surface of the ship. The bulge became a huge door that rotated open and tilted to one side. A flood of brilliance spilled out of the opening.

There was a pause, and then a dozen two-legged beings came into view. They wore almost transparent armor, and they dragged, or guided, great floating machines. Swiftly, the machines were concentrated around a small area on the ship's surface. From a distance, the flames that poured forth seemed small, but their dazzling brightness indicated either enormous heat or else a titanic concentration of other radiation. What was obviously repair work proceeded at an alarming rate.

Frantically, Ixtl probed the screen that barred him from the ship, looking for weak spots. He found none. The force was too complex, its coverage too wide, for anything that he could muster against it. He had sensed that at a distance. Now he faced the reality of it.

The work—Ixtl saw they had removed a thick section of the outer wall and replaced it with new material—was finished almost as quickly as it had begun. The incandescent glare of the welders died spluttering into darkness. Machines were unclamped, floated toward the opening, down into it, and out of sight. The two-legged beings scrambled after them. The large, curved plain of metal was suddenly as deserted and lifeless as space itself.

The shock of that nearly unseated Ixtl's reason. He couldn't let them escape him now, when the whole universe was in his grasp—a few short yards away. His arms reached out, as if he would hold the ship by his need alone. His body ached with a slow, rhythmical hurt. His mind spun toward a black, bottomless pit of despair, but poised just before the final plunge.

The great door was slowing in its swift rotation. A solitary being squeezed through the ring of light and ran to the area that had been repaired. He picked up something and started back towards the open air lock. He was still some distance from it when he saw Ixtl.

He stopped as if he had been struck. Stopped, that is, in a physically unbalanced fashion. In the glow from the portholes, his face was plainly visible through his transparent space suit. His eyes were wide, his mouth open. He seemed to catch himself. His lips began to move rapidly. A minute later, the door was rotating again, outward. It swung open, and a group of the beings came out and looked at Ixtl. A discussion must have followed, for their lips moved at uneven intervals, first one individual's, then another's.

Presently, a large metal-barred cage was floated up out of the air lock. There were two men sitting on it, and they seemed to be steering it under its own power. Ixtl guessed that he was to be captured.

Curiously, he had no sense of lift. It was as if a drug were affecting him, dragging him down into an abyss of fatigue. Appalled, he tried to fight the enveloping stupor. He would need all his alertness if his race, which had attained the very threshold of ultimate knowledge, was to live again.

**14**

"How in the name of all the hells can anything live in intergalactic space?"

The voice, strained and unrecognizable, came through the communicator of Grosvenor's space suit as he stood with the others near the air lock. It seemed to him that the question made the little group of men crowd closer together. For him, the proximity of the others was not quite enough. He was too aware of the impalpable yet inconceivable night that coiled about them, pressing down to the very blazing portholes.

Almost for the first time since the voyage had begun, the immensity of that darkness struck home to Grosvenor. He had looked at it so often from inside the ship that he had become indifferent. But now he was suddenly aware that man's farthest stellar frontiers were but a pin point in this blackness that reached billions of light-years in every direction.

The voice of Director Morton broke through the scared silence. "Calling Gunlie Lester inside the ship...Gunlie Lester..."

There was a pause; then, "Yes, Director?"

Grosvenor recognized the voice of the head of the astronomy department.

"Gunlie," Morton went on, "here's something for your astro-mathematical brain. Will you please give us the ratio of chance that blew out the drivers of the *Beagle* at the exact point in space where that thing was floating? Take a few hours to work it out."

The words brought the whole scene into even sharper focus. It was typical of mathematician Morton that he let another man have the limelight in a field in which he himself was a master.

The astronomer laughed, then said in an earnest tone, "I don't have to do any figuring. One would need a new system of notation to express the chance arithmetically. What you've got out there can't happen, mathematically speaking. Here we are, a shipload of human beings, stopping for repairs halfway between two galaxies—the first time we've ever sent an expedition outside our own island universe. Here we are, I say, a tiny point intersecting without prearrangement exactly the path of another, tinier point. It's impossible, unless space is saturated with such creatures."

It seemed to Grosvenor that there was a more likely explanation. The two events could conceivably be in the simple relationship of cause and effect. A huge hole had been burned in the engine-room wall. Torrents of energy had poured out into space. Now they had stopped to repair the damage. He parted his lips to say as much, and then closed them. There was another factor, the factor of the forces and probabilities involved in *that* assumption. Just how much power would be needed to drain the output of a pile in a few minutes? Briefly he considered the formula applicable, and shook his head slightly. The figures that came through were so enormous that the hypothesis he had intended to offer seemed automatically ruled out. A thousand coeurls among them couldn't have handled energy in such quantities, which suggested that machines, not individuals, were involved.

Somebody was saying, "We ought to turn a mobile unit on anything that looks like that."

The shudder in his voice stirred a like emotion in Grosvenor. The reaction must have run along the communicators, because, when Director Morton spoke, his tone indicated he was trying to throw off the chill of the other man's words. Morton said, "A regular blood-red devil spewed out of a nightmare, ugly as sin—and possibly as harmless as our beautiful pussy a few months ago was deadly. Smith, what do you think?"

The gangling biologist was coldly logical. "This thing, as far as I can make it out from here, has arms and legs, a development of purely planetary evolution. If it is intelligent, it will begin to react to the changing environment the moment it is inside the cage. It may be a venerable old sage, meditating in the silence of space where there are no distractions. Or it may be a young murderer, condemned to exile, consumed with desire to get back home and resume life in his own civilization."

"I wish Korita had come out with us," said Pennons, the chief engineer, in his quiet, practical fashion. "His analysis of pussy on the cat planet gave us an advance idea of what we had to face and—"

"Korita speaking, Mr. Pennons." As usual, the Japanese archeologist's voice came over the communicators with meticulous clarity. "Like many of the others, I have been listening to what is happening, and I must admit I am impressed by the image I can see of this creature on the vision plate before me. But I'm afraid analysis on the basis of cyclic history would be dangerous at this factless stage. In the case of pussy, we had the barren, almost foodless planet on which he lived, and the architectural realities of the crumbled city. But here we have a being living in space a quarter of a million light-years from the nearest planet, existing apparently without food, and without means of spatial locomotion. I suggest the following: Keep the screen up, except for an opening for the cage to be taken out. When you have your creature actually in the cage, study him—every action, every reaction. Take pictures of his internal organs working in the vacuum of space. Find out everything about him, so that we shall know what we are bringing aboard. Let us avoid killing, or being killed. The greatest precautions are in order."

"And that," said Morton, "is sense."

He began to issue orders. More machines were brought up from inside the ship. They were set up on a smooth, curving expanse of the outer surface, except for a massive fluorite camera. That was attached to the mobile cage.

Grosvenor listened uneasily while the Director gave final instructions to the men guiding the cage. "Open the door as wide as possible," Morton was saying, "and drop it over him. Don't let his hands grab the bars."

Grosvenor thought, It's now or never. If I have any objections, I've got to offer them.

There seemed nothing to say. He could outline his vague doubts. He could carry Gunlie Lester's comment to its logical conclusion and say that what had happened could not be an accident. He might even suggest that a shipload of the red, devillike beings was possibly waiting in the distance for their fellow to be picked up.

But the fact was that all the precautions against such eventualities had been taken. If there were a ship, then by opening the protective screen only enough to admit the cage, they were offering a minimum target. The outer skin might be seared, the men on it killed. But the vessel itself would surely be safe.

The enemy would find that his action had served no useful purpose. He would find arrayed against him a formidable armed and armored vessel, manned by members of a race that could pursue a battle to a remorseless conclusion.

Grosvenor reached that point in his speculation, and decided to make no comment. He would hold his doubts in reserve.

Morton was speaking again. "Any final remarks from anyone?"

"Yes." The new voice belonged to von Grossen. "I'm in favor of making a thorough examination of this thing. To me, thorough means a week, a month."

"You mean," said Morton, "we sit here in space while our technical experts study the monster?"

"Of course," said the physicist.

Morton was silent for several seconds, then he said slowly, "I'll have to put that up to the others, von Grossen. This is an exploratory expedition. We are equipped to take back specimens by the thousand. As scientists, all is grist for our mill. Everything must be investigated. Yet I feel sure that the objection will be made that if we sit out in space an entire month for each specimen we plan to take aboard, this journey will take five hundred years instead of five or ten. I do not offer that as a personal objection. Obviously, every specimen must be examined and dealt with on its own merits."

"My point," said von Grossen, "is let's think it over."

Morton asked, "Any other objections?" When none was made, he finished quietly, "All right, boys, go out and get him!"

# 15

Ixtl waited. His thoughts kept breaking up into kaleidoscopic memories of all the things he had ever known or thought. He had a vision of his home planet, long ago destroyed. The picture brought pride, and a gathering contempt for these two-legged beings who actually expected to capture him.

He could remember a time when his race could control the movement of entire sun systems through space. That was before they dispensed with space travel as such and moved on to a quieter existence, building beauty from natural forces in an ecstasy of prolonged creative production.

He watched as the cage was unerringly driven towards him. It passed successfully through an opening in the screen, which closed instantly behind it. The transition was smoothly made. Even had he wanted to, he could not have taken advantage of the opening in the screen during the brief moment it existed. He had no desire to do so. He must be careful not to make a single hostile move until he was inside the ship. Slowly, the metal-barred construction floated towards him. Its two operators were wary and alert. One held a weapon of some kind. Ixtl sensed that it discharged an atomic missile. It made him respectful, but he also recognized its limitations. It could be used against him out here, but they would not dare employ such a violent energy within the confines of the ship.

More sharply, more clearly, that focused his purpose. Get aboard the ship! Get inside!

Even as the determination struck deeper, the gaping mouth of the cage closed over him. The metal door snapped noiselessly shut behind him. Ixtl reached for the nearest bar, caught it, and held on grimly. He clung there, dizzy from reaction. For he was safe! His mind expanded with the force of that reality. There was a physical as well as a mental effect. Free electrons discharged in swarms from the chaos of spinning atom systems inside his body, and frantically sought union with other systems. He was safe after quadrillions of years of despair. Safe on a material body. No matter what else happened, control of the energy source of this power-driven cage forever freed him from his past inability to direct his movements. He would never again be subject only to the pull and equally feeble counterpull of remote galaxies. Henceforth, he could travel in any direction he desired. And that much he had gained from the cage alone.

As he clung to the bars, his prison started to move toward the surface of the ship. The protective screen parted as they came to it, and closed again behind them. Close up, the men looked puny. Their need of space suits proved their inability to adapt themselves to environments radically different from their own, which meant that they were physically on a low plane of evolution. It would be unwise, however, to underestimate their scientific achievements. Here were keen brains, capable of creating and using mighty machines. And they had now brought up a number of those machines, evidently with the purpose of studying him. That would reveal his purpose, identify the precious objects concealed within his breast, and expose at least a few of his life processes. He could not allow such an examination to be made.

He saw that several of the beings carried not one but two weapons. The instruments were attached to holsters, which were fitted in with the hand-arm mechanisms of each space suit. One of the weapons was the atomic-missile type with which he had already been threatened. The other had a sparkling, translucent handle. He analyzed it as a vibration gun. The men on the cage were also armed with the latter type of weapon.

As the cage settled into the hastily arranged laboratory, a camera was pushed towards the narrow opening between two of the bars. That was Ixtl's cue. With effortless ease, he jerked himself to the ceiling of the cage. His vision intensified, and became sensitive to very short frequencies. Instantly, he could see the power source of the vibrator as a bright spot well within his reach.

One arm, with its eight wirelike fingers, lashed out with indescribable swiftness at the metal, *through* it; and then he had the vibrator from the holster of one of the men on the cage.

He did not attempt to readjust its atomic structure as he had adjusted his arm. It was important that they should not be able to guess who had fired the weapon. Straining to maintain his awkward position, he aimed the weapon at the camera and at the group of men behind it. He pressed the trigger.

In one continuous movement, Ixtl released the vibrator, withdrew his hand, and, by the act, pushed himself to the floor. His immediate fear was gone. The purely molecular energy had resonated through the camera and had affected to some extent most of the equipment in the makeshift laboratory. The sensitive film would be useless; meters would have to be reset, gauges examined, and each machine tested. Possibly the entire lot of paraphernalia would have to be replaced. And best of all, by its very nature, what had happened would have to be regarded as an accident.

Grosvenor heard curses in his communicator, and he guessed, with relief, that the others were fighting, as he was, the stinging vibration that had been only partly stopped by the material of their space suits. His eyes adjusted slowly. Presently, he could see again the curved metal on which he stood, and beyond that the brief, barren crest of the ship, and the limitless miles of space—dark, fathomless, unthinkable gulfs. He saw, too, a blur among the shadows, the metal cage.

"I'm sorry, Director," one of the men on the cage apologized. "The vibrator must have fallen out of my belt and discharged."

Grosvenor said quickly, "Director, that explanation is unlikely in view of the virtual absence of gravity."

Morton said, "That's a good point, Grosvenor. Did anybody see anything significant?"

"Maybe I knocked against it, sir, without noticing," volunteered the man whose weapon had caused the turmoil.

There was a spluttering sound from Smith. The biologist muttered something that sounded like "That erysipelatous, strabismic, steatopygian..." Grosvenor didn't catch the rest, but he guessed that it was a biologist's private curse. Slowly, Smith straightened. "Just a minute," he mumbled, "and I'll try to remember what I saw. I was right here in the line of fire—ah, there, my body has stopped throbbing." His voice became sharp as he went on. "I can't swear to this, but just before that vibrator shocked me, the creature moved. I have an idea he jumped to the ceiling. I admit it was too black to see more than a blur, but..." He left the sentence unfinished.

Morton said, "Crane, turn the cage light on, and let's see what we've got here."

With the others, Grosvenor faced about as a blaze of light showered down upon Ixtl crouching at the bottom of the cage. And then he stood silent, shocked in spite of himself. The almost metallic red sheen of the creature's cylindrical body, the eyes like coals of fire, the wirelike fingers and toes, and the overall scarlet hideousness of it startled him.

Through the communicator, Siedel said breathlessly, "He's probably very handsome—to himself!"

The halfhearted attempt at humor broke the spell of horror. A man said stiffly, "If life is evolution, and nothing evolves except for use, how can a creature living in space have highly developed legs and arms? Its insides should be interesting. But now—the camera's useless. That vibration would have the effect of distorting the lens, and of course the film has been ruined. Shall I have another sent up?"

"No-o-o!" Morton sounded doubtful, but he continued in a firmer tone. "We've been wasting a lot of time; and, after all, we can recreate vacuum of space conditions inside the ship's laboratories, and be traveling at top acceleration while we're doing it."

"Am I to understand that you are going to ignore my suggestion?"

It was von Grossen, the physicist. He went on. "You will recall that I recommended at least a week's study of this creature before any decision is made about taking him aboard."

Morton hesitated, then said, "Any other objections?" He sounded concerned.

Grosvenor said, "I don't think we should jump from the extreme of precaution to no precaution at all."

Morton said quietly, "Anybody else?" When no one replied, he added, "Smith?"

Smith said, "Obviously, we're going to take him aboard sooner or later. We mustn't forget that a creature existing in space is the most extraordinary thing we've run across. Even pussy, who was equally at home with oxygen and chlorine, needed warmth of a kind, and would have found the cold and lack of pressure in space deadly. If, as we suspect, this creature's natural habitat is not space, then we must find out why and how he came to be where he is."

Morton was frowning. "I can see we'll have to vote on this. We could enclose the cage in metal that will take a limited amount of the energy that makes up the ship's outer screen. Would that satisfy you, von Grossen?"

Von Grossen said, "Now we are talking sensibly. But we shall have more arguments before the energy screen is taken down."

Morton laughed. "Once we're on our way again, you and the others can discuss the pro and con of that from now till the end of the voyage." He broke off. "Any other objections? Grosvenor?"

Grosvenor shook his head. "The screen sounds effective to me, sir."

Morton said, "All those against, speak up." When no one spoke, he directed a command to the men on the cage. "Move that thing over here, so we can start preparing it for energization."

Ixtl felt the faint throb in the metal as the motors started. He saw the bars move. Then he grew conscious of a sharp, pleasant, tingling sensation. It was a physical activity inside his body, and while it was in progress it hampered the working of his mind. When he could think again, the cage floor was rising above him—and he was lying on the hard surface of the space ship's outer shell.

With a snarl, he scrambled to his feet as he realized the truth. He had forgotten to readjust the atoms in his body after firing the vibrator. And now he had passed through the metal floor of the cage.

"Good heavens!" Morton's bass exclamation almost deafened Grosvenor.

A scarlet streak of elongated body, Ixtl darted across the shadowy reach of the impenetrable metal of the ship's outer wall to the air lock. He jerked himself down into its dazzling depths. His adjusted body dissolved through the two inner doors. And then he was at one end of a long, gleaming corridor, safe for the moment. And one fact stood out.

In the imminent struggle for control of the ship, he would have one important advantage, aside from his individual superiority. His opponents did not yet know the deadliness of his purpose.

# 16

It was twenty minutes later. Grosvenor sat in one of the auditorium seats in the control room and watched Morton and Captain Leeth consulting together in low tones on one of the tiers leading up to the main section of the instrument board.

The room was packed with men. With the exception of guards left in key centers, everybody had been ordered to attend. The military crew and its officers, the heads of science departments and their staffs, the administrative branches, and the various technical men who had no departments—all were either in the room or congregated in the adjoining corridors.

A bell clanged. The babble of conversation began to fade. The bell clanged again. All conversation ceased. Captain Leeth came forward.

"Gentlemen," he said, "these problems keep arising, do they not? I am beginning to feel that we military men have not properly appreciated scientists in the past. I thought they lived out their lives in laboratories, far from danger. But it's beginning to dawn on me that scientists can find trouble where it never existed before."

He hesitated briefly, then went on in the same dryly humorous tone. "Director Morton and I have agreed that this is not a problem for military forces alone. So long as the creature is at large, every man must be his own policeman. Go armed, go in pairs or groups—the more the better."

Once more he surveyed his audience, and his manner was grimmer when he continued. "It would be foolish for you to believe that this situation will not involve danger or death for some among us. It may be me. It may be you. Nerve yourself for it. Accept the possibility. But if it is your destiny to make contact with this immensely dangerous creature, defend yourself to the death. Try to take him with you. Do not suffer, or die, in vain.

"And now"—he turned to Morton—"the Director will guide a discussion regarding the utilization against our enemy of the very considerable scientific knowledge which is aboard this ship. Mr. Morton."

Morton walked slowly forward. His large and powerful body was dwarfed by the gigantic instrument board behind him, but nevertheless he looked imposing. The Director's gray eyes flicked questioningly along the line of faces, pausing at none, apparently simply assessing the collective mood of the men. He began by praising Captain Leeth's attitude, and then he said, "I have examined my own recollections of what happened, and I think I can say honestly that no one—not even myself—is to blame for the creature's being aboard. It had been decided, you may remember, to bring him aboard in the confines of a force field. That precaution satisfied our most precise critics, and it was unfortunate that it was not taken in time. The being actually came into the ship under his own power by a method which could not be foreseen." He stopped. His keen gaze once more swept the room. "Or did anybody have something stronger than a premonition? Please hold up your hand if you did."

Grosvenor craned his neck, but no hands were raised. He settled back into his seat, and was a little startled to see that Morton's gray eyes were fixed on him. "Mr. Grosvenor," said Morton, "did the science of Nexialism enable you to predict that this creature could dissolve his body through a wall?"

In a clear voice, Grosvenor said, "It did not."

"Thank you," said Morton.

He seemed satisfied, for he did not ask anyone else. Grosvenor had already guessed that the Director was trying to justify his own position. It was a sad commentary on the ship's politics that he should have felt it necessary. But what particularly interested Grosvenor was that he had appealed to Nexialism as a sort of final authority.

Morton was speaking again. "Siedel," he said, "give us a psychologically sound picture of what has happened."

The chief psychologist said, "In setting about to capture this creature, we must first of all straighten our minds about him. He has arms and legs, yet floats in space and remains alive. He allows himself to be caught in a cage, but knows all the time that the cage cannot hold him. Then he slips through the bottom of the cage, which is very silly of him if he does not want us to know he can do it. There is a reason why intelligent beings make mistakes, a fundamental reason that should make it easy for us to do some shrewd guessing as to where he came from, and, of course, to analyze why he is here. Smith, dissect his biological make-up!"

Smith stood up, lank and grim. "We've already discussed the obvious planetary origin of his hands and feet. The ability to live in space, if evolutionary at all, is certainly a remarkable attribute. I suggest that here is a member of a race that has solved the final secrets of biology; and if I knew how we should even begin to start looking for a creature that can escape from us through the nearest wall, my advice would be: Hunt him down, and kill him on sight."

"Ah..." Kellie, the sociologist, said. He was a baldheaded man, fortyish, with large, intelligent eyes. "Ah—any being who could fit himself to live in a vacuum would be lord of the universe. His kind would dwell on every planet, clutter up every galaxy. Swarms of him would be floating in space. Yet we know for a fact that his race does not infest our galactic area. A paradox that is worthy of investigation."

"I don't quite understand what you mean, Kellie," said Morton.

"Simply—ah—that a race which has solved the ultimate secrets of biology must be ages in advance of man. It would be highly sympodial, that is, capable of adaptation to any environment. According to the law of vital dynamics, it would expand to the farthest frontier of the universe, just as man is trying to do."

"It is a contradiction," acknowledged Morton, "and would seem to prove that the creature is not a superior being. Korita, what is this thing's history?"

The Japanese scientist shrugged, but he stood up and said, "I'm afraid I can be of only slight assistance on present evidence. You know the prevailing theory: that life proceeds upward—whatever we mean by upward—by a series of cycles. Each cycle begins with the peasant, who is rooted to his bit of soil. The peasant comes to market; and slowly the market place transforms into a town, with ever less 'inward' connection to the earth. Then we have cities and nations, finally the soulless world cities and a devastating struggle for power, a series of frightful wars which sweep men to fellahdom, and so to primitiveness, and on to a new peasanthood. The question is: Is this creature in the peasant part of his particular cycle, or in the big-city, megalopolitan era? Or where?"

He stopped. It seemed to Grosvenor that some very sharp pictures had been presented. Civilizations did appear to operate in cycles. Each period of the cycle must in a very rough fashion have its own psychological background. There were many possible explanations for the phenomenon, of which the old Spenglerian notion of cycles was only one. It was even possible that Korita could foresee the alien's actions on the basis of the cyclic theory. He had proved in the past that the system was workable and had considerable predictability. At the moment, it had the advantage that it was the only historical approach with techniques that could be applied to a given situation.

Morton's voice broke the silence. "Korita, in view of our limited knowledge of this creature, what basic traits should we look for, supposing him to be in the big-city stage of his culture?"

"He would be a virtually invincible intellect, formidable to the ultimate possible degree. At his own game, he would make no errors of any kind, and he would be defeatable only through circumstances beyond his control. The best example"—Korita was suave—"is the highly trained human being of our own era."

"But he has already made an error!" von Grossen said in a silken tone. "He very foolishly fell through the bottom of the cage. Is that the kind of thing a peasant would do?"

Morton asked, "Suppose he was in the peasant stage?"

"Then," Korita replied, "his basic impulses would be much simpler. There would first of all be the desire to reproduce, to have a son, to know that his blood was being carried on. Assuming great fundamental intelligence, this impulse might, in a superior being, take the form of a fanatic drive toward race survival."

He finished quietly, "And that's all I will say, on available evidence." He sat down.

Morton stood stiffly on the tier of the instrument board and looked over his audience of experts. His gaze paused at Grosvenor. He said, "Recently, I have personally come to feel that the science of Nexialism may have a new approach to offer to the solution of problems. Since it is the whole-istic approach to life, carried to the nth degree, it may help us to a quick decision at a time when a quick decision is important. Grosvenor, please give us your views on this alien being."

Grosvenor stood up briskly. He said, "I can give you a conclusion based on my observations. I could go into a little theory of my own as to how we made contact with this creature—the way the pile was drained of energy, with the result that we had to repair the outer wall of the engine room—and there were a number of significant time intervals—but rather than develop on such backgrounds, I'd like to tell you in the next few minutes how we should kill—"

There was an interruption. Half a dozen men were pushing their way through the group that crowded the doorway. Grosvenor paused, and glanced questioningly at Morton. The Director had turned and was watching Captain Leeth. The captain moved towards the new arrivals, and Grosvenor saw that Pennons, chief engineer of the ship, was one of them.

Captain Leeth said, "Finished, Mr. Pennons?"

The chief engineer nodded. "Yes, sir." He added in a warning tone, "It is essential that every man be dressed in a rubberite suit and wear rubberite gloves and shoes."

Captain Leeth explained. "We've energized the walls around the bedrooms. There may be some delay in catching this creature, and we are taking no chances of being murdered in our beds. We—" He broke off, asking sharply, "What is it, Mr. Pennons?"

Pennons was staring at a small instrument in his hand. He said slowly, "Are we all here, Captain?"

"Yes, except for the guards in the engine and machine rooms."

"Then…then something's caught in the wall of force. Quick, we must surround it!"

# 17

To Ixtl, returning to the upper floors from exploring the lower ones, the shock was devastating, the surprise complete. One moment he was thinking complacently of the metal sections in the hold of the ship, where he would secrete his guuls. The next moment he was caught in the full sparkling, furious center of an energy screen.

His mind went black with agony. Clouds of electrons broke free inside him. They flashed from system to system, seeking union, only to be violently repelled by atom systems fighting stubbornly to remain stable. During those long, fateful seconds, the wonderfully balanced flexibility of his structure nearly collapsed. What saved him was that even this dangerous eventuality had been anticipated by the collective genius of his race. In forcing artificial evolution upon his body—and their own—they had taken into account the possibility of a chance encounter with violent radiation. Like lightning, his body adjusted and readjusted, each new-built structure carrying the intolerable load for a fraction of a microsecond. And then he had jerked back from the wall, and was safe.

He concentrated his mind on the immediate potentialities. The defensive wall of force would have an alarm system connected to it. That meant the men would be bearing down on all the adjacent corridors in an organized attempt to corner him. Ixtl's eyes were glowing pools of fire as he realized the opportunity. They would be scattered, and he would be able to catch one of them, investigate him for his guul properties, and use him for his first guul.

There was no time to waste. He darted into the nearest unenergized wall, a tall, gaudy, ungraceful shape. Without pausing, he sped through room after room, keeping roughly parallel to a main corridor. His sensitive eyes followed the blurred figures of the men as they raced by. One, two, three, four, five in this corridor. The fifth man was some distance behind the others. Comparatively, it was a slight advantage, but it was all Ixtl needed.

Like a wraith he glided through the wall just ahead of the last man and pounced forth in an irresistible charge. He was a rearing, frightful monstrosity with glaring eyes and ghastly mouth. He reached out with his four fire-colored arms, and with his immense strength clutched the human being. The man squirmed and jerked in one contorted effort; and then he was overwhelmed, and flung to the floor.

He lay on his back, and Ixtl saw that his mouth opened and shut in an uneven series of movements. Every time it opened, Ixtl felt a sharp tingling in his feet. The sensation was not hard to identify. It was the vibrations of a call for help. With a snarl, Ixtl pounced forward. With one great hand he smashed at the man's mouth. The man's body sagged. But he was still alive and conscious as Ixtl plunged two hands into him.

The action seemed to petrify the man. He ceased to struggle. With widened eyes, he watched as the long, thin arms vanished under his shirt and stirred around in his chest. Then, horrified, he stared at the blood-red, cylindrical body that loomed over him.

The inside of the man's body seemed to be solid flesh. And Ixtl's need was for an open space, or one that could be pressed open, so long as the pressing did not kill his victim. For his purposes, he needed living flesh.

Hurry, hurry! His feet registered the vibrations of approaching footsteps. They came from one direction only, but they came swiftly.

In his anxiety, Ixtl made the mistake of actually speeding up his investigation. He hardened his searching fingers momentarily into a state of semisolidity. In that moment, he touched the heart. The man heaved convulsively, shuddered, and slumped into death.

An instant later, Ixtl's probing fingers discovered the stomach and the intestines. He drew back in a violence of self-criticism. Here was what he wanted; and he had rendered it useless. He straightened slowly, his anger and dismay fading. For he had not anticipated that these intelligent beings could die so easily. It changed and simplified everything. They were at his mercy, not he at theirs. No need for him to be more than casually cautious in dealing with them.

Two men with drawn vibrators whipped around the nearest corner and slid to a halt at the sight of the apparition that snarled at them across the dead body of their companion. Then, as they came out of their momentary paralysis, Ixtl stepped into the nearest wall. One instant he was a blur of scarlet in that brightly lighted corridor, the next he was gone as if he had never been. He felt the transmitted vibration from the weapons as the energy tore futilely at the walls behind him.

His plan was quite clear now. He would capture half a dozen men and make guuls of them. Then he could kill all the others, since they would not be necessary to him. That done, he could proceed on to the galaxy towards which the ship was evidently heading and there take control of the first inhabited planet. After that, domination of the entire reachable universe would be a matter of a short time only.

Grosvenor stood in front of a wall communicator with several other men, and watched the image of the group that had gathered around the dead technician. He would have liked to be on the scene, but it would have taken him several minutes to get there. During that time he would be out of touch. He preferred to watch, and see and hear everything.

Director Morton stood nearest the sending plate, less than three feet from where Dr. Eggert was bending over the dead man. He looked tense. His jaw was clenched. When he spoke, his voice was little more than a whisper. Yet the words cut across the silence like a whiplash.

"Well, Doctor?"

Dr. Eggert rose up from his kneeling position beside the body and turned to Morton. The action brought him to face the sending plate. Grosvenor saw that he was frowning.

"Heart failure," he said.

"Heart failure?"

"All right, all right." The doctor put up his hands as if to defend himself. "I know his teeth look as if they've been smashed back into his brain. And, having examined him many times, I know his heart was perfect. Nevertheless, heart failure is what it looks like to me."

"I can believe it," a man said sourly. "When I came around that corner and saw that beast, I nearly had heart failure myself."

"We're wasting time." Grosvenor recognized the voice of von Grossen before he saw the physicist standing between two men on the other side of Morton. The scientist continued. "We can beat this fellow, but not by talking about him and feeling sick every time he makes a move. If I'm next on his list of victims, I want to know that the best damned bunch of scientists in the system are not crying over my fate but instead are putting their brains to the job of avenging my death."

"You're right." That was Smith. "The trouble with us is we've been feeling inferior. He's been on the ship less than an hour, but I can see clearly that some of us are going to get killed. I accept my chance. But let's get organized for combat."

Morton said slowly, "Mr. Pennons, here's a problem. We've got about two square miles of floor space in our thirty levels. How long will it take to energize every inch of it?"

Grosvenor could not see the chief engineer. He was not within range of the plate's curving lens. But the expression on the officer's face must have been something to witness. His voice, when he responded to Morton, sounded aghast. He said, "I could sweep the ship, and probably wreck it completely within an hour. I won't go into details. But uncontrolled energization would kill every living thing aboard."

Morton's back was partly to the communicating plate that was transmitting the images and voices of those who stood beside the body of the man who had been killed by Ixtl. He said questioningly, "You could feed more energy to those walls, couldn't you, Mr. Pennons?"

"No-o!" The ship's engineer sounded reluctant. "The walls couldn't stand it. They'd melt."

"*The walls couldn't stand it!*" a man gasped. "Sir, do you realize what you're making this creature out to be?"

Grosvenor saw that there was consternation in the faces of the men whose images were being transmitted. Korita's voice cut across the pregnant silence. He said, "Director, I am watching you on a communicator in the control room. To the suggestion that we are dealing with a super-being, I want to say this: Let us not forget that he did blunder into the wall of force, and that he recoiled in dismay without penetrating into the sleeping quarters. I use the word 'blunder' deliberately. His action proves once again that he does make mistakes."

Morton said, "That takes me back to what you said earlier about the psychological characteristics to be expected at the various cyclic stages. Let us suppose he's a peasant of his cycle."

Korita's reply was crisp for one who usually spoke with such care. "The inability to understand the full power of organization. He will think, in all likelihood, that in order to gain control of the ship he need only fight the men who are in it. Instinctively, he would tend to discount the fact that we are part of a great galactic civilization. The mind of the true peasant is very individualistic, almost anarchic. His desire to reproduce himself is a form of egoism, to have his own blood, particularly, carried on. This creature—if he is in the peasant stage of his development—will very possibly want to have numbers of beings similar to himself to help him with his fight. He likes company, but he doesn't want interference. Any organized society can dominate a peasant community, because its members never form anything more than a loose union against outsiders."

"A loose union of those fire-eaters ought to be enough!" a technician commented acidly. "I...aaa-a-a..."

His words trailed into a yell. His lower jaw sagged open. His eyes, plainly visible to Grosvenor, took on a goggly stare. All the men who could be seen in the plate retreated several feet.

Full into the center of the viewing plate stepped Ixtl.

# 18

He stood there, forbidding specter from a scarlet hell. His eyes were bright and alert, though he was no longer alarmed. He had sized up these human beings, and he knew, contemptuously, that he could plunge into the nearest wall before any one of them could loose a vibrator on him.

He had come for his first guul. By snatching that guul from the center of a group, he would to some extent demoralize everybody aboard.

Grosvenor felt a wave of unreality sweep over him as he watched the scene. Only a few of the men were within the field of the plate. Von Grossen and two technicians stood nearest Ixtl. Morton was just behind von Grossen, and part of the head and body of Smith could be seen near one of the technicians. As a group, they looked like insignificant opponents of the tall, thick, cylindrical monstrosity that towered above them.

It was Morton who broke the silence. Deliberately, he held his hand away from the translucent handle of his vibrator, and said in a steady voice, "Don't try to draw on him. He can move like a flash. And he wouldn't be here if he thought we could blast him. Besides, we can't risk failure. This may be our only chance."

He continued swiftly, in an urgent tone. "All emergency crews listening in on this get above and below and around this corridor. Bring up the heaviest portables, even some of the semiportables, and burn the walls down. Cut a clear path around this area, and have your beams sweep that space at narrow focus. Move!"

"Good idea, Director!" Captain Leeth's face appeared for a moment on Grosvenor's communicator, superseding the image of Ixtl and the others. "We'll be there if you can hold that hellhound three minutes." His face withdrew as swiftly as it had come.

Grosvenor deserted his own viewing plate. He had been acutely aware that he was too far from the scene for the kind of precise observation on which a Nexialist was supposed to base his actions. He was not part of any emergency crew, and so his purpose was to join Morton and the other men in the danger area.

As he ran, he passed other communicators, and realized that Korita was giving advice from a distance. "Morton, take this chance, but do not count on success. Notice that he has appeared once again before we have been able to prepare against him. It doesn't matter whether he is pressing us intentionally or accidentally. The result, whatever his motivation, is that we are on the run, scurrying this way and that, futilely. So far, we have not clarified our thoughts."

Grosvenor had been in an elevator, going down. Now he flung open the door and raced out. "I am convinced," Korita's voice continued from the next corridor communicator, "that the vast resources of this ship can defeat any creature—I mean, of course, any single creature— that has ever existed..." If Korita said anything after that, Grosvenor didn't hear it. He had rounded the corner. And there, ahead, were the men and beyond them Ixtl.

He saw that von Grossen had just finished sketching something in his notebook. As Grosvenor watched with misgivings, von Grossen stepped forward and held the sheet out to Ixtl. The creature hesitated, then accepted it. He took one glance at it, and stepped back with a snarl that split his face.

Morton yelled, "What the devil have you done?"

Von Grossen was grinning tensely. "I've just shown him how we can defeat him," he said softly. "I—"

His words were cut off. Grosvenor, still to the rear, saw the entire incident merely as a spectator. All the others in the group were involved in the crisis.

Morton must have realized what was about to happen. He stepped forward, as if instinctively trying to interpose his big body in front of von Grossen. A hand with long, wirelike fingers knocked the Director against the men behind him. He fell, unbalancing those nearest him. He recovered himself, clawed for his vibrator, and then froze with it in his hand.

As through a distorted glass, Grosvenor saw that the thing was holding von Grossen in two fire-colored arms. The two-hundred-and-twenty-pound physicist squirmed and twisted, vainly. The thin, hard muscles held him as if they were so many manacles. What prevented Grosvenor from discharging his own vibrator was the impossibility of hitting the creature without also hitting von Grossen. Since the vibrator could not kill a human being but could render him unconscious, the conflict inside him was: Should he activate the weapon in the hope that Ixtl would also be knocked unconscious, or try in a desperate bid to get information from von Grossen? He chose the latter.

He called to the physicist in an urgent voice, "Von Grossen, what did you show him? How can we defeat him?"

Von Grossen heard, because he turned his head. That was all he had time for. At that moment, a mad thing happened. The creature took a running dive and vanished into the wall, still holding the physicist. For an instant, it seemed to Grosvenor that his vision had played a trick on him. But there were only the hard, smooth, gleaming wall and eleven staring, perspiring men, seven of them with drawn weapons, which they fingered helplessly.

"We're lost!" a man whispered. "If he can adjust our atomic structures and take us with him through solid matter, we can't fight him."

Grosvenor saw that Morton was irritated by the remark. It was the irritation of a man who is trying to maintain his balance under trying circumstances. The Director said angrily, "While we're living, we can fight him!" He strode to the nearest communicator, and asked, "Captain Leeth, what's the situation?"

There was a delay, then the commander's head and shoulders came into focus on the plate. "Nothing," he said succinctly. "Lieutenant Clay thinks he saw a flash of scarlet disappearing through a floor, going down. We can, for the time being, narrow our search down to the lower half of the ship. As for the rest, we were just lining up our units when it happened. You didn't give us enough time."

Morton said grimly, "We didn't have anything to say about it."

It seemed to the listening Grosvenor that the statement was not strictly true. Von Grossen had hastened his own capture by showing the creature a diagram of how he could be defeated. It was a typically egotistical human action, with little survival value. More than that, it pointed up his own argument against the specialist who acted unilaterally and was incapable of cooperating intelligently with other scientists. Behind what von Grossen had done was an attitude centuries old. That attitude had been good enough during the early days of scientific research. But it had a limited value now that every new development required knowledge and coordination of many sciences.

Standing there, Grosvenor questioned that von Grossen had actually evolved a technique for defeating Ixtl. He questioned that a successful technique would be limited to the field of a single specialist. Any picture von Grossen had drawn for the creature would probably have been limited to what a physicist would know.

His private thought ended as Morton said, "What I'd like is some theory as to what was drawn on the sheet of paper von Grossen showed the creature."

Grosvenor waited for someone else to reply. When no one did, he said, "I think I have one, Director."

Morton hesitated the barest moment, then said, "Go ahead."

Grosvenor began. "The only way one could gain the attention of an alien would be to show him a universally recognized symbol. Since von Grossen is a physicist, the symbol he would have used suggests itself."

He paused deliberately and looked around him. He felt as if he were being melodramatic, but it was unavoidable. In spite of Morton's friendliness, and the Riim incident, he was not recognized as an authority aboard this ship, and so it would be better if the answer would occur spontaneously at this point to several people.

Morton broke the silence. "Come, come, young man. Don't keep us in suspense."

"An atom," said Grosvenor

The faces around him looked blank. "But that doesn't mean anything," said Smith. "Why would he show him an atom?"

Grosvenor said, "Not just any atom, of course. I'll wager that von Grossen drew for the creature a structural representation of the eccentric atom of the metal that makes up the outer shell of the *Beagle*."

Morton said, "You've got it!"

"Just a minute." Captain Leeth spoke from the communicator plate. "I confess I'm no physicist, but I'd like to know just what is it that he's got."

Morton explained. "Grosvenor means that only two parts of the ship are composed of that incredibly tough material, the outer shell and the engine room. If you had been with us when we first captured the creature, you would have noticed that when it slipped through the floor of the cage it was stopped short by the hard metal of the outer shell of the ship. It seems clear that it cannot pass through such metal. The fact that it had to run for the air lock in order to get inside is further proof. The wonder is that we didn't all of us think of that right away."

Captain Leeth said, "If Mr. von Grossen was showing the creature the nature of our defenses, couldn't it be that he depicted the energy screens we put up in the walls? Isn't that just as possible as the atom theory?"

Morton turned and glanced questioningly at Grosvenor. The Nexialist said, "The creature had already experienced the energy screen at that time and had survived it. Von Grossen clearly believed he had something new. Besides, the only way you can show a field of force on paper is with an equation involving arbitrary symbols."

Captain Leeth said, "This is very welcome reasoning. We have at least one place aboard where we are safe—the engine room—and possibly somewhat lesser protection from the wall screens of our sleeping quarters. I can see why Mr. von Grossen would feel that gave us an advantage. All personnel on this ship will hereafter concentrate only in those areas, except by special permission or command." He turned to the nearest communicator, repeated the order, and then said, "Heads of departments should be prepared to answer questions relating to their specialties. Necessary duties will probably be assigned to suitably trained individuals. Mr. Grosvenor, consider yourself in this latter category. Dr. Eggert, issue anti-sleep pills where required. No one can go to bed until this beast is dead."

"Good work, Captain!" Morton said warmly.

Captain Leeth nodded, and disappeared from the communicator plate.

In the corridor, a technician said hesitantly, "What about von Grossen?"

Morton said harshly, "The only way we can help von Grossen is by destroying his captor!"

# 19

In that vast room of vast machines, the men seemed like dwarfs in a hall of giants. Grosvenor blinked involuntarily at each burst of unearthly blue light that sparkled and coruscated upon the great, glistening sweep of ceiling. And there was a sound that rasped his nerves as much as the light affected his eyes. It was imprisoned in the air itself. A hum of terrifying power, a vague rumble like thunder from beyond the horizon, a quivering reverberation of an inconceivable flow of energy.

The drive was on. The ship was accelerating, going ever deeper and faster through the gulf of blackness that separated the spiral galaxy, of which Earth was one tiny, spinning atom, from another galaxy of almost equal size. That was the background to the decisive struggle that was now taking place. The largest, most ambitious exploratory expedition that had ever set out from the solar system was in the gravest danger of its existence.

Grosvenor believed that firmly. This was no Coeurl, whose over-stimulated body had survived the murderous wars of the dead race that had performed biological experiments upon the animals of the cat planet. Nor could the danger from the Riim folk be compared. After their first misguided effort at communication, he had controlled every subsequent action in what he had thought of as the struggle between one man and a race.

The scarlet monster was clearly and unmistakably in a class by himself.

Captain Leeth climbed up a metal stairway that led to a small balcony. A moment later Morton joined him and stood looking down at the assembled men. He held a sheaf of notes in his hand, divided by one interposed finger into two piles. The two men studied the notes, then Morton said, "This is the first breathing spell we've had since the creature came aboard less than—incredible as it may seem—less than two hours ago. Captain Leeth and I have been reading the recommendations given us by heads of departments. These recommendations we have roughly divided into two categories. One category, being of a theoretical nature, we will leave till later. The other category, which concerns itself with mechanical plans for cornering our enemy, naturally takes precedence. To begin with, I am sure that we are all anxious to know that plans are afoot to locate and rescue Mr. von Grossen. Mr. Zeller, tell the rest of the men what you have in mind."

Zeller came forward, a brisk young man in his late thirties. He had succeeded to the headship of the metallurgy department after Breckenridge was killed by Coeurl. He said, "The discovery that the creature cannot penetrate the group of alloys we call resistance metals automatically gave us a clue as to the type of material we would use in building a space suit. My assistant is already working at the suit, and it should be ready in about three hours. For the search, naturally, we'll use a fluorite camera. If anybody has any suggestions..."

A man said, "Why not make several suits?"

Zeller shook his head. "We have only a very limited amount of material. We could make more, but only by transmutation, which takes time." He added, "Besides, ours has always been a small department. We'll be fortunate to get one suit completed in the time I have set."

There were no more questions. Zeller disappeared into the machine shop adjoining the engine room.

Director Morton raised his hand. When the men had settled again to silence, he said, "For myself, I feel better knowing that, once the suit is built, the creature will have to keep moving von Grossen in order to prevent us from discovering the body."

"How do you know he's alive?" someone asked.

"Because the damned thing could have taken the body of the man he killed, but he didn't. He wants us alive. Smith's notes have given us a possible clue to his purpose, but they are in category two, and will be discussed later."

He paused, then went on, "Among the plans put forward for actually destroying the creature, I have here one offered by two technicians of the physics department, and one by Elliott Grosvenor. Captain Leeth and I have discussed these plans with chief engineer Pennons and other experts, and we have decided that Mr. Grosvenor's idea is too dangerous to human beings, and so will be held as a last resort. We will begin immediately on the other plan unless important objections to it are raised. Several additional suggestions were made, and these have been incorporated. While it is customary to let individuals expound their own ideas, I think time will be saved if I briefly outline the plan as it has finally been approved by the experts."

"The two physicists"—Morton glanced down at the papers in his hand—"Lomas and Hindley, admit that their plan depends on the creature's permitting us to make the necessary energy connections. That appears probable on the basis of Mr. Korita's theory of cyclic history, to the effect that a 'peasant' is so concerned with his own blood purposes that he tends to ignore the potentialities of organized opposition. On this basis, under the modified plan of Lomas and Hindley, we are going to energize the seventh and ninth levels—only the floor and not the walls. Our hope is this. Until now, the creature has made no organized attempt to kill us. Mr. Korita says that, being a peasant, the thing has not yet realized that he must destroy us or we will destroy him. Sooner or later, however, even a peasant will realize that killing us should come first, before anything else. If he doesn't interfere with our work, then we'll trap him on the eighth level, between the two energized floors. There, under circumstances where he won't be able to get down or up, we'll search him out with our projectors. As Mr. Grosvenor will realize, this plan is considerably less risky than his own, and therefore should take precedence."

Grosvenor swallowed hard, hesitated, and then said grimly, "If it's the amount of risk we're considering, why don't we just crowd together here in the engine room and wait for him to develop a method of coming in after us?" He went on earnestly, "Please don't think I'm trying to push my own ideas. But personally"—he hesitated, then took the plunge—"I consider the plan you outlined as worthless."

Morton looked genuinely startled. Then he frowned. "Isn't that rather a sharp judgment?"

Grosvenor said, "I understand the plan as described by you was not the one originally put forward, but a modified version of it. What was taken out?"

"The two physicists," said the Director, "recommended energizing four levels—seven, eight, nine, and ten."

For the third time, Grosvenor hesitated. He had no desire to be overcritical. At any moment, if he persisted, they would simply cease asking his opinion. He said finally, "That's better."

From behind Morton, Captain Leeth interrupted. "Mr. Pennons, tell the group why it would be inadvisable to energize more than two floors."

The chief engineer stepped forward. He said with a frown, "The principle reason is that it would take an extra three hours, and we are all agreed that time is of the essence. If time were not a factor, it would be much better to energize the entire ship under a controlled system, walls as well as floors. That way, he couldn't escape us. But it would require about fifty hours. As I stated previously, uncontrolled energization would be suicide. There's another factor involved that we discussed purely as human beings. The reason the creature will seek us out will be that he wants more men, so that when he starts down, he'll have one of us with him. We want that man, whoever he is, to have a chance for life." His voice grew harsh. "During the three hours it will take us to put the modified plan into effect, we'll be helpless against him except for high-powered mobile vibrators and heat projectors. We dare not use anything heavier inside the ship, and those will have to be used with care since they can kill human beings. Naturally, each man is expected to defend himself with his own vibrator." He stepped back. "Let's get going!"

Captain Leeth said unhappily, "Not so fast. I want to hear more of Mr. Grosvenor's objections."

Grosvenor said, "If we had time, it might be interesting to see how this creature reacts to such energized walls."

A man said irritably, "I don't get the argument. Why, if this creature ever gets caught between two energized levels, that's the end of him. We know he can't get through."

"We don't know anything of the kind," Grosvenor said firmly. "All we know is that he got into a wall of force, and that he escaped. We assume he didn't like it. In fact, it seems clear that he definitely could not remain in such an energy field for any length of time. It is our misfortune, however, that we cannot use a full force screen against him. The walls, as Mr. Pennons pointed out, would melt. My point is, *he escaped from what we've got.*"

Captain Leeth looked disconcerted. "Gentlemen," he said, "why was this point not brought out at the discussion? It is certainly a valid objection."

Morton said, "I was in favor of inviting Grosvenor to the discussion, but I was voted down on the basis of a long-standing custom, whereby the man whose plan is under consideration is not present. For the same reason, the two physicists were not invited."

Siedel cleared his throat. "I don't think," he said, "that Mr. Grosvenor realizes what he has just done to us. We have all been assured that the ship's energy screen is one of man's greatest scientific achievements. This has given me personally a sense of well-being and security. Now he tells us this being can penetrate it."

Grosvenor said, "I didn't say the ship's screen was vulnerable, Mr. Siedel. In fact, there is reason to believe the enemy could not and cannot get through it. The reason is that he waited beyond it till we brought him inside it. The floor energization, now being discussed, is a considerably weaker version."

"Still," said the psychologist, "don't you think the experts unconsciously assumed a similarity between the two forms? The rationale would be: If this energization is ineffective, then we are lost. Therefore, it must be effective."

Captain Leeth broke in wearily. "I'm afraid that Mr. Siedel has accurately analyzed our weakness. I recall now having such a thought."

From the center of the room, Smith said, "Perhaps we'd better hear Mr. Grosvenor's alternative plan."

Captain Leeth glanced at Morton, who hesitated, then said, "He suggested that we divide ourselves into as many groups as there are atomic projectors aboard— "

That was as far as he got. A physics technician said in a shocked voice, "Atomic energy—inside a ship!"

The uproar that began then lasted for more than a minute. When it died away, Morton went on as if there had been no interruption.

"We have forty-one such projectors at the moment. If we accepted Mr. Grosvenor's plan, each one would be manned by a nucleus of military personnel, with the rest of us spread out as bait within sight of one of the projectors. Those manning the projector would be under orders to activate it even if one or more of us is in the line of fire."

Morton shook his head slightly, and went on. "It is possibly the most effective suggestion that has been put forward. However, the ruthlessness of it shocked us all. The idea of firing at one's own people, while not new, strikes much deeper than Mr. Grosvenor—I think— realizes. In fairness, though, I must add that there was one other factor that decided the scientists against it. Captain Leeth stipulated that those who acted as bait must be unarmed. To most of us, that was carrying the thing too far. Every man should be entitled to defend himself." The Director shrugged. "Since there was an alternative plan, we voted for it. I am now personally in favor of Mr. Grosvenor's idea, but I still object to Captain Leeth's stipulation."

At the first mention of the commander's suggestion, Grosvenor had swung around and stared at the officer. Captain Leeth looked back steadily, almost grimly. After a moment, Grosvenor said aloud in a deliberate tone, "I think you ought to take the risk, Captain."

The commander acknowledged the words with a slight, formal bow. "Very well," he said, "I withdraw my stipulation."

Grosvenor saw that Morton was puzzled by the brief interchange. The Director glanced at him, then at the captain, then back again to Grosvenor. Then a startled look flashed into his heavy-set face. He came down the narrow metal steps and over to Grosvenor. He said in a low tone, "To think that I never realized what he was getting at. He obviously believes that in a crisis..." He stopped, and turned to stare up at Captain Leeth.

Grosvenor said placatingly, "I think he now realizes he made a mistake in bringing up the matter."

Morton nodded, and said reluctantly, "I suppose, when you come right down to it, he's right. The impulse to survive, being basic, could supersede all subsequent conditionings. Still"—he frowned—"we'd better not mention it. I think the scientists would feel insulted, and there's enough bad feeling aboard."

He turned and faced the group. "Gentlemen," he said resonantly, "it seems clear that Mr. Grosvenor has made a case for his plan. All in favor of it, raise their hands."

To Grosvenor's intense disappointment, only about half a hundred hands came up. Morton hesitated, then said, "All against, raise theirs."

This time, just over a dozen hands were raised.

Morton pointed at a man in the front line. "You didn't put yours up either time. What seems to be the trouble?"

The man shrugged. "I'm neutral. I don't know whether I'm for it or against it. I don't know enough."

"And you?" Morton indicated another individual.

The man said, "What about secondary radiation?"

Captain Leeth answered that. "We'll block it off. We'll seal the entire area." He broke off. "Director," he said, "I don't understand why this delay. The vote was fifty-nine to fourteen in favor of the Grosvenor plan. While my jurisdiction over scientists is limited even during a crisis, I regard that as a decisive vote."

Morton seemed taken aback. "But," he protested, "nearly eight hundred men abstained."

Captain Leeth's tone was formal. "That was their privilege. It is expected that grown men know their own minds. The whole idea of democracy is based on that supposition. Accordingly, I order that we act at once."

Morton hesitated, then said slowly, "Well, gentlemen, I am compelled to agree. I think we'd better get about our business. It'll take time to set up the atomic projectors, so let's start energizing levels seven and nine while we're waiting. As I see it, we might as well combine the two plans, and abandon one or the other depending on the developing situation."

"Now that," said a man, with evident relief, "makes sense."

The suggestion seemed to make sense to a lot of the men. Resentful faces relaxed. Somebody cheered, and presently the great human mass was flowing out of the huge chamber. Grosvenor turned to Morton.

"That was a stroke of genius," he said. "I was too set against such limited energization to have thought of such a compromise."

Morton acknowledged the compliment gravely. "I was holding it in reserve," he said. "In dealing with human beings, I've noticed there is usually not only a problem to be solved but the matter of tension among those who have to solve it." He shrugged. "During danger, hard work. During hard work, relaxation in every practicable form."

He held out his hand. "Well, good luck, young man. Hope you come through safely."

As they shook hands, Grosvenor said, "How long will it take to roll out the atomic cannon?"

"About an hour, perhaps a little longer. Meanwhile, we'll have the big vibrators to protect us..."

The reappearance of the men brought Ixtl up to the seventh level with a rush. For many minutes, he was an abnormal shape that flitted through the wilderness of walls and floors. Twice he was seen, and projectors flashed at him. They were vibrators as different from the hand weapons he had faced so far as life from death. They shattered the walls through which he jumped to escape them. Once, the beam touched one of his feet. The hot shock from the molecular violence of the vibration made him stumble. The foot came back to normal in less than a second, but he had his picture of the limitations of his body against these powerful mobile units.

And still he was not alarmed. Speed, cunning, careful timing and placing of any appearance he made—such precautions would offset the effectiveness of the new weapons. The important thing was: What were the men doing? Obviously, when they had shut themselves up in the engine room, they had conceived a plan, and they were carrying it out with determination. With glittering, unwinking eyes, Ixtl watched the plan take form.

In every corridor, men slaved over furnaces, squat things of dead-black metal. From a hole in the top of each furnace, a white glare spewed up, blazing forth furiously. Ixtl could see that the men were half blinded by the white dazzle of the fire. They wore space armor, but the ordinarily transparent glassite of which it was made was electrically darkened. Yet no light-metal armor could ward off the full effect of that glare. Out of the furnaces rolled long, dully glowing strips of material. As each strip emerged, it was snatched by machine tools, skillfully machined to exact measurements, and slapped onto the metal floors. Not an inch of floor, Ixtl noted, escaped being enclosed by the strips. And the moment the hot metal was down, massive refrigerators hugged close to it and drew its heat.

His mind refused at first to accept the result of his observations. His brain persisted in searching for deeper purposes, for a cunning of vast and not easily discernible scope. Presently, he decided that this was all there was. The men were attempting to energize two floors under a system of controls. Later, when they realized that their limited trap was not effective, they would probably try other methods. Just when their defensive system would be dangerous to him, Ixtl wasn't certain. The important thing was that as soon as he did regard it as dangerous, it would be a simple matter to follow the men about and tear loose their energization connections.

Contemptuously, Ixtl dismissed the problem from his mind. The men were only playing into his hands, making it easier for him to get the guuls he still needed. He selected his next victim carefully. He had discovered in the man he had unintentionally killed that the stomach and intestinal tract were suitable for his purposes. Automatically, the men with the largest stomachs were on his list.

He made his preliminary survey, and then launched himself. Before a single projector could be turned towards him, he was gone with the writhing, struggling body. It was simple to adjust his atomic structure the moment he was through a ceiling, and so break his fall to the floor beneath. Swiftly, he let himself dissolve through that floor also, and down to the level below. Into the vast hold of the ship, he half fell, half lowered himself. He could have gone faster, but he had to be careful not to damage the human body.

The hold was familiar territory now to the sure-footed tread of his long-toed feet. He had explored the place briefly but thoroughly after he first boarded the ship. And, in handling von Grossen, he had learned the pattern he needed now. Unerringly, he headed across the dim-lit interior toward the far wall. Great packing cases were piled up to the ceiling. He went through them or around them, as it suited him, and presently found himself in a great pipe. The inside was big enough for him to stand up in. It was part of the miles-long system of air conditioning.

His hiding place would have been dark by ordinary light. But to his infrared-sensitive vision, a vague twilight glow suffused the pipe. He saw the body of von Grossen, and laid his new victim beside it. Carefully, then, he inserted one of his wiry hands into his own breast, removed a precious egg, and deposited it into the stomach of the human being.

The man was still struggling, but Ixtl waited for what he knew must happen. Slowly, the body began to stiffen. The muscles grew progressively rigid. In panic, the man squirmed and jerked as he evidently recognized that paralysis was creeping over him. Remorselessly, Ixtl held him down until the chemical action was completed. In the end, the man lay motionless, every muscle rigid. His eyes were open and staring. There was sweat on his face.

Within hours, the eggs would be hatching inside each man's stomach. Swiftly, the tiny replicas of himself would eat themselves to full size. Satisfied, Ixtl darted up out of the hold. He needed more hatching places for his eggs, more guuls.

By the time he had put a third captive through the process, the men were working on the ninth level. Waves of heat rolled along the corridor. It was an inferno wind. Even the refrigeration unit in each space suit was hard put to it to handle the superheated air. Men sweated inside their suits. Sick from the heat, stunned by the glare, they labored almost by instinct.

Beside Grosvenor a man said suddenly, harshly, "Here they come now!"

Grosvenor turned in the direction indicated, and stiffened in spite of himself. The machine that was rolling towards them under its own power was not big. It was a globular mass with an outer shell of wolfram carbide, and had a nozzle that protruded from the globe. The strictly functional structure was mounted on a universal bearing, which, in its turn, rested on a base of four rubber wheels.

All around Grosvenor, men had ceased work. Their faces pale, they stared at the metal monstrosity. Abruptly, one of them came over to Grosvenor and said angrily, "Damn you, Grove, you're responsible for this. If I'm due to get irradiated by one of those things, I'd like to punch you one in the nose first."

"I'll be right here," said Grosvenor in a steady voice. "If you get killed, so will I."

That seemed to take some of the anger out of the other. But there was still violence in his manner and tone, as he said, "What the hell kind of nonsense is this? Surely there must be better plans than to make bait out of human beings."

Grosvenor said, "There is another thing we can do."

"What's that?"

"Commit suicide!" said Grosvenor. And he meant it.

The man glared at him, then turned away muttering something about stupid jokes and moronic jokesters. Grosvenor smiled mirthlessly and went back to work. Almost immediately, he saw that the men had lost their zest for the job. An electric tension leaped from one individual to another. The slightest untoward action on the part of one person brought the others tautly erect.

They were bait. All over the various levels, men would be reacting to the death fear. No one could be immune, for the will to survive was built-in in the nervous system. Highly trained military men like Captain Leeth could put on an impassive front, but the tension would be there just under the surface. Similarly, people like Elliott Grosvenor could be grim but determined, convinced of the soundness of a course of action and prepared to take their chance.

"Attention, all personnel!"

Grosvenor jumped with the rest as that voice came out of the nearest communicator. It took a long moment before he recognized it as belonging to the commander of the ship.

Captain Leeth continued. "All projectors are now in position to levels seven, eight, and nine. You will be glad to know that I have been discussing the dangers involved with my officers. We make the following recommendations: If you see the creature, don't wait, don't look around! Throw yourself instantly to the floor. All weapon crews—right now—adjust your nozzles to fire at 50:1$\frac{1}{2}$. That gives you all a clearance of one and a half feet. This will not protect you from secondary radiation, but I think we can honestly say that if you hit the floor in time, Dr. Eggert and his staff in the engine room will save your life.

"In conclusion"—Captain Leeth seemed more at ease, now that his main message had been delivered—"let me assure all ranks that there are no shirkers aboard. With the exception of the doctors and three invalid patients, every individual is in as great danger as you. My officers and I are divided among the various groups. Director Morton is down on the seventh level. Mr. Grosvenor—whose plan this is— is on level nine, and so on. Good luck, gentlemen!"

There was a moment's silence. Then the leader of the gun crew near Grosvenor called in a friendly voice, "Hey, you fellows! We've made the adjustments. You'll be safe if you can hit the deck in nothing flat."

Grosvenor called, "Thanks, friend."

Just for a moment, then, the tension eased. A mathematical-biology technician said, "Grove, butter him up some more with soft talk."

"I always did love the military," said another man. In a hoarse aside, he said loud enough for the gun crew to hear, "That ought to hold 'em off for that extra second I need."

Grosvenor scarcely heard. Bait, he was thinking again. And no group would know when the moment of danger came for some other group. At the instant of "guncrit"—a modified form of critical mass, in which a small pile developed enormous energy without exploding—a tracer light would leap out of the muzzle. Along it and around it would pour the hard, silent, invisible radiation.

When it was all over, the survivors would notify Captain Leeth on his private band. In due course, the commander would inform the other groups.

"Mr. Grosvenor!"

Instinctively, as the sharp voice sounded, Grosvenor dived for the floor. He struck painfully, but came up almost immediately as he recognized Captain Leeth's voice.

Other men were climbing ruefully to their feet. One man muttered, "Dammit, that wasn't fair."

Grosvenor reached the communicator. He kept his gaze warily on the corridor ahead of him, as he said, "Yes, Captain?"

"Will you come down to level seven at once? Central corridor. Approach from nine o'clock."

"Yes, sir."

Grosvenor went with a sense of dread. There had been a tone in the captain's voice. Something was wrong.

He found a nightmare. As he approached, he saw that one of the atomic cannon was lying on its side. Beside it, dead, burned beyond recognition, lay what had been three of the four military crewmen of the projector. On the floor beside them, unconscious but still twitching and squirming, all too evidently from a vibrator discharge, was the fourth crewman.

On the far side of the cannon, twenty men lay unconscious or dead, among them Director Morton.

Stretcher-bearers, wearing protective clothing, were dashing in, picking up a victim, and then racing off with him on a loading mule.

The rescue work had clearly been going on for several minutes, so there were probably more unconscious men already being tended in the engine room by Dr. Eggert and his staff.

Grosvenor stopped at a barrier that had been hastily erected at a turn in the corridor. Captain Leeth was there. The commander was pale but calm. In a few minutes, Grosvenor had the story.

Ixtl had appeared. A young technician—Captain Leeth did not name him—forgot in panic that safety lay on the floor. As the muzzle of the cannon came up inexorably, the hysterical youngster fired his vibrator at the crew, stunning them all. Apparently they had hesitated slightly when they saw the technician in their line of fire. The next instant, each crewman was unknowingly contributing his bit to the disaster. Three of them fell against the cannon, and, instinctively clinging to it, swung it over on its side. It rolled away from them, dragging the fourth man along.

The trouble was he had hold of the activator, and for what must have been nearly a second he pressed it.

His three companions were in the direct line of fire. They died instantly. The cannon finished rolling over on its side, spraying one wall.

Morton and his group, though never in the direct line of fire, were caught by the secondary radiation. It was too soon to tell how badly they were injured, but at a conservative estimate they would all be in bed for a year. A few would die.

"We were a little slow," Captain Leeth confessed. "This apparently happened a few seconds after I finished talking. But it was nearly a minute before somebody who heard the crash of the cannon toppling grew curious and glanced around this corner." He sighed wearily. "At the very worst, I never expected anything as bad as an entire group being wiped out."

Grosvenor was silent. This was why, of course, Captain Leeth had wanted the scientists unarmed. In a crisis, a man protected himself. He couldn't help it. Like an animal, he fought blindly for his life.

He tried not to think of Morton, who had realized that the scientists would resist being disarmed and who had thought up the *modus operandi* that would make the use of atomic energy acceptable to all. He said steadily, "Why did you call me?"

"My feeling is that this failure affects your plan. What do you think?"

Grosvenor nodded reluctantly. "The surprise element is gone," he said. "He must have come up without suspecting what was waiting for him. Now, he'll be careful."

He could picture the scarlet monster poking his head through a wall, surveying a corridor—then boldly coming out beside one of the cannon and snatching one of the crew men. The only adequate precaution would be to set up a second projector to cover the first one. But that was out of the question—there were only forty-one available for the whole ship.

Grosvenor shook his head. Then he said, "Did he get another man?"

"No."

Once more Grosvenor was silent. Like the others, he could only guess at the creature's reason for wanting living men. One of those guesses was based on Korita's theory that the being was in a peasant stage and intent on reproducing himself. That suggested a bloodcurdling possibility, and a pressure of need on the part of the creature that would drive him after more human victims.

Captain Leeth said, "As I see it, he'll be up again. My idea is that we leave the cannon where they are for the time being and finish energizing three levels. Seven is completed, nine is almost ready, and so we might as well go on to eight. That will give us three floors altogether. As far as the possible effectiveness of such a plan goes, we should consider that the creature has now captured three men in addition to von Grossen. In each case, he was seen to take them in what we call a downward direction. I suggest that, as soon as we have energized all three levels, we go to the ninth floor and wait for him. When he captures one of us, we wait momentarily; and then Mr. Pennons will throw the switch that sets up the force field in the floors. The creature will strike the eighth level, and find it energized. If he tries to go through, he will find that seven is also energized. If he comes up, he finds nine in the same deadly state. Either way, we force him to make contact with two energized floors." The commander paused, looked thoughtfully at Grosvenor and then said, "I know you considered that contact with only one level would not kill him. You were not so positive about two." He stopped, and waited questioningly.

Grosvenor said, after a moment of hesitation, "I'll buy that. Actually, we can only guess how it will affect him. Maybe we'll all be pleasantly surprised."

He didn't believe that. But there was another factor in this developing situation: the convictions and hopes that men had. Only an actual event would change the minds of some people. When their ideas were altered by reality, then—and then only—they would be emotionally ready for more drastic solutions.

It seemed to Grosvenor that he was learning slowly but surely how to influence men. It was not enough to have information and knowledge, not enough to be right. Men had to be persuaded and convinced. Sometimes that might take more time than could safely be spared. Sometimes it couldn't be done at all. And so civilizations crumbled, battles were lost, and ships destroyed because the man or group with the saving ideas would not go through the long-drawn-out ritual of convincing others.

If he could help it, that was not going to happen here.

He said, "We can keep the atomic projectors in place till we finish energizing the floors. Then we'll have to move them. Energization would bring guncrit even without the nozzle being open. They'd blow up."

As deliberately as that he withdrew the Grosvenor plan from the battle against the enemy.

# 20

Ixtl came up twice during the hour and three quarters that was needed to do level eight. He had six eggs left, and he intended to use all except two of them. His only annoyance was that each guul took more time. The defense against him seemed more alert, and the presence of atomic cannon made it necessary for him to go after the men who actually manned the projectors.

Even with that limitation rigidly observed, each escape turned out to be an achievement in timing. Nevertheless, he was not worried. These things had to be done. In due course, he would attend to the men.

When the eighth level was completed, the cannon withdrawn, and everyone on the ninth level, Grosvenor heard Captain Leeth say curtly, "Mr. Pennons, are you ready to use power?"

"Yes, sir." The engineer's voice was a dry rasp on the communicators. He finished even more harshly. "Five men gone, and one to go. We've been lucky, but there is at least one more to go."

"Do you hear that, gentlemen? One to go. One of us will be bait whether he likes it or not." It was a familiar voice, but one that had long been silent. The speaker went on gravely. "This is Gregory Kent. And I'm sorry to have to say that I am speaking to you from the safety of the engine room. Dr. Eggert tells me it'll be another week before I'm off the invalid list. The reason I am speaking to you now is that Captain Leeth has turned Director Morton's papers over to me, and so I'd like Kellie to elaborate on the note of his that I have here. It will clear up something very important. It will give us a sharper picture of what we're facing. We might as well all know the worst."

"Ah..." The cracked voice of the sociologist sounded on the communicators. "Here's my reasoning. When we discovered the creature, it was floating a quarter of a million light-years from the nearest star system, apparently without means of spatial locomotion. Picture that appalling distance, and then ask yourself how long it would require, relatively, for an object to move it by chance alone. Lester gave me my figures, so I would like him to tell you what he told me."

"Lester speaking!" The voice of the astronomer sounded surprisingly brisk. "Most of you know the prevailing theory of the beginnings of the present universe. There is evidence to believe that it came into being as a result of the breakup of an earlier universe several million million years ago. It is believed today that a few million million years hence, our universe will complete its cycle, and blow up in a cataclysmic explosion. The nature of such an explosion can only be surmised."

He went on, "As for Kellie's question, I can only offer a picture to you. Let us suppose that the scarlet being was blown out into space when the great explosion occurred. He would find himself heading out into intergalactic space, with no means of changing his course. Under such circumstances, he could float along forever without coming nearer to a star than a quarter of a million light-years. That is what you wanted, Kellie?"

"Ah, yes. Most of you will recall my mentioning before that it was a paradox that a pure sympodial development, such as this creature is, did not populate the entire universe. The answer to that is, logically, if his race *should* have controlled the universe, then it *did* control it. We can see now, however, that they ruled a previous universe, not our present one. Naturally, the creature now intends that his kind shall also dominate our universe. This at least is a plausible theory, if no more."

Kent said in a placating tone, "I'm sure that all the scientists aboard realize that we are speculating by necessity on matters about which little evidence is as yet available. I think it is a good thing for us to believe that we are confronted with a survivor of the supreme race of a universe. There may be others like him in the same predicament. We can only hope that no other ship ever comes near one. Biologically, this race could be billions of years ahead of us. Thinking thus, we can feel justified in demanding the utmost contribution in effort and personal sacrifice from every person aboard—"

The shrill scream of a man interrupted him. "Got me!... Quick!...ripping me out of my suit—" The words ended in a gurgle.

Grosvenor said tensely, "That was Dack, chief assistant in the geology department." He spoke the identification without thinking. His recognition of voices was now as quick and automatic as that.

Another voice sounded shrilly on the communicators. "He's going down. I saw him go down!"

"The power," said a third, calmer voice, "is on." That was Pennons.

Grosvenor found himself staring curiously at his feet. Sparkling, brilliant, beautiful blue fire shimmered there. Little tendrils of the pretty flame reared up hungrily a few inches from his rubberite suit, as if baffled by some invisible force protecting the suit. Now there was no sound. With almost blank mind, he gazed along a corridor that was alive with the unearthly blue fire. Just for a moment, he had the illusion that he was looking not out at it but down into the depths of the ship.

With a rush, his mind came back into focus. And with fascinated eyes he watched the blue ferocity of the energization that was struggling to break through his protected suit.

Pennons spoke again, this time in a whisper. "If the plan worked, we've now got that devil on the eighth or seventh levels."

Captain Leeth commanded efficiently, "All men whose last names begin with the letters 'A' to 'L,' follow me to the seventh level! Group 'M' to 'Z,' follow Mr. Pennons to the eighth level! All projector crews remain at their posts! Camera teams, carry on as ordered!"

The men ahead of Grosvenor stopped short at the second corner from the elevators on the seventh level. Grosvenor was among those who went forward and stood staring down at the human body that sprawled on the floor. It was seemingly held to the metal by brilliant fingers of blue fire. Captain Leeth broke the silence.

"Pull him loose!"

Two men stepped gingerly forward and touched the body. The blue flame leaped at them, as if trying to fight them off. The men jerked, and the unholy bonds yielded. They carried the body up in an elevator to the unenergized tenth level. Grosvenor followed with the others, and stood silently by as the body was laid on the floor. The lifeless thing continued to kick for several minutes, discharging torrents of energy, then gradually took on the quietness of death.

"I'm waiting for reports!" Captain Leeth spoke stiffly.

Pennons said after a second's silence, "The men are spread out over the three levels, according to plan. They're taking continuous pictures with fluorite cameras. If he's anywhere around, he'll be seen. It will take at least thirty more minutes."

Finally the report came. "Nothing!" Pennons's tone reflected his dismay. "Commander, he must have got through safely."

Somewhere a voice sounded plaintively on the momentarily open circuit of the communicators, "Now what are we going to do?"

It seemed to Grosvenor that the words probably expressed the doubt and anxiety of every person on the *Space Beagle*.

# 21

The silence grew long. The great men of the ship, who were ordinarily so articulate, seemed to have lost their voices. Grosvenor shrank a little from the purpose, the new plan, in his own mind. And then, slowly, he faced up to the reality that now confronted the expedition. But still he waited. For it was not up to him to speak first.

It was chief chemist Kent who finally broke the spell. "It would appear," he said, "that our enemy can pass through energized walls as easily as through unenergized ones. We can continue to assume that he does not care for the experience, but that his recuperation is so swift that what he feels in one floor has no effect on him by the time he falls through the air to the next one."

Captain Leeth said, "I should like to hear from Mr. Zeller. Where are you now, sir?"

"Zeller speaking!" The brisk voice of the metallurgist sounded on the communicators. "I've finished the resistance suit, Captain. And I've started my search at the bottom of the ship."

"How long would it take to build resistance suits for everybody on the ship?"

Zeller's reply was slow in coming. "We'd have to set up a production unit," he said finally. "First we'd have to make the tools to make the tools that would make such suits in quantity from any metal. Simultaneously, we would start one of the hot piles to the task of making resistance metal. As you probably know, it comes out radioactive with a half life of five hours, which is a long time. My guess is that the first suit would roll off the assembly line about two hundred hours from now."

To Grosvenor, it sounded like a conservative estimate. The difficulty of machining resistance metal could hardly be overstated. Captain Leeth seemed to have been struck into silence by the metallurgist's words. It was Smith who spoke.

"Then that's out!" The biologist sounded uncertain. "And since the complete energization would also take too long, we've shot our bolt. We've got nothing else."

The usually lazy voice of Gourlay, the communications expert, snapped, "I don't see why those ways are out. We're still alive. I suggest we get to work, and do as much as we can as soon as we can."

"What makes you think," Smith asked coldly, "that the creature is not capable of smashing down resistance metal? As a superior being, his knowledge of physics probably transcends our own. He might find it comparatively simple to construct a beam that could destroy anything we have. Don't forget, pussy could pulverize resistance metal. And heaven knows there are plenty of tools available in the various laboratories."

Gourlay said scornfully, "Are you suggesting that we give up?"

"No!" The biologist was angry. "I want us to use common sense. Let's not just work blindly towards an unrealizable goal."

Korita's voice sounded on the communicators, and ended the verbal duel. "I am inclined to agree with Smith. I say further that we are now dealing with a being who must shortly realize that he cannot allow us time for anything important. For that and other reasons, I believe the creature would interfere if we attempted to prepare the ship for complete controlled energization."

Captain Leeth remained silent. From the engine room, Kent's voice came again. "What do you think he will do when he begins to understand that it's dangerous to let us continue organizing against him?"

"He'll start to kill. I can't think of any method by which we can stop him, short of retreating into the engine room. And I believe, with Smith, that he will be able to come in there after us, given time."

"Have you any suggestions?" That was Captain Leeth.

Korita hesitated. "Frankly, no. I would say we mustn't forget we are dealing with a creature who seems to be in the peasant stage of his particular cycle. To a peasant, his land and his son—or, to use a higher level of abstraction—his property and his blood are sacred. He fights blindly against encroachment. Like a plant, he attaches himself to a piece of property, and there he sinks his roots and nourishes his blood."

Korita hesitated, then said, "That is the generalized picture, gentlemen. At the moment, I have no idea how it should be applied."

Captain Leeth said, "I seriously can't see how it can help us. Will each department head consult on his private band with his lower-echelon executives? Report in five minutes if anybody has come up with a worthwhile idea."

Grosvenor, who had no assistants in his department, said, "I wonder if I could ask Mr. Korita a few questions while the departmental discussions are in progress."

Captain Leeth shook his head. "If no one else objects, you have my permission."

There were no objections, so Grosvenor said, "Mr. Korita, are you available?"

"Who is this?"

"Grosvenor."

"Oh, yes, Mr. Grosvenor. I recognize your voice now. Proceed."

"You mentioned that the peasant clings with an almost senseless tenacity to his plot of land. If this creature is in the peasant stage of one of his civilizations, could he imagine our feeling differently about our property?"

"I'm sure he could not."

"He would make his plans in the full conviction that we cannot escape him, since we are cornered aboard this ship?"

"It is a fairly safe assumption on his part. We cannot abandon the ship and survive."

Grosvenor persisted. "But we are in a cycle where any particular property means little to us? We are not blindly attached to it?"

"I still don't think I understand what you mean." Korita sounded puzzled.

"I am," said Grosvenor steadily, "pursuing your notion to its logical conclusion in this situation."

Captain Leeth interrupted. "Mr. Grosvenor, I think I am beginning to get the direction of your reasoning. Are you about to offer another plan?"

"Yes." In spite of himself, his voice trembled slightly.

Captain Leeth sounded taut. "Mr. Grosvenor," he said, "if I'm anticipating you correctly, your solution shows courage and imagination. I want you to explain it to the others in—" he hesitated, and glanced at his watch—"as soon as the five minutes are up."

After a very brief silence, Korita spoke again. "Mr. Grosvenor," he said, "your reasoning is sound. We can make such a sacrifice without suffering a spiritual collapse. It is the only solution."

A minute later, Grosvenor gave his analysis to the entire membership of the expeditionary force. When he finished, it was Smith who said in a tone that was scarcely more than a loud whisper, "Grosvenor, you've got it! It means sacrificing von Grossen and the others. It means individual sacrifice for every one of us. But you're right. Property is not sacred to us. As for von Grossen and the four with him"—his voice grew stern and hard—"I haven't had a chance to tell you about the notes I gave Morton. He didn't tell you because I suggested a possible parallel with a certain species of wasp back home on Earth. The thought is so horrible that I think quick death will come as a release to those men."

"The wasp!" a man gasped. "You're right, Smith. The sooner they're dead the better!"

It was Captain Leeth who gave the command. "To the engine room!" he said. "We—"

A swift, excited voice clamoring into the communicators interrupted him. A long second went by before Grosvenor recognized it as belonging to Zeller, the metallurgist.

"Captain—quick! Send men and projectors down to the hold! I've found them in the air-conditioning pipe. The creature's here, and I'm holding him off with my vibrator. It's not doing him much damage, so—hurry!"

Captain Leeth snapped orders with machine-gun speed as the men swarmed toward the elevators. "All scientists and their staffs proceed to the air locks. Military personnel take the freight elevators and follow me!" He went on, "We probably won't be able to corner him or kill him in the hold. But, gentlemen"—his voice became grave and determined—"we're going to get rid of this monster, and we're going to do so at any cost. We can no longer consider ourselves."

Ixtl retreated reluctantly as the men carried off his guuls. The first shrinking fear of defeat closed over his mind like the night that brooded beyond the enclosing walls of the ship. His impulse was to dash into their midst and smash them. But those ugly, glittering weapons held back the desperate urge. He retreated with a sense of disaster. He had lost the initiative. The men would discover his eggs now, and, in destroying them, would destroy his immediate chances of being reinforced by other ixtls.

His brain spun into a tightening web of purpose. From this moment, he must kill, and kill only. He was astounded that he had thought first of reproduction, with everything else secondary. Already he had wasted valuable time. To kill he must have a weapon that would smash anything. After a moment's thought, he headed for the nearest laboratory. He felt a burning urgency, unlike anything he had ever known.

As he worked, tall body and intent face bent over the gleaming metal of the mechanism, his sensitive feet grew aware of a difference in the symphony of vibrations that throbbed in discordant melody through the ship. He paused and straightened. Then he realized what it was. The drive engines were silent. The monster ship of space had halted in its headlong acceleration and was lying quiescent in the black deeps. An indefinable sense of alarm came to Ixtl. His long, black, wirelike fingers became flashing things as he made delicate connections deftly and frantically.

Suddenly, he paused again. Stronger than before came the sensation that something was wrong, dangerously, terribly wrong. The muscles of his feet grew taut with straining. And then he knew what it was. He could no longer feel the vibrations of the men. *They had left the ship!*

Ixtl whirled from his almost completed weapon and plunged

through the nearest wall. He knew his doom with a certainty that found hope only in the blackness of space.

Through deserted corridors he fled, slavering hate, a scarlet monster from ancient, ancient Glor. The gleaming walls seemed to mock him. The whole world of the great ship, which had promised so much, was now only the place where a hell of energy would break loose at any moment. With relief, he saw an air lock ahead. He flashed through the first section, the second, the third—and then he was out in space. He anticipated that the men would be watching for him to appear, so he set up a violent repulsion between his body and the ship. He had a sensation of increasing lightness as his body darted from the side of the ship out into that black night.

Behind him, the porthole lights were snuffed out and were replaced by an unearthly blue glow. The blue fire flashed out from every square inch of the ship's immense outer skin. The blue glow faded slowly, almost reluctantly. Long before it died away completely, the potent energy screen came on, blocking him forever from access to the ship. Some of the porthole lights came on again, flickered weakly and then slowly began to brighten. As mighty engines recovered from that devastating flare of energy, the lights already shining grew stronger. Others began to flash on.

Ixtl, who had withdrawn several miles, drove himself nearer. He was careful. Now that he was out in space, they could use atomic cannon on him and destroy him without danger to themselves. He approached to within half a mile of the screen, and there, uneasy, stopped. He saw the first of the lifeboats dart out of the darkness inside the screen into an opening that yawned in the side of the big vessel. Other dark craft followed, whipping down in swift arcs, their shapes blurred against the background of space. They were vaguely visible in the light that glowed steadily again from the lighted portholes.

The opening shut, and without warning the ship vanished. One instant it was there, a vast sphere of dark metal. The next, he was staring through the space where it had been at a spiral-shaped, bright splotch, a galaxy that floated beyond a gulf of a million light-years.

Time dragged drearily towards eternity. Ixtl sprawled unmoving and hopeless in the boundless night. He couldn't help thinking of the young ixtls, who now would never be born, and of the universe that was lost because of his mistakes.

Grosvenor watched the skillful fingers of the surgeon as the electrified knife cut into the fourth man's stomach. The last egg was deposited in the bottom of the tall resistance-metal vat. The eggs were round, grayish objects, one of them slightly cracked.

Several men stood by with drawn heat blasters as the crack widened. An ugly, round, scarlet head with tiny, beady eyes and a tiny slit of a mouth poked out. The head twisted on its short neck and the eyes glittered up at them with hard ferocity. With a swiftness that almost took them by surprise, the creature reared up and tried to climb out of the vat. The smooth walls defeated it. It slid back and dissolved in the flame that was poured down upon it.

Smith, licking his lips, said, "Suppose he'd got away and dissolved into the nearest wall!"

No one answered that. Grosvenor saw that the men were staring into the vat. The eggs melted reluctantly under the heat from the blasters, but finally burned with a golden light.

"Ah," said Dr. Eggert; and attention turned to him and to the body of von Grossen, over which he was bending. "His muscles are beginning to relax, and his eyes are open and alive. I imagine he knows what's going on. It was a form of paralysis induced by the egg, and fading now that the egg is no longer present. Nothing fundamentally wrong. They'll be all right shortly. What about the monster?"

Captain Leeth replied, "The men in two lifeboats claim to have seen a flash of red emerge from the main lock just as we swept the ship with uncontrolled energization. It must have been our deadly friend, because we haven't found his body. However, Pennons is going around with the camera staff taking pictures with fluorite cameras, and we'll know for certain in a few hours. Here he is now. Well, Mr. Pennons?"

The engineer strode in briskly and placed a misshapen thing of metal on one of the tables. "Nothing definite to report yet—but I found this in the main physics laboratory. What do you make of it?"

Grosvenor was pushed forward by department heads who drew in around the table for a closer look. He frowned down at the fragile-looking object with its intricate network of wires. There were three distinct tubes that might have been muzzles running into and through three small, round balls that shone with a queer, silvery light. The light penetrated the table, making it as transparent as glassite. And, strangest of all, the balls absorbed heat like a thermal sponge. Grosvenor reached out toward the nearest ball, and felt his hands stiffen as the heat was drawn from them. He drew back quickly.

Beside him, Captain Leeth said, "I think we'd better leave this for the physics department to examine. Von Grossen ought to be up and around soon. You say you found it in the laboratory?"

Pennons nodded. And Smith carried on the thought. "It would appear that the creature was working on it when he suspected that something was amiss. He must have realized the truth, for he left the ship. That seems to discount your theory, Korita. You said that, as a true peasant, he couldn't even imagine what we were going to do."

The Japanese archeologist smiled faintly through the fatigue that paled his face. "Mr. Smith," he said politely, "there is no question but that this one did imagine it. The probable answer is that the peasant category amounted to an analogy. The red monster was, by all odds, the most superior peasant we have yet encountered."

Pennons groaned. "I wish we had a few peasant limitations. Do you know that it will take us three months at least to get this ship properly repaired after those three minutes of uncontrolled energization? For a time I was afraid that..." His voice trailed off doubtfully.

Captain Leeth said with a grim smile, "I'll finish that sentence for you, Mr. Pennons. You were afraid the ship would be completely destroyed. I think that most of us realized the risk we were taking when we adopted Mr. Grosvenor's final plan. We knew that our lifeboats could be given only partial anti-acceleration. So we'd have been stranded here a quarter of a million light-years from home."

A man said, "I wonder whether, if the scarlet beast had actually taken over this ship, it would have gotten away with its obvious intent to take over the galaxy. After all, man is pretty well established in it—and pretty stubborn, too."

Smith shook his head. "It dominated once, and it could dominate again. You assume far too readily that man is a paragon of justice, forgetting, apparently, that he has a long and savage history. He has killed other animals not only for meat but for pleasure; he has enslaved his neighbors, murdered his opponents, and obtained the most unholy sadistical joy from the agony of others. It is not impossible that we shall, in the course of our travels, meet other intelligent creatures far more worthy than man to rule the universe."

"By heaven!" said a man, "no dangerous-looking creature should ever be allowed aboard this ship again. My nerves are all shot; and I'm not so good a man as I was when I first came aboard the *Beagle*."

"You speak for us all!" came the voice of Acting Director Kent over the communicator.

# 22

Somebody whispered in Grosvenor's ear, so softly that he could not catch the words. The whisper was followed by a trilling sound, as gentle as the whisper and equally meaningless.

Involuntarily, Grosvenor looked around.

He was in the film room of his own department, and there was nobody in sight. He walked uncertainly to the door that led to the auditorium room. But no one was there either.

He came back to his workbench, frowning, wondering if someone had pointed an encephalo-adjuster at him. It was the only comparison he could think of, for he had seemed to hear a sound.

After a moment, that explanation struck him as improbable. Adjusters were effective at short ranges only. More important, his department was shielded against most vibrations. Besides, he was only too familiar with the mental process involved in the illusion he had experienced. That made it impossible for him to dismiss the incident.

As a precaution, he explored all five of his rooms and examined the adjusters in his technique room. They were as they ought to be, properly stored away. In silence, Grosvenor returned to the film room and resumed his study of the hypnotic light-pattern variations, which he had developed from the images that the Riim had used against the ship.

Terror struck his mind like a blow. Grosvenor cringed. And then there was the whisper again, as soft as before, yet somehow angry now, and unthinkably hostile.

Amazed, Grosvenor straightened. It *must* be an encephalo-adjuster. Somebody was stimulating his mind from a distance with a machine so powerful that the protective shielding of his room was penetrated.

With a frown, he considered who it might be, and finally called up the psychology department as the most likely offender. Siedel answered personally, and Grosvenor started to explain what had happened. He was cut off.

"I was just about to contact you," said Siedel. "I thought you might be responsible."

"You mean everybody's affected?" Grosvenor spoke slowly, trying to imagine the implications.

"I'm surprised you got any of it at all in that specially constructed department of yours," said Siedel. "I've been receiving complaints for more than twenty minutes, and some of my instruments were affected several minutes before that."

"Which instruments?"

"Brain-wave detector, nerve-impulse register, and the more sensitive electrical detectors." He broke off. "Kent is going to call a meeting in the control room. I'll see you there."

Grosvenor did not let him go so quickly. "Has there been any discussion as yet?" he asked.

"We-e-l-ll, we're all making an assumption."

"What's that?" he asked quickly.

"We're about to enter the great galaxy M-33. We're assuming this comes from there."

Grosvenor laughed grimly. "It's a reasonable hypothesis. I'll think about it, and see you in a few minutes."

"Be prepared for a shock when you first go out into the corridor. The pressure out here is continuous. Sounds, light flashes, dreams, emotional turmoil—we're really getting a dose of stimulation."

Grosvenor nodded, and broke the connection. By the time he had put away his films, Kent's announcement of the meeting was coming over the communicator. A minute later, as he opened his outer door, he realized what Siedel had meant.

He paused as the barrage of excitations instantly began to affect his brain. Then, uneasily, he headed for the control room.

He sat presently with the others; and the night whispered, the immense night of space that pressed against the hurtling ship. Capricious and deadly, it beckoned and it warned. It trilled with frenzied delight, then hissed with savage frustration. It muttered in fear and growled in hunger. It died, reveling in agony, and burgeoned again into ecstatic life. Yet always and insidiously it threatened.

"This is an opinion," said somebody behind Grosvenor. "The ship ought to go home."

Grosvenor, unable to identify the voice, glanced around to see who had spoken. Whoever it was said nothing more. Facing forward again, Grosvenor saw that Acting Director Kent had not turned from the eyepiece of the telescope through which he was peering. Either he considered the remark had been unworthy of reply, or else he hadn't heard it. Nor did anyone else comment.

As the silence continued, Grosvenor manipulated the communicator in the arm of his chair, and presently he was seeing a slightly blurred image of what Kent and Lester were gazing at directly through the telescope. Slowly, then, he forgot the spectators and concentrated on the night scene shown by the plate. They were near the outer environs of an entire galactic system, yet the nearest stars were still so far away that the telescope could barely resolve the myriad needle points of brilliance that made up the spiral nebula, M-33, in Andromeda, their destination.

Grosvenor glanced up just as Lester turned from the telescope. The astronomer said, "What is happening seems incredible. Vibrations we can actually sense, spilling out from a galaxy of billions of suns." He paused, then said, "Director, it seems to me this is not a problem for an astronomer."

Kent released his own eyepiece and said, "Anything that embraces an entire galaxy comes under the category of astronomical phenomena. Or would you care to name the science that is involved?"

Lester hesitated, then replied slowly, "The scale of magnitude is fantastic. I don't think we should assume galactic scope as yet. This barrage may be coming on a beam which is concentrated on our ship."

Kent turned toward the men who sat in the tiers of cushioned seats facing the broad and colorful control panel. He said, "Has anyone a suggestion or a thought?"

Grosvenor glanced around, hoping that the unidentified man who had spoken earlier would explain himself. But whoever it was remained silent.

Undeniably, the men no longer felt so free to speak up as they had under the leadership of Morton. One way or another, Kent had made it rather plain that he deemed the opinions of those other than department heads impertinent. It was also evident that he personally declined to regard Nexialism as a legitimate department. For several months, he and Grosvenor had been polite to each other on a basis of minimum contact. During that time, the Acting Director had, by way of consolidating his position, introduced several motions in the council giving his office more authority in certain activities, the ostensible reason being to avoid duplication of effort.

The importance to this ship's morale of encouraging individual initiative, even at the cost of some efficiency, was a point that could have been demonstrated only to another Nexialist, Grosvenor had felt sure. He had not bothered to protest. And so a few more slight restrictions had been imposed on the already dangerously regimented and confined shipload of human beings.

From the rear of the control room, Smith was the first to answer Kent's request for suggestions. The angular and bony biologist said dryly, "I notice Mr. Grosvenor is twisting about in his chair. Can it be that he is politely waiting for the older men to have their say? Mr. Grosvenor, what's on your mind?"

Grosvenor waited until the faint wave of laughter—in which Kent did not join—had died away. Then he said, "A few minutes ago, someone suggested that we turn around and go home. I'd like whoever did so to give his reasons."

There was no reply. Grosvenor saw that Kent was frowning. It did seem strange that there was anyone aboard unwilling to acknowledge an opinion, however briefly held, however quickly discarded. Other men were glancing about in astonishment.

It was the sad-faced Smith who said finally, "When was that statement uttered? I don't recall hearing it."

"Nor I!" echoed half a dozen voices.

Kent's eyes were gleaming. It seemed to Grosvenor that he moved into the discussion like a man anticipating personal victory. He said, "Let me get this straight. There was such a statement, or there wasn't. Who else heard it? Raise hands."

Not a single hand went up. Kent's voice was subtly malicious as he said, "Mr. Grosvenor, what exactly did you hear?"

Grosvenor said slowly, "As I remember them, the words were: 'This is an opinion. The ship should go home.'" He paused. When there was no comment, he went on. "It seems clear that the words themselves came as the result of stimulation of the auditory centers of my brain. Something out there feels strongly that it wants us to go home, and I sensed it." He shrugged. "I do not, of course, offer this as a positive analysis."

Kent said stiffly, "The rest of us, Mr. Grosvenor, are still trying to understand why you should have heard this request, and no one else."

Once again Grosvenor ignored the tone in which the words were spoken, as he replied earnestly, "I've been considering that for the past few seconds. I can't help but remember that during the Riim incident my brain was subjected to sustained stimulation. It is possible that I am now more sensitive to such communication." It struck him that his special sensitivity could also explain why he had been able to receive the whisper in his shielded rooms.

Grosvenor was not surprised at Kent's slight frown. The chemist had shown that he preferred not to think about the bird people and what they had done to the minds of the members of the expedition. Now Kent said acidly, "I had the privilege of listening to a transcription of your account of the episode. If I recall correctly, you stated that the reason for your victory was that these Riim beings did not realize that it was difficult for a member of one race to control the nervous system of a member of an alien life form. How then do you explain that whatever is out there"—he waved in the direction the ship was heading—"reached into your mind and stimulated with pinpoint accuracy those areas in your brain that produced exactly the warning words you have just repeated to us?"

It seemed to Grosvenor that Kent's tone, his choice of words, and his attitude of satisfaction all seemed unpleasantly personal. Grosvenor said pointedly, "Director, whoever stimulated my brain could be aware of the problem presented by an alien nervous system. We don't have to assume that it can speak our language. Besides, its solution of the problem was a partial one, because I'm the only person who responded to the stimulation. My feeling is that we should not at the moment discuss how I received it, but why, and what are we going to do about it."

Chief geologist McCann cleared his throat and said, "Grosvenor is right. I think, gentlemen, we had better face the fact that we have entered somebody else's stamping ground. And it's *some* somebody!"

The Acting Director bit his lip, seemed about to speak, then hesitated. In the end, he said, "I think we should be careful about letting ourselves believe that we have evidence enough to draw a conclusion. But I do feel that we should act as if we are confronted by an intelligence larger than man—larger than life as we know it."

There was silence in the control room. Grosvenor noticed that men were unconsciously bracing themselves. Their lips tightened and their eyes narrowed. He saw that others also had observed the reaction.

Kellie, the sociologist, said softly, "I am glad—ah—to see that no one shows any sign of wanting to turn back. That is all to the good. As servants of our government and our race, it is our duty to investigate the potentialities of a new galaxy, particularly now that its dominating life form knows *we* exist. Please note that I am adopting Director Kent's suggestion and talking as if we actually are dealing with a sentient being. Its ability to stimulate more or less directly the mind of even one person aboard indicates that it has definitely observed us and therefore knows a great deal about us. We cannot permit that type of knowledge to be one-sided."

Kent was at ease again, as he said, "Mr. Kellie, what do you think of the environment we're heading into?"

The balding sociologist adjusted his pince-nez. "That—ah—is a large order, Director. But this whispering could be the equivalent of crisscrossing radio waves that blanket our own galaxy. They—ah—may be simply the outward signs, like coming out of a wilderness into an area of cultivation."

Kellie paused. When no one commented, he went on. "Remember, man also has left his imperishable imprint on his own galaxy. In the process of rejuvenating dead suns, he has lighted fires in the form of novae that will be seen a dozen galaxies away. Planets have been led from their orbits. Dead worlds have come alive with verdure. Oceans now swirl where deserts lay lifeless under suns hotter than Sol. And even our presence here in this great ship is an emanation of man's power, reaching out farther than these whispers around us have ever been able to go."

Gourlay, of the communications department, said, "Man's imprints are scarcely permanent in the cosmic sense. I don't see how you can speak of them in the same breath with this. These pulsations are alive. They're thought forms so strong, so all-pervading, that the whole of space whispers at us. This is no tentacled pussy, no scarlet monstrosity, no fellah race confined to one system. It could be an inconceivable totality of minds speaking to each other across the miles and the years of their space-time. This is the civilization of the second galaxy; and if a spokesman for it has now warned us—" Gourlay broke off with a gasp, and flung up an arm as if to defend himself.

He was not the only one who did just that. All over the room, men crouched or slumped in their seats—as Director Kent, in a single spasmodic movement, snatched his vibrator and fired it at his audience. It was not until Grosvenor had instinctively ducked that he saw that the tracer beam from the weapon pointed over his head, and not at it.

Behind him, there was a thunderous howl of agony, and then a crash that shook the floor.

Grosvenor whirled with the others, and stared with a sense of unreality at the thirty-foot armored beast that lay squirming on the floor a dozen feet behind the last row of seats. The next instant, a red-eyed replica of the first beast materialized in mid-air and landed with a thud ten feet away. A third devil-faced monster appeared, slid off the second, rolled over and over—and got up, roaring.

Seconds later, there were a dozen of the things.

Grosvenor drew his own vibrator and discharged it. The bestial roaring redoubled in intensity. Metal-hard scales scraped metal walls and metal floors. Steely claws rattled, and heavy feet stamped.

All around Grosvenor now, men were firing their vibrators. And still more beasts materialized. Grosvenor turned and scrambled over two rows of seats, then leaped to the lowest platform of the instrument board. The Acting Director ceased firing as Grosvenor climbed up to his level, and yelled angrily, "Where the hell do you think you're going, you yellow dog?"

His vibrator swung around—and Grosvenor knocked him down, mercilessly kicking the weapon out of his hand. He was furious, but he said nothing. As he leaped to the next platform, he saw Kent crawling after the vibrator. There was no doubt in Grosvenor's mind that the chemist would fire at him. It was with a gasp of relief that he reached the switch that activated the great multiple-energy screen of the ship, pulled it all the way over, and flung himself to the floor— just in time. The tracer beam of Kent's vibrator impinged on the metal of the control panel where Grosvenor's head had been. Then the beam snapped off. Kent climbed to his feet and shouted above the uproar, "I didn't realize what you were trying to do."

As an apology, it left Grosvenor cold. The Acting Director had evidently believed that he could justify his murderous action on the grounds that Grosvenor was running from the battle. Grosvenor brushed by the chemist, too angry to talk. For months he had tolerated Kent, but now he felt that the man's behavior proved him unfit to be director. In the critical weeks ahead, his personal tensions might act as a trigger mechanism that could destroy the ship.

As Grosvenor came down to the lowest platform, he again added the energy from his vibrator to that of the other men's. From the corner of one eye, he saw that three men were wrestling a heat projector into position. By the time the projector's intolerable flame poured forth, the beasts were unconscious from the molecular energy, and it was not difficult to kill them.

The danger past, Grosvenor had time to realize that these monstrous things had been transported alive across light-centuries. It was like a dream, too fantastic to have happened at all.

But the odor of burning flesh was real enough. And so was the bluish-gray beast blood that slimed the floor. The final evidence was the dozen or so armored and scaly carcasses that were sprawled about the room.

# 23

When Grosvenor saw Kent again a few minutes later, the Acting Director was coolly and efficiently giving orders into a communicator. Cranes floated in and began to remove bodies. Communicators buzzed with a crisscross of messages. Swiftly, the whole picture clarified.

The creatures had been precipitated only into the control room. The ship's radar registered no material object such as an enemy ship. The distance to the nearest star in any direction was a thousand light-years. All over the room, sweating men cursed as those scanty facts penetrated.

"Ten light-centuries!" Selenski, the chief pilot, said. "Why, we can't even transmit messages that far without relays."

Captain Leeth came hurrying in. He talked briefly to several scientists, then called a council of war. The commander began the discussion.

"I need hardly emphasize the hazard confronting us. We are one ship against what seems to be a hostile galactic civilization. For the moment we are safe behind our energy screen. The nature of the menace requires us to set ourselves limited, though not too limited, objectives. We must discover why we are being warned away. We must ascertain the nature of the danger and measure the intelligence behind it. I see our chief biologist is still examining our late adversaries. Mr. Smith, what kind of beasts are they?"

Smith turned from the monster he had been studying. He said slowly, "Earth could have produced something like their type during the dinosaur age. Judging by the minute size of what appears to be the brainpan, the intelligence must have been extremely low."

Kent said, "Mr. Gourlay tells me the beasts could have been precipitated through hyperspace. Perhaps we could ask him to develop on that."

Captain Leeth said, "Mr. Gourlay, you have the floor."

The communications expert said in his familiar drawl, "It's only a theory, and fairly recent at that, but it likens the universe to an expanded balloon. When you prick the skin, the balloon instantly starts to deflate, and simultaneously begins to repair the break. Now, oddly enough, when an object penetrates the outer skin of the balloon, it does not necessarily come back to the same point in space. Presumably, if one knew some method of controlling the phenomenon, he might use it as a form of teleportation. If all this sounds fanciful, remember that what has actually happened seems equally so."

Kent said acidly, "It's hard to believe that anyone is that much smarter than we are. There must be simple solutions to the problems of hyperspace, which human scientists have missed. Maybe we'll learn something." He paused, then said, "Korita, you've been singularly silent. How about telling us what we're up against?"

The archeologist stood up and spread his hands in a gesture of bewilderment. "I can't even offer a guess. We shall have to learn somewhat more about the motivation behind the attack before we can make comparisons on the basis of cyclic history. For example, if the purpose was to seize the ship, then to assail us as they did was a mistake. If the intent was merely to scare us, the attack was a howling success."

There was a flurry of laughter as Korita sat down. But Grosvenor noticed that the expression on Captain Leeth's face remained solemn and thoughtful.

"As to motivation," the captain said slowly, "one unpleasant possibility has occurred to me that we should be prepared to face. It fits the evidence to date. It is this: Supposing this potent intelligence, or whatever it is, would like to know where we came from?"

He paused, and from the way feet shifted and men stirred in their seats, it was clear that his words had struck a responsive chord. The officer went on. "Let's look at it from—his—point of view. Here is a ship approaching. In the general direction from which it is coming, within ten million light-years, are a considerable number of galaxies, star clusters, and nebulae. Which is us?"

There was silence in the room. The commander turned to Kent. "Director, if it's all right with you, I suggest we proceed to examine some of the planetary systems of this galaxy."

Kent said, "I have no objection. But now, unless someone else..."

Grosvenor raised his hand.

Kent continued, "I declare the meeting—"

Grosvenor stood up, and said loudly, "Mr. Kent!"

"—adjourned!" said Kent.

The men remained sitting. Kent hesitated, and then said lamely, "I beg your pardon, Mr. Grosvenor, you have the floor."

Grosvenor said firmly, "It is hard to believe that this being will be capable of refined interpretation of our symbols, but I think we should destroy our star maps."

"I was about to suggest the same thing," said von Grossen excitedly. "Continue, Grosvenor."

There was a chorus of approval. Grosvenor went on. "We are taking action in the belief that our main screen can protect us. Actually, we have no choice but to carry on as if that were true. But when we finally land, we might be advised to have available some large encephalo-adjusters. We could use them to create confusing brain waves, and so prevent any further mind reading."

Once more, the audience made enough noise to show that they favored the suggestion.

Kent said in a flat voice, "Anything else, Mr. Grosvenor?"

"A general comment only," said Grosvenor. "The department heads might make a survey of matériel they control with a view to destroying any that might endanger our race if the *Beagle* were captured."

He sat down amid a chilling silence.

※

As time went on, it seemed clear that the inimical intelligence was deliberately refraining from further action, or else that the screen was doing an effective job. No further incident occurred.

Lonely and remote were the suns at this distant rim of the galaxy. The first sun grew big out of space, a ball of light and heat that burned furiously into the great night. Lester and his staff located five planets close enough to the parent body to be worth investigating. One of the five—all were visited—was habitable, a world of mists and jungles and giant beasts. The ship left it after flying low over an inland sea and across a great continent of marsh growth. There was no evidence of civilization of any kind, much less the stupendous one whose existence they had reason to suspect.

The *Space Beagle* sped three hundred light-years, and came to a small sun with two planets crowding up close to its cherry-red warmth. One of the two planets was habitable, and it also was a world of mists and jungles and saurianlike beasts. They left it, unexplored, after darting down low over a marshy sea and a land choked with riotous growth.

There were more stars now. They pinpointed the blackness of the next hundred and fifty light-years. A large blue-white sun, with a retinue of at least twenty planets, attracted Kent's eye; and the swift ship flashed towards it. The seven planets nearest the sun were burning hells, without hope of supporting life. The ship spiraled past three close-together planets that were habitable, and then sped off to interstellar vastness without investigating the others.

Behind them, three steamy jungle planets whirled in their orbits around the hot sun that had spawned them. And, on board, Kent called a meeting of the heads of departments and their chief assistants.

He began the discussion without preamble. He said, "Personally, I don't think the evidence is very significant as yet. But Lester has urgently requested me to call you." He shrugged. "Perhaps we'll learn something."

He paused, and Grosvenor, watching him, was puzzled by a faint aura of satisfaction that radiated from the little man. He thought, What is he up to? It seemed odd that the Acting Director had taken the trouble to disclaim in advance all credit for any good results that might come from the meeting.

Kent was speaking again, and his tone was friendly. "Gunlie, will you come up here and explain yourself?"

The astronomer climbed to the lower platform. He was a man as tall and thin as Smith. He had eyes of royal blue set in an expressionless face. But there was a hint of emotion in his voice as he spoke.

"Gentlemen, the three habitable planets of that last system were identical triplets, and it was an artificially induced state. I don't know how many of you are familiar with the current theory regarding the formation of planetary systems. Those of you who are not will perhaps take my word for it that the distribution of mass in the system we have just visited is dynamically impossible. I can say definitely that two of the three habitable planets of that sun were moved into their present position. In my opinion, we should go back and investigate. Somebody seems to be deliberately creating primeval planets; for what reason I don't pretend to guess."

He stopped and glared belligerently at Kent. The chemist came forward, a faint smile on his face. He said, "Gunlie came to me and asked me to order that we return to one of those jungle planets. In view of his feeling on the matter, I now call for a discussion, and a vote."

So that was it. Grosvenor sighed, not exactly with admiration for Kent, but at least with appreciation. The Acting Director had made no attempt to build up a case for his opposition. It was quite possible that he did not really oppose the astronomer's plan. But by calling a meeting where his own views would be overruled, he was proving that he regarded himself as subject to democratic procedure. It was an adroit if somewhat demagogic means of maintaining the good will of his supporters.

Actually, there were valid objections to Lester's request. It was hard to believe that Kent knew of them, for that would mean he was deliberately ignoring possible danger for the ship. He decided to give Kent the benefit of the doubt, and waited patiently while several scientists asked the astronomer questions of minor importance. When those had been answered, when it seemed clear that the discussion was over except for himself, Grosvenor stood up and said, "I should like to argue in favor of Mr. Kent's viewpoint in this matter."

Kent replied coldly, "Really, Mr. Grosvenor, the attitude of the group seems to be indicated by the briefness of the discussion so far, and taking up any more time—"

At that point, he stopped. The real meaning of Grosvenor's words must finally have penetrated. A thunderstruck expression came into his face. He made an uncertain gesture toward the others, as if appealing for help. When no one spoke, he dropped his arm to his side and muttered, "Mr. Grosvenor, you have the floor."

Grosvenor said firmly, "Mr. Kent is right. It is too soon. So far we have visited three planetary systems. It should be not less than thirty, taken at random. This is the minimum number, with respect to the order of magnitude of our search, that could have any conclusive significance. I shall be glad to turn over my mathematics to the mathematics department for corroboration. Moreover, in landing we would have to come out from inside our protective energy screen. We would have to be prepared to resist a surprise attack by an intelligence that can use the instantaneous medium of hyperspace to deliver his forces. I have a mental picture of a billion tons of matter projected down upon us as we sit helpless on some planet. Gentlemen, as I see it, there is a good month or two of detailed preparation ahead of us. During that time, naturally, we should visit as many suns as we can. If their habitable planets also are exclusively—or even predominantly—the primeval type, then we shall have a sound basis for Mr. Lester's idea that it is an artificial state." Grosvenor paused, then finished. "Mr. Kent, have I expressed what you had in mind?"

Kent had full control of himself again. "Almost precisely, Mr. Grosvenor." He glanced about him. "Unless there are any further comments, I move that we vote on Gunlie's proposal."

The astronomer stood up. "I withdraw it," he said. "I confess I hadn't considered some of the points against an early landing." He sat down.

Kent hesitated, then said, "If someone cares to take up Gunlie's proposal…" When, after several seconds, no one had spoken, Kent continued confidently. "I want each department head to prepare for me a detailed account of what he can contribute to the success of the landing we must eventually make. That's all, gentlemen."

In the corridor outside the control room, Grosvenor felt a hand on his arm. He turned and recognized McCann, the chief geologist. McCann said, "We've been so busy doing repair work these last few months that I haven't had a chance to invite you to come to my department. I anticipate that when we finally make a landing, the equipment of the geology department will be used for purposes for which it was not precisely intended. A Nexialist could come in very handy."

Grosvenor considered that, then nodded his acceptance. "I'll be there tomorrow morning. I want to prepare my recommendations for the Acting Director."

McCann looked at him quickly, hesitated, and then said, "You don't think he'll be interested, do you?"

So others had noticed Kent's dislike of him. Grosvenor said slowly, "Yes, because he won't have to give individual credit."

McCann nodded. "Well, good luck to you, my boy."

He was turning away when Grosvenor stopped him. Grosvenor said, "What, in your opinion, is the basis for Kent's popularity as a leader?"

McCann hesitated, and seemed to be deliberating. Finally he said, "He's human. He has likes and dislikes. He gets excited about things. He has a bad temper. He makes mistakes, and tries to pretend that he didn't. He's desperately anxious to be director. When the ship gets back to Earth, the publicity will flow around the executive officer. There's something of Kent in all of us. He's—well—he's a human being."

"I notice," said Grosvenor, "you didn't say anything about his qualifications for the job."

"It's not a vital position, generally speaking. He can get advice from experts on anything he wants to know." McCann pursed his lips. "It's hard to put Kent's appeal into words, but I think that scientists are constantly on the defensive about their alleged unfeeling intellectualism. So they like to have someone fronting for them who is emotional but whose scientific qualifications cannot be questioned."

Grosvenor shook his head. "I disagree with you about the director's job not being vital. It all depends on the individual as to how he exercises the very considerable authority involved."

McCann studied him shrewdly. He said finally, "Strictly logical men like you have always had a hard time understanding the mass appeal of the Kents. They haven't much chance against his type, politically."

Grosvenor smiled grimly. "It's not their devotion to the scientific method that defeats the technologists. It's their integrity. The average trained man often understands the tactics that are used against him better than the person who uses them, but he cannot bring himself to retaliate in kind without feeling tarnished."

McCann frowned. "That's too pat. Do you mean you have no such qualms?"

Grosvenor was silent.

McCann persisted. "Suppose you decided that Kent ought to be ousted, what would you do?"

"At the moment my thoughts are quite constitutional," Grosvenor said carefully.

Grosvenor was surprised to see that there was relief in McCann's expression. The older man gripped his arm in a friendly gesture. "I'm glad to hear your intentions are legal," he said earnestly. "Ever since that lecture you gave, I've realized what hasn't yet dawned on anyone else that you are potentially the most dangerous man on this ship. The integrated knowledge you have in your mind, applied with determination and purpose, could be more disastrous than any outside attack."

After a moment of astonishment, Grosvenor shook his head. "That is an overstatement," he said. "One man is too easy to kill."

"I notice," said McCann, "you don't deny possessing the knowledge."

Grosvenor held out his hand in farewell. "Thanks for your high opinion of me. Although considerably exaggerated, it's psychologically uplifting."

The thirty-first star they visited was Sol-size, Sol-type. Of its three planets, one followed an orbit at eighty million miles. Like all the other habitable worlds they had seen, it was a steaming mass of jungle and primeval sea.

The *Space Beagle* settled through its gaseous envelope of air and water vapor, and began to fly along at a low level, a great alien ball of metal in a fantastic land.

In the geology laboratory, Grosvenor watched a bank of instruments that metered the nature of the terrain below. It was a complex job which demanded the closest attention, since much of the interpretation of the data called for the associative processes of a highly trained mind. The constant stream of reflections of the ultrasonic and short-wave signals being sent out had to be channeled into the proper computing devices at precisely the right time for comparative analysis. To the standard techniques with which McCann was familiar, Grosvenor had added certain refinements in accordance with Nexial principles, and an amazingly complete picture of the planet's outer crust was being tabulated.

For an hour Grosvenor sat there, deeply involved in his educated guesswork. The facts emerging varied widely in detail, but consideration of molecular structure, arrangement, and distribution of the different elements indicated a certain geologic sameness: mud, sandstone, clay, granite, organic debris—probably coal deposits—silicates in the form of sand overlying rock, water—

Several needles on the dials before him swung over sharply and held steady. Their reaction showed indirectly the presence of metallic iron in large quantities with traces of carbon, molybdenum—

Steel! Grosvenor snatched at a lever which precipitated a series of events. A bell started to ring. McCann came running. The ship stopped. A few feet from Grosvenor, McCann began to talk to Acting Director Kent.

"Yes, Director," he was saying, "steel, not just iron ore. We've got an observer who can detect differences like that." He did not mention Grosvenor by name, but went on, "We set our instruments at a hundred feet maximum. This could be a city buried—or hidden—in jungle mud."

Kent said matter-of-factly, "We'll know in a few days."

Cautiously, the ship was kept well above the surface, and the necessary equipment was lowered through a temporary gap in its energy screen. Giant shovels, cranes, mobile conveyors were set up, along with supplementary devices. So carefully had everything been rehearsed that thirty minutes after the ship started to disgorge material it was again heading out into space.

The entire excavating job was done by remote control. Trained men watched the scene in communicator plates and operated the machines on the ground. In four days, the highly integrated mass of implements had dug a hole two hundred and fifty feet deep by four hundred feet wide and eight hundred feet long. What was exposed then was not so much a city as the incredible rubble of what had been a city.

The buildings looked as if they had crumbled under the weight of a burden too great for them to carry. The street level was at the full two-hundred-and-fifty-foot depth, and there they began to turn up bones. Cease-digging orders were given, and several lifeboats made their way down through the muggy atmosphere. Grosvenor went along with McCann, and presently he was standing with several other scientists beside what was left of one of the skeletons.

"Rather badly crushed," said Smith. "But I think I can piece it together."

His trained fingers arranged bones into a rough design. "Four-legged," he said. He brought a fluoroscopic device to bear on one of the limbs. He said presently, "This one seems to have been dead about twenty-five years."

Grosvenor turned away. The shattered relics that lay around might hold the secret of the fundamental physical character of a vanished race. But it was unlikely that the skeletons held any clue to the identity of the unimaginably merciless beings who had murdered them. These were the pitiful victims, not the arrogant and deadly destroyers.

He made his way gingerly to where McCann was examining soil dug up from the street itself. The geologist said, "I think we'll be justified in taking a stratigraphical survey from here on down several hundred feet."

At his word, a drill crew sprang into action. During the next hour, as that machine tore its way through rock and clay, Grosvenor was kept busy. A steady trickle of soil samplings passed under his eyes. Occasionally, he put a bit of rock or earth through a chemical-breakdown process. By the time the lifeboats headed back to the parent ship, McCann was in a position to give a fairly accurate generalized report to Kent. Grosvenor stayed out of the receptive field of the communicator plate while McCann gave the report.

"Director, you will recall that I was particularly asked to check if this could be an artificial jungle planet. It seems to be. The strata below the mud appears to be that of an older, less primitive planet. It is hard to believe that a layer of jungle could have been skimmed from some distant planet and superimposed on this one, but the evidence points in that direction."

Kent said, "What about the city itself? How was it destroyed?"

"We have made a few of the calculations, and we can say cautiously that the enormous weight of rock and soil and water could have done all the damage we saw."

"Have you found any evidence to indicate how long ago this catastrophe took place?"

"We have a little geomorphological data. In several places we examined, the new surface has formed depressions in the old one, indicating that the extra weight is forcing down weaker areas below. By identifying the type of land fault that would sag under such circumstances, we have some figures that we intend to feed into a computing machine. A competent mathematician"—he meant Grosvenor—"has roughly estimated that the pressure of the weight was first applied not more than a hundred years ago. Since geology deals in events that require thousands and millions of years to mature, all the machine can do is to check the manual calculation. It cannot give us a closer estimate."

There was a pause, and then Kent said formally, "Thank you. I feel that you and your staff have done a good job. One more question: In your investigation, did you find anything that might be a clue to the nature of the intelligence that could bring about such a cataclysmic destruction?"

"Speaking only for myself, without having consulted with my assistants—no!"

It was, Grosvenor reflected, just as well that McCann had so carefully limited his denial. For the geologist, the investigation of this planet was the beginning of the search for the enemy. For himself, it had proved to be the final link in a chain of discovery and reasoning that had started when they first began to hear the strange murmurings in space.

He knew the identity of the most monstrous alien intelligence conceivable. He could guess its terrible purpose. He had carefully analyzed what must be done.

His problem was no longer: What is the danger? He had reached the stage where he needed, above all, to put over his solution without compromise. Unfortunately, men who had knowledge of only one or two sciences might not be able, or even willing, to comprehend the potentialities of the deadliest danger that had ever confronted all the life of the entire intergalactic universe. The solution itself might become the center of a violent controversy.

Accordingly, Grosvenor saw the problem as both political and scientific. He analyzed, with a sharp awareness of the possible nature of the forthcoming struggle, that his tactics must be carefully thought out and carried through with the utmost determination.

It was too soon to decide how far he would have to go. But it seemed to him that he dared not place any limitation upon his actions. He would do what was necessary.

When he was ready to act, Grosvenor wrote a letter to Kent:

## ACTING DIRECTOR
## ADMINISTRATIVE OFFICES
## EXPEDITIONARY SHIP Space Beagle

> DEAR MR. KENT:
> I HAVE AN IMPORTANT COMMUNICATION TO MAKE TO ALL HEADS OF
> DEPARTMENTS. THE COMMUNICATION RELATES TO THE ALIEN
> INTELLIGENCE OF THIS GALAXY, ABOUT THE NATURE OF WHICH I
> HAVE ACCUMULATED EVIDENCE ADEQUATE FOR ACTION ON THE
> LARGEST SCALE.
> WOULD YOU PLEASE CALL A SPECIAL MEETING, SO THAT I MAY
> PRESENT MY SUGGESTED SOLUTION?

He signed it, "Sincerely yours, Elliott Grosvenor," and wondered
if Kent would notice that he was offering a solution, but not
supportive evidence. While he waited for a reply, he quietly moved
the rest of his personal belongings from his cabin to the Nexial

department. It was the last act in a defense plan that included the possibility of a siege.

The answer arrived the following morning.

> DEAR MR. GROSVENOR:
>
> I HAVE COMMUNICATED TO MR. KENT THE GIST OF YOUR MEMO OF YESTERDAY AFTERNOON. HE SUGGESTS THAT YOU MAKE A REPORT ON THE ENCLOSED FORM, A-16-4, AND EXPRESSED SURPRISE THAT YOU HAD NOT DONE SO AS A MATTER OF COURSE.
>
> WE ARE IN RECEIPT OF OTHER EVIDENCE AND THEORY ON THIS MATTER. YOURS WILL BE GIVEN CAREFUL CONSIDERATION ALONG WITH THE REST.
>
> WILL YOU PLEASE SUBMIT THE FORM, PROPERLY FILLED OUT, AS SOON AS POSSIBLE.

YOURS TRULY,
JOHN FOHRAN
FOR MR. KENT

Grosvenor read the letter grimly. He did not doubt that Kent had made sharp remarks to the secretary about the only Nexialist on the ship. Even as it was, Kent had probably restrained his language. The turmoil, the reservoir of hatred that was in the man, was still suppressed. If Korita was right, it would come out in a crisis. This was the "winter" period of man's present civilization, and entire cultures had been torn to pieces by the vaulting egotism of individuals.

Although he had not intended to offer factual information, Grosvenor decided to fill in the form the secretary had sent him. However, he only listed the evidence. He did not interpret it, nor did he offer his solution. Under the heading, "Recommendations," he wrote, "The conclusion will be instantly obvious to any qualified person."

The titanic fact was that every item of evidence he had presented was known to one or another of the various science departments aboard the *Space Beagle*. The accumulated data had probably been on Kent's desk for weeks.

Grosvenor delivered the form in person. He didn't expect a prompt reply, but he remained in his department. He even had his meals sent up. Two twenty-hour periods went by, and then a note arrived from Kent.

DEAR MR. GROSVENOR:

IN GLANCING OVER FORM A-16-4, WHICH YOU HAVE SUBMITTED FOR CONSIDERATION OF THE COUNCIL, I NOTICE THAT YOU HAVE FAILED TO SPECIFY YOUR RECOMMENDATIONS. SINCE WE HAVE RECEIVED OTHER RECOMMENDATIONS ON THIS MATTER, AND INTEND TO COMBINE THE BEST FEATURES OF EACH INTO A COMPREHENSIVE PLAN, WE WOULD APPRECIATE RECEIVING FROM YOU A DETAILED RECOMMENDATION.

WILL YOU PLEASE GIVE THIS YOUR PROMPT ATTENTION?

It was signed, "Gregory Kent, Acting Director." Grosvenor took Kent's personal signature to the letter to mean that he had scored a direct hit, and that the main action was about to begin.

He doctored himself with drugs that would produce symptoms indistinguishable from influenza. While he waited for his body to react, he wrote another note to Kent, this time to the effect that he was too sick to prepare the recommendations—"which are necessarily long, since they would have to include a considerable body of interpretive reasoning based on the known facts of many sciences. Still, it might be wise to start immediately on the preliminary propaganda in order to accustom the members of the expedition to the notion of spending an extra five years in space."

As soon as he had slipped the letter into the mail chute, he called Dr. Eggert's office. His timing, as it turned out, was sharper than he had anticipated. In ten minutes Dr. Eggert came in and put down his bag.

As he straightened, footsteps sounded in the corridor. A moment later, Kent and two husky chemistry technicians entered.

Dr. Eggert glanced around casually, and nodded cheerfully as he recognized the chemist chief. "Hello, Greg," he said in his deep voice. Having acknowledged the other's presence, he gave his full attention to Grosvenor. "Well," he said finally, "looks like we've got a bug here, my friend. It's amazing. No matter how much protection we give on these landings, some virus or bacteria break through occasionally. I'll have you taken down to the isolation ward."

"I'd rather stay up here."

Dr. Eggert frowned, then shrugged. "In your case, it's feasible." He packed his instruments. "I'll have an attendant up right away to look after you. We don't take any chances with strange bugs."

There was a grunt from Kent. Grosvenor, who had glanced occasionally at the Acting Director with simulated puzzlement, looked up questioningly. Kent said in an annoyed tone, "What seems to be the trouble, Doctor?"

"Can't tell yet. We'll see what the lab tests bring out." He frowned. "I've taken samples from almost every part of him. So far, the symptoms are fever and some evidence of fluid in the lungs." He shook his head. "I'm afraid I can't let you talk to him now, Greg. This may be serious."

Kent said brusquely, "We'll have to take the risk. Mr. Grosvenor is in possession of valuable information and"—he spoke deliberately—"I feel sure he is still strong enough to give it."

Dr. Eggert looked at Grosvenor. "How do you feel?" he asked.

"I can still talk," Grosvenor said weakly. His face felt hot. His eyes ached. But one of the two reasons why he had made himself sick was the hope that it would impel Kent to come up, as he now had.

The other reason was that he didn't want to attend in person any meeting of scientists Kent might call. Here in this department and here alone he could defend himself from hasty actions the others might decide to take against him.

The doctor glanced at his watch. "Tell you what," he said to Kent and, more indirectly, to Grosvenor, "I'm sending up an attendant. The conversation has to be over by the time he gets here. All right?"

Kent said with false heartiness, "Fine!"

Grosvenor nodded.

From the door, Dr. Eggert said, "Mr. Fander will be up here in about twenty minutes."

When he had gone, Kent came slowly to the edge of the bed and looked down at Grosvenor. He stood like that for a long moment, and then said in a deceptively mild voice, "I don't understand what you're trying to do. Why are you not giving us the information you have?"

Grosvenor said, "Mr. Kent, are you really surprised?"

Once more there was silence. Grosvenor had the distinct impression of a very angry man restraining himself with difficulty. Finally, Kent said in a low, tense voice, "I am the Director of this expedition. I demand that you make your recommendations at once."

Grosvenor shook his head, slowly. He suddenly felt hot and heavy. He said, "I don't know just what to say to that. You're a pretty predictable man, Mr. Kent. You see, I expected you to handle my letters the way you did. I expected you to come up here with"—he glanced at the other two men—"a couple of hatchetmen. Under the circumstances, I think I'm justified in insisting on a meeting of the heads, so that I can personally present my recommendations."

If he had had time, he would have jerked up his arm then to defend himself. Too late, he saw that Kent was more furious than he had suspected.

"Pretty smart, eh!" the chemist said savagely. His hand came up. He struck Grosvenor in the face with his palm. He spoke again through clenched teeth. "So you're sick, are you? People sick with strange diseases sometimes go out of their heads, and they sometimes have to be severely handled because they insanely attack their dearest friends."

Grosvenor stared at him blurrily. He put his hand up to his face. And, because he was feverish and genuinely weak, he had trouble slipping the antidote into his mouth. He pretended to be holding his cheek where Kent had struck him. He swallowed the new drug, and then said shakily, "All right, I'm insane. Now what?"

If Kent was surprised by the reaction, his words did not show it. He asked curtly, "What do you really want?"

Grosvenor had to fight a moment of nausea. When that was past, he replied, "I want you to start propaganda to the effect that, in your judgment, what has been discovered about the enemy intelligence will require the members of this ship to adjust themselves to staying in space five years longer than was anticipated. That's all for now. When you've done that, I'll tell you what you want to know."

He was beginning to feel better. The antidote was working. The fever was down. And he meant exactly what he had said. His plan was not inflexible. At any stage, Kent or, later on, the group could accept his proposals, and that would end his series of stratagems.

Twice, now, Kent parted his lips as if he intended to speak. Each time, he closed them again. Finally, he said in a choked voice, "Is this all you're going to offer at this time?"

Grosvenor's fingers under the blanket were poised on a button at one side of the bed, ready to press it. He said, "I swear you'll get what you want."

Kent said sharply, "It's out of the question. I couldn't possibly commit myself to such madness. The men won't stand for even a one-year extension of the voyage."

Grosvenor said steadily, "Your presence here indicates that you don't think I have a mad solution."

Kent clenched and unclenched his hands. "It's impossible! How could I possibly explain my action to the department heads?"

Watching the little man, Grosvenor suspected that the crisis was imminent. "You don't have to tell them at this point. All you have to do is promise the information."

One of the technicians, who had been watching Kent's face, spoke up. "Look, chief, this man doesn't seem to realize he's speaking to the Director. How about us working him over?"

Kent, who had been on the point of saying something more, stopped himself. He stepped back, licking his lips. Then he nodded vigorously. "You're right, Bredder. I don't know how I came to start arguing with him. Just a minute while I lock the door. Then we'll—"

Grosvenor warned, "I wouldn't shut it if I were you. It'll set off alarms all over the ship."

Kent, one hand on the door, stopped and turned. There was a set smile on his face. "All right, then," he said stiffly, "we'll take you apart with the door open. Start talking, my friend."

The two technicians stepped forward quickly. Grosvenor said, "Bredder, have you ever heard of a peripheral electrostatic charge?" As the two men hesitated, he went on grimly. "Touch me and you'll burn. Your hands will blister. Your face—"

Both men were straightening, pulling away. The blond Bredder glanced uneasily at Kent. Kent said angrily, "The amount of electricity in a man's body couldn't kill a fly."

Grosvenor shook his head. "Aren't you a little out of your field, Mr. Kent? The electricity isn't in my body, but it will be in yours if you lay a hand on me."

Kent took out his vibrator and deliberately made an adjustment on it. "Stand back!" he said to his assistants. "I'm going to give him a timed spray of one-tenth of a second. It won't knock him unconscious, but it'll jar every molecule in his body."

Grosvenor said quietly, "I wouldn't try it, Kent. I'm warning you."

The man either did not hear him or was too angry to pay any attention. The tracer beam dazzled Grosvenor's eyes. There was a hiss and a crackle, and a cry of pain from Kent. The light blinked out. Grosvenor saw that Kent was trying to shake the weapon from his hand. It clung stickily, but finally dropped to the floor with a metallic clatter. In evident agony, Kent grabbed his injured hand and stood there swaying.

Grosvenor said with a kind of angry sympathy, "Why didn't you listen? Those wall plates are carrying a high electric potential. And since a vibrator ionizes the air, you got an electric shock that simultaneously nullified the energy you discharged, except near the muzzle. I hope it didn't burn you too badly."

Kent had control of himself. He was white and tense, but calm. "This will cost you dearly," he said in a low voice. "When the others find out that one man is trying to force his ideas—" He broke off and gestured imperiously to his two henchmen. "Come along, we're through here for the time being."

Fully eight minutes after they had gone, Fander came in. It was necessary for Grosvenor to explain patiently several times that he was no longer sick. And it required even longer to persuade Dr. Eggert, whom the young man summoned. Grosvenor did not worry about being found out. It would take a definite suspicion plus considerable research to identify the drug he had used.

In the end, they left him alone, with the advice that he remain in his quarters for a day or so. Grosvenor assured them that he would follow their instructions, and he meant it. In the hard days ahead, the Nexial department would be his fortress.

He didn't know just what might be done against him, but here he was as ready as he could be.

About an hour after the doctors had departed, there was a click in the mail-delivery chute. It was from Kent, an announcement of a meeting called, according to the wording, at the request of Elliott

Grosvenor. It quoted from Grosvenor's first letter to Kent, and ignored all subsequent events. The printed form ended: "In view of Mr. Grosvenor's past performances, the Acting Director feels that he is entitled to a hearing."

At the bottom of Grosvenor's notice, Kent had written in longhand: "Dear Mr. Grosvenor: In view of your illness, I have instructed Mr. Gourlay's staff to connect your communicator with the control-room auditorium, so that you may participate from your sickbed. The meeting will otherwise be private."

At the designated hour, Grosvenor tuned into the control room. As the image came on, he saw that the whole room was spread before him in sharp focus, and that the receiving plate must be the large communicator just above the massive control board. At this moment, his face was a ten-foot image looking down at the men. For once, he realized wryly, he was going to be present at a meeting in a con-spicuous way.

A quick glance over the room showed that most of the department heads were already seated. Directly below the receiving plate, Kent was talking to Captain Leeth. It must have been the end, not the beginning of a conversation, because he looked up at Grosvenor, smiled grimly, and then turned to face his small audience. Grosvenor saw that he wore a bandage on his left hand.

"Gentlemen," said Kent, "without further preamble, I am going to call on Mr. Grosvenor." Once more he looked up at the communicator plate, and the same savage smile was on his face. He said, "Mr. Grosvenor, you may proceed."

Grosvenor began, "Gentlemen, about a week ago, I had enough evidence to justify this ship's taking action against the alien intelligence of this galaxy. That may seem like a tremendous statement, and it is an unfortunate fact that I can merely give you my interpretation of the available evidence. I cannot prove to everybody present that such a being does actually exist. Some of you will realize that my reasoning is sound. Others, lacking knowledge of certain sciences, will feel that the conclusions are distinctly controversial. I have racked my brain over the problem of how to convince you that my solution is the only safe one. Telling you what experiments I made happens to be one of the steps which it seemed reasonable to take."

He made no mention of the fact that he had already had to evolve an elaborate ruse in order to obtain a hearing at all. In spite of what had happened, he had no desire to antagonize Kent any more than was necessary.

He continued, "I want now to call on Mr. Gourlay. I am sure you will not be too surprised when I tell you that all this goes back to automatic C-9. I wonder if you would tell your colleagues about it."

The communications chief looked at Kent, who shrugged and nodded. Gourlay hesitated, then said, "It's impossible to say just when C-9 came on. For the benefit of those who are feeling ignorant right now, C-9 is a minor screen that is activated automatically when the dust in the surrounding space reaches a density that could be dangerous to a ship on the move. The apparent density of the dust in any given volume of space is of course relatively greater at high velocities than at low. The fact that there was enough dust around to affect C-9 was first noticed by a member of my staff shortly before those lizards were precipitated into the control room."

Gourlay leaned back in his seat. "That's it," he said.

Grosvenor said, "Mr. von Grossen, what did your department find out about the space dust in this galaxy?"

The bulky von Grossen shifted in his chair. He said without getting up, "There's nothing about it that we could regard as being characteristic or unusual. It's a little denser than that in our own galaxy. We collected a small amount of the dust by means of ionizing plates with a very high potential, and scraped off the deposits. It was mostly solid, a few simple elements being present and traces of many compounds—which could have been formed at the moment of condensation—and a little free gas, mostly hydrogen. Now, the trouble is that what we got probably bears very little resemblance to the dust as it exists outside, but the problem of collecting it in its original form has never been satisfactorily solved. The very process used in capturing it causes it to change in many ways. We can never more than guess at how it functions in space." The physicist lifted his hands helplessly. "That's all I can say now."

Grosvenor continued. "I could go on asking various department heads what they found out. But I believe I can summarize their discoveries without doing anyone an injustice. Both Mr. Smith's and

Mr. Kent's departments ran into much the same problem as did Mr. von Grossen's. I believe that Mr. Smith by various means saturated the atmosphere of a cage with the dust. The animals he put into the cage showed no ill effects, so he finally tested it on himself. Mr. Smith, have you anything to add to that?"

Smith shook his head. "If it's a life form, you can't prove it by me. I admit that the closest we got to getting the real stuff was when we went out in a lifeboat, opened all the doors, then closed them, and let air into the boat again. There were slight changes in the chemical content of the air, but nothing important."

Grosvenor said, "So much for the factual data. I also, among other things, performed the experiment of taking out the lifeboat and letting the space dust drift in through open doors. What I was interested in was: If it's life, what does it feed on? So after I had pumped the air back into my lifeboat, I analyzed it. Then I killed a couple of small animals, and again analyzed the atmosphere. I sent samples of the atmosphere as it was before and after to Mr. Kent, Mr. von Grossen, and Mr. Smith. There were several very minute chemical changes. They could be attributed to analytical error. But I should like to ask Mr. von Grossen to tell you what he found."

Von Grossen blinked and sat up. "Was that evidence?" he asked in surprise. He turned in his seat, and faced his colleagues with a thoughtful frown. "I don't see the significance," he said, "but the molecules of air in the sample marked 'After' carried a slightly higher electric charge."

It was the decisive moment. Grosvenor gazed down at the upturned faces of the scientists and waited for the light of understanding to come to at least one pair of eyes.

The men sat stolid, puzzled expressions on their faces. One individual said finally, in a wry voice, "I suppose we're expected to jump to the conclusion that we are dealing with a nebular-dust intelligence. That's too much for me to swallow."

Grosvenor said nothing. The mental jump he wanted them to make was even more farfetched than that, though the difference was subtle. Already, the feeling of disappointment was strong in him. He began to stiffen himself for the next step.

Kent said sharply, "Come, come, Mr. Grosvenor. Explain yourself, and then we will make up our minds."

Grosvenor began reluctantly. "Gentlemen, your failure to see the answer at this point is very disturbing to me. I foresee that we are going to have trouble. Consider my position. I have given you the available evidence, including a description of the experiments which led me to identify our enemy. It is already clear that my conclusions will be regarded as distinctly controversial. And yet, if I am right—and I'm convinced of it—failure to take the action I have in mind will be disastrous for the human race and for all other intelligent life in the universe. But here is the situation: If I tell you, then the decision is out of my hands. The majority will decide, and there will be no legal recourse from their decision, so far as I can see."

He paused to let that sink in. Some of the men glanced at each other, frowning. Kent said, "Wait. I have already come up against the stone wall of this man's egotism."

It was his first hostile comment of the meeting. Grosvenor glanced at him quickly, then turned away, and went on. "It is my unhappy lot to inform you, gentlemen, that under the circumstances, this problem ceases to be scientific and becomes political. Accordingly, I have to insist that my solution be accepted. A satisfactory propaganda must be launched, in which Acting Director Kent and every head of a department commits himself to the notion that the *Space Beagle* will have to remain in space the equivalent of five Earth years extra, though we should act as if it were five star years. I am going to give you my interpretation, but I want each head to adjust himself to the notion that he must irrevocably stake his reputation and good name on this matter. The danger, as I see it, is so all-embracing that any petty squabbling we do will be disgraceful according to the time we spend on it."

Succinctly, he told them what the danger was. Then, without waiting for their reaction, he outlined his method of dealing with it.

"We'll have to find some iron planets and set the productive capacity of our ship to the making of atomically unstable torpedoes. I foresee that we will have to spend nearly a year traversing this galaxy and sending out such torpedoes in great numbers at random. And then, when we have made this entire sector of space virtually untenable for him, we depart and offer him the opportunity of following us, this last at a time when he will have literally no recourse but to pursue our ship in the hope that we will lead him to another and better source of food than is available here. Most of our time will be taken up in making sure that we do not guide him back to our own galaxy."

He paused, then said quietly, "Well, gentlemen, there you have it. I can see on various faces that the reaction is going to be a split one and that we are in for one of those deadly controversies."

He stopped. There was silence, and then a man said, "Five years."

It was almost a sigh, and it acted like a cue. All over the room, men stirred uneasily.

Grosvenor said quickly, "Earth years."

He had to keep pressing that. He had deliberately chosen what seemed the longer way of estimating time, so that, when translated into star years, it would seem somewhat less. The fact was that Star Time, with its hundred-minute hour, its twenty-hour day, and its three-hundred-and-sixty-day year, was a psychological device. Once adjusted to the longer day, people tended to forget how much time was passing according to their older ways of thinking.

In the same way, now, he expected them to feel relieved when they realized that the extra time would amount to just about three years, Star Time.

Kent was speaking. "Any other comments?"

Von Grossen said unhappily, "I cannot honestly accept Mr. Grosvenor's analysis. I have great respect for him in view of his past performances. But he is asking us to take on faith what I am sure we could understand if he actually had valid evidence. I reject the notion that Nexialism provides so sharp an integration of sciences that only individuals trained by its methods can hope to understand the more intricate interrelated phenomena."

Grosvenor said curtly, "Aren't you rejecting rather hastily something which you have never troubled to investigate?"

Von Grossen shrugged. "Perhaps."

"The picture I have," said Zeller, "is of us spending many years and much effort, and yet not once will we have anything but the most indirect and insubstantial evidence that the plan is working."

Grosvenor hesitated. Then he realized that he had no alternative but to continue to make antagonistic statements. The issue was too important. He could not consider their feelings. He said, "*I'll* know when we've been successful, and if some of you people will deign to come to the Nexial department and learn a few of our techniques, you'll know it also when the time comes."

Smith said grimly, "Mr. Grosvenor has this in his favor. He is always offering to teach us how to be his equal."

"Any more comments?" It was Kent, his voice shriller, and edged with triumph.

Several men made as if to speak, but seemingly thought better of it. Kent went on, "Rather than waste any time, I think we should take a vote as to what the majority feels about Mr. Grosvenor's proposal. I'm sure we all want to have a general reaction."

He walked forward slowly. Grosvenor could not see his face, but there was arrogance in the way the man held himself. Kent said, "Let's have a showing of hands. All in favor of accepting Mr. Grosvenor's method—which involves remaining five extra years in space—please raise your hands."

Not a single hand came up.

A man said querulously, "It'll take a little while to think this through."

Kent paused to answer that. "We're trying to get the as-of-now opinion. It's important to all of us to know what the chief scientists of this ship think."

He broke off, and called out, "Those definitely against, raise your hands!"

All except three hands came up. In a lightning glance, Grosvenor identified the three who had abstained. They were Korita, McCann, and von Grossen.

Belatedly, he saw that Captain Leeth, who stood near Kent, had also abstained.

Grosvenor said quickly, "Captain Leeth, this is surely a moment when your constitutional right to take control of the ship would apply. The danger is obvious."

"Mr. Grosvenor," said Captain Leeth slowly, "that would be true if there were a visible enemy. As it is, I can act only on the advice of the scientific experts."

"There is only one such expert aboard," said Grosvenor coldly. "The others are a handful of amateurs who dabble around on the surface of things."

The remark seemed to stun most of those in the room. Abruptly, several men tried to speak at once. They spluttered into angry silence.

It was Captain Leeth who said, finally, in a measured tone, "Mr. Grosvenor, I cannot accept your unsupported claim."

Kent said satirically, "Well, gentlemen, we now have Mr. Grosvenor's true opinion of us."

He seemed unconcerned with the insult itself. His manner was one of ironic good humor. He seemed to have forgotten that he had a duty as Acting Director to maintain an atmosphere of dignity and courtesy.

Meader, head of the botany subsection, reminded him angrily. "Mr. Kent, I do not see how you can tolerate such an insolent remark."

"That's right," said Grosvenor, "stand up for your rights. The whole universe is in deadly danger, but your sense of dignity must be maintained."

McCann spoke for the first time, uneasily. "Korita, if there were a kind of entity out there such as Grosvenor has described, how would that fit in with cyclic history?"

The archeologist shook his head unhappily. "Very tenuously, I'm afraid. We could postulate a primitive life form." He looked around the room. "I am far more concerned with the evidences of the reality of cyclic history among my friends. Pleasure in the defeat of a man who has made us all feel a little uneasy because of his achievements. The suddenly revealed egomania of that man." He gazed regretfully up at Grosvenor's image. "Mr. Grosvenor, I am very disappointed that you have seen fit to make the statements that you have."

"Mr. Korita," said Grosvenor soberly, "if I had adopted any other course than the one I have actually pursued, you would not even have had the privilege of hearing me tell these honorable gentlemen— many of whom I admire as individuals—what I have told them, and what I have still to say."

"I feel confident," said Korita, "that the members of this expedition will do what is necessary, regardless of personal sacrifice."

"It's hard to believe that," said Grosvenor. "I feel that many of them were influenced by the fact that my plan would require five extra years in space. I confess it's a cruel necessity, but I assure you there is no alternative."

He broke off, curtly. "Actually, I expected this outcome, and prepared for it." He addressed himself to the group as a whole. "Gentlemen, you have compelled me to take an action which, I assure you, I regret more than I can ever say. Here is my ultimatum."

"Ultimatum!" That was Kent, surprised, suddenly pale.

Grosvenor ignored him. "If by 1000 hours tomorrow my plan has not been accepted, I shall take over the ship. Everybody aboard will find himself doing what I order whether he likes it or not. Naturally, I expect that the scientists aboard will pool their knowledge in an attempt to prevent my carrying out such a stated purpose. Resistance, however, will be useless."

The uproar that began then was still going on when Grosvenor broke the connection between his communicator and the control room.

# 26

It was about an hour after the meeting when Grosvenor received a call on his communicator from McCann.

"I'd like to come up," said the geologist.

Grosvenor was cheerful. "Come along."

McCann looked doubtful. "I'm assuming you have the corridor booby-trapped."

"We-e-l-ll, yes, I suppose you could call it that," Grosvenor agreed, "but you'll not be troubled."

"Suppose I came with the secret intention of assassinating you?"

"Here in my rooms," said Grosvenor with a positiveness which he hoped would impress any listeners-in, "you couldn't even kill me with a club."

McCann hesitated, then said, "I'll be right up!" He broke the connection.

He must have been very near, for it was less than a minute later that the hidden corridor detectors began to report his approach. Presently, his head and shoulders flashed across a communicator plate, and a relay switch closed into position. Since it was part of an automatic defense process, Grosvenor deactivated it manually.

A few seconds later, McCann came through the open door. He paused on the threshold, and then came forward shaking his head.

"I was worried there. Despite your reassurance, I had the feeling that batteries of weapons were pointing at me. And yet I saw nothing." He looked searchingly into Grosvenor's face. "Are you pulling a bluff?"

Grosvenor said slowly, "I'm a little worried myself. Don, you've shaken my faith in your integrity. I honestly didn't expect you to come up here carrying a bomb."

McCann looked blank. "But I'm not. If your instruments show any such—" He stopped. He took off his coat. He began to search himself. Suddenly, his movements slowed. His face was pale as he brought up a wafer-thin gray object about two inches long. "What is it?" he asked.

"A stabilized plutonium alloy."

"*Atomic!*"

"No, it's not radioactive, not as it is. But it can be dissolved into a radioactive gas by the beam from a high-frequency transmitter. The gas would give us both radiation burns."

"Grove, I swear to you that I knew nothing of this."

"Did you tell anyone you were coming?"

"Naturally. This whole part of the ship is blocked off."

"In other words, you had to get permission?"

"Yes. From Kent."

Grosvenor hesitated, then said, "I want you to think hard about this. At any time during the interview with Kent did you feel that the room was hot?"

"W-why, yes. I remember now. I had the feeling that I was going to suffocate."

"How long did that last?"

"A second or so."

"Hmmm, that means you were out probably ten minutes."

"Out?" McCann was scowling. "Well, I'll be damned. That little wretch drugged me."

"I could probably find out for sure just how much of a dose you were given." Grosvenor spoke deliberately. "A blood test would do it."

"I wish you'd make it. That would prove—"

Grosvenor shook his head. "It would only prove that you actually underwent such an experience. It wouldn't prove that you didn't do so willingly. Far more convincing to me is the fact that no man in his right senses would permit plutonium alloy Pua-72 to be dissolved in his presence. According to my automatic nullifiers, they've been trying to dissolve it now for at least a minute."

McCann was white. "Grove, I'm through with that vulture. I admit I was in a state of conflict, and I agreed to report to him the result of my conversation with you—but I intended to warn you that I was bound to make such a report."

Grosvenor smiled. "It's all right, Don. I believe you. Sit down."

"What about this?" McCann held out the small metal "bomb."

Grosvenor took it and carried it to the little vault he had for his radioactive material. He came back and seated himself. He said, "I imagine there'll be an attack. The only way Kent could justify to the others what he's done is to make sure that we are rescued in time for us to be given medical treatment for radioactive burns."

He finished, "We can watch it in that plate."

The attack registered first on several electronic detectors of the electric-eye type. Faint lights flashed on a wall instrument board, and a buzzer sounded.

They saw the attackers presently as images on the large plate above the instruments. About a dozen men in space suits rounded a distant corner and approached along the corridor. Grosvenor recognized von Grossen and two of his assistants from the physics department, four chemists, of whom two were from the biochemistry division, three of Gourlay's communications experts, and two weapon officers. Three soldiers brought up the rear, riding, respectively, a mobile vibrator, a mobile heat gun, and a large gas-bomb dispenser.

McCann stirred uneasily. "Isn't there another entrance to this place?"

Grosvenor nodded. "It's guarded."

"What about down and up?" McCann indicated the floor and the ceiling.

"There's a storeroom above, and a motion-picture theater below. Both are taken care of."

They fell silent. Then, as the group of men in the corridor stopped, McCann said, "I'm surprised to see von Grossen out there. I think he admires you."

Grosvenor said, "I stung him when I called him and the others amateurs. He's come to see for himself what I can do."

Out in the corridor, the group of attackers seemed to be consulting. Grosvenor went on. "What, specifically, brought you up here?"

McCann's gaze was on the plate. "I wanted you to know you were not completely alone. Several executives asked me to tell you they were with you." He broke off distractedly. "Let's not talk now, not while that's going on."

"Now is as good a time as any."

McCann seemed not to hear. "I don't see how you're going to stop them," he said uneasily. "They've got enough power out there to burn down your walls."

Grosvenor made no comment, and McCann faced him. "I've got to be frank with you," he said. "I'm in a state of conflict. I feel sure you're right. But your tactics are too unethical for me." He appeared unaware that he had turned his attention from the viewing plate.

Grosvenor said, "There's only one other possible tactic, and that is to run for election against Kent. Since he's only Acting Director, and was not himself elected, I could probably force an election within about a month."

"Why don't you?"

"Because," said Grosvenor with a shudder, "I'm afraid. The thing—out there—is practically starving to death. At any time it's liable to make a try for another galaxy, and it might very well go for ours. We can't wait a month."

"And yet," McCann pointed out, "your plan is to drive it from this galaxy, and you've estimated that will take a whole year."

"Have you ever tried to snatch food from a carnivore?" Grosvenor asked. "It tries to hold on to it, doesn't it? It will even fight for it. My idea is that when this being realizes we're trying to drive him off, he'll hang on as long as he can to what he's got."

"I see." McCann nodded. "Besides, you'll have to admit your chance of winning an election on your platform is pretty close to zero."

Grosvenor shook his head vigorously. "I'd win. You may not believe that on my say-so. But the fact is that people who are wrapped up in pleasure, excitement, or ambition are easily controlled. I didn't devise the tactics I'd use. They've been around for centuries. But historical attempts to analyze them just didn't get at the roots of the process. Until recently the relation of physiology to psychology was on a fairly theoretical basis. Nexial training reduced it to definite techniques."

McCann was silent, studying him. He said finally, "What kind of future do you envisage for man? Do you expect us all to become Nexialists?"

"On board this ship it's a necessity. For the race as a whole, it's still impractical. In the long run, however, there can be no excuse for any individual not knowing what it is possible for him to know. Why shouldn't he? Why should he stand under the sky of his planet and look up at it with the stupid eyes of superstition and ignorance, deciding vital issues on the basis of somebody's fooling him? The smashed civilizations of Earth's antiquity are evidence of what happens to a man's descendants when he reacts blindly to situations, or if he depends on authoritarian doctrines."

He shrugged. "At the moment a lesser goal is possible. We must make men skeptical. The shrewd though illiterate peasant who has to be shown concrete evidence is the spiritual forebear of the scientist. On every level of understanding, the skeptic partly makes up for his lack of specific knowledge by his attitude of 'Show me! I've got an open mind, but what you say cannot by itself convince me.'

McCann was thoughtful. "You Nexialists are going to break through the cyclic-history pattern, is that what you have in mind?"

Grosvenor hesitated, then said, "I confess I was not too conscious of its importance till I met Korita. I've been impressed. I imagine the theory can stand a great deal of revision. Such words as 'race' and 'blood' are particularly meaningless, but the general pattern seems to fit the facts."

McCann had returned his attention to the attackers. He said, puzzled, "They seem to be taking a long time getting started. You'd think they'd have made their plans before they came this far."

Grosvenor said nothing. McCann glanced at him sharply. "Just a moment," he said. "They haven't run up against your defenses, have they?"

When Grosvenor still made no reply, McCann jumped to his feet, walked nearer to the plate, and peered into it at close range. He stared intently at two men who were down on their knees.

"But what are they doing?" he asked helplessly. "What is stopping them?"

Grosvenor hesitated, then explained, "They're trying to keep from falling through the floor." Despite his effort to remain calm, excitement put a tremor into his voice.

The others didn't realize that what he was doing was new to him. He had had the knowledge, of course, for a long time. But this was practical application. He was taking action that had never been taken before, anywhere, in quite the same way. He had used phenomena from many sciences, improvising to fit his purpose and to suit the exact environment in which he was operating.

It was working—as he had expected it would. His understanding, so sharp, so broadly based, left little room for error.

But the physical reality exhilarated him in spite of his preknowledge.

McCann came back and sat down. "Will the floor actually collapse?"

Grosvenor shook his head. "You're not getting it. The floor is unchanged. They are sinking into it. If they proceed much farther, they'll fall through." He laughed in sudden glee. "I'd just like to have a good look at Gourlay's face when his assistants report the phenomenon. This is his 'balloon,' teleportation, hyperspace notion, with an idea added from oil geology and two techniques of plant chemistry."

"What's the geology notion?" McCann began. He stopped. "Well, I'll be damned. You mean the way we get oil these days without drilling. We just create a condition on the surface to which all oil in the vicinity has to come." He frowned. "But, just a minute. There's a factor that—"

"There are a dozen factors, my friend," said Grosvenor. He went on soberly, "I repeat, this is laboratory stuff. A lot of things work at close quarters on very little power."

McCann said, "Why didn't you use a little of this trickery against pussy and the scarlet monster?"

"I've told you. I've rigged this situation. I worked through many a sleep hour installing my equipment, something which I never had a chance to do against our alien enemies. Believe me, if I had had control of the ship, we wouldn't have lost so many lives in either of those incidents."

"Why didn't you take control?"

"It was too late. There wasn't time. Besides, this ship was built several years before there was a Nexial Foundation. We were lucky to get a department aboard."

McCann said presently, "I don't see how you're going to take over the ship tomorrow, since that'll involve coming out of your laboratory." He stopped and stared at the plate. Then he said breathlessly, "They've brought up de-gravity rafts. They're going to float over your floor."

Grosvenor made no reply. He had already seen.

# 27

De-gravity rafts operated on the same principle as the anti-acceleration drive. The reaction that occurred in an object when inertia was overcome had been found on examination to be a molecular process, but it was not inherent in the structure of matter. An anti-acceleration field shifted electrons in their orbits slightly. This, in turn, created a molecular tension, resulting in a small though all-embracing rearrangement.

Matter so altered acted as if it were immune to the normal effects of speeding up or slowing down. A ship proceeding on anti-acceleration could stop short in mid-flight, even if it had been traveling at millions of miles a second.

The group attacking Grosvenor's department merely loaded their weapons onto the long, narrow rafts, climbed aboard themselves, and activated them to a suitable field intensity. Then, using magnetic attraction, they drew themselves forward toward the open door two hundred feet away.

They proceeded about fifty feet, then slowed, came to a full stop, and began to back. Then they stopped again.

Grosvenor, who had been busy at his instrument board, came back and sat down beside the puzzled McCann.

The geologist asked, "What did you do?"

Grosvenor answered without hesitation. "As you saw, they propelled themselves forward by pointing directional magnets at the steel walls ahead. I set up a repeller field, which is nothing new in itself. But actually this version of it is part of a temperature process more related to the way you and I maintain our body heat than it is to heat physics. Now they'll have to use jet propulsion, or ordinary screw propellers, or even"—he laughed—"oars."

McCann, his gaze on the viewing plate, said grimly, "They're not going to bother. They're going to turn their heater loose. Better shut the door!"

"Wait!"

McCann swallowed visibly. "But the heat will come in here. We'll roast."

Grosvenor shook his head. "I've told you; what I did was part of a process involving temperature. Fed new energy, the whole metal environment will seek to maintain its equilibrium on a somewhat lower level. There—look."

The mobile heat blaster was turning white. It was a white that made McCann curse softly under his breath. "Frost," he mumbled. "But how…"

As they watched, ice formed on the walls and the floors. The heater gleamed in its frozen casing, and a chill blast of air came through the door. McCann shivered.

"Temperature," he said vaguely. "A somewhat lower equilibrium."

Grosvenor stood up. "I think it's time they went home. After all, I don't want anything to happen to them."

He walked to an instrument that stood against one wall of the auditorium room, and sank into a chair in front of a compact keyboard. The keys were small and different colors. There were twenty-five to a row, and twenty-five rows.

McCann came over and stared down at the instrument. "What is it?" he asked. "I don't recall seeing it before."

With a quick, rippling, almost casual movement, Grosvenor depressed seven of the keys, then reached over and touched a main release switch. There was a clear, yet soft, musical note. Its overtones seemed to stay in the air for several seconds after the basic note had died away.

Grosvenor looked up. "What association did that bring to your mind?"

McCann hesitated. There was an odd expression on his face. "I had a picture of an organ playing in a church. Then that changed, and I was at a political rally where the candidate had provided fast, stimulating music to make everybody happy." He broke off, and said breathlessly, "So this is how you could win an election."

"One of the methods."

McCann was tense. "Man, what terrific power you have."

Grosvenor said, "It doesn't affect me."

"But you're conditioned. You can't expect to condition the whole human race."

"A baby is conditioned when it learns to walk, move its arms, speak. Why not extend the conditioning to hypnotism, chemical responses, the effects of food? It was possible hundreds of years ago. It would prevent a lot of disease, heartache, and the kind of catastrophe that derives from misunderstanding of one's own body and mind."

McCann was turning back to the mounted, spindle-shaped instrument. "How does it work?"

"It's an arrangement of crystals with electrical circuits. You know how electricity can distort certain crystalline structures. By setting up a pattern, an ultrasonic vibration is emitted which bypasses the ear and directly stimulates the brain. I can play on that the way a musician plays on his instrument, creating emotional moods that strike too deep for any untrained person to resist."

McCann returned to his chair and sat down. He looked suddenly pale. "You frighten me," he said in a low voice. "I regard that as unethical. I can't help it."

Grosvenor studied him; then, turning, he bent down and made an adjustment on the instrument. He pressed the button. The sound was sadder, sweeter, this time. It had a cloying quality, as if endless vibrations continued to throb in the air around them, though the sound itself was gone. Grosvenor said, "What did you get that time?"

McCann hesitated again, then said uneasily, "I thought of my mother. I had a sudden desire to be back home. I wanted—"

Grosvenor frowned. "That's too dangerous," he said. "If I intensified that enough, some of the men might curl up again in the womb position." He paused. "How about this?"

Rapidly, he set up a new pattern, and then touched the activating switch. He drew a bell-like sound, with a soft, soft tinkling in the distant background.

"I was a baby," said McCann, "and it was bedtime. Gosh, I'm sleepy." He seemed not to notice that he had reverted to the present tense. Involuntarily, he yawned.

Grosvenor opened a drawer in a table beside the machine, and took out two plastic headpieces. He handed one to McCann. "Better put that on."

He slipped the other over his own head, while his companion, with evident reluctance, did the same. McCann said gloomily, "I guess I'm just not made to be Machiavellian. I suppose you'll try to tell me that meaningless sounds have been used before to evoke emotions and influence people."

Grosvenor, who had been setting a dial pointer, paused to answer. He said earnestly, "People think a thing ethical or unethical depending on the associations that come to their minds at the moment, or while they're considering the problem in retrospect. That doesn't mean that no system of ethics has any validity. I personally subscribe to the principle that our ethical measuring rod should be that which benefits the greatest number, provided that it doesn't include extermination or torture of, or denial of rights to, individuals who do not conform. Society has to learn to salvage the man who is ill or ignorant."

He was intent now. "Please note that I have never used this device before. I have never used hypnosis except when Kent invaded my department—though of course I intend to do so now. From the moment the trip began, I could have lured people up here by stimulating them in a dozen unsuspected ways. Why didn't I? Because the Nexial Foundation laid down a code of ethics for itself and its graduates, which is conditioned right into my system. I can break through that conditioning, but only with the greatest difficulty."

"Are you breaking through it now?"

"No."

"It seems to me, then, that it's pretty elastic."

"That's exactly right. When I firmly believe, as I do now, that my actions are justified, there is no internal nervous or emotional problem."

McCann was silent. Grosvenor went on. "I think you've got a picture in your mind of a dictator—myself—taking over a democracy by force. That picture is false, because a ship on a cruise can be run only by quasi-democratic methods. And the greatest difference of all is that at the end of the voyage I can be brought to account."

McCann sighed. "I suppose you're right," he said. He glanced at the plate. Grosvenor followed his gaze, and saw that the space-suited men were trying to propel themselves forward by pushing against the wall. Their hands tended to go right into the walls, but there was some resistance. They were making slow progress. McCann was speaking again. "What are you going to do now?"

"I intend to put them to sleep—like this." He touched the activating switch.

The bell sound seemed no louder than before. Yet in the corridor the men slumped over.

Grosvenor stood up. "That will repeat every ten minutes, and I've got resonators spread all through the ship to pick up the vibrations and echo them. Come along."

"Where are we going?"

"I want to install a circuit breaker in the main electric-switch system of the ship."

He secured the breaker from the film room, and a moment later was leading the way into the corridor.

Everywhere they went, men lay sleeping. At first, McCann marveled out loud. Then he grew silent and looked troubled. He said finally, "It's hard to believe that human beings are basically so helpless."

Grosvenor shook his head. "It's worse than you think."

They were in the engine room now, and he crawled onto a lower tier of the electric switchboard. It required less than ten minutes to fit in his circuit breaker. He came down silently, nor did he subsequently explain what he had done or what he intended to do.

"Don't mention that," he said to McCann. "If they find out about it, I'll just have to come down and put in another one."

"You're going to wake them now?"

"Yes. As soon as I get back to my rooms. But first I'd like you to help me cart von Grossen and the others to their bedrooms. I want to make him disgusted with himself."

"You think they'll give in?"

"No."


His estimate was right. And so, at 1000 hours the following day, he pressed home a switch that rechanneled the main electric current through the circuit breaker he had installed.

All over the ship, the constantly burning lights flickered ever so slightly in a Nexial version of the Riim hypnotic pattern. Instantly, without knowing it, every man aboard was deeply hypnotized.

Grosvenor began to play on his emotion-educing machine. He concentrated on thoughts of courage and sacrifice, duty to the race in the face of danger. He even evolved a complex emotional pattern that would stimulate the feeling that time was passing at double, even treble, what had been normal before.

The basis laid, he activated the "General Call" of the ship's communicator, and gave exact commands. The main instructions stated, he then told the men that each and every one would thereafter respond instantly to a cue word without ever knowing what that cue word was, or remembering it after it was given.

Then he gave them amnesia for the entire hypnotic experience.

He went down to the engine room and removed the circuit breaker.

He returned to his own room, wakened everyone, and called Kent. He said, "I withdraw my ultimatum. I'm ready to give myself up. I've suddenly realized that I cannot bring myself to go against the wishes of the other members of the ship. I would like another meeting, at which I will appear in person. Naturally, I intend to urge once more that we wage all-out warfare against the alien intelligence of this galaxy."

He was not surprised when the ship's executives, strangely unanimous in their change of heart, agreed that after consideration they could see that the evidence was clear, and that the danger was compellingly urgent.

Acting Director Kent was instructed to pursue the enemy relentlessly, and without regard for the comfort of the members of the ship.

Grosvenor, who had not interfered with the overall personality of any individual, observed with grim amusement the reluctance with which Kent himself acknowledged that the action should be taken.

The great battle between man and alien was about to begin.

# 28

The Anabis existed in an immense, suffused, formless state, spread through all the space of the second galaxy. It writhed a little, feebly, in a billion portions of its body, shrinking with automatic adjustment away from the destroying heat and radiation of two hundred billion blazing suns. But it pressed tightly down against the myriad planets, and strained with a feverish, insatiable hunger around the quadrillion tingling points where were dying the creatures that gave it life.

It was not enough. The dread knowledge of an imminent starvation seeped to the farthest reaches of its body. Through all the countless, tenuous cells of its structure came messages from near and far, proclaiming that there was not enough food. For long now, all the cells had had to do with less.

Slowly, the Anabis had come to realize that it was either too big—or too small. It had made a fatal mistake in growing with such abandon during its early days. In those years, the future had seemed limitless. The galactic space, where its form could wax ever huger, had appeared of endless extent. It had expanded with all the vaunting, joyous excitement of a lowborn organism grown conscious of stupendous destiny.

It *was* lowborn. In the dim beginning it had been only gas oozing from a mist-covered swamp. It was an odorless, tasteless, colorless gas, yet somehow, someway, a dynamic combination was struck. And there was life.

At first it was nothing but a puff of invisible mist. Ardently, it darted over the muggy, muddy waters that had spawned it, twisting, diving, pursuing incessantly and with a gathering alertness, a gathering need, striving to be present while something—anything—was being killed.

For the death of others was its life.

Not for it was the knowledge that the process by which it survived was one of the most intricate that had ever been produced by a natural life chemistry. Its interest was in pleasure and exhilaration, not in information. What a joy it felt when it was able to swoop over two insects, as they buzzed in a furious death struggle, envelop them, and wait, trembling in every gassy atom, for the life force of the defeated to spray with tingling effect against its own insubstantial elements.

There was a timeless period then, when its life was only that aimless search for food. And its world was a narrow swamp, a gray, nubiferous environment, where it lived its contented, active, idyllic, almost mindless existence. But even in that area of suffused sunlight it grew bigger imperceptibly. It needed more food, more than any haphazard search for dying insects could bring it.

And so it developed cunning, special little bits of knowledge that fitted the dank swamp. It learned which were the insects that preyed, and which were the prey. It learned the hunting hours of every species, and where the tiny, nonflying monsters lay in wait—the flying ones were harder to keep track of. Though—as the Anabis discovered—they, also, had their eating habits. It learned to use its vaporous shape like a breeze to sweep unsuspecting victims to their fate.

Its food supply became adequate, then more than adequate. It grew, and once more it hungered. Of necessity, it became aware that there was life beyond the swamp. And, one day, when it ventured farther than ever before, it came upon two gigantic armored beasts at the bloody climax of a death struggle. The sustained thrill that came as the defeated monster's life force streamed through its vitals, the sheer quantity of energy it received, provided ecstasy greater than it had experienced during all its previous lifetime. In a few hours, while the victor devoured the writhing vanquished, the Anabis grew by ten thousand times ten thousand.

During the single day and night period that followed, the steaming jungle world was enveloped. The Anabis overflowed every ocean, every continent, and spread up to where the eternal clouds gave way to unadulterated sunlight. Later, in the days of its intelligence, it was able to analyze what happened then. Whenever it gained in bulk, it absorbed certain gases from the atmosphere around it. To bring this about, two agents were needed, not just one. There was the food it had to search for. And there was the natural action of ultraviolet radiation from the sun. In the swamp, far below the upper reaches of that water-laden atmosphere, only a minute quantity of the necessary short waves had come through. The results were correspondingly tiny, localized, and potentially only planetary in scope.

As it emerged from the mist, it was increasingly exposed to ultraviolet light. The dynamic expansion that began then did not slow for eons. On the second day, it reached the nearest planet. In a measurable time, it spread to the limits of the galaxy, and reached out automatically for the shining stuff of other star systems. But there it met defeat in distances that seemed to yield nothing to its groping, tenuous matter.

It took in knowledge as it took in food. And in the early days it believed the thoughts were its own. Gradually, it grew aware that the electrical nerve energy it absorbed at each death scene brought with it the mind-stuff of both a victorious and a dying beast. For a time, that was its thought level. It learned the animal cunning of many a carnivorous hunter, and the evasive skill of the hunted. But, here and there on different planets, it made contact with an entirely different degree of intelligence: beings who could think, civilization, science.

It discovered from them, among many other things, that by concentrating its elements it could make holes in space, go through, and come out at a distant point. It learned to transport matter in this fashion. It began to junglize planets as a matter of course because primeval worlds provided the most life force. It transported great slices of other jungle worlds through hyperspace. It projected cold planets nearer their suns.

It wasn't enough.

The days of its power seemed but a moment. Wherever it fed, it grew vaster. Despite its enormous intelligence, it could never strike a balance anywhere. With horrendous fear, it foresaw that it was doomed within a measurable time.

The coming of the ship brought hope. By stretching dangerously thin in one direction, it would follow the ship to wherever it had come from. Thus would begin a desperate struggle to remain alive by jumping from galaxy to galaxy, spreading ever farther into the immense night. Throughout those years its hope must be that it would be able to junglize planets, and that space had no end...

To the men, darkness made no difference. The *Space Beagle* crouched on a vast plain of jagged metal. Every porthole shed light. Great searchlights poured added illumination on rows of engines that were tearing enormous holes into the all-iron world. At the beginning the iron was fed into a single manufacturing machine, which turned out unstable iron torpedoes at the rate of one every minute, and immediately launched them into space.

By dawn of the next morning, the manufacturing machine itself began to be manufactured, and additional robot feeders poured raw iron into each new unit. Soon, a hundred, then thousands of manufacturing machines were turning out those slim, dark torpedoes. In ever greater numbers they soared into the surrounding night, scattering their radioactive substance to every side. For thirty thousand years those torpedoes would shed their destroying atoms. They were designed to remain within the gravitational field of their galaxy, but never to fall on a planet or into a sun.

As the slow, red dawn of the second morning brightened the horizon, engineer Pennons reported on the "General Call."

"We're now turning out nine thousand a second; and I think we can safely leave the machines to finish the job. I've put a partial screen around the planet to prevent interference. Another hundred iron worlds properly located, and our bulky friend will begin to have a hollow feeling in his vital parts. It's time we were on our way."

The time came, months later, when they decided that their destination would be Nebula NGC-50,347. Astronomer Lester explained the meaning of the selection.

"That particular galaxy," he said quietly, "is nine hundred *million* light-years away. If this gas intelligence follows us, he'll lose even his stupendous self in a night that almost literally has no end."

He sat down, and Grosvenor rose to speak.

"I'm sure," he began, "we all understand that we are not going to this remote star system. It would take us centuries, perhaps thousands of years, to reach it. All we want is to get this inimical life form out where he will starve. We'll be able to tell if he's following us by the murmurings of his thoughts. And we'll know he's dead when the murmurings stop."

That was exactly what happened.

Time had passed. Grosvenor entered the auditorium room of his department, and saw that his class had again enlarged. Every seat was occupied, and several chairs had been brought in from adjoining rooms. He began his lecture of the evening.

"The problems which Nexialism confronts are whole problems. Man has divided life and matter into separate compartments of knowledge and being. And, even though he sometimes uses words which indicate his awareness of that wholeness of nature, he continues to behave as if the one, changing universe has many separately functioning parts. The techniques we will discuss tonight…"

He paused. He had been looking out over his audience, and his gaze had suddenly fastened on a familiar figure well to the rear of the room. After a moment's hesitation, Grosvenor went on.

"…will show how this disparity between reality and man's behavior can be overcome."

He went on to describe the techniques, and in the back of the room Gregory Kent took his first notes on the science of Nexialism.

And, carrying its little bit of human civilization, the expeditionary ship *Space Beagle* sped at an ever increasing velocity through a night that had no end.

And no beginning.

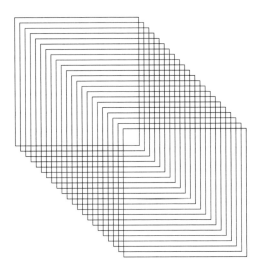

INTRODUCED BY JACK DANN
AFTERWORD BY MARTA RANDALL
EPILOGUE AGAIN BY BARRY N. MALZBERG

# GALAXIES

BY BARRY N. MALZBERG

# INTRODUCTION

It's 1994, and I've just arrived at the Sky Garden Room of the St. Moritz Hotel on Central Park. I'm standing cheek-to-jowl with a clutch of writers, editors, publishers, and agents; it's the annual Science Fiction Writers of America Authors-Editors Reception, and it's a cold Monday night in November. But it's warm and close in this room at the top of New York. Writers are cruising around, looking fresh and intent, drinks in hand, searching for editors to "do business with," while most of the editors are standing around in rumpled suits, being polite, putting in the requisite appearance after a heavy day's work in the office. The views from the balconies are breathtaking: New York City in all its splendour, clouds and avenues of Christmas lights, and from this height, Manhattan Island takes on the outline of a great ship cruising through the darkness.

I look around for Barry N. Malzberg. He promised to meet me here.

I push through the crowd and slowly make my way across the room. I talk with old friends, do a little business, shake hands, and then I hear a deep, low voice, a voice that somehow combines humour and resignation and absolute finality—"Hello, Jack." I turn around, and there he is beside me, thin and hunched over and looking uncomfortable and miserable in a black suit. He's taller than anyone else in the room, a stork standing among the penguins. "You're late. I've been here for ninety minutes."

We talk and try to catch up, for we've known each other for a lifetime; but Barry grows more uncomfortable and more nervous with every second, as if he's trapped and doing all he can to hold back the panic and, perhaps, revulsion; and finally he says, "This is it, Jack, an hour and a half is my limit, that's all I can take, I'm out of it, out of it, it's over for me, I'm sorry, I wanted to see you, but"—he glances quickly around the room and says, "Why do we do this to ourselves?" and then he bolts for the door.

I follow him to the elevators.

As the elevator doors close, we stare at each other.

Goodbye, Barry...

He will calm down in the cool darkness of a concert hall where he will lose himself in Mahler or Berlioz or Bach; and as I walk back into the humid, noisy room, into the comforting swell of dear friends and old acquaintances, I imagine him striding down the streets alone.

Barry...the quintessential outsider.

Over a period of four decades, Barry N. Malzberg has written mainstream fiction, erotic fiction, and mystery and suspense, but his considerable reputation rests on his science fiction novels and short stories. He is the author of over seventy novels and over two hundred short stories; some of his short fiction may be found in the collections *Final War and Other Fantasies* (as K. M. O'Donnell, 1969), *In the Pocket and Other Science Fiction Stories* (as K. M. O'Donnell, 1971), *Out From Ganymede* (1974), *The Many Worlds of Barry Malzberg* (1975), *Down Here in the Dream Quarter* (1976), *The Best of Barry Malzberg* (1976), *Malzberg at Large* (1979), *The Man Who Loved the Midnight Lady* (1980), and *The Passage of the Night: The Recursive Science Fiction of Barry N. Malzberg*, edited by Mike Resnick and Anthony R. Lewis (1994).

Malzberg began as a playwright, but turned to writing science fiction consistently and prolifically for about seven years after his first sale to Fred Pohl at *Galaxy* magazine. The story was "We're Coming Through the Windows" and it appeared in the August 1967 issue. But it was his second story that established him as an innovator who would come to exemplify the literary experimentation and questioning of traditional values that was associated with the "New Wave" movement of the late sixties and early seventies. "Final War" was a dark and caustic reflection on war as a game that never ends; it was published in the April 1968 issue of *The Magazine of Fantasy & Science Fiction*.

Malzberg's first novel of note was *Oracle of the Thousand Hands* (1968), which was published by the controversial Olympia Press. He wrote nine other novels for Olympia, which include *Screen* (1970), *In my Parents' Bedroom* (1970), and *Confessions of Westchester County* (1971). As Malzberg writes in his autobiographical sketch in *Contemporary Authors*: "'You son of a bitch,' Maurice Girodias said to me in a restaurant, a week after I had delivered *Screen* to his Olympia Press…. 'You son of a bitch, you give me literature, you give me horse racing and decadence and death and impotence and darkness! So I have, you see, no nice little book of porno-graffee as I wish; I have this *literature*. I cannot publish it in paperback, of course; they would throw it across the room. I publish in hardcover then, and I lose all my money.'"

In 1969 Malzberg began publishing science fiction under the pseudonym K. M. O'Donnell. * Besides the two pseudonymous short-story collections mentioned above, he wrote the novels *The Empty People* (1969), *Dwellers of the Deep* (1970), *Universe Day* (1971), and *Gather in the Hall of the Planets* (1971). His first sf novel under his own name was *The Falling Astronauts* (1971), which was followed by *Beyond Apollo* (1972). This controversial novel about the first manned expedition to Venus is narrated by the only survivor of the mission, who is probably insane. Robert Silverberg wrote that "Barry Malzberg's dark, bleak vision of the future is one of the most terrifying ever to come out of science fiction." When *Beyond Apollo* won the first John W. Campbell, Jr. Memorial Award, traditional science fiction fans were incensed: this was *not* the kind of science fiction that

* MALZBERG HAS WRITTEN UNDER A NUMBER OF PSEUDONYMS, WHICH INCLUDE MIKE BARRY, FRANCINE DE NATALE, CLAUDINE DUMAS, MEL JOHNSON, LEE W. MASON, AND GERROLD WATKINS.

the editor of *Astounding Stories* (later *Analog Science Fiction*) would have ever bought.

*Beyond Apollo* established Malzberg as a major science fiction writer.

Malzberg's most prolific period was during the '70s when he produced some of his most brilliant work, which would include the aforementioned *Beyond Apollo*, *Overlay* (1972), *The Men Inside* (1973), *Herovit's World* (1973), *The Destruction of the Temple* (1974), *Underlay* (1974), *Guernica Night* (1974), *Chorale* (1978), and *Galaxies* (1975). If I had to choose only the very best of Malzberg's work at novel length, it would have to be *Beyond Apollo*, *Herovit's World*, *Guernica Night*, *Galaxies*, which is included here, and his last published novel *The Remaking of Sigmund Freud* (1985).

Barry Malzberg has also edited a number of important anthologies, which include the groundbreaking *Final Stage: The Ultimate Science Fiction Anthology* (with Edward L. Ferman, 1974, 1975), *The Arbor House Treasury of Horror and the Supernatural* (with Bill Pronzini and Martin H. Greenberg, 1981), and *The Arbor House Treasury of Mystery and Suspense* (with Bill Pronzini and Martin H. Greenberg, 1981).

I should also mention and recommend Malzberg's dark retrospective volume *The Engines of the Night* (1982), which won the Locus Award for nonfiction and was a Hugo Award finalist. It is one of the most important personal histories in the genre. When the book was published, writer, editor, and critic Algis Budrys wrote: "Destined to be misunderstood and misused, this cry from the heart will prove once more that honesty is suicidal."

Barry's pain and revelation and genius have had a profound impact on science fiction, yet his dark, stabbing, autobiographical work has not received nearly the attention it deserves. Almost all of his titles are out of print; and now, at the very height of his powers, he has almost stopped writing.

How did this happen to the author who wrote *Herovit's World*, *Overlay*, *Guernica Night*, *The Remaking of Sigmund Freud*, *Beyond Apollo*, *Down Here in the Dream Quarter*, *The Engines of the Night*, and *Galaxies*?

One answer might be that Malzberg had no business being a genre writer. As a writer and editor once remarked, "Only Barry would try to become a commercially successful science fiction writer by grinding out great quantities of depressing science fiction novels and stories." And, indeed, Malzberg has more in common with writers such as Gogol, Kafka, and Rilke, or modern writers such as Barth, Barthelme, Bellows, Pynchon, and Oates. In a different timeline, in some alternate world, Barry N. Malzberg is having a career like the prolific Joyce Carol Oates, whose dark, alienated, internalised fiction has earned her a place in the current pantheon of literary lions. But whereas Oates (who admires Malzberg's work) directs some of her large output into the genre magazines and anthologies, Malzberg has never crossed over into the literary market.

In a candid interview with Charles Platt, he said:

"I became a science-fiction writer because I failed in my attempts to succeed in the literary world. I quit the largest writing fellowship in the country—the Cornelia Ward Creative Writing Fellowship—in 1965 because I was being rejected. I was writing literary short stories and drowning in rejections and I just did not want to go any further.

"In October or November of that year I read in *Galaxy* magazine Norman Kagan's story 'Laugh Along with Franz.' It was a brilliant, savage piece of science fiction, except it wasn't science fiction at all, it was a serious, savage work of American fiction by a young American fiction writer. I shook my head as I read it and I cynically said to myself, if this son of a bitch can get away with this kind of stuff in the commercial science fiction genre then I've got a future because I can do this just as well myself right now, and I can do it a little better in a couple of years, given a little training. If he can get away with this, I can too. And it was at that moment that I knew, viscerally, that I could sell science fiction."

If Malzberg had been patient…if he had kept sending out his work to the commercial markets…if he had kept writing plays…if he had submitted short stories to the literary quarterlies, which he didn't want to be in because "nobody read them and they didn't pay, so why bother"…would he have broken through to the literary mainstream firmament? Perhaps. Probably. But Barry Malzberg isn't patient. He paces around his home and office like a trapped animal and transforms his high anxiety into fiction, into diabolically self-referential and obsessive metafiction, postmodern fiction, humour, and autobiography. Although he now works on a computer, he used to type on an old portable Smith-Corona manual, and he'd punch at those keys like a boxer going for a knockout.

He has written some of the darkest fiction in the genre, so dark that once the shock wears off, we realise we've been reading comedy by a master.

But is it *really* science fiction?

Malzberg uses the tropes of science fiction to catalogue his own inadequacies (and, by extension, our own) and—as Brian Stableford has said—to dramatise "relationships between the human mind and its social environment in an sf theatre of the absurd." His fiction is also profoundly political, but as critic Jeffrey M. Wallmann has written: "To say that…Malzberg is criticising meaningless bureaucracy and arbitrary government in general, and the space program and space colonisation in particular, may be correct but too easy. By leaving riddles unresolved at the end, and by rejecting the tenet that the aim of space travel is primarily pragmatic, Malzberg abandons a cornerstone of science fiction: the leading to a confirmation, not to a questioning, of the concept of reality and identity."

It has often been suggested that Malzberg's work isn't science fiction so much as postmodern fiction—a category that is as difficult to define as science fiction and would include fiction that "resists the very idea of boundaries," "regards distinctions as undesirable and even impossible," and "adopts a self-conscious intertextuality sometimes verging on pastiche, which denies the formal propriety of authorship and genre," to quote from the *Prentice-Hall Guide to English Literature*.

If you are fortunate enough to find a copy of *The Engines of the Night* in a second-hand bookstore, flip to the last chapter entitled "Corridors." Is it an essay disguised as a short story, or a short story disguised as an essay? Is it autobiography or pastiche? For that matter is *Galaxies* a novel or an essay on the process of writing a novel with fictional episodes as illustration?

⚛

The first incarnation of *Galaxies* was the novella entitled "A Galaxy Called Rome," which was first published in *The Magazine of Fantasy & Science Fiction* in July 1975. It was reprinted a year later in his short story collection *Down Here in the Dream Quarter*. In the afterword to the story, Malzberg wrote:

> Here I address an old (maybe oldest) question in our tortured category which will never be resolved: *what is science fiction?* And if we can ever define it, does it 'mean' anything in the sense that commercial and literary fiction which deals with objective verifiable fact can be said to 'mean' if not precisely 'be'? Is science fiction merely another slightly distorted paradigm of common reality or is it something else which, at its best, can mysteriously assume the reality of a future we will never have?
>
> Difficult questions but I think that some tentative answers are here. I believe that good fiction can unfold its truths only on its own terms, that it cannot be paraphrased in terms other than its own and that the answers cannot be summarised. But perhaps there are given some suggestions.

When *Galaxies* was published in 1975, the reviews were few; but the one by Robert Silverberg is for the ages, since it confronts issues in the writing of science fiction that will not go away:

"What Malzberg tells us, on every page, is that neither he nor Heinlein nor Doc Smith nor anybody can convey the reality of what it is like to be the pilot of a fortieth-century spaceship bearing a cargo of dead souls, that is toppling into a black hole. It is audacious enough, says Malzberg, for a writer to think that he can show us the reality of a middle-class New Jersey suburb in our own time; how then to handle all these unfathomable cosmic wonders? He can't. Yet he is a science-fiction writer, and he must try. So try he does, magnificently, approaching his inconceivable thematic matter elliptically, obliquely, poking at it, toying with it, trying to seduce it into plausibility. Conventional science fiction novels of the kind this is packaged to look like bang straightforwardly away at their themes, hero, villain, problem, conflict, obstacles, complication, resolution, and if we have not lost the knack of willing suspension of disbelief we accept what their authors are saying, at least for the nonce. Malzberg can no longer suspend his own disbelief, and yet, oddly, as he wrestles with his impossibly grandiose conceptual burden of black holes and tachyonic drive, he achieves a kind of acceptance in the reader anyway. He persuades us, somehow, to glimpse the fortieth century. Of all his many novels, this is, I think, the most completely realised work of art, the most moving, the most profound, and despite its ostensible refusal to handle its material straightforwardly, the most successful work of science fiction he has produced.

"Of course, I've lived on into the fourth generation myself, both as a reader and a writer, and my reaction to *Galaxies* may well be colored by my own accumulated troubles. Be warned by that confession of bias. *Galaxies* will probably not please the new reader of science fiction, the undemanding one, or the unsophisticated one. I think it will amaze and delight those who have grown and deepened since the days of Blackie Duquesne and Giles Habibula, and that it will altogether flabbergast the current generation of s-f writers who will find their private struggles to make sense out of the unimaginable laid bare here in unforgettable manner."

Whatever you might think of Malzberg's oeuvre—whatever you might think it is, or what it means, or what it means to accomplish— you should know that Barry N. Malzberg walked into all this with his eyes open. He chose his own way and disregarded the consequences. He didn't cave in to the demands of the market. He became the prince of the remainder bookshelf and the Cassandra of the genre. He wrote reams, for he's an extraordinarily prolific writer, and he thought, wrongly, that if he wrote a lot of fiction, even if it was uncompromisingly dark, he'd be able to make a good middle-class living.

It worked…for a few glorious, prosperous years.

He had the house in the 'burbs and the great symbol of the '60s middle class: the Cadillac.

"A 1973 Calais Coup. Burnt Sienna. $6,500.00 plus tax."

He still has the house in the 'burbs...and he can still write fiction that is as brilliant and disconcerting and uncomfortable as anything he ever wrote in his salad days of the seventies and eighties. While most fiction reinforces our values, prejudices, and beliefs, Malzberg's work still makes us uncomfortable about everything we take for granted. His new work—what little there is of it—is still uncomfortable and sometimes revelatory. It is still bleak and funny and contradictory...and new. And the humour is still black as the pit at midnight.

But, as he once remarked, "I just won't keep throwing the work into a black hole." He recently wrote: "We learn and we learn and our knowledge reduces us to silence. (Or ascends to silence like the dead or the Just.)"

Certainly, to this reader, none of it has been in vain. The work remains, even if we must excavate the dark recesses of second-hand bookstores to find it. And in recent years, something has occurred that has even surprised Malzberg: he has become the acknowledged conscience of the genre.

For almost thirty years he told it like it was.

He didn't lie to us...or bullshit us. We found that all out later.

And it's all there in the fiction...and in the life.

The work only awaits rediscovery.

Jack Dann
Melbourne, Australia
May, 1997

# GALAXIES

## BY BARRY N. MALZBERG

**IN MEMORY OF ISIDORE ZELNICK:**
5/17/05—9/19/74

**IN MEMORY OF LILLIAN ZELNICK:**
5/16/06—5/31/73

FIRST THE CORPUS, THEN THE MIND, THE CONSCIOUSNESS, THEN SELF-AWARENESS
AND ITS EXTENSIONS: THE ENVIRONMENT, THE ABSTRACT ENVIRONMENT, IMMORTALITY,
MATTERS OF THE SPIRIT. WE CAN ASSUME A CONTINUITY OF THESE QUALITIES AND WE
CAN EVEN ASSUME THAT THAT WHICH WOULD INSIST UPON IMPOSING ORDER WOULD CONTINUE
TO DO SO EVEN AFTER THE POINT OF PHYSICAL DEATH.

BUT IN ORDER TO BE COMPLETELY SECURE WITH THESE ASSUMPTIONS WE WOULD
HAVE TO DEFINE SOME TERMS. WHAT IS "CONSCIOUSNESS" OR THE "SPIRIT"?
WHAT IS "ORDER"? FOR THAT MATTER, WHAT IS "PHYSICAL DEATH"?

H. H. BRENNER
THE LAST POSSESSOR

To define terms at the outset, this will not be a novel so much as a series of notes toward one. Nevertheless pay attention, for it will cease to become a novel exactly at the point where it seems to be at last gathering force. Up until that time (which I will never tell), it will be as much of a novel as *The Rammer of Arcturus* or *Slinking Slowly on the Slime Planet's Sludge*, titles which flank this to left and right with covers offering inducements—let me be honest about this—they will never fulfill.

The novel itself cannot be written, at least by this writer, nor can it be encompassed by any techniques currently available, because it partakes of its time and that time is of the fortieth century, a time unimaginably distant...and it could be perceived only through the idiom and devices of that era which, to be sure, will not exist for more than eighteen hundred years.

Nor—continuing to be straightforward—will that idiom or those devices ever exist because science fiction is not a series of working models for the future but merely a subgenre of romantic fiction which employs the future as historicals would use the past, as Westerns would use the West, as pornography would use fornication—in short as a convention, which is the focus of their appeal. By virtue of these reasons then, not to say others which are more personal—but which will be revealed—these fifty-five thousand words are little more than a set of constructions toward a construction even less substantial. It, as the writer himself, will not be finished in this world.

Let us talk about the writer a little if I may. Writers are not machines, you know, or disembodied personae, part of the printers' workshops: we have our qualities, we are people, we suffer, we *hurt*, although not as much, perhaps, as we would like you to believe. Still the writer is entitled to some explication. As he writes this novel he has slid past his thirty-fifth birthday and now confronts the not-distant monument of his thirty-sixth with bewilderment. Thirty-five is practically more than he can handle. He knows that forty is bad and fifty is worse, he has heard grim reports from even further on, but the writer has always thought of himself as being such a *young* man and ever-youthful; he has lurched through twenty-one, twenty-five, thirty years and similar landmarks in his shambling way, but nothing, either inherited or anticipated, has quite prepared him for the understanding that by Biblical calculation—by calculation, too, of much heredity—his life is fully at the halfway point. How can this be? The writer for many years was always the youngest person in the class. He finds his state hard to reckon with and he does not know with whom he can commiserate. Those older think he is young; those younger think he is old; his contemporaries have similar difficulties. Psychoanalysis is expensive and the writer has never had much faith in it.

The writer has struggled to order his life just as he is struggling now to order his sequence of notes for a novel entitled *Galaxies,* and yet no less than the wild and wonderful concepts which are surely to follow, he wonders whether he is really under control or whether it matters at all how he contemplates his death. His passage would be of little more consequence than his birth, which did not by much antedate the rape of Poland. Were the two somehow causally linked? Did the writer by being born cause Warsaw to be sealed off, reports moving toward the front lines on fine and invisible connection? Did he, by being born, cause the world to exist and by dying will he end it? This is the kind of megalomania with which he must deal—and yet it is this megalomania which is the key—God help him—to fiction which itself creates or manipulates worlds.

The reader may sit tight, however. The author is not a character in *Galaxies*. You need not worry that he will intrude into the body of the work which will be fast-moving (when it gets into the action sequences) and exceedingly detached. I introduce myself, in truth, only to remind you that these engines of creation are indeed powered by an individual no less idiosyncratic, difficult or painful to himself than you, although I have learned through tormenting years of apprenticeship ruthlessly to suppress all that is truly mine in the service of detached and transmuted work. (Even this use of "author" as character is a device, then; it is an invented persona which is in certain ways a metaphor for the real writer and in other ways not; it is a thing of spring and cheap bailing wire which, if it is handled correctly, will give you the impression that you know me when all you know is what I wish to present. So there.)

The author has been writing, with some success, for seven years now, but he was writing without success for a long time before that, and, therefore, his failure ratio, even taking into account his recent modest rise in reputation, is still convincing. Not only has the author always felt himself to be a young person, he has thought himself to be a young *failure*; but there is more strength in that because our youth and possibility may be stripped from us, but our failure can remain shining and constant forever. Sustained by his failure—to say nothing of a modest advance from his publisher—the author moves forward.

Galaxies will be based heavily on two articles published in *Analog: Science Fiction—Science Fact* by the late John W. Campbell. Campbell for the last thirty-three years of his life (he died on 7/11/71) was the editor of that magazine under its present title and earlier identity, *Astounding Science Fiction*. He was a difficult man but not a dishonest one.

Campbell's articles put forth the existence of a "black" or lightless galaxy which would result from the implosion of a neutron star, the implosion unleashing terrible forces, causing a gravitational influence so strong as the star collapsed upon itself that the galaxy in which this occurred would trap not only light but space, and possibly time. A spaceship trapped within this black galaxy would be unable to get out. Escape velocity would, to counter gravity, have to exceed the unplausible speed of light. All interstellar paths of flight would lead toward the gravitational field of this galaxy; none would lead away. Such a galaxy, Campbell pointed out, would be called Rome.

Neutron stars are white dwarves, inconceivably hot and dense, which burn furiously through their resources only to exhaust their fuel at a much earlier stage of their cycle of existence than so called "normal" stars like our own humble Sol which, when its light is exhausted in several billion years, will probably decoalesce and disperse gently, therefore signaling the day of judgment, to say nothing of the rising of the dead and the sacred priests. Neutron stars cannot look forward to a long senility and a whimpering old age; they will depart to no nursing home of the heavens but instead are at a consistently *accelerating* combustion in order to maintain their existence, and when this acceleration reaches a point of no supply, matters do become rather cataclysmic. A day of judgment controlled by the life of a neutron star would be brief and would result, doubtless, in the recremation of the dead who, presumably, have already suffered enough.

The novel to be based on this material would concern itself with a faster-than-light spaceship in the year 3902 which would tumble into the black galaxy and be unable to leave by tachyonic drive. ("Tachyonic" meaning *faster* than light, a device long beloved by science-fiction writers, since we can keep our characters shuttling through the galaxies much as writers for the *Quarterly Review* can use subways and taxicabs for understandably slighter terrain, but a device useful here only if the ship can accelerate *up to* before moving beyond light speed.) Falling into the galaxy would be easy or at least inevitable, since one of the characteristics of the black galaxy is its invisibility, the implosive forces having contained light. Leaving, however, would be much more difficult. Leaving will be the concern of this novel.

Consider. Science fiction, since its formal inception as a romantic subgenre in this country in 1926 with the publication of the first issues of Hugo Gernsback's *Amazing Stories*, has best been known for its simple and melodramatic plots which demonstrate man's mastery (or later on, loss of control) of technology. The conventions of the genre then demand that the novel pivot upon the attempts of the crew to leave this entrapment and return to their planet of origin.

The ship is known—to us at least—as the *Skipstone*. It was completed in 3895 after a century-long effort of construction that involved the resources of many worlds and billions of the Systematized Forces. It is one of only fifteen faster-than-light ships now operating. Obviously something like this cannot be cheaply abandoned. The crew must return it to the fleet.

This problem-solving pivot is not one which I might attempt given my own devices. I am not a problem-solver by profession, let alone in my personal life. Left to myself I would be more interested in showing how the ship's inhabitants and cargo adjust to their new dwelling, how they set up light housekeeping in this unknown and difficult sector of the universe, but this would not do for the purposes of the science-fiction novel. We must compete with, sell on the racks against *The Rammers of Arcturus*. It is important to understand, and I am sure that all of you do, that classically this field of science fiction was meant by its American originators to provide a road map from technological impasse, a map which would show us the way from a confusing and overpowering technology, to the wondrous society it could give us. Science fiction, then, is *technological fiction*; it is an attempt to relieve anxieties about the encroaching machinery by showing people how that machinery may be usefully applied. Science as benign instrumentation. *Amazing*'s earliest competitor was *Astounding Stories of Super-Science*. *Super-Science* brings us super-solutions. Thrilling Wonder. Astonishing Stories.

Details of the submission of *Skipstone*'s crew to the unknown should be dystopian. While the dystopian has an honorable tradition in science fiction, reaching earlier than *Amazing* to the works of Olaf Stapledon and H. G. Wells, it has really had a difficult time making its way, and even now, at a time of technological impasse and collapsed institutions, science-fiction writers who go against the protechnological format have a more difficult time in finding audiences and publishers than the traditionally oriented.

My own decision has been made, however: I would rather command an audience than not, to say nothing of publisher's advances, and therefore this construct, despite its bleaker aspects and a certain aura of cynicism which may occasionally drift off the pages, will be essentially cheerful, essentially hopeful, quite problem-solving and possessed of qualities of adventurousness. No writer of integrity with a wife and two helpless children could do less for the sake of his controlling artistic vision. This is to be kept in mind at all times.

The Campbell articles were found by others and given to me; I did not locate them myself. There was a time in the late 1960s, early seventies, when I gave up altogether on *Analog*. Through no fault of my own (I felt), I was unable to read or relate to the contents of the magazine. Now I am back to reading it but not quite up to back issues. The articles were sent by people who thought I might be interested in basing a technologically oriented S F story on their contents. "Hard" science fiction they call it.

I have always had a certain awe for this kind of science fiction, and, although I cannot really do it well myself, wish that the genre had more of it. Unhappily "hard" science fiction is largely a myth; there is almost no science in science fiction and never has been. The recollected masterpieces of the 1940s were fantasies whose scientific basis was almost completely invented or could have been found in a general research work in five or ten minutes. At low word-rates, research is neither desirable nor profitable, since all markets pay the same for all stories that they publish, rewarding merit as they do the incompetent with a standard rate. Consequently, James Blish's science-fiction writer is quoted as saying, "All the science I ever needed to know I got out of a bottle of scotch."

But how we could use it! Science, that is to say. We could indeed profit by technologically accurate science fiction. The awful expansion of our machinery, the technological manual as the poetics of the age, the rhythms of the machine as analogous to those of the newly discovered spirit...we need writers who can show us what the machines are doing to us in terms more systematized than those of random paranoia. A writer who could combine the techniques of modern fiction with a genuine command of science could be at the *top* of this field in no more than a few years. He would also stand alone.

There are a few among us who know science and a few more who understand fiction, but there is not a single science-fiction writer who can do both. The one who has come closest, at least in his later work, is A—but A, although his undoubted gifts are the equal of any writer in America, is exhausted by a career of hackwork in his youth and embittered by the fact that his newer, important work has not distanced him from the hackwork but to most readers simply extends and reaffirms it. In any event A, like all science-fiction writers, is invisible to the academic/literary nexus which controls judgments of literary reputation in America. He made wrong choices at the beginning. It is all his fault, of course, but one may nevertheless have sympathy for A.

B, a writer of equal technical range and even greater delicacy than A, also comes close to this ideal, but his science is weak and his output diminishing; he has, in any event, no interest in continuing to write science fiction and is making desperate attempts to leave the genre. Then there is C who has won a major literary award and is considered by many to be at the level of A or B, but C is clumsy and impenetrable and has little sense of compression. X Y and Z have all in their way done interesting work but are burned out at the ages of, respectively, 2-, 2- and 2- and little can be expected of them. R had promise, of course, but has been dead for many years, and in terms of their literary contribution, O, P and T might just as well be—although one may wish them long life and health of days. Commercial writing is a difficult field for even its few successes. Ask A about this sometime.

Still, we deal not with A, B or the others (although they would make for an interesting study which I might someday do) but only with this writer, thirty-five years old and stricken M, easy to quick judgments of his contemporaries, slow to wrath or judgment of himself. I would like to accept that challenge: the welding of hard, technological insight with the full range of modern literary technique, but even so, a first confrontation with this material made me feel that I should pass it by. My personal life—I wanted to say this and in an earlier draft, in fact, did—my personal life is my black hole; my two daughters provide more correct and stiffening implosion than does any neutron star, and as far as the song of the pulsars, it is as nothing, as nothing at all to the sounds which come from the paddock area at Aqueduct Race Track in the Borough of Queens, New York, on a dark summer Tuesday. *Get me out, Angel; get that seven horse out flying.*

"No," I could have said like Cheever's adolescent in *Bullet Park,* "No, enough of your breathtaking concepts, infinite distances, quasar leaps, binding messages from the Crab Nebula; be away with your light years, asteroids, Van Allen belts, methane systems and heavy planets. No, I am aware that there are those who find an ultimate truth there and would bend their lives toward their perception, but this is not for me. Where is the *pain*, the *remorse*, the *regret* and *guilt* and *terror?* No, I would rather dedicate the years of my productive life which remain to an understanding of the agonies of this middle-class suburb in northern New Jersey. Until I deal with those how can I comprehend Ridgefield Park, to say nothing of Scarsdale, Shaker Heights or the unknown lands of the west? Give me not the year two million which I will not see; give me now. The year two million can say nothing to me, but I may address it if, of course, the collected works can be carefully preserved. At least one writer will survive from this era and if not the notorious Q or the obscure N or the unfortunate A, why could it not be me?"

Nicely put. Cheever's adolescent would have approved, if not Cheever. Indeed, I found it convincing, until it occurred to me in one of those quick changes of consciousness which control the lives of all of us yet which may never be acknowledged in fiction, that Ridgefield Park would forever be as mysterious to me as the swamp of lights perceived through the refinery smog which are known to my children as "stars"...and that one should never deny infinity to pursue a particular which until the day of one's death—if not for longer than that—would always be a mystery.

So I decided to try *Galaxies* after all, although with some trepidation. I felt better when I came to understand that it did not have to be a novel but merely a set of notes for one. Knowing this I was not shamed nor did I grieve, for one's life is merely a set of notes for a life and Ridgefield Park merely a rough working model of Trenton in which nonetheless several thousand people live unable to divine their right hand from their left, and also some cattle. Shalt thou have not pity on the cattle? For they too grew up and perished in a night.

# 8

So in the novel, which takes place in 3902, the spacecraft *Skipstone*, on an exploratory flight through the major and minor galaxies surrounding the Milky Way, falls into the black galaxy of a neutron star and is lost forever.

The captain of *Skipstone* and the only living consciousness aboard is its woman commander, Lena Thomas. True now, all true: the hold of the ship carries five hundred and fifteen of the dead, sealed in their gelatinous fix, absorbing the unshielded ultraviolet of space which will at some future time hearken their reconstitution. True that yet another part of the enormous hold contains inactivated prostheses in which have been installed the personalities of seven skilled engineers who could be switched on at only slight inconvenience, who would provide Lena not only with answers to any problems technical but also with companionship to while away the long and grave hours of this flight; true also that Lena's consciousness would, if it were so directed, reel and teem with memory, the rich and variegated colors of all the associations she has had through her twenty-eight years, aided by a whiff of psychogenics to augment the totality of her recall. True that, as has been explained to her during training, solitude is merely a state of mind and has little to do with the interior geography of the soul in which we all must reside.

True. All of it. Lena, however, does not use the prostheses until the time that *Skipstone* falls into the black galaxy, nor has she had any desire to. She is a willful person, highly skilled and competent at least in relation to the routine tasks of this testing flight, and quite self-reliant. To call upon artificial engineers for aid would be an admission of weakness, as would any resort to the dead who are, of course, dead and cannot be reached. She feels that to lean upon anything outside of herself would only be an admission of weakness, would be carried back to the Bureau by the monitors which constantly scan the ship to report gross physical functions and only the Bureau knows what else and this would lessen her chances for promotion at the end of the voyage. Lena is reasonably ambitious and propelled by self-interest; it is not unfair to her to say this or to point out that much of what occurs in her mind and actions from henceforth are spurred by selfish motives. In this sense her humanity is merely increased; witness is borne to it.

(In her suspicions she is quite right. The Bureau monitors everything. Not only are there biological readouts, but also visual scanners which transmit all activities aboard to tape at headquarters which when fed through another machine can reconstitute the interior of the ship. One can barely conceive the efficacy of the monitors to which Lena is exposed. Our own astronauts could have functioned under a sheath of independence, so complete is the Bureau's fashioning of images. To be sure the monitoring ceases immediately as the ship falls into the black galaxy...but Lena is not sure of this and even then moderates her responses with caution. She has lived too long in *Skipstone* under the assumption that she has been spread out into a series of charts on a desk somewhere which reveal everything, even desires of which she is unaware.)

Sometimes Lena thinks that she would like to talk to the dead. Her feelings toward them are not as ruthless as those toward the Bureau or toward the prostheses; her condition, as she rattles in the hold of the ship moving on tachyonic drive, often seems to approximate theirs. Although they are deprived of consciousness, that quality seems almost irrelevant to the condition of hyperspace, and if there were any way in which she could bridge their mystery, she might well address them. What would she say to the dead? Anything, of course; just whatever comes into your mind, but she does not wish the Bureau to think she is mad. Surely they would adduce dialogues with the dead as evidence of insanity. So, caught between desire and necessity, she must settle for imaginary dialogues deep within the cells of consciousness and for long, quiescent periods when she will watch the monitors, watch the rainbow of hyperspace, witness the collisions of the spectrum. And say nothing whatsoever. Deny her life. It is a ship, at times, like this: utterly of the dead and yet beyond.

Lena, however, is not always mute. On certain occasions she will talk incessantly, as a matter of fact, if only to herself. (Her interior dialogue at these rare and explosive moments—when thoughts of the Bureau fall from her mind and she is only a lonely and frightened woman—is helpful, because in *Galaxies* dialogue will be important, both to heighten dramatic incident and to break up the long and inevitably difficult sections of expository prose.)

No device better than dialogue has been found to persuade the paperback reader, skimming a book on the newsstand, to opt for purchase. It gives a book a look of accessibility, gives the reader the assurance that he can penetrate it, and to say this is not to cast aspersion but to pay the reader the respect due his simple deductive insight. We must, all of us, become more human and can communicate our humanity only in the way that we deal with one another.

"Is that not so?" Lena asks the monitors, whispering in the darkness.

"Oh, it is surely so," she imagines that they say to her; "we become human only by approaching those who are of ourselves and by sharing our thoughts with them."

"Well then, there is nothing wrong in talking to you."

"Not at all."

"I need to talk to you."

"You should. You certainly should."

"Who can make judgments that it is wrong to talk? Does Bureau know what is going on here?"

"Of course not."

"Do the dead? Do the engineers?"

"No. No again."

"Only I know."

"You and we, Lena, you and we."

"Of course. So I will continue to talk to you when I wish to do so."

"You should."

"I will."

"Thank you."

"Thank *you*."

Thus dialogue to open the partitions of the novel. It will play the same role here that repetitive sex scenes play in the pornographic novel. We cannot use sex here, since sex could hardly be conducted in *Skipstone*. With whom would she have it? Also the role of sex in science fiction is uncertain; it is an uneasy addition to a category of literature many of whose readers find sex (or at least written sex) directly uncomfortable.

Sex does not play an insignificant role in Lena's inner life, and eventually this issue will have to be discussed, in the best taste of course, but for now we consider merely the matter of dialogue. Lena talks to herself. She has dialogues with herself, with the monitors, often with the dead. She roams the ship and declaims. She maintains soliloquies, sometimes for hours. "Consider," she will for instance say to the dead this time, "consider what is going on here," the dead quiescent in the hold, some of them here for eight hundred years, others scaled down from that to only a few weeks, the recent dead and the far-gone dead nestled in the same gelatinous container that has been transferred wholly into the ship, "Consider where we are now," pointing through the hold, the colors gleaming through the portholes onto her wrist, colors dancing in the air, her eyes full and maddened in this light which is not to say that she *is* mad but that the condition of hyperspace is itself insane. The Michelson-Morley effect has a psychological as well as physical reality. "Why now," she says, "it could be *me* dead and in the hold and all of you here in the dock watching the colors spin, all the same, living and the dead together as we move faster than light," she says...and indeed she is right. The tachyonic drive has such a profound effect upon subjective reality that the living can become the dead, the dead the living.

Faster-than-light speed drives all things toward the center of the bell curve of existence, you see. Here the dead live, the living are dead, all together in that mix as she has pointed out, and were it not that the objective poles of her consciousness remain fixed intensely by her years of trained discipline, she would press the levers, eject one by one the dead into the larger coffin of space, something which is indicated only as an emergency procedure under the gravest of circumstances and which would result in her removal from command post immediately upon her return. It would be an outrageous action, for the dead are precious cargo: their accumulated estates, willed toward preservation and revival have, in essence, funded the faster-than-light experiments.

"I will handle you with the greatest delicacy," Lena says; "I will treat you with great respect, and I will never, oh, I will never let you go, little packages in your little prisons, exquisite goods, delightful cargo, precious weight," and so and on and on as the *Skipstone* moves in excess of one hundred and eighty-six thousand miles per second. Indeed it now moves at two point three million miles per second, still accelerating...and yet except for the colors, the nausea, the disorienting swing, her own mounting insanity, the terms of this novel as it must be written, were it not for all of this, Lena might be in the IRT Lenox Avenue local at rush hour moving slowly uptown as circles of illness track her in the fainting car in the bowels of summer in New York in 1975 as mortality, known over and again, presses in.

But the novel is not of mortality but immortality. It is of the vaulting extension of human life as it will be known not only within the spaces of the ship, but also in the minds that one by one, painfully in that hold, are being freed by radiation to tenant the cyborgs that have been constructed precisely against such an emergency. Of the dead, Lena will learn much more. Of herself she knows much already. As *Galaxies* opens she is twenty-eight years old.

It is almost two thousand years in the future. Man has established colonies on forty planets in the Milky Way, including the system of Sirius, the well-known Dog Star; he has fully populated the solar system, except for Jupiter whose methane gases are not only inimical to life, but also destructive to the gearing of life support. Jupiter, thus, was given up for lost in 2814, but all of the other planets are populated and on several of them—Venus, Neptune, Titan, largest moon of Saturn notably—there is already severe evidence of overpopulation and the breakdown of social and technological systems. For this reason great emphasis has been placed upon the faster-than-light experiments which will, hopefully, open up worlds outside the few already known that might not be inimical to human life. The three planets of Sirius already have a fragile colony, the Antares Cluster has twenty worlds upon which autonomous colonists are presumed to exist, but this is not sufficient, and now the social engineers and philosophers of this time, who are no more numerous or farsighted than those of our present, predict the collapse of the multitechnological system within a century unless more space is found.

The colonies of the solar system are under the government of Earth, and on Earth a feudal system has been reconstituted, an autocracy with nobles, vassals and a hereditary monarchy...but fortunately none of these need be developed in the novel. They will merely lurk in the background, a set of assumptions underlying, perhaps, Lena's character or the necessity of certain confrontations, but not developed. It will be understood, of course, that the alienation produced by a feudal/hierarchical system works upon almost all those not high in the hierarchy and that much of Lena's anguish is social as well as metaphysical.

It is 3902. Still, the medical science of that distant time is not notably superior to that of our own in terms of human mortality. The life-span has not been significantly extended, and although certain serious illnesses have been almost eradicated—heart seizure by cortisone derivatives in the late twentieth century, cancer through horse antibodies in the middle 2500s, cerebrovascular accident by glandular therapy only two hundred years ago—others have risen to take their place as if certain universal laws of mortality must be served, diseases only being their humble agents. So nephritis is killing people now, and arteriosclerosis and pancreatitis are major killers. Meningitis, transmuted into a hereditary disease, is a common cause of mortality over eighty. All in all the life-span is only five or ten years longer than what it is during our time, say seventy-seven years for men, eighty-four or eighty-five for women. Perhaps this is tragic, but perhaps it is not; there is no way that humanity would ever have been able to deal with the social chaos produced by a greatly extended life-span or practical immortality; the systems in which men have always lived are geared to common mortality tables as are the institutions.

Indeed, most of the dead embalmed in the hold were merely in their sixties or seventies. There is irrelevant irony in the fact that man can have at least established peripheral colonies through sections of the Milky Way, can travel through most of it, can have solved the mysteries of the FTL drive and constructed such a craft as *Skipstone* and yet finds his own biology as stupefying and mysterious as he did in Elizabethan times. But, then, every sociologist understands that those who live in a culture are least qualified to judge it, because they have so fully assimilated the codes of the culture that they are unable to be objective, and Lena does not see this irony any more than it is necessary for the reader to in order to appreciate the deeper and more metaphysical irony of *Galaxies*. Which is this:

That greater speed, greater space, greater progress, greater sensation has not resulted in any real expansion of the limits of consciousness and personality...and that Lena, much less than appreciating the wonders of the FTL drive, merely perceives it as a form of further entrapment and delimitation.

(This is a familiar theme in my work: that the expansion of technology will only delimit consciousness, create greater feelings of alienation, impotence, hopelessness and so on, and that the neurological/psychological equipment of our species is programmed to record sensations equally alien in the stars or on the sea. Although many literary critics and philosophers tend toward this vision, most science-fiction readers or writers do not, since science fiction is about control, not dysfunction. Still, I beg your various indulgences, pointing out that, even if matters are not hopeless, writing *about* hopelessness may serve cautionary ends just as the sermons of John Calvin enabled Puritans of the seventeenth century to better appreciate their lot on Earth. I am doing the best I can, just as each of you is doing the best you can, and I am as much in awe of *Skipstone* as is Lena; in fact my awe is greater than hers, since *Skipstone* is my creation.)

# 10

Lena is merely a technician. Let us not misunderstand this; it is crucial. Although she is highly skilled and has been trained by Bureau personnel for many years, she really does not need to possess much more than the knowledge of any graduate physicist of her time. Her role, which is essentially to maintain the ship on its preselected course and respond to computer check-out, could be done by any of our own astronauts; could, in fact, be done by anyone capable of flying a single-engine plane. The nature of the investment, however, has demanded that Lena be intellectually qualified far beyond the true demands of her job, and this leads to boredom, depression and further alienation, the Bureau not understanding in the fortieth century what NASA does not understand now: that there is no one happier than he or she who is in a position utilizing fullest capacity; no one more prone to depression and incompetence than the overqualified.

Lena is doing it for the money, to be sure. It is the only rational motive with which she can live. Certainly she is not an idealist. No idealist would study for a decade in order to take on cargo of the dead.

When she is finished with this latest probe, three months hence, she has decided that she will return to her quarters on Uranus and request a six-month leave. She is entitled to it, and surely the Bureau will not object; after her debriefing is concluded, it cannot hold her. She will not be denied and she will insist upon the leave. She is only twenty-eight, as young or a little younger in her culture than she would be in ours, and she does not like having been sent with the dead to tumble through the spectrum of the tachyons for weeks at a time. She would like to be, at least for a while now, a young woman. She would like to be at peace. She would like to be taken for herself and not merely as a lever of FTL manipulation. She would not mind being loved. She would not mind a physical relationship. Her needs are the needs of any of you.

Saying that Lena "would not mind a physical relationship," which is a delicate way of saying for the category market that she would enjoy some sex, means that we must confront the element of sex in this novel if only because it deals with a female protagonist. Culture is culture, Ti-Grace to the contrary, and readers would not stand for the idea of asepsis with a young woman, although they would not be similarly suspicious if Lena were an attractive young man. Still, this is *modern, literary* science fiction where some credence is given to the entire inferred range of human needs and desires. One cannot ignore the issue of the sexuality of the protagonist.

And the easy scenes could be included and to stunning literary effect; perhaps in the final draft they might be. The writer could win high marks for his poetic vision if not his subtlety. Lena masturbating as she stares through the porthole at the colored levels of hyperspace, that space a series of steps that seem to lead her, twitch by twitch upon the lever of the clitoris to the very altar of self. Lena dreaming thickly of intercourse, as deep in sleep she massages her nipples, the ship plunging deeper this instant (as she could not possibly know) toward the black galaxy, the black galaxy itself some sort of ultimate vaginal symbol whose Freudian overcast would not be ignored in the imagery of the novel as it has been ignored in the imagery of little modern science fiction. Indeed one can envision Lena stumbling toward the evictors at the depths of her panic in the black galaxy as she tries to bring out one of the dead, struggling with it in the blocks, her grim and necrophiliac fantasies as the body moves slowly on its glistening slab, the way her eyes would look as she slowly comes to the awareness that, through the devices of autoeroticism, she has become one of the dead, indistinguishable from the body that is risen...oh, this could be a powerful scene indeed; almost anything having to do with sex in space is powerful, and one must conjure also with the possible effects of hyperspace upon the orgasm. I would face the issue unintimidated and in line with the use to which the novel can place powerful and effective dialogue.

Dialogue:

"For God's sake," Lena would say at the end, the music of her entrapment squeezing, coming over her, rending her toward extinction, "for God's sake, all that we ever sought was sex, that was what must have sent us into the tiers of space as well, that was all space ever meant to us, another level of extension. I've got to have it, do you understand?"

"Oh, yes," her partner, perhaps the dead itself would say, "I agree with you; you've got to have it."

"Then give it to me!"

"Oh, I will," her partner would say thoughtfully, "I will give it to you, but then think of sex being the life-force and representing so many other things. Are you *sure* you want it? You had better think this through very carefully."

"You're mad," she says, "you are mad; I'm pleading for you."

"But what are you pleading for?" her partner says, moving slowly; "unless you know, I'm afraid that I had better not cooperate; I wouldn't want to give you what you think you're seeking only for you to learn that all of this was a lie; we can't be lied to; we have got to face the truth now," lying across her, odors coming in little whiffs from his body, which is, of course, utterly corrupt, the cryonic factor being lock to death rather than its obliteration. "I'd like to do it very much you understand; I agree with you that this may be the only freedom that we can find—"

"Must you talk?"

"But of course! Inexhaustibly. It may be our only freedom, but I can't quite give it to you. I can't give you what you want. I'm not quite right you see," he would point out, his wasted little limbs like the wings of a ruined bird fluttering upon her. "Terribly sorry."

"Sorry?"

"Yes, surely, but after all you are demanding more than you can possibly be given. You are—"

"No," she would say, "no, I don't want to hear your excuses, don't want to hear any of that at all. It does no good, it excuses nothing, get inside me, get inside me, damn it! Don't you understand this is the only thing we ever wanted?" seizing his wasted organs, dropping them with disgust as she sees them like a pendulum hung within her hand, giving up then and pushing him away with revulsion to jam her fingers instead through her aqueous surfaces, slippery and waiting, opening up the walls to the image of a culmination that if she could only touch she could have then, swimming through the surfaces of the self, but the nearer she gets to it the further seems the climax, and not only that but there is something else wrong, something nagging at the periphery of realization, if she could only touch it—

Well, if she could touch it, then she would, but this is not the direction that the novel would take, at least in the present conceptualization. Attempts at poetry fall into the pornographic tumble, one variety of pulp becomes another, organs are substituted for machinery and the center takes hold of all. Say it and be done then: space *is* asepsis; it cancels differences, renders sexuality barren. That has been the secret of the power of science fiction for almost fifty years. It is not deceit or its adolescent audience or publication codes or difficult editors which have deprived our literature of the range of human sexuality, but the fact that in the clean and abysmal spaces between the stars, sex, that demonstration of our perverse and irreplaceable humanity, would have no role at all. For we are not human out there in any way which can join with another; our humanity, frail at best, is fully concentrated within ourselves to defend ourselves against the void.

Consider. It was not casual that our astronauts returned to give us their vision of otherworldliness, not casual that they staggered in their thick landing gear as they came under the salute on board, not casual that White screamed on his space walk and begged to return to the capsule or Carpenter shouted *get me out of here!* Not for nothing did all of those marriages, all of those wonderful kids undergo such terrible strains as many went undersea or toward poetry, hypnosis, transcendental meditation. Sex was squeezed out of them up there and many have not yet recovered. It does not fit. It will never occupy any meaningful role in all of the history of space travel.

Lena knows this. Somewhere toward the end of the novel she would in fact come to terms. "I never thought of sex," she would say, "never thought of it once, not even at the very end when everything was exploding around me and I was falling."

Naturally when we speak of the absence of sex at this time we are dealing only with the faster-than-light craft and their solitary voyagers; the conventional ferry ships, those that take people at sublight speeds from planet to planet, from star to star within the galaxies, are populated by the ordinary voyagers of their time and like ordinary voyagers of any time, they couple randomly or otherwise, stare through the portholes and think of their wasted lives, perform their hasty scuttling in the dark. In all cultures at any stage of their history, sex will be important, but it does not seem to have anything to do with the opening of new frontiers, which is, of course, Lena's mission and which will similarly be the mission of this novel.

Thirty-nine zero two. There has yet been no contact with intelligent extraterrestrial life, although humanity has colonized many planets and investigated several thousand more. This seeming exclusivity of human intelligence baffles cosmologists and mathematicians while pleasing the theologians; perhaps humanity is unique in the universe, perhaps by the laws of chance it is to be expected that, in nearly two thousand years of exploration, contact with an intelligence other than our own in a limitless universe would be highly unlikely. Bovine animals found on a planet of Sirius have turned out to have an intelligence close to that of birds and are the most intelligent race yet encountered, but these animals—called Sirians by the uninventive colonists—have enough xenophobia to be dying off slowly, their grazing culture succumbing to fires which the colonists have set for the purposes of atmospheric balance. It would be nice to compound the myth of faster-than-light drive with deeper and richer myths of strange races amidst the great stars, but this cannot be.

The farther humanity voyages, then, the more it seems merely to confront itself. At least this is the point of view which *Galaxies* will take. This is merely one of a set of alternatives. One could write colorful chapters about the many strange, civilized races colonists have encountered, all of them celebrative of man and his works, except for those few misguided who would fight him and so would have to be destroyed. That would be polemic, however. Despite the excesses of my youth, polemic has no place even in a science-fiction novel. Leave those innocent races alone. Upon investigation they would be found out to be not so damned innocent at all. Too, the higher the level of innocence, the more room there is for corruption.

# 14

Because of the asepsis and the fact that she is alone on the ship when the novel opens and there are no intelligent aliens, it will be necessary to obtain characterization for Lena, definable idiosyncrasy, in some other fashion. Some channel then, will have to be found to trigger conflict and color and that opportunity will come only through the moment of crisis, that moment at which *Skipstone* is drawn slowly into the black galaxy of the neutron star.

Now this moment will occur fairly early into the novel. Perhaps only eight or nine thousand words of expository material will precede the disaster. There will be a shade of exposition in which the spectra of hyperspace are interwoven with Lena's fantasy and then, her only indication a quiver in the gut of the ship, *Skipstone* will fall. It will fall for twenty-five billion miles with its load of the dead and its screaming pilot. It will fall not only through space, but also through time, but of time Lena will know nothing at all, only of her pain and her astonishment.

To explain why she screams during the fall, it is important to explain hyperspace. To Lena the tachyonic drive is merely to draw the curtains across the portholes and to be in a cubicle. There is no cessation of motion in hyperspace; there could not possibly be, the drive taking the ship past any concept of light or motion and into an area where there is no language to encompass nor glands to register. Were Lena to draw these curtains (similar in their frills and pastels to what at one time hung in the author's own familial home), she would be deprived of any sensation; but of course she cannot; she must open them to the portholes and through them she can then see the song of the colors.

Inside, in tachyonic drive, there is for Lena a deep and painful wretchedness, a feeling of terrible loss not unlike the emotions of the unknowing and invisible dead which may be ascribed to the effects of hyperspace upon the psyche. But these sensations can be shielded. They are not visible from the outside and can be completely controlled by the phlegmatic personalities who comprise most of the pilots of these interstellar flights. Lena herself is phlegmatic. She reacts more to stress than do some of her counterparts, but she is well within the normal range prescribed by the Bureau, which, it must be admitted, tends to do a rather superficial job of profiling.

But phlegmatic or not, contained or not, the effects of falling into the black galaxy are entirely different from the hyperspace in which *Skipstone* "normally" dwells, and it is here where Lena's emotional equipment comes apart.

# 15

And it is here where the *writer's* emotional equipment begins to come apart as well; the writer, no mere engine of creation, has his own problems with which to deal. His powers fail, likewise his will, his desire, a welter of personal difficulties which are rightfully no concern of the reader (do not worry about them) similarly overwhelm. He is exploited by a series of weaknesses which his own novels savagely probe and exploit the way that a surgeon's cunning tool might burst rather than remove a cyst. The writer's background in physics is slight, his astronomy shaky, his astronautics shakier yet nor does he grasp chemistry. He has a certain feeling for the scientific spirit, but surely this cannot carry him through. What he lacks is that systematized and rigorous grasp of the hard sciences which the novel will have to utilize in order to succeed, and the writer cannot rely, at least this one time, upon his stylistic gifts to carry him through.

The writer's stylistic gifts are notable. Even he will testify to that. For many years he has been able to write in the style and vision of almost any writer living or preferably dead: he is a skillful parodist, a creator of pastiche so smooth as to be almost undetectable from the original. He has access to rhetorical tricks and devices which have time and again enabled him to force his way through a difficult novel on technique alone. From publisher to publisher the writer has carried his little carnival with its cheap masks, greasepaint, assortment of mirrors and depressed freaks; even when the spirit has failed him yea unto the very sinuses, his magic and revolving light shows, with the energetic cooperation of his freaks, never have. But for reasons which the writer cannot quite understand—is it possible that he has been smitten by artistic integrity?—he does not want magic and revolving freak and light show inc. to perform its wondrous if somewhat mechanical convolutions this time. He would like to do this novel the difficult way, which is to say upon the basis of its rather awesome and terrible concept, but he does not know if he has the courage, he does not know if he can summon the will to work on his research base or even to command the material. He is not sure, like Lena herself, that he belongs in a project of this sort at all, and therefore only with much moaning and groaning does he address himself to the task which this one time he will not write himself out of but into…and courage, he has decided, has nothing to do with this at all. Ignore everything above. Courage is facing a man with a gun or protecting your wife against attack or risking your job to protest policies you despise or running a mile in three fifty-seven flat when the heart seems turned to ashes. Nothing to do with the writing of fiction, particularly science fiction, has anything to do with courage. Do not let anyone tell you otherwise. Most science-fiction writers are drunks and almost all of them have unhappy lives. A, B and C.

# 16

The *Skipstone* falls into the black galaxy. Needed here are great gobs of physics; astronautic and mathematical data must likewise be transmitted. If they are not, *Galaxies* would be a space romance, a work of fantasy, and this is no fantasy at all. The heavy-science data must be furnished in a way, however, which will illuminate the reader without repelling him.

In traditional literature this is not so easy, in science fiction it never is quite so difficult. A science-fiction writer does not have to worry as much as a literary writer about repelling his audience by trying to teach it. Readers of this genre *expect* to be bored; in fact they are seeking boredom as a means of release from too much self-confrontation. They *want* bad writing as well, because bad writing does not energize; it makes almost no one (except stuffy critics and jealous fellow writers) uncomfortable. Science-fiction readers, thus, will sit for a lecture much more willingly than would, say, the sophisticated readers of the esteemed John Cheever who could hardly bear sociological diatribes spliced into those already difficult landscapes. Thus it would be possible without awkwardness or the need to dramatize to put down a hard body of facts, and these facts could indeed be set off from the novel. They would be a separate chapter.

Through all of the time that these facts are being articulated, Lena is in the black galaxy, stunned and suffering, and this is certainly too bad for her, but life is cruel, art is everlasting, one must treat characters cruelly in order to make a point. They are, after all, constructions; they have no existence. A writer with compassion for his characters is a writer without guile or control, uninterested in the truth. Fictional characters must be manipulated coldly; they permit this, having no choice. Would that this were true for all characters and not those merely confined to the contract between writer and reader.

In some of the myriad galaxies which revolve through the known portion of the universe, a universe which is either finite, expanding or circular (the debate continues in 3902; perceptions of the size of the universe have expanded through the millennia, but there are those who say that a limit has been found), there exist phenomena known as neutron stars.

Neutron stars, several hundred times the size of "average" stars such as Sol or Sirius, must, because of their gigantic dimension, create and consume energy at a fearsome rate of atomic combustion merely to sustain themselves. In this sense, neutron stars, like all heavenly constructions, are sentient: they fight for self-preservation in the way that our near planets fight for life by spinning faster than those distant; if they did not do so, they would fall into the Sun and be consumed. So does the neutron star ferociously consume its energy.

But as the energy is being eaten away by the violence of combustion, so it must run out, and for this reason the neutron star will collapse in a mere ten to fifteen thousand years as opposed to the hundreds of millions which a "normal" star will have...and as that neutron star reaches the end of its cycle, its hydrogen fuses to helium, then nitrogen and even heavier elements, the atoms grabbing stray electrons in a frantic attempt to maintain atomic reaction, and then with an implosion of cosmic force, all power gone, the neutron star collapses upon itself.

All is disaster.

Ah, the lamentations of Jeremiah! It is not merely that the dying neutron stars destroy themselves, collapsing inward at the speed of light, layers of gases crowding, grappling with one another, falling into that diminished core...that is a pretty enough sight in itself—we may see it in our spectroscopes and telescopes as the nova—but this is merely the beginning of what the neutron star, ending, can do. For it can destroy the galaxy by which it was enveloped.

The gravitational force created by this implosion would be so vast as to literally seal in light. Small planets have slight gravity, larger objects heavier; the gravity on Jupiter greatly exceeds that of our Earth...but how much greater than Jupiter's is Sol's, how much greater than Sol's the gravity of massive Antares into which almost all of our solar system in its orbit would fit? And the neutron star, which could contain five or ten thousand Antares before its collapse, could create a gravity which would overcome all speeds presently understood. Light travels at a hundred and eighty-six thousand miles per second. That might not be sufficient to escape from the ruined core.

And not only light. Sound, heat, the properties of all the stars would be sucked into that great tube of force. The galaxy itself might be drawn into the funnel of gravitation created by the collapse and be absorbed slowly into the flickering and desperate heart of the extinguished star.

# 18

Most of this theory would be news to Lena, of course. Even two thousand years in the future. She is not a theorist but a technician, and as the *Skipstone* begins its descent into the black galaxy, all that she would know would be pain, but it would be pain of such dimension that she would not have the language for it, a pain so profound that it might be interpreted as pleasure or as any one of a hundred other things. Tumbling, tumbling, as the animal in the center claws for her.

# 19

The existence of neutron stars and their disastrous outcome would make several extrapolations reasonable. Of the existence of these stars there is no doubt; they are being dealt with (along with ruined celebrities and the politics of Mozambique and the political fallout of the radical middle) in our most prominent Sunday supplements. The articles on which the astronomic theory of *Galaxies* is in part based are in themselves based upon a body of theory which has been widely accepted as a result of the researches of the last decade.

Just a few extrapolations follow:

*One:* The gravitational forces created by the implosion would, like great spokes wheeling from the star, drag in all sections of the galaxy within their compass, and because of the force of that gravitation, the galaxy would be invisible. Gravitation would contain light. Hit a certain section of space as has *Skipstone* where nothing has been mapped and find a galaxy. Galaxies themselves, of course, are merely interruptions in the lightless canvas of the universe.

*Two:* The neutron star, functioning as a cosmic vacuum cleaner (all right, this is homey imagery but then good science fiction should make the mysterious, the terrible, the inviolable as comfortable and accessible as one's own possessions, just as pornography should make the fires of sex little more than a twitch, easily untwitched, in the familiarly tumescent genitalia), might literally destroy the universe. *The entire universe*. Indeed, the universe may be in the process at this moment of being broken down as hundreds of millions of its planets and their suns are being inexorably drawn in the mesh of their galaxies toward the great vortices of the neutron stars. It would be a slow process, to be sure; here one is talking about many billions of years...but one is also talking about a span of time that may someday be measured in finite terms and which thus gives inexorable cast to all human endeavor.

("Hey, Joe, look at this! The print-out says that in two billion, three hundred and fifty-two million years and change the universe is going to be destroyed!")

("Let me look at that, Tom. Hey, this is frightening! This is terrible news but it all seems to check out.")

("We'd better tell the President. We'd better go right in there now and tell him.")

("No. Wait.")

("What?")

("I said wait, Tom. I do not know if they can handle information like this at the present time.")

("It is our obligation.")

("Our obligation to what? Make science a mere servant of the state? No...we must conform to a higher ethic.")

("Only two billion, three hundred and fifty-two million to go. I don't know what to say. Only that...only that we'll miss it all terribly.")

A single neutron star, at least theoretically, could absorb the universe given limitless time and of that there would be nothing in the universe as we know it. There are quite a few neutron stars.

*Three:* But, then, the universe may have, looking at it the other way, been *created* by such an implosion, that implosion throwing out enormous cosmic filaments, which in flickering instants of time which are as eons to us but mere instants to the cosmologists, are now being drawn in like a child's paddle ball extended on a rubber string, now falling back. Those filaments lead to the neutron star. The galaxies may be a by-product of the implosion; existence as we know it may be an accidental offshoot, an interruption in the cycle controlled by the neutron star whose creation and expulsion are the true ordering force of the universe.

This would either cancel vanity or make it stronger.

*Four:* Consider this astronautically for a moment, ignoring questions of cosmology. A ship trapped in such a vortex, such a black or invisible galaxy, drawn toward the deadly source of the neutron star, would be unable to leave through normal faster-than-light drive; because the gravitation would absorb light it would be impossible to build up through acceleration to escape velocity. (Accelerative velocities are sub-faster-than-light.) If it were then possible to emerge from the field, it could be done so only by an immediate switch to the tachyonic drive without acceleration. This is a process which could well drive the occupants of the ship insane and which would, in any case, give no clear destination. At the point of breakout the flight would be uncontrollable. The black hole of the dead star is a literal vacuum in space. One could fall through the hole but where, then, where would one go?

And when? To what time?

*Five:* The mere process of *falling* toward the dead star would be a state incomprehensible to current understanding of biophysics or chronology. It would certainly make one insane.

# 20

So one can understand now why Lena would not know that *Skipstone* had fallen into the black galaxy until, with no sense of transition, she would simply be there. Not that anticipation would have done her much good. There is literally no way to plan for events like this. One cannot create vectors for madness.

# 21

These fragments of technological data having been stated, the crisis of the novel—the fall into the black galaxy—having already occurred, it would be necessary in terms of a smoothly plotted story line with a rising level of excitement to describe then the actual sensations incurred by *Skipstone*'s entrapment in the field of the neutron star.

This is not unreasonable. Science fiction, after all, is all that most of us will ever be able to know of the technological wonders of the future, and although it is true that the majority of us are not *interested* in the future, having more than we can handle, mostly, in coming to terms with the unspeakable present, there is a small and dedicated group of readers to whom the future has at least as much meaning as their circumstances and these, the science-fiction audience for the most part, should not be disappointed. One would not want to skimp on the details. Even at its relatively low word rates, and this must be understood, they are quite low in relation to the amount of invention needed and time expended, science fiction in the hands of its best writers has always been a generous medium, offering more detail than would strictly speaking be necessary from the standpoint of mere plotting, of simple manipulation of characters through obstacles. Indeed, science fiction often suffers from the weakness of too much background, too little foreground, skimping of characterization in favor of unassimilated futurological details, but at this point the construct hints at breaking down into a series of grumbling little essays about the state of the art and this is not the author's intention.

I will resist this. Polemic, after all, is not fiction nor does fiction serve didactic purposes and remain art, and the author's opinions, artistic or polemical alike, are worthless; only his ability to transmute them through the material matters, and this is the contract with the reader. He will not be led away from *Skipstone* (not far, anyhow), the author will stay with the point, the novel will be science fiction and not merely *about* science fiction, and if the reader will stay around, I promise a smooth and satisfying read containing effortless little blocks of scientific data which will be of personal use. A little hard fact is by no evidence dangerous; it may be the last legitimate refuge of those of us who would still espouse—as does your suffering, tormented, lecherous and self-pitying author—the colorful tenets of Calvinism.

I would use, then, a surrealistic mode to describe Lena's descent into the galaxy. Conceive of what is happening now as *Skipstone* is gathered to that palm and crushed like sand downward: she sees, perhaps, grotesques slithering in dimensions on the walls, monsters that are really little recoveries of her past, plastered there in descent. Watching them whirl in pattern, scuttle on the bulkheads, she could reenact her life in full consciousness from birth to death, the grotesques merely being triggering projections of events from her history. She could indeed be turned inside out anatomically; she could perform in her imagination or in the flesh gross physical acts upon herself; she could live or die a thousand times in the lightless, timeless expanse of the pit...all of this could be done within the confines of this one section, the descent toward the neutron star. It would lead to some powerful insights if only properly handled.

One could do it in many ways. Picaresque would be a possibility, an episodic framework one should say, one perversity or lunacy to a chapter, the chapters interwoven with flatter, more expository sections on the gravitational effects, the biochemistry of descent, the physics of the force field. For instance, there might be a point at which Lena could take herself to be back in training, preparing for the ordeal of *Skipstone*.

In only a little while, she thinks, she will be responsible for the great ship and for its cargo of the dead, but now, staggering from the tube of the simulator, her vision is somewhat more limited. She sees the man who is responsible for her training, a man whom we will call John. Slightly disoriented, nauseated from the experiments, she finds herself speaking to him in a way that she has never before. "Why the dead?" she says. She moves her hands across the slate of cheekbones, whoops with little convulsions of nausea. "Why must we carry the dead?"

"There are many reasons."

"Tell me. Tell me one. Why must I take death into the stars when the stars were to bring us life?"

"Because it is the dead who have paid for much of this," John says, holding her tentatively. He is a wise and embittered man who believes that it is necessary for him to see and tell the truth at all times, and for these reasons he lives in great pain because his is not a truthful culture. "Without the moneys that are paid from the great trusts of the dead to make possible this first stage of their revival, they would be unable to finance the probes."

"It's not right."

"The conditions are stringent. The ultraviolet will restore them, with other things, to life someday. It is fortunate that their needs and ours have so meshed."

"But it is not right," Lena says, "it's not right; the dead are the dead and should not be tied to life. And what happens if something goes wrong in space? Am I responsible for all of them, then? What will become of me?"

"Waivers," John says. "There are careful and complete waivers which are signed, Lena; you can be sure of that. All will be taken care of."

He takes her, then, from the simulating crate, trying to ease her toward calm with many little pats and touches on her back, but Lena moves from him and says, "I don't want to travel with the dead. I can't bear it to feel that they're all in there with me."

"They have no consciousness."

"They're still *dead*." Old fears and revulsions—the word is atavism, I suppose—persist.

"They are merely cargo."

"Cargo is cargo but these were people once."

"Lena, the costs of this are more enormous than anyone can grasp. The dead at least subsidize a little part of it, make it that much easier. Is it their fault that this is for them another opportunity to live again someday? Lena, we will all be dead someday. Are you prepared to say what you will do?"

She shakes her head. "I'm not going to be dead for a long time," she says, "but if I were to die now, I would accept it; I would not take down the living."

"How do you know?"

"I *know*," she says, "I know what I am, what I would do; you have no right to say that I don't," and she then goes on to explain to John in a lucid fashion that makes a good deal of sense why this is so: why she cannot bear the presence of the dead on what she takes to be (she believes this if only to sustain her own mood) a mission that is life-seeking, but as she tries to explain this in a level, reasonable tone to John, something opens darkly within her, restraint vanishes and she is weeping convulsively against him.

John makes brusque, useless little gestures across her arms and shoulders, hoping that he will not break down himself and cry with her and for the *Skipstone,* for the dead in space. If he were to do this, he knows, he would never stop, that single lunge of feeling would take him all the way over the precipice of detachment and he would be gone forever; no good for Lena either; he must take care of her and so he gets hold of himself, swaddling Lena against him, leading her away from there under the confused gaze of other, less senior technicians who cannot possibly imagine the meaning of this scene but know that something has happened to their pilot and to their supervisor which will change the course of all preparations. Except that in this world nothing changes.

# 22

No, the technicians are wrong again; anyone who functions under the supposition of change surrounding these experiments would be wrong. The schedule for the mission is as rigorous and controlled as any of our own countdowns. So diabolically cunning are those in this Bureau of 3902 that they have even programmed into the countdown emotional breakdowns of the minor sort which Lena has just experienced, which has so unsettled John. (They have worked up the psychometrics; they know there will be no major breakdowns.) Not only the engineering but personalities have been taken into account by the cunning and nearly omniscient Bureau so that, while Lena and John feel that they have undergone a series of reactions, they are merely enacting what the psychologists had long since forecast as a momentary stress-tremor. Nothing that they have done since the beginning of training, not even the hasty and uncertain intercourse which they now undertake in the sterile cell of Lena's quarters, is not charted by the Bureau.

Of course Lena would like to feel that it is. If she were to know that her sudden coupling with John was part of her program and that the

Bureau has calculated it almost to the minute of entrance, if John were to know that he occupies his position as training superior only because he has been judged most likely to give Lena a satisfactory sexual recollection to hold to herself in the void, both of them would be overcome with revulsion and their plotted coupling would not have taken place. They would have sprung from one another.

For these reasons the Bureau tries to make its involvement in the lives of its principals as subtle as possible, although every now and then, particularly in the matter of monitoring—on which it is adamant—its true impulse to control can be glimpsed. Still, who can blame it? From the vantage point of 1975, none of us can comprehend the forces which made it this way. The future of humanity, or so their computers and technicians hold, is dependent on the outcome of these FTL experiments. Unless the tachyonic drive can be used by the hundreds of thousands sent routinely voyaging to colonize, unless the space of *Skipstone* can someday, much enlarged, shield inexperienced travelers from the horrors of hyperdrive, humanity will remain confined to its precarious hold only upon portions of the Milky Way. The tachyons must work. The flight must be accomplished. The investment in *Skipstone* and in Lena is absolute.

So who is to begrudge these two or the Bureau their desperate moments of communion in her quarters? Not now; not these two. Certainly not the author who here would bring out his rhetorical arsenal to prove that sex in the future is very much the same as sex in the present or past. (This kind of approach is very reassuring to readers of science fiction, to say nothing of the author himself who has the feeling that he has been missing something most of his life.) And then, too, the author has a wicked hand with a sex scene, always did, is a master of the pornographic literary or the literary pornographic, depending upon your point of view.

"Oh, my God, you must do it to me," Lena would shriek, a little floridly, but floridity under stress is one of her more charming habits; she becomes more rather than less dignified when excited and indulges in archaisms of speech. "You must do it to me quickly, you must do it to me now, you must penetrate me swiftly to the core and make me close upon you in the arc of my need," her nipples bursting like little flowers, or, more in tune with the material, one might say that they are the dull purple of methane. "I want it now, I really do want it now, John; you have got to give it to me, for I cannot, truly cannot stand it anymore," and John, grunting not only with need but with a reluctance which he has always felt with her, finds her desirable, yet there is something within her that he cannot touch, something which he thinks of as eternally *measuring*, moves toward the task, poised on his knees, running his hands over the slab of her body, his flesh seeming to retract as nevertheless he covers the pilot of *Skipstone* and begins to move upon her slowly, unrhythmically, pausing now and then to wipe his streaming brow with a veined, competent supervisor's hand. Silent during sex—the clinical opposite of Lena, he finds himself speechless during the act, performing it in a reverent manner—he nevertheless conducts an interior monologue. I don't know why I'm doing this, he thinks; I can't imagine what the point of this is; it isn't having her for the meaning of the act but only to satisfy something within her, and he comes close in that instant to an understanding of the uses to which the Bureau has put them, but he pushes this away, not able, as he never will be, to confront what the Bureau has made of him. But I must do it, I must do the best for her that I can because, well, because that is what is expected of me and I must always meet my obligations. He is obsessed with the thought that his obligations must be fulfilled; in a simpler age he would have been a slave to duty.

"Oh, now it is coming," Lena says, "it is coming upon me hard and fast, I can feel it growing within, do not abandon me now nor let me fail, but rather penetrate me more deeply, more darkly, until at last suspension is over and all is done." John, not unwillingly, humps and jumps over her, rising and sinking to various heights and depths, the surfaces of his body gleaming with the honesty of his efforts as underneath Lena begins to twitch and contract. "Here it is," she says, "here it is now and now and now and known again," and, in a falling scream, goes into her small and at last silent spasms which are all that she will ever know of pleasure, nipples gleaming, teeth gleaming, eyes flat and widened, and she climaxes with a groan, reaches her hands toward him, puts her fingers in his shoulders as if she were adjusting various levers shipside and sets off again. Patiently, doing the best that he can, John stalks her.

If these passages give the impression that Lena is not attractive, they have been poorly handled, because the fact is that she is quite beautiful. The aesthetic standards of this age are very close to those of our own, history tending to reenact itself more often than not, history having an impoverished invention, and Lena would certainly compare well with a movie star of the late 1950s to the middle 1960s, before anachronisms invaded our own life cycle. She has huge breasts, a tiny waist, full lips, lush thighs, large nipples which stand up under the most superficial kind of titillation.... She is, in sum, wildly attractive in terms of those sexual obsessions which framed the author, and perhaps a few of his fantasies have slid into the confrontation here.

The author is not being prurient. I can no more imagine myself having intercourse with Lena than I could conceive of myself as being in *Skipstone*; it is all detached in the extreme. I am not one of those writers whose creations become so vital to him that he literally laughs, weeps, argues, confers with them. My literary influences are more Russian than Mediterranean, so to speak, and I can therefore derive only the slightest prurient feedback from the depiction of Lena.

Nor, the contract with the reader being firm, is this description for prurient release upon the reader either. The author has other and far easier devices of arousal and so, for that matter, do his publishers; I refer you to the rack of books slightly to the right of here and above eye level if you are seeking an easy release and good luck to you as well; I have surely been there myself in one guise or another. No, Lena's beauty is more cleansing than sensual; she is one of those women who induce reverence rather than lust, at least with the majority of partners, and I can offer no better evidence of this than how little pleasure John is really obtaining from sex with her. This is a profound commentary not only upon his character—which is in many ways more interesting than hers and it is a pity, accordingly, that he is a minor figure in this novel—but upon the society from which both of them have evolved. For here sex is little more than a medium of social exchange, an extension of the contract which all humans make with one another to give no pain, at least superficially, unless forced, and far more could be read into this coupling than is truly there. Sex is not that important in the fortieth century, although it's important enough to make possible even here, even then, their own kind of pornography.

Regardless. John is able at last to achieve his orgasm; with a whine and cry so feeble that he might be a child, he tumbles in and out of her, falls away so that Lena, clutching at him, still seeking that last lunge of his which will touch off her final satisfaction (but she will not find it and would not have found it if he had stayed atop her for an hour), gives a bleat of anguish as he revolves upon the pallet to look through the dome and then, putting her disappointment aside, turns onto her own back. She is a controlled woman, she has a sense of proportion about these matters and knows the triviality of seeking orgasm.

"I'm afraid of the dead," she says.

It is as if they have not copulated at all She merely picks up on the conversation. "I'm frightened of them," she says again as if John had argued with her. "I have a right to feel that way if I want."

"You shouldn't be."

"I don't want to go with them. They have no right to make them cargo."

"They become companions in space," John says. These are indeed the reports brought back by commanders of the other FTL craft, that at times they feel that they are close to the dead, that there is a true communion, space being so alien that living and dead are more possessed of the humanity that once touched them than separated by mortality. "If anything you will be glad to have them there. And if things get too bad you have the prostheses to keep you company, to talk to."

John wonders vaguely why he is arguing this point with Lena. Any pilot who so resists the conditions of the voyage should be relieved of the command; that is the policy that he would adopt if he had any true influence. He does not, however; he is merely another functionary of the Bureau and the Bureau's dictates are quite clear, have been explained to him: it is absolutely imperative that Lena take the *Skipstone*. Too much has been invested in her for command to be shifted now.

"That's the other thing," she is saying. "The prostheses *aren't* company. Metallic frames. Machines which work on tape. They're horrible."

"But they have the personalities and the memories of some very wonderful people, skilled technicians, counselors, advisors, supportive people who can—"

"That doesn't matter. They're still machines. Dead and machines in space; that's all that they give me."

"Lena," John says, although this disturbs him, too; he has long thought that the craft should be dual-controlled even though the Bureau insists that the costs and the intrapersonal tensions would be unmanageable, "they can't send more than one live person into space. That's always been the case. The support systems would not carry more than one person. Within those limits, Bureau is trying their best." He is careful to say *Bureau*. Under normal role-provisions he would say *we*, but increasingly John is separating himself from the Bureau in his mind. He does not agree with how it has handled Lena's preparations. More than before, he is severely disturbed by what he feels to be a lack of comprehension on its part of her real anguish, an anguish he is beginning to apprehend. "They want you to be happy."

"But I'm not happy."

"Happiness is not that necessary," John says reasonably. "No one empowers us to be happy; it is not part of your training, not part of our life. All that is necessary is that you be able to handle the circumstances of the voyage and in that regard Bureau has done its best."

"I know that," she says a little sullenly, "I know that; I realize what you're saying, but it isn't fair, John, it just isn't right," and she goes on then to make certain statements about the Bureau, express certain opinions of what she thinks it has made the true purpose of her mission which are perhaps best excluded from the text of the novel since they are, let us understand this, merely the paranoid outpourings of a young woman who is under a good deal of strain, who possesses only modest intellectual gifts and whose emotional state has begun to buckle under the impact of the voyage and her realization of its importance. If there were anything useful in these meanderings, the author would be the first to put them down (and John, he says to himself, would be the first to report them to the Bureau; he would have no choice; he would have to tell them everything because that is his responsibility, but he does not think that there is anything significant here; he wishes to believe that).

Also beside the point would be text on what happens later, how John and Lena in these last days before the flight of *Skipstone* stumble into a slightly deeper emotional relationship, how John manages to find her desirable after all, how certain commitments are stressed in their final coupling which, although instantly forgotten the day the ship departs, are taken very seriously by both at the time that they are said.

And, since it falls outside Lena's point of view, it will not be necessary to describe John's uneasy relationship with the Bureau, the careful reports he hands it almost daily, the intimate and terrible nature of his confessions. To probe his mind superficially is one thing, but to reproduce these confessions is quite another. In order to approach the material, I would have to use full multiple point of view—a largely discredited technique which can only work in odd snippets and flashes—or worse yet the archaic, omniscient author, and although there has been a little of both here, *Galaxies* really needs a more intense focus, a narrowing. Multiple points of view are obviously unacceptable.

Suffice it to say that John omits discussion of Lena's mental state from his reports, that the Bureau, in any case, files those reports without reading, keeping them merely as a procedural hedge against *Skipstone*'s failure so that there will be someone to blame. It would be John's fault for not reporting emotional or psychic inadequacies to his superiors, the Bureau would say. John feels somewhat guilty for omitting the many disturbing things that Lena has said, but this guilt is hardly to the point where he would leave anything out of the reports that he felt the Bureau really ought to know. Instead he discusses her sexual behavior, material which he knows has never failed to interest the clerks. (He would be most distressed to know that nothing interests the clerks and that his reports are unread.)

Of Lena's relationship with John little more will be made of here, but it is one of those details which come upon her as she relives her life while falling into the neutron star and should be included on that account. By no means has the material been incorporated for the sake of prurience, since the sexual material is relevant to understanding Lena.

# 23

Many years ago I appeared in concert on a radio talk show attended by two grim-faced men representing the Citizens' League for Decent Literature who were attempting to hold a Mother's Day rally in a local stadium celebrating, with the help of bicyclists and Miss Teenage America, the temporarily outflanked but risen-to-anger forces of virtue. "The thing that I hold against pornography," one of the grim-faced men pointed out, "is that any hack can write it, any *hack* can turn out a scene describing sex and the human body and create a perverted interest, but that isn't *writing*. That isn't *art*. That isn't what a *novel* is all about."

I raged toward the microphone to destroy the grim-faced Decent Citizen with an aphorism which would wrap him into the wire, but as I started to speak, I realized that I agreed with him. The man was right. "I agree with you. You are right," I said. The Decent Citizen smiled. "But, of course, the First Amendment covers all that," I added hastily. The Decent Citizen smiled again. The Mother's Day rally, however, fell through. Not enough financial support from the public.

# 24

As *Skipstone* dives, the relationship with John is merely one of the events which pass stately across the panels of Lena's mind. There are many others, events that is, and if I were interested in a little discreet padding, I would have no difficulty in filling many pages with exposition. Lena's whole life could be placed here in a terse but endless number of scenes, dropped in to bulk up the word count. (Any professional learns things like this almost before he has started selling.) I could flash back and flash forward, depict Lena at work and at play in many postures through her young life, could feed in colorful dramatic snippets which would illuminate the strange and wonderful nature of the society from which she comes. There are at least twelve thousand words available here, and perhaps I would be a fool not to do it, depending, of course, on how short the novel would look in first draft. There may be enough already. Then again the book may be short and under deadline pressure, and I may have to add those twelve thousand words. It all depends. Everything depends. It is a wholly dependent universe except in the matter of morality where there may be certain absolutes.

Fortunately this is merely a set of notes for a novel and not the novel itself, and therefore I should not have to concern myself with what will be padding and what will not be. I can put in precisely what I want, what will advance the plot and no more. There is little plot in these early moments of falling, and therefore the material will be held down.

Then, too, I am not terribly interested in Lena or her society. They have little to do with what is going on here which could be at any time.... I only want to posit a technology which makes possible FTL craft that can find the neutron stars. The word for this 3902 is *arid*. It is hard to conceive that a system which could populate the numerous stars could be homogenous, rigid, dull and puritanical, but that is really what humanity has become, even though it numbers fifty billions on one hundred and seven separate worlds, moons and asteroids. The polyglot variety of our time, which comes from relatively high social mobility and institutions in decay, is really an aberrant event in man's history. Institutions tend to stabilize and control; socioeconomic levels tend to stratify. Goods are distributed unequally by heredity; religious or state sanctions merely function to keep the system in place. The years from 1900 through 2155 happen to mark one of those infrequent periods of our history when this was not the case, because the technological devices are far ahead of the ability of the culture to absorb them; but 3902 is deep in a period of stability. Under the hand of the Bureau which controls everything related to space, there have been no conflicts in several hundred years, except for minor disputes between governments of colonies too widely separated to engage in warfare.

The Bureau should not be thought of as tyrannical—it merely occupies a place; it is a quality of the environment. Those in its service have no sense of being oppressors, nor does the Bureau adopt the attitudes of the totalitarian.

These are dull times. Despite the infinite variety which they would seem to have for us, the people of the fortieth century find them unremarkable and similarly dull. Because of the functionality of the system, the tight integration of institutions and individuals, most are rather well compensated. It is just as well that this is so and that Lena has been drawn from a pool of people even more stable than the norm.

Thirty seconds in FTL would drive any of our contemporary astronauts mad. A month under the devices of the Bureau would give any of us severe social illness. Different times, different conditions...the gladiators would not have done very well in the New York subway system.

This all taken into account, there will be little time spent on explication of Lena's past life. Lena is as unremarkable as most of her contemporaries, and her training has acted to flatten her further, it being sickening, repetitive, technical and dull. Material could be put in for padding if conditions forced, but it would seem better to pad the novel in other areas, areas in which the extraneous material could react more vitally with its theme.

For instance, as the ship falls, there could be some elaboration on the suggestion that neutron stars might be pulsars which would be most intriguing, if the reader has not been intrigued sufficiently already by the notion that all of "life" as we understand it when we glimpse the heavens may be merely an incidental by-product of the cycle of neutron glare.

So *there*, Cheever, Barth, Barthelme, Oates. What in the collected works would touch *that* for *angst*?

# 25

Pulsars occur on spectrographs or other sophisticated receivers as rhythmic messages from space, messages which may be defined as light or sound but which have no visual counterpart. In short, their signals give evidence of their existence, but they cannot be seen, which, in the early days of their discovery, led to the theory that they might indeed be coded messages sent by intelligent aliens.

Later it was found that the pulsars do not emanate from single stars but are probably impulses received from entire galaxies, galaxies so many light-years distant that they can be traced by no telescopic equipment available and which are indeed so unimaginably far that their light may not yet have reached us, may not yet reach us for billions of years, although they may well have a history equivalent to our own.

New theories suggest that, while some of the pulsars may be galaxies, others may represent the dying neutron stars or, then again, a neutron star in collapse might *become* a galaxy. What we receive, then, are messages of the imminent collapse of the universe. The neutron stars chatter out their little warnings in clear spectrographic pattern. This concept, that the pulsars are the squalling of failed stars, causes anguish. This possibility would not be evaded during the course of *Galaxies*, and the period of *Skipstone*'s fall would be the proper place of insertion, since it is here, finally, where all the strands of the novel meet, no tension at the center, all of it in the filigree and dark of its suggestion.

# 26

And, then, too, this is Lena's novel. The focus must be kept on her; it would serve no purpose to wander further from her because to the degree that *Galaxies* generates power, it will come from its portrait of the protagonist who is the filter of all impressions. So let it be known, let it be taken into account, that all of the time that *Skipstone* is falling, Lena is in terrible pain. She is suffering. Her anguish is real and her desolation barely a measure of her fear.

For this novel is about people. Evolution is about people; so are neutron stars, pulsars and even the machinations of the Bureau: at the center is always the frail, human form under the lash of brutality or the light-years, and in the hold of the ship which falls interminably in a flight which may go on forever because not only light but time is contained by gravitation, Lena is screaming. She comes in and upon herself over and over again, ripped from end to end, her joints like sealing wax, her eyes torn out like water, lots not being cast over her vestments only because she has no vestments, and there is no one alive, no one alive in the hold of the ship to cast lots over her. But this will come. All of this will happen to her, and since she knows not only the past but the future, she sees this, and it adds to her anguish, although she cannot express it. She can express nothing. She merely holds and falls.

And falling she sees the dead, falling she hears them, the dead address her from the hold and they, too, are screaming. In this new gravitation, the dead and the living have, as John has predicted, merged, the dead not knowing their condition nor the living, everything the same; meat distended, and yet the old distinction somehow holds if only in attitude, for the dead are other than Lena and they shout.

They shout: "Release us, release us, we are alive. What is happening? We are in terrible pain. What is happening? Why are we in such torment?" and so on and so forth, their many voices speaking with one through the hold, revolving speech marking passage from one to the other, poor baffled creatures coming to consciousness after centuries of emptiness in a condition which means that every dream that they have ever known of horror has come true. (Perhaps this is the secret of death itself; we live in the hope of a merciful God who looks upon us with benevolence, but what do we know of the disposition of souls or what is planned for us?) So there they lie, there in that gelatinous flux, their distended limbs sutured finger and toe to the membranes which have held them. Their decay has, if not reversed, at least been halted and imploded as the neutron star has itself imploded; the warp into which they have fallen has reversed time so that now they are alive (or at least they are not dead), and they beg Lena to release them from anguish which they cannot express, so profound is it.

The voices are in her head, they peal and bang like oddly shaped bells and where, oh, where, is she? She does not know. She has no sense of partition but seems, instead, to exist in all space.

"Release us," they scream. "We are no longer dead; the trumpet has sounded and we have been raised; we have been raised incorruptible in a moment, in the twinkling of an eye, at the last trumpet!" and so on and so forth; perhaps they do not shout this but some other theological scrap or snippet, but this is how their cries are referred to Lena who is familiar with some of the old texts. She knows, then, she knows exactly what is happening and maintains consciousness of what has occurred, but then again, she does *not*, there is no circumstantial function. In the larger sense she is aware, but in the matter of particular she is not.

Not only the issue of her pain holds her here. She is merely the ferryman on this passage, not a medical specialist, and she knows nothing of the mysteries of return, of the effect of supergravitational properties upon the corpus of the dead. All that she knows of those dead is that their passage through hyperspace has, in some way unknown to her, changed the very ions of which they are constituted so that they will be in a state of preanimacy and that the process will be further extended upon their return. This is the very latest and most sophisticated of all the experiments in unlocking the dead which have been going on for several hundred years, and although it has returned a scattering of them to perilous life, the expense of carrying them as cargo has been so high, the chances of their continued animation (most of the restored die for a second and final time very quickly) so slight, that the process can be considered to be only at its most rudimentary stages. It may be a false pursuit which will then be abandoned. On all the planets and galaxies no more than twenty of the previous dead exist, and their lives can hardly be said to be satisfactory, since their chemistry has become so precarious that they exist only in tanks, immobilized. Was it for this that they willed enormous sums to have themselves preserved hundreds of years ago? Lena cannot possibly answer this. She cannot speak for them.

She could not, in any event, grant them release. Despite their cries, their vows of life restored, their departure from the medium which nourishes them would surely destroy. She would explain this to them if only she could, take it patiently step by step through the process of causing them to know what has happened, but her technical knowledge is entirely too slender and she has succumbed to her own responses.

Those responses overwhelm her.

For here, in this black hole, if the dead indeed are risen (and this is a question which the novel just cannot confront, staggering in the thin and shrinking line between metaphysics and science where little but the hope for rationality can be said to exist), then the risen can be considered the dead. For she, too, dies in this space. She dies a thousand times over a period of seventy thousand years. There is no objective time here; chronology is controlled only by the psyche, and so Lena has a thousand full lives, a thousand individual and richly textured deaths, and it is awful of course as only something like this can be, but it is also interesting, because for every cycle of death there is also a life. Seventy thousand years, one thousand times seventy upon which she may meditate, if not reenact, her condition.

# 27

And this is a concept so broad, so (as the old pulp magazines might have billed it) mind-shattering, that it is worth considering for just a little while. As the ship, past its initial lurch into the field of the neutron star, becomes part of the black galaxy, as the ship partakes of the energies and properties of a gravitation so immense, Lena begins to live not only her life again, but also the life of various separate identities which are not hers.

Some of these are identities transferred from the dead in the hold, others are taken from those that she has known in her previous life and others still (like this novel itself) have been completely constructed, fictional lives that nevertheless have all the reality and omnipresence of truth. Self-invention, spontaneous creation are as pervasive as anything that has happened, Lena finds, and as she lives a thousand lives over these seventy thousand years (give or take a few years overall and falling well within the bell curve of chances), she has the time to find out a great deal.

It is quite painful. It would have to be this way. Who can possibly describe or imagine what it would be like to live seventy years in solitude, let alone one thousand times seventy, let alone the complete recall of all the previous lives available to the present? There is simply no language for this within the present, and although the author's technical resources are well to the level of any of his peers, he would not even make the attempt. It is simply beyond him. Before something like this, a decent sense of awe must be kindled.

But it can be said that the black galaxy not only repeats and intensifies time, but also compresses so that although seventy thousand years are in one sense quite extended, in another they are short enough for Lena to undergo all of the sensations of her various lives in what she knows—as a dreamer might be able to make assessment outside his dreams—to be a shorter span. Knowledge and memory are not so much enacted through her as implanted. She knows in every way what those seventy lives were like, then, but it is a knowledge of recollection rather than partaking, much as one might stagger from a dream, recollecting for the instant all of its myriad details without, however, having experienced them. What can one say? The black hole, like dreams, destroys time.

Here, in short, is the point at which the novel could be extended. To put it another way, it could be padded out to almost any length demanded by the publisher. One could conceive of a whole cycle of novels here, a *recherche pas du space âge*, seventy volumes interrelated, each of them dealing with another of Lena's lives, all of them locked together by the prologue—title it *Before the Black Galaxy*—and the novel of epilogue which would conclude everything in a fulfilled and satisfying manner. An author with a modicum of energy, a modest scale of expenses and moderate pretensions might well be able to draw a publisher's advance on this scheme for the rest of his working life, for, in the way that all series in genre fiction can be said to be, these novels would be self-reinforcing. The audience would build from book to book as well as sending its newer readers in search of the earlier works of the series.

So, then, one could compose a work which would span the centuries and the world, which would describe all of human history in chiaroscuro from the present day or a little earlier right through the year 3902, and the series would mesh cleverly, since a character in one novel could share certain memories and events with characters in the other, a complex, towering fugal arrangement which would keep the author lunging from novel to subsequent novel until, in simple exhaustion, from audience apathy or in search of better things to do, the author would abandon the series in midcareer. Or drive it to a fast conclusion: Lena rescued from the black hole, *Skipstone* falls through and out the other end, Lena resigns herself to an eternity of plunge and so on. There would be as many ways to finish it off, in short, as to expand, and even at a relatively modest advance, the author would find the temptation hard to put off. Security and the middle class beckoning. As Lena's problems multiply so could the author's be said to have come under control.

This, however, is not the line that *Galaxies* would take. Put it down not to an excess of integrity nor laziness: I simply do not want the work moving in that direction. The point, after all, is not what happens to Lena as a side effect of her fall but what she does to get out of her predicament and what effect those struggles have not only upon her own consciousness, but also upon that of the reader. The true basis of the novel then, would not be found in the side effects which are merely peripheral to these basic points.

Besides, the author confesses to a certain boredom. His own life is at least as difficult to manage as Lena would find her seventy; too much of his energy is involved with assuming mastery of his own existence. Why create false proposals? *Galaxies* will assume Lena's multiple lives without undue explication and leave the reader, that collaborator, to judge the effects of all this upon her.

Sufficient to say that, although Lena is neither stupid nor insensitive, she is not one of the strongest personalities available in this culture. If she were, she would not be in what is essentially a technician's job. [The effect of the multiple existences upon her thus might be crushing, but then again it might only inspirit her to a deeper characteriological and metaphysical framework than she had ever known previously.] Who is to say? There are certain areas which even science-fiction writers are not equipped to explore with any certainty, and before the mysterious curtains which shroud the one, discrete human soul, it may be best, after all, to stay silent.

# 28

*Galaxies*, having set up its background, having reached its crisis early on (in conformation with the basic principles of good plotting), would then plunge into its basic argument and conflict which would occur when Lena at last decides that she must summon help. She must obtain from the prostheses an evaluation, or, failing that, she must in some way establish communication with the dead.

Now, the fact that it has taken her seventy thousand years to reach this decision is in one way incredible, and yet in another and more significant way it is simple and miraculous. In an infinite universe, possibilities similarly multiplied, only a fraction of them reconstituted even now, it is highly unlikely that even once in seventy thousand years of lives and reenactments she would have intercepted a personality which would seek help in this way, and had it not been for the fact that she is unusually strong-willed and that the personality which she inhabits is so weak that she can override it, it might not have happened yet—*Skipstone* and its denizens might be plunging onward instead of having reached a point of resolution which, later on, we will be able to explicate.

Before she has summoned the prostheses, Lena has had time to think, and she decides that the prostheses might provide her with the only set of answers. There has been an accretion of memory from life to life so that she has been able to do some almost conterminous thinking, and when the moment comes when she may act, she is prepared to do so.

Some of her previous personalities have also been weak but not in this way, in a fashion to encourage override. Others have been strong, not a few have been insane, but there has been a little residue even in the worst of them to carry forth the knowledge of what she must do, and so in the seventy thousandth and first year, when the cumulative truth of the matter has come upon her, Lena realizes what has happened and what will happen next and what she must do to deal with this.

She summons all of her strength and will. She is, in this thousandth existence, occupying the persona of a sniveling, whining old man of the 3200s who had enough money to embalm but not quite enough to seal off his body from relatives who, for profit, put it on exhibition in their temple for many years as an artifact and the center of a sect, until one by one the members of the family left the temple, the cult fell into disgrace and the institutions of the time began to confiscate its property. Meanwhile the corpus was immaculately preserved, the society of all times having had one consistency: to protect and perpetuate the bodies of the embalmed so that they could enjoy the possibility of revival.

In this persona she summons John. As he did not tell her until the very moment of her embarkation, his personality is also on *Skipstone*, one of the prostheses, implanted within a metallic block approximately but not truly in the shape of a man. (It was deliberate that the prostheses not appear human. It prevents the ferryman, who may at the time of summoning be in a near-psychotic stage, from reacting to them as if they were people; at one time there were some terrible incidents which need not be described here.) Sensors turn, little lights and wiring play, and as the machine whirs, coughing into the block the preserved persona of John, Lena gasps in relief, too weak even to respond with pleasure to the fact that in this condition of null time, canceled light, ruined causality, the machinery still works.

But, then, the machinery would. It would function. Even in this final and most dreadful of situations, the machinery continues to function. This has always been the point of science fiction: that if we did not master the future, it would be from our own incapacities and never those of the machines. They may have been right, they may have been wrong, but those old science-fiction writers had one core insight: whatever happened would eventually devolve upon technology. Fail in that and everything fails.

"Hello," John says within a shimmering, silver block, crudely sculptured into a parody of human form, little blind lights winking at one end, little extensions balancing at the other. "I'm glad to see you."

Fully implanted with the personality and memories of he who has been obtained, the prosthesis assumes at this moment of summoning the condition of her superior. Of course it is *not* John. Lena must remember this at all times and also must know that the prosthesis has no memory of the voyage. Its recollections have been shut off from the time that John fed the log of his personality, piece by aching piece, into the receptors during the weeks before the voyage. She cannot, then, fall upon this contrivance and beg for salvation. It would literally not know what she was talking about; it is there to provide technical and humanitarian assistance only to the point that information can be given to it. That is true, Lena says to herself, moving her lips, subvocalizing these assurances; that is true, I must remember this at all times, I must not think that this thing is human.

This knowledge is wrenching, and the old man with whom she shares the cavern of consciousness is similarly distressed and somehow she maintains enough control to keep the two in balance, to maintain her sense of control and identity and to address John in a slow, reasonable tone. This is no small accomplishment. It cannot be dismissed easily. Possibly I have underestimated Lena to this point. She is showing a kind of behavioral control and absolute discipline which would be beyond anyone of this time and highly exceptional even in hers.

"What is the matter, Lena?" John says. He knows—it knows, whatever the device may be called—that he would only be summoned if there were some kind of serious trouble in flight. "Can you tell me what's wrong? What can I do for you?" Her mentor would have phrased it just this way, yet—in the context—it seems absolutely stupid to her.

And the blundering nature of this question, its naïveté and irrelevance in the midst of what she has occupied, stuns Lena, and yet more when she compares this mask to the actual John who would never (well, would he? could he be this way?) act so stupidly, but she realizes even through the haze of blockage that this John would, of course, join her without any memory of immediate circumstance. He would have to be told what is happening. He knows nothing at all.

Inevitably, then, she must brief him. It is hard to maintain control over that other personality which once again has panicked and is scrambling desperately against the walls of consciousness, trying to get out of there, trying to find sleep once again but of course it cannot, not until the genetic allotment of its mortality has been exhausted. She must reassert her own personality. Whining and sniveling, she manages to brief the thing that is John, half in one voice, half in another, as to what has happened.

(Some comment should be made on background: the awful stillness of the ship in the fall, an absolute cancellation of motion, even a placidity in the grip of collapse which gives an almost pastoral stillness to the interior whose support systems continue to function. It also should be clearly stated that seventy thousand years is *subjective* time to Lena; no such period has actually elapsed. No time at all can be said to have passed since the fall began, and the biological systems are frozen. Naturally she could not have survived seventy thousand years or even seventy thousand seconds in plunge. All event is perceived only through the engineering which controls the subjective time-belt; it is by no means implied that the objective passage of time can be measured at all.)

Lena does know what has happened. A thousand lives, seventy thousand years, have enabled her to reconstruct, quite painfully but piece by piece, the cosmology which has put her in this position. It has not been easy, but then again in seventy thousand years of thought almost anyone could reconstruct the cosmos. This, in any event, is the premise of the novel, take or leave its essential optimism as you will. She tells John, then, about the neutron star, about the implosion which has brought her to this condition, about gravitation. About light and pain. John in metallic frame stands there quietly, listening to this. Indeed there is little else that he can do; the prostheses are triggered only by pauses in conversation, will otherwise stand mute, and Lena's jumble of recollection, explanation and hysteria goes on without pause. Finally she is done, and when it is certain that this is so, the device moves its rudimentary head in what might be a very human gesture or then again might only represent its projection by Lena of her need to have it be human.

"Remarkable," it says.

"Yes."

"That's really remarkable. And terrible, of course. You've shown a great deal of strength in being able to assess the situation."

"Yes."

"And not to panic. That's remarkable also. You've met this test with real strength." The programs, of course, are slanted to be encouraging and supportive, this being Bureau's conception of how users might best be served. "You're a remarkable woman. I'm really proud of you. Then, too, you have a right to be proud of yourself. Are you? I truly hope you are."

"That has nothing to do with anything," Lena says. "You've got to help me."

"You say that this falling continues still? That at this moment we're diving?"

"Falling now, falling forever."

"How terrible for you."

Lena looks at the blank masking which covers the portholes, wondering what would happen now if she were to strip that masking away so that she could see the black hole itself. She does not think that she could bear it, and yet at some point, even past seventy thousand years, she knows that she will have to do it. The compulsion is absolute.

"Would you care to talk some more about your feelings, Lena? Why don't you talk?"

"You've got to help me," she says. "This has nothing to do with feelings."

"What would you like me to do? What do you think that I *could* do?

How long have you had these feelings that you could derive help from me, Lena? Do you really think that the solution lies outside yourself?"

"You've got to have a function," she says. "All of you were placed here in order to help with some emergency; this is an emergency. Do something. Tell me what can be done to end this."

"Well, now," John says, "well, now, Lena, let's consider that a little if we may." It addresses her with superb calm which has also been programmed in, the only emotion which is picked up on the tapes. It would hardly be supportive, the Bureau has long since calculated, to have prostheses capable of other emotions on these flights; they would lead to vast complications far beyond the ability of the Bureau itself to contain. At one time it was argued at the highest levels that emotions of warmth, affection, passion might meet the program, but in the end it had been decided against, since none of them would serve any technological purpose.

"Let us consider," the prosthesis is saying. "I could hardly help you, although I know that to you I represent a factor that you always looked to for help. Still, the means for release are beyond me."

"Are they?"

"If beyond you, beyond me," John points out. "That would stand to reason, wouldn't it?"

"But you've got to have an answer! You were installed to be called upon, so that you could help."

"Only in those matters which would fall within my experience," John says with a little regret. "Really, I am little more than a mechanical contrivance, a data bank as it were which can give you faster access to facts of a certain kind than you could obtain by research. I mean I'm perfectly willing to be supportive—that's what we're here for after all, to render support—but you'd be wrong in looking at me as much more than a catalog or perhaps a synthesis of information. So you see I'm not capable of that kind of action."

"You must be."

"But I'm not." Although the crude metal is not designed for expression, she seems to think that John is betraying grief, but this is undoubtedly emotional; she is being emotional once again. "I'm truly not."

"Impossible."

"Not impossible. Objective fact. In truth your problem is that you are projecting on me certain emotional needs which I cannot possibly fulfill."

"Emotional needs?"

"Of course. I am not your mentor, your lover John, but merely a representation of his personality, a simulacrum of this real person who is certainly not at all here."

"I know that."

"But perhaps you are not sure. At an emotional level, Lena, you may be shielding yourself from this fact. Be honest with yourself. You did not call upon me for intellectual advice but emotional support, and I cannot yield that at all."

Consider this: they tumble into a black hole in an eternity of pain and yet the prosthesis is engaging in elemental casework procedure. Surely this appears confusing to the reader—how, after all, can the sense of wonder be congealed with the principles of modern social work?—but this is among the points the novel has to make; that the Bureau's attack upon the universe has been to obliterate its pain and hence its parameters by acting as if it could be handled with routine techniques of therapeutic approach which have not changed at all in two thousand years, have merely become ritualized.

"You're going to have to deal with this yourself, Lena," the metallic thing points out. "There is quite little that the cyborg technique can do for you; you can no longer displace the responsibility for your condition upon machines. In fact I seem to recall raising this very point in discussions at the Bureau a long, long time ago, but no one ever listened to me. They never listened at all there."

"What are you talking about?" Lena says. "I have no idea what you're saying." This is only a partial truth. She knows quite well indeed what is being suggested—that she is alone, that she is in a void, that this metal merely simulates companionship and that no one can save her—but at the level of emotional acceptance she has indeed become blank. Something impenetrable within her through all the subjective centuries of pain has finally shifted, and she now feels open in a way which hardly dignifies her. "Help me," she says again.

"I can't."

"You must. Otherwise this will go on forever."

There is, here, a pathos which I cannot really transmit. Open sentiment has never been one of my virtues; the ironic sense is too strong for me to bring off a scene at the level of simple emotional clarity which gives sentiment its often despised power. I could say that what gives this scene much of its horror is that Lena yearns toward a lover whose very form mocks that yearning, a form the Bureau has designed to parody that emotion. "Oh," she says, "if you don't help me, who will? Who can?"

"There are others," the device says. "Engineers, tutors, advisors are also in the bank, and they might be able to give you more practical advice, although I doubt this. But there's no reason for you to feel that everything begins and ends here; truly it does not have to. It's merely your emotional condition running away with you."

"I hate you," she says then. "I hate you."

"Don't hate me. I am merely an abstraction; that would get you nowhere. Get hold of yourself."

"I have hold of myself. I hate you now."

"You can only find these feelings of hatred destructive. In any case," the cyborg continues, "the situation as you've put it is frightening and upsets me no less than it does you. In fact, although no decent machine should ever confess to something like this, I'm beginning to feel my own balance starting to disappear. This is a very tenuous creation here, weak and frozen circuitry, levels of fusion which can hardly put up with any severe stress. I am going to disconnect."

"You can't do that."

"Of course I can do that. Don't be silly; I can do anything that I want. We have a complete range of free-willed choices available to us; we can regulate our own participation. Otherwise we would be dominated and utilized in such a way as to make yourself quite mad. By free will I must detach myself before something drastic happens, and of course I obey it absolutely."

The cyborg labors in a rather clumsy way toward one of the portholes and lifts its tentacles to part the curtains.

Lena can do nothing. She is astonished by the action, does not understand it and yet, unwillingly, as she stares, she begins to see the sense. She can see what the cyborg has said to her and realize that it is quite right: it could hardly bear this staggering situation. It was not made for it; Bureau did not anticipate black galaxies or their interception when the lists for *Skipstone* were compiled. She had no right to expect anything; it was foolishness even to summon, but then again, what choice did she have? What could she have done? She needed help and thought that it could be provided here, and the weakness, then, is not that of the cyborg but her own. She must understand this. She remains in place as the thing rolls to a porthole, tears open the curtains and takes a long look at the aspect glinting through, an aspect which Lena herself will not witness even though she has seen it in her mind for seventy thousand years; she will not look at it, and then a cry both human and metallic emerges from the thing at the porthole.

It bellows in a pain which might be pleasure so acute is the sound, and then the very joints seem to decompose (although Lena knows that this must be, it would have to be, an illusion; sight could not destroy steel nor could sensation alone break an engine, could it? Could this happen?), and then it leans and staggers against a bulkhead, arches in upon itself and collapses. It does not, after that first stricken bellow, make any sound at all, as if all feeling had been drawn from it on that one single line. Lena manages to stand, move in that direction and, her hand become a tentacle, her eyes closed, she seizes the curtain and draws it closed, shutting off the light and the death of the black galaxy, and then she is alone.

"I am alone," she says with just a hint of self-dramatization (but she can be pardoned this); I am alone, she thinks, and knows that she is not, not in any sense which will profit her. Because somewhere below her the cyborg that was once John lies, but she neither sees nor touches; instead her body shrinks and then she scuttles away. The personality of the dead with which her persona has shared this momentarily becomes the stronger, and she begins to whine and mumble then like an old incontinent, shudder within the container of her flesh as if it were despicable, and this may go on for years and then again it may go on for moments (there is no time in the black galaxy, except the time that she feels has elapsed; time is a function of condition), but eventually, like all things, it stops, and she must confront her basic problem again. Always she will have to do this.

She is alone in the ship. Her descent continues. Her pain does not remit. She is out of control and yet she is in control. Nothing can be understood and yet in another way all is comprehensible. All. All can be known. Something must be done. She cannot bear this eternally.

BARRY N. MALZBERG                                    335

# 29

And here could run yet another moody flashback concerning Lena's relationship with John, dropped in to provide color and poignance, augmenting the mood of despair. Long sexual passages here could alternate with painful streams of consciousness in the present. Sex and space, orgasm and isolation could run counterpoint, and the author's gifts for irony, which are not modest, would be exhibited to their fullest range. Also, in the traditions of modern science fiction, the sex scenes could be quite titillating, render the novel some extraliterary interest. A construct like this could use all the extraliterary interest it could get.

But this would not work. *Space is asepsis:* straddling this simple and irrevocable insight, the temptation to write long and easy scenes of coupling falls to ash. How can I show sex, even retrospectively, against a background where light and history are themselves contained?

I cannot. I would not even attempt it; that is all there is to say about the matter, and in addition to this Lena's thoughts have already veered far from John. They are less retrospectively concerned than fixed on the immediacy and difficulty of her situation, the need to deal with it and obtain escape.

She wants to change her condition. She wants to get out of this. Of course she does, how natural a need; but consider the measure of her entrapment in that it has taken seventy thousand years for her to have reached this point of decision. There are monolithic writers and those who pace slowly, but even a Jamesian standard weakens by comparison here. This is a character who has taken a thousand selves and seventy times that to decide that her situation is unbearable. Science fiction must truly be a superior medium if it can involve such an extension, such a superimposition of leisurely pace upon material. Nothing else in any other form could begin to approach it.

Still, if it is understood that the black galaxy does indeed contain time as well as light and sensation, memory as well as all sub-FTL speeds, then it is not unreasonable that it would take Lena this long to reach any point of decision. Indeed, it is quite a substantial declaration that she would come through all of these stresses alive. There is nobody of our time who could have survived what has happened, yet training methods and the undoubted factor of evolution have produced many Lenas, individuals whose capacity for experience and the weight it bears goes far beyond our own. They can, in our terms, tolerate anything. Governments throughout history, in fact, have sought a population with Lena's patience and malleability; to many of them she would have been the ideal citizen. Her tolerance levels are quite high.

Nor (because she considers her survival unexceptional, because it is merely a concomitant of her training) can she truly understand the remarkable nature of her survival. She does not consider herself to be an exceptional individual, and this is one of the bitterest of all factors.

The thing that contained John's persona lies near a bulkhead. It makes no gesture. Dead before, it is more dead now, containing nothing. Again she is alone in the ship and overwhelmed once more by the cries of the dead.

# 30

"You were foolish," a dead says to her. "You asked more than could be given."

"I did not."

"Yes, you did. It fit not the programs. There is nothing that they can do for you."

"Then I had no choice. I had to call upon them. I was instructed to call upon them if I needed help."

"Even here you have choices," the dead says. "No matter what your condition, no matter what has happened to you, you exist in a scheme of choice. You must remember this."

The seventy thousand years have had their effect upon the dead as well. At least some of them, it would seem, have learned something. The one to whom she is speaking is extremely patient: he seems to have moved to a new plane of knowledge, but then again the dead may not truly exist in a sentient condition; their apparent existence may simply be a projection of Lena's wild and altered mental state upon their abstraction, or then again the factor of change in the field of the neutron star may make all of her impressions merely hallucinative along with any questions of growth or choice. That would lend *Galaxies* yet another series of levels, of course. The possibility that the acts described may be occurring only as patterns falsely encoded within the protagonist renders everything in it liable to suspicion, although I can give assurance that there are certain poles in this work, that the work can be said to exist in revolution around them. One of the poles is the neutron star and the other is the hypocrisy of the Bureau and the way in which they mesh—becoming, ultimately, the same thing. Also significant is the statement that both Lena and *Skipstone* do exist; they exist at this moment in the sense that all that will be can be said to have already existed, sending back its reverberations to the time before it was created.

"Choices," the dead repeats, since Lena's stream of consciousness has been wandering as it is prone to do. "And you are compelled to make them."

"He did not try to help me."

"He could not have helped you. How could you have expected that he would? You are being very naïve; they are not programmed to deal with anything like this."

"I thought he would."

"You are a fool."

"I thought he would help me—"

"*He* is not John. You called upon John but found only a mechanical recreation," the dead says gently. "How can you be brought to realize that what you thought happened did not happen? Everything was based upon a set of false expectations."

"It cannot be."

"It can and it is. If you did not face the truth of the matter, you would not have summoned him. You know where you are and what is happening to us, but you must continue to face that truth, Lena."

"What truth?"

"The truth of resolution. It lies wholly within yourself. Only you may change this."

"How can you say that? How can you tell me that the truth lies within myself? Who are you?" she says and does not know what she is addressing, fearful that she may be talking to herself. "I don't know what qualifies you to say something like this, how you can put on me the responsibility—"

"The truth is the responsibility," the dead says. "And your responsibility is the truth."

And then it says no more. Whether it actually goes away or merely becomes silent when it is finished speaking is something she does not know; she cannot gauge the temper of the dead any more than she can judge the veracity of their address. The murmurs of others surround, the voice blends into all of the voices of the hold and she is shrouded once again in the music and the darkness.

She wanders toward the console again, an action that may take her ten minutes or ten years or (such is the characteristic of time which I am trying to get across here) *both* and looks at it for a while, her fingers trembling. Beside the prosthesis of John in the storage tank lay all of the others, each with its separate abilities and gifts, and she decides to summon them, to try to obtain advice in that way, but the will to call them forth is, for the time, beyond her, and she must gird herself to this for long, struggling instants, because if these cyborgs, too, fail to help her, if they desert her as did John, then she truly does not know if she will be able to contend further with the situation.

Yet. Her desire to survive is still there. Indeed, it must have never left her. It chews away like a rat, busily snipping little raw chunks of personality and she is in its thrall; she is, in fact, astonished by the realization of how desperately she wants to live, somehow to get out of this. It may have been seventy thousand years reaching this point of urgency, but now that it is here it cannot be wasted, she thinks, if they have led to this. She sheds the personality she has inhabited. It falls from her like a cloak and she is once again and fully herself.

Lena places her hands upon the console and summons, simultaneously, three cyborgs.

Here the novel obviously veers toward religious allegory, an abused area but one which is obviously inevitable within the difficult context and in terms, too, of the author's personality. Not for nothing has he spent all of those difficult and perilous hours during the period of the High Holy Days, even though it cannot be said that his religious experience is rich in conclusion. Still, for all his ambivalence, complaint and seizures of doubt, the author does not regret his religious affiliation; within his rather secular frame a small and battered *chassid* in cantorial regalia is trying to get out. He will *not* get out, of course; where would he go? There is not a Reform temple in the area which would suit and Orthodoxy is too time consuming, but he will not stay in place either, this *chassid*, and from the tension between his desires and his practice, the author can wring the usual amounts of irony. Nothing at all is easy once you begin to take the thematic subtext seriously, something which applies to science fiction as well as religion. It would be best concentrating on the ritual without excessive attention to its significance. *Slogging Through the*

*Slime Planet* might have been a better investment after all. Ethical Culture certainly involves less than Reform.

But religious disquisition to one side, the allegory will obviously be tempting in that chapter involving the three cyborgs which Lena summons to confer further on her problem. The parallels are indeed clear, and the selection of *three* rather than a single cyborg at a time approaches the level of conscious intention. The resemblance of these summoned to the three comforters of Job could hardly be ignored and would indeed be worked through the material cunningly.

Job. He is that Old Testament figure of faith and submission, or then again he may only be a symbol of cosmic abandonment, God's Fool. For his pains he was subjected by Satan (God having approved the deal with eager curiosity; would Job bend or would he not?) to a series of trials in order to determine whether Job's faith truly came from love of God or merely upon the wealth that God had lavished upon him. Satan in succession lays Job's fields, cattle and children low, leading his wife to suggest that Job curse God and die.

Do not be restless; this is all important. The parable of Job brought the concept of justice into the Old Testament as even Adam's trials did not. Job refuses his wife's demand—although severely tried—and his wife abandons him in disgust. In her place come three wise men from a neighboring province who join him upon the ground to tell sad stories of the death of kings. These are the three comforters, figures of satire, since they fall outside the pain and terror of Satan's vengeance and approach the unspeakable in a burlesque of intellectualism which is, in fact, comic. They give Job the most reasonable, persuasive reasons for his condition and offer reasonable encouragements as to why he should no longer silently bear his grief. They do not prevail, at least not quite, but probably only because the text, like so much of the Old Testament, has been shaped toward the purpose of the didactic. They certainly do not take Job's positions with grace.

In the story of the comforters is the conscious origin of the section in which Lena and the three new prostheses discuss her condition and that of *Skipstone*. Summoned one by one, activated, they are briefed by Lena as she briefed John, and they listen as patiently as that device did, making no interjection. They are not, as I have pointed out, geared toward interruption; their whole supportive presence is for that reason a fraud perpetuated by the Bureau. They are not there to help but merely to grant relief; however this is the way that the Bureau has always done things on these interstellar sweeps, and who is to say that if it had changed its procedures anything would have been different? Almost assuredly there would have been no difference at all.

None of them is quite as bright as John. This is understandable; John was Lena's supervisor directly on merit. They are, however, bright enough by far to absorb her explanation as well as to understand its seriousness. When she warns them not to go to the portholes, they agree. When she tells them not to look at the galaxy, they do not protest. When she says that the sight of space in this fall will drive even a prosthesis insane, they nod. When she points at the crushed heap of John, they murmur to one another. They construe her remarks correctly, and they do not protest when she says that they must attend to her. And when she is done, they stand in their line of rigid and curious mortification and seem able to say nothing.

"I've now told you everything," she says.

Indeed she has told them everything. They nod solemnly.

"I have nothing to add. That is what has happened here and I can tell you no more."

They seem to shrug. She has nothing to add and can say no more. Of course. Who would have thought otherwise? If she had something else to say, she would have said it. Wouldn't she? All of that seems reasonable.

Her long, thick pause, which in time-dilation effect may be no more than a few seconds but then again may be several years (perhaps I am forcing this point, but it must be emphasized again and again that normal considerations of chronology just do not apply here), extends and then she says, "I was waiting now to hear from you."

They seem to look at one another. Perhaps an illusion of light. Then they look back at her.

"Well," she says, "well? You're all highly trained and qualified, not as qualified as John, perhaps, but surely amongst the three of you you ought to be able to come up with something. I'm waiting. How do I get out of this?"

Still they say nothing. From the helpful, even eager aspect which can be seen glinting in the façade they present, it is obvious that they are not hostile, that they present no menace. They simply do not know what to do. Perhaps they make a few more shrugging gestures, if metal blocks can be said to shrug.

"Come on," Lena says.

They look as if they would be quite pleased to go on. But they say nothing.

"Well, look here, then," she says. "You can't just stay there. You must talk to me; I insist on it. You must have some good ideas."

"Well," one says and pauses, "well, then. The only means of escape would be to go directly into the tachyonic drive. To shift to faster-than-light speed without acceleration."

"That is true," another says. "Moving into faster-than-light speed without acceleration, that is. No tardyons, no gathering of force, but a clear shift."

"I've thought of that," Lena says. "The black hole contains all speeds below the speed of light, we can assume, since it is inhibiting light itself. But we don't know up to what limit it controls. It may contain even infinite speed."

"Nothing is infinite," one says. They really cannot be distinguished from one another. It would be nice to do those authorial things, neatly individuate the devices, even hint at a wisp of conflict between them, make them come alive through traits of character and argument, but how can this be done? You simply cannot make machines live, although the Bureau, in its reverence for its devices, has tried; and you cannot make machines different from one another except in technological specifications. No, there is nothing to be done; the situation must be accepted as it is. When one speaks, the others are quiet; when the three speak, they all sound the same. There is no difference. "Everything is finite," this one concludes.

"We don't know," she says; "nobody knows. That's why I've called on you."

Yet again they nod, slowly, bleakly. In truth their programs have not yet absorbed what she is talking about. They have only the dimmest grasp of the situation, but then again they have not had seventy thousand years to ponder the point. Even if they had had that amount of time, they function within a very slight range.

"Tardyons and tachyons, you see," Lena says. "Tardyons represent particles that move at less than the speed of light, tachyons those that move faster. Tardyons obviously won't work at all, not in terms of escape velocity here. I don't even know what state the craft is in at this point. I can't evaluate. I can't get a reading on any of this, although you can be sure that I've tried. Nothing about this is easy, you see."

"Tachyons," a cyborg says. "Yes, you are making that point clear. I can now understand what you are saying. It is difficult to grasp but it seems to make a certain sense." It confers with the others; they exchange information in little mumbles. If they were hooked up to the same computer bank, exchange would be immediate, but they are not, this being one of the Bureau's small economies. They cannot pool their information directly but must act in the halting fashion of humans.

"Unless you can think of something different," Lena says after they finish their discussion and have turned expectant blank cylinders to her once again. "Otherwise I'm going to be in here infinitely, and I just don't think that I can take much more of this really. Not with the dead."

"The dead? What about the dead?"

"You don't hear them?" Lena says. "You don't hear what's going on all the time?"

"I'm really afraid not," the cyborg assures her. It turns to the others. "Do you sense anything?" They make negative gestures. "What dead?" the cyborg says.

"Those in the hold."

"They would mean nothing. They are the dead and have no existence. Now I truly do not know what you are talking about."

"Here," she says, "here they have existence."

"I am afraid that you are wrong. The specifications are quite clear and you are misconceiving something."

"Perhaps I'm completely insane," Lena says quickly enough. "I've certainly had the opportunity to give that a lot of thought. That could very well be. It's a possibility anyway. Anyone could have been made crazy by this."

"Indeed."

"I've been in this field for seventy thousand years, and it's taken me almost all of this time simply to understand what's happening to us."

"Well," the same cyborg says, "ah, well." It seems to have assumed the role of speaker while the others stand by, rolling lightly in the motion of the ship which continues evenly as in a series of pulses which Lena can feel as pain to the depth of her senses but does not block thought. "Have you ever considered that it might be your destiny to *spend* infinity in this black hole."

"No."

"Maybe it is ordained in some fashion. Then again it may be inevitable. There might have been some cosmic disaster about which we know nothing but which has brought this on. In that case it would be impossible to get out. Anyway, the situation seems pretty hopeless as far as I'm concerned. Why don't you just relent? There seems to be a kind of immortality to it anyway, subjective immortality, of course, but what's the difference? It isn't everyone who could live seventy thousand years in any circumstances. Maybe you should just accept this fate."

"No," she says again. "No, I cannot. There is no cosmic accident. It is only *Skipstone* intercepting the field."

"Are you sure? Are you really sure of that? Perhaps you are in some way determining the condition, the force, the very *fate* of the universe."

"I don't understand."

"Don't you?"

"No," she says, "I don't. I don't know what you're talking about. Why does everything have to be concerned with the fate of the universe?" It is a cry not only from Lena, but also from the heart of the science-fiction writer. "Why can't something just mean what it simply *means*? Why can't it be my own problem to suffer and to solve; why does it have to get tied in with the *universe*? Isn't my condition enough?"

"It was you who said that this might all be a gigantic accident," the cyborg points out. "Now didn't you say that? All existence might be an accidental by-product of the force of the implosion."

"I didn't know what I was saying," she says a little sulkily. "I'm not always responsible for everything that I say; everything doesn't have to *mean*—"

"Of course it does. Everything is related, you know that. Every act everywhere affects everything else, and perhaps your suffering here gives the universe purpose. Did you ever think of that?"

"No."

"Perhaps the implosion would not exist unless you were here to observe it. How can one tell about something like this? There are no easy answers. It is all very difficult and metaphysical."

"Metaphysical," the others say together, contrapuntally. "It is all metaphysical."

"At least you ought to consider it," the leader/spokesman says. "I wouldn't ignore anything that I'm saying here. Who can tell about something like this?"

"And then, too," the second cyborg/comforter says with just a slight lisp. (Possibly this is an individuating characteristic; in the absence of genuine inventive powers, one can always toss in a limp, a lisp, a cigarette, a stutter, a hint of bigotry. Look for these as the sign of an author or comic in trouble.) "If you say that the dead down there are alive—of course *we* can't hear a thing and you're probably quite mad, you know—but assuming that you're right and that they do have some kind of objective, external existence, well, then. What about that, I want to ask? Wouldn't that change the situation?"

"What situation?"

"Everything," the cyborg says rather grandly. "Nothing. The totality of it. You can't expect me to be specific about a matter like this; the conception is too grand to necessitate explanations. It just would be very important."

"I still don't understand," Lena says tensely. "I don't know what you're trying to tell me. I've come to you for answers and instead you're asking questions that are nonsense. Be practical. I'm trying to be; you could at least be the same."

Speaking at such length after seventy thousand years of subjective silence has made her weak. Cautiously she clears her throat, rasps, hawks, then spits. She runs a hand across her forehead, and it comes away glistening with sweat; she finds it amusing in a distant way that even here, in these circumstances, the ancient biological factors will nonetheless assert themselves. There is something important here. Even in a black hole one becomes weak, one sweats, one's throat tends to burn. An organism can become exposed to any kind of exotic parasites or bacteria but will always feel sick in a conventionally symptomatic fashion. His skin will not turn green nor will he be able to fly. The keyboard of human response is large but finite, and only certain harmonies can be played upon it no matter the impetus. Always, pain is referred back to the system; the system does not alter with the pain.

Abruptly she is filled with a revulsion so great that it becomes a palpable network which she feels glowing dimly within her. I should not have called upon them, she thinks, as if in the midst of illuminated wire, enfolding her, binding her inward, but then if I had not called upon them, what then? Would I have done it myself? What they are saying may be right. Possibly they have spoken nothing but the truth: that all of the universe swirls around this single pivot. If that is what has happened, then what am I to do? I do not know if I can manage a decision like this alone. I was not trained to make decisions; that was never the function for which the Bureau prepared us.

"I don't know about the deads," she says. "Maybe you're right about that; maybe I didn't hear them."

"Oh? Is that so?"

"I seem to have been in communication with one of them, but it may be an illusion. This could be. It is possible. I can accept and understand that I might be imagining them. But not entirely. And not the rest of it."

"But what if not?" the second says with a little urgency. "What if you do hear them? If somehow the black galaxy has brought them back to life, then an immediate vault into the tachyonic would destroy them for good."

"I don't know. I can't tell about anything like that. Why can't you leave me alone?"

"It would be a lot of meat lost," the third rumbles in a rather self-important way. "One could say that about the dead. They are very valuable; they make possible all of the FTL experiments. If you were able somehow to return to Earth after this jolt, if it worked and you escaped the galaxy at whatever cost, I doubt very much if the Bureau would be congratulatory. It would be ruined cargo in that hold and they would be completely liable."

"So what?"

"So what? The estates would be litigious, the institutions which support the Bureau would be thrown into ruin. The legal complications alone would be enormous. It would be quite bad for you, Lena. You had better consider the dead, take them into account in all of your considerations here."

"I have been thinking of them."

"Not enough, then."

"I have, but I also have to think of *Skipstone* and of myself. Aren't *we* valuable?"

"Not so much."

"Don't I matter?"

"Not as much as the dead," the second says cheerfully; "not anywhere near them. If I were you, in fact, I think that I'd stay with them. Better to be lost and a mystery than to return and cause this kind of situation. Why, it would be the end of the project! Bureau would be unable to deal with this."

On his tiny conveyances the second, which has moved forward, moves back then against the bulkhead, much like an actor who has completed a monologue, and the others move in closer as if to confer with congratulatory murmurs. It is almost, Lena thinks, it is almost as if deep within their programs was implanted the need to preserve these dead at all costs, even from life which could take them only as a disease...but what else could she have expected? She knows the nature of this Bureau for which she works.

And as they do this, as she thinks that, a clamorous murmur seems to arise from the hold as if all of the dead were shrieking in exquisite pain, but whether this is coincidentally triggered or whether they have heard what the cyborg has said and this is their reaction is not known. And then, too, she might be imagining this. The cyborgs give no indication. How expressive can the dead be? How much can they tell? How much of this can be said to exist and what of it is dreams?

She listens and listens for that voice that has been in her mind for centuries...but she hears nothing, although her call beats against her chest like a bird, mingling with the lump of revulsion, binding, breaking and flowing then toward epiphany.

To what degree can she disentangle from what she inhabits? This is part of her problem, and the other part is how much of what she inhabits has overtaken her so that she is no longer herself? She may have no more reality than the cyborgs. She may be a cyborg herself, of a more sophisticated type and without memory of how she was created; how otherwise could she have survived this? The originals would have the answer to this; so would the Bureau, but there is no way to make contact. What has been done to her? Are all of them here merely machines and the *Skipstone* a living being which contains them? Where is the line of demarcation between humanity and the machines?

"Well," the third cyborg says, not in response to this (the devices are certainly not telepathic), "well, I feel that I should make a statement here, *too*." In a rather nervous gesture, absurd because these things are said not to feel, it twitches one of its cubes, revolves it slowly in position as it averts its line of sight from the omnipresent and dreadful portholes covered again. Do they really see, these things, or do they receive sensory impressions in a code which she could not understand? What is the quality of their consciousness, are they indeed conscious or merely feeding tape in a predetermined way for responses…and does it matter? Does any of this matter at all? For all the difference that it would make to her, they might see nothing.

"Ah, yes," the first says, "there is another point of view to be presented here that I think we should all attend to very closely."

"Right," the second lisps, "that's definitely right. There should be a whole range of points of view, after all. All articles of faith should be represented. What I am saying is right; it is the full and final truth of the matter, but I will be happy to know that other positions are represented and they should be, they should all be given their say. After all this is an important decision here, very crucial."

"Crucial," the first whispers, "absolutely crucial. Everything is crucial and becoming increasingly so. Nothing will ever be trivial here."

"Indeed," the third says. It inclines its surfaces toward the second. "That has been stated very well, and as a matter of fact I couldn't have done it better myself. It really should be taken into consideration. I wanted to discuss what could be called the more cosmic implications of what is going on here."

"You should," the first says, "and so you very definitely should. I'm glad that you had the courage to bring it up. That shows very rare courage."

"Right," the third says and then to Lena: "Now listen here. Listen to me and attend this. You've fallen into a neutron star, a black funnel. It's utterly beyond your puny capacities to escape it, and the dimensions of what has happened here would reduce you to inconsequence. What can be done against forces like these? You've got to submit, got to accept the situation."

"I don't want to believe that," Lena says.

"You had better."

"Man can overcome anything. He can voyage anywhere."

"But he cannot voyage out."

"What he sees, he understands; what he understands, he can master. Nothing is beyond us."

"That's puerile thinking."

"No, it isn't."

"Certainly it is. It's the same puerility which put you here to begin with, and you still don't seem willing to accept the truth. Can the dead overcome death?"

"They have."

"*They have not.* It is all in your imagination. There are places man was not meant to go, objects he was not meant to touch, emotions beyond his ability to interpret, and this is all of them. You must yield. You must face the futility of the situation. I would recommend that you look for a religious solution. That would probably serve you better than anything at this time."

"He's quite right," the second adds. "That's a very good point that's just been made up here. Surrendering, absolutely yielding control of the situation, is *always* a reasonable option, and here it's been forced upon you. It would be stupid not to interpret the signals, wouldn't it? After all, you'd just be doing what you've been told."

"That's easy for you to say," Lena says. She is responding blindly now, no longer thinking, merely continuing the disputation by reflex as it were. "After all, you're just machines. You aren't even that; you're a series of tapes and memories. How could you suffer as I am? Furthermore, you don't have my responsibilities. You won't be the ones to have to deal with the Bureau; I will. You won't be held responsible for this at all."

"Now how do you know?" the third says reasonably. "How can you make an easy statement like that? Can you judge the suffering of machines? Have you ever been one? Part of all of us was once human so that we can make some comparison, but have you ever been a machine? Now think of *that*."

"Maybe I'm a machine now and I'm dreaming all of this. Maybe this is another simulation."

"Don't be ridiculous," the first says snappishly. "Just face the realities here and give up. It's been the only real option that has been presented to you from the start of this hopeless situation: to give up and accept your fate. If I were in your position, I would. You're just being stubborn."

"The Bureau will understand," the second lisps. "Believe me, they'd appreciate what you're up against here. They'd approve of this and they'd be proud of you for doing what was best to protect *their* interests."

"The Bureau never gave up," Lena says. "The Bureau sent me out here. If it weren't for them, this wouldn't have happened to begin with, just remember that. It's their responsibility, not mine. Anything that I do, I'm doing for them as much as for myself, and they'll know it."

"But it's too late now anyway," the third says. "That's just sophistry, and that kind of thing doesn't work these days. These are modern times, hard-boiled, practical, you've got to come to terms with the way things are and deal with them as they are. This is no time for idealism or whining around. As you know I used to be a physicist; I was originally made part of the equipment so that I would be able to advise you on any emergencies that had a physical science basis. I'm the expert in that area, and you have to take my word on anything that is said, and I've had plenty of opportunity now to calculate what's happened here. If I were you, I'd accept it. I'd just give up and let the ship fall and try to make the best of what is admittedly a very bad situation. The other way lies madness and futility, and you don't want to pursue that."

"I'm already mad."

"No, you're not. Not if you've been able to make presentation the way you have."

"That's nonsense."

"But, Lena, you are brilliantly, totally sane! Your mental facilities are absolutely intact. Despite the chaos here, there is not a sign of schizoid break."

"I'm suffering," she says. Her voice takes on inflection for the first time during this. "I'm suffering terribly. The dead are suffering also; I've taken on their condition. I share it with them now. There's at least a theoretical possibility that we can get free of this."

"How? Not at all."

"I exit without acceleration."

"Utterly destructive."

"Switch directly to tachyonic drive. Move immediately beyond light speed."

"There's no precedent for that, Lena. It's never been heard of; it goes counter to all the established rules of physical motion. Even if it isn't theoretically impossible, which it may well be, but even if it weren't, you can't do that. You cannot gauge the effects."

"This is a situation unlike any before. It demands new and special measures. How can we know what we can do until we've faced doing it? How can we say what our limits are until we've gone beyond to test them?"

"You're talking nonsense, Lena. Vainglorious nonsense which does not befit you."

"And then, too," the first says, "what if you do attempt this hasty and disastrous course, this selfish and stupid blunder? Where will you emerge?"

She has thought of that. She has given it a good deal of consideration, more than she would want to concede to the comforters. "I don't know," she says.

"You could land in the heart of a star. You could land at an edge of the universe where at no speed could you ever return. You might come out embalmed in rock on some planet. You might put *Skipstone* into explosion."

"I know that."

"You might destroy the foundations of the cosmos. The destabilization might be that profound. Have you thought of what might happen if you land in another neutron star?"

"Yes."

"You argue that all rules of space and time have been destroyed here and that only gravity persists. But would the fall not end eventually? There must be finite limits; at some point you will be drawn into the black hole and come out the other end of it into some other universe or some part of this one."

"No," she says, "I've thought about that. It took me a long time to work that one through, but if the very shape of space is changed by the gravitational field, then the fall would be infinite. It would have to be. There would be no point of termination, because we are falling inside curved space, a null space which lacks any of the properties which we can associate—"

"All right," the physicist cyborg says, cutting her off as if disturbed. "You've had a chance to evaluate and come to that explanation. You may be right, although I disagree, but we won't argue that at this time;

we'll defer to the thought you've given. It doesn't matter. The point still is, where will you come out if you break free?"

"And I told you," she says, "I told you that already. I don't know. I have no idea."

"In truth there's no way to calculate it, is there? It just becomes chance; the coordinates are beyond computation and you could be anywhere at all."

"That's possible."

"You had better think of that. If I were you, I would have given that serious thought."

"I have."

"And what then?"

"Anything would be better than this, that's what I think. This can't go on."

"Why can't it?"

"Because it's unbearable."

"You cannot gauge where you would show up, you fool. Can't you understand the scope of the universe? You're heading into infinite possibilities of which all human life occupies the tiniest sector. Your coordinates are antihuman and antilife."

"What do you care?"

"We care about the fate of the universe. You might unbalance the cosmos. A sudden matter transfer. There is no way of gauging these things, Lena. There is no way in which the shifts could be anticipated. The dropping of mass—"

"Oh, go to hell," she says furiously. "Damn it, go to hell. You're supposed to help me here, not fight. You were put here so that I could call on you, so that I wouldn't have to fight this alone, and what have you done? What has happened to me? All you want to do is to do things to convenience the Bureau. That's all the Bureau cares about."

"It cares about not destroying the universe."

"Why does everything have to do with the destruction of the universe?" she says again. "Can't you just deal with people, can't you understand that there are *people* here? I matter; I matter more than the Bureau does."

"You know you really don't mean that."

"I do mean it. I didn't activate you for you to tell me what not to do or how impractical I was. I wanted you to go over the thinking with me and tell me that I was right."

"But you're not right," the third says. "Your thinking is entirely wrong."

"I'm the captain!"

"You are not in a command position. You are merely another piece of equipment on *Skipstone* responsible for the maintenance of the other equipment. You are the servant of the ship not its master, and you are," the third says with a sigh which has personality, it is as if the full burden of humanity had come upon it if only for an instant, certain tapes activated which thrust upon it the mannerisms of the person it had been, "you are to remain here," it says, "and maintain the ship in a standby alert position. You are to do nothing to try to leave the field. It is unfortunate that this has happened, but it was a chance that you took when you assumed the responsibility, and you can't get out of it now."

"I am not," Lena says, "I am not going to stay here. I am going to do exactly what I want."

"You are willfull."

"I don't care. I don't care what I am. I'm going to do this no matter what you say. I'm going to gear the ship up to tachyonic drive and try to get all of us out of here."

"No," the second says, similarly inflected. It is remarkable how the context of the discussion has changed; now it is Lena who is calm, the cyborgs who are screaming, "No, I really wouldn't want to do that. You and the dead are joined together now. It is a shared fate and was always meant to be this way. You must remain with them. You are part of the dead."

"No, I am not."

"Ah, well," the first cyborg says. "You have to consider the mysteries here. What is life? What is death? What is the difference between the two, where do they meet and where does the division begin? Consider these questions."

"That's a good point, Lena. Those are good questions. I really would."

"Impenetrable mysteries."

"Darkness, theology."

"You can penetrate the very core of existence with this, Lena. Life and death existing together in this fall. Think of it: the symbolic fall heightening the symbolism here if you want to pursue it. Why, it's fascinating! You may be able to work out the full and final answers here."

"An exquisite opportunity."

"Exquisite, I'd say."

"Remarkable. Wholly remarkable. You will be able to glimpse, as no other human ever has, the eternal and the essential."

"You will never regret this, Lena."

"We'll stay with you, if you desire. We'll render you all the companionship you could need."

"Oh, definitely. Definitely. We'll give you a great deal of support."

"We can share this. Together."

"I wouldn't pass this up if I were you, Lena. It's never been offered anyone before."

"Oh, no. Never."

"Never again, either. What a small price to pay for understanding! It's remarkable."

"No," she says again, dazzled by the comforts, their interchangeability in dialogue, their persuasiveness, their solidity of purpose now that they seem finally to have accepted her own seriousness. But she knows, too, that the historical and theological role of comforters has always been to mislead (and if she does not know it then the author, busily straining over the levers of the plot in the cockpit of his own attention certainly does), and she will not be dissuaded. "No, I will not listen to you. There are no solutions. You offer me no solutions at all."

"We do. We—"

"There are only mysteries," she says, "and they can never be solved, but we can cultivate a decent respect for them and try to deal with them in relation to the mystery of our own humanity," and then she turns from them, breaking their hold upon her with a mere suspension of attention, goes to the place where the thing that was John lies, crouches over it like an animal and just for a little while she weeps. For herself, for him, for the lies, for the flight. For the dead in space. For the failure of her own belief that the Bureau, at one time, must have cared for her.

But shortly she feels better and the time is done for weeping. Furthermore, she knows that what has been discharged is more profound than tears; it is a whole level of feeling which she will never have again and without which, like a swimmer, she will be able to move more swiftly through the dark waters of purpose. The conversation has discommoded her as the Bureau intended the comforters to do, but it has also brought her to a new level; now, past disorientation and the shaken poles of faith, she begins to sense a new order. She must depend wholly upon herself. In one sense it is posited that this dialogue is taking place in a ship falling madly in a quality of space which could never be described, but in another it can be seen as one of those elegant and terrible drawing-room exchanges so popular with the discredited practitioners of the well-made play in which the slightest alteration of point of view or opinion is supposed to create great tension.

Any tension, however, is that generated between the furnaces of the dying star, ten million explosions a minute, and *Skipstone*, an arc in its heavens. Lena, knowing this, feels numb. Having moved beyond the comforters, she feels that she has learned little, and yet she must persist. She cannot turn over the very little she has learned to the iron hearts of the machines.

"Fuck you," she says.

They say nothing. Scatology does not move them any more than reason. If anything, their efforts have drained them and left them without visible effect. They lurk like crouched animals, only the slight whirring of their transistors indication that they are still functioning.

"Fuck you all," she says again. "I'm going to do it and I always was from the beginning. I'm going to get us out of here. It's all a plot of the Bureau, anyway, to prevent me from getting back should I run into some disaster. I'll come out all right; I don't care what you told me. It's all lies. Bureau just doesn't want the embarrassment of my returning to tell the tales. They don't want anyone to know what's going on in space, what it's really like. They were plotting this from the beginning; they just want a smooth path so that they can conquer the world. They don't give a damn about the universe." She realizes that, although she has phrased this crudely, she probably believes it, that she has always believed it. She puts her hands near the console. All along she hated those in the Bureau. She should have known. If she had only touched her feelings, she would have known the nature of that with which she was dealing. "I'm going to turn you off now," she says. "You'll never know the difference anyway when we escape. You'll be dismantled when we get back, so you'll never know a thing. What do you care? It's going to be much easier for you than for me; I'm going to have to go through."

The first says, almost agreeably, "You're right. We have no instinct of self-preservation."

"Indeed," the second says with similar amiability. "I'm finding this quite wearying, and I never did have a forceful personality, even at the best."

"If we had self-preservative instincts, it would be too difficult and painful," the first says cheerfully. "Fortunately, we're willing to be deactivated. As far as we're concerned, we did our absolute best. The problem is not ours now."

"Me, too," says the third. "I can go along with that completely. I mean, just because we have an argument here, because we tell you a few things that we were programmed to say, don't think that we don't have any feelings, because we do, or at least if we did, we'd feel very badly about this. We're just trying to do what we can in your own best interests, that's all."

"Liars," Lena says. "Now you're trying to win my confidence and get me to go along with you by pretending to agree. I don't believe anything that you're saying. You'll never make me believe it, no matter what you do. I won't cooperate with any of your schemes; I see through you."

"But it's true," the first says, "all true. You don't have to get paranoid about this just because we've lost an argument and are willing to admit it. You know, you're entitled to do what you want to; it's your decision. Stay here or, if you wish, leave. Of course it would be much nobler of you, in probability, to remain here. For all we know your condition gives substance and vitality to the universe. Maybe the basic stresses here are those from which all existence itself came to begin with and you are now at the beginning of time. How do you like that? Good irony, no, and certainly of a large scale! But if time is suspended, *you* may have caused the universe, Lena, you and *Skipstone*. You and the ship have generated everything. From your accident came everything including those very conditions which led to the accident. Hah!"

"Madness," Lena says, shaking her head, "that's utter madness," but the author, busily pulling the handles of his little dumb show, sweating behind the canvas, casting a nearsighted, astigmatic eye every now and then through the cardboard of the set to see whether the audience is paying attention, how the audience is taking all of this, is thinking take *that* Barth, Barthelme, Roth or Oates! *Pace* Bellow and Malamud, and may your Guggenheims multiply, but what have any of you or those unnamed created to compare with this? *Angst*, this is the sigh from which all self-pity once must have come. But the author ducks away, keeps his mind on business, modestly looks away from the audience and then down, transmuting (as he tries to except at very weary moments) his responses, histories, revulsion or envy to his characters. That is, after all, the more lasting and satisfying way to do this. "That would be insane." Lena says; "it would reduce all circumstance, *all* of it, to a circular accident caused by that accident. It would mean that there was no purpose in anything other than to create purposes and that—"

"But why not? What other reason would be as sufficient? You might have created the universe, you might even *be* the universe, come to think of it, but," the first concludes, "you aren't going to listen to any of this so I won't argue the point. We agreed to end disputation; it won't get us anywhere. You win, we lose. You'll have to handle this your way."

"Not so. I want to *save* the mission. I want; don't you understand that I want to return the dead—"

"Rationalization, Lena. Shut off the console now. Shut it off, deactivate us."

"All right," she says, "all right then, I will. You want me to do that—"

"*You* want to do it, Lena. You'll be much happier then and so will we. What do you care if you deny all existence by following this course? But we won't argue the point further. We really won't. It's in your hands, it always was, we were never anything more than abstractions anyway," the first concludes rather mysteriously and then makes a gesture to the other two, something sly and secret in the glint, some level of communication between cyborgs that Lena could not enter, would not understand if she could. In tandem they roll solemnly to the porthole like children trundling their awkward way across a floor. "We'll just have ourselves a good look at this," the cyborg says; "we'll have a look at this so-called black galaxy that you've warned us about."

"Don't," Lena says, "now please don't do that. There's no need, no need at all—"

"Of course we will," says the second.

"You bet your life we will," the third says.

"We're absolutely unanimous on this point," says the spokesman; "you can see that if it's going to be done your way then it has to be done ours as well," and the first thrusts aside the curtain again, poking its cylindrical snout, and Lena has an idea. She will get to the console and deactivate the cyborgs manually before they can do what they are seeking, but she does not have enough time to do so. In midlunge she is cut off, and then the pure, spectral range of the black galaxy pours through.

She shrieks, covers her eyes, fights with the switches and so at last, by accident, hits the lever of cancellation, shutting off the power in the cyborgs, and they collapse then in sequence by the porthole, curtains swinging closed, lying there in metallic disarray, clutching one another in a human and dependent fashion as if the moment of confrontation had driven them out of metal and wire and made them human again, made them seek one another. Lena begins, not unemotionally, to weep. It is manufactured sheerly by emotion and pity; there is nothing else to it.

But her weeping will pass, everything will pass, there are only certain limits past which emotional anguish can be carried before the psyche seals off, the reflexes of pain are numbed and the reader, too, loses belief, and so in time, kicking the machines aside so that they need not distract her anymore, Lena returns to the business at hand which is now clear to her. She knows what she must do.

She must will herself to the controls and begin the dance of the tachyons. She must concentrate on dangerous eviction that might destroy all.

# 34

So this can be said: that the novel sits upon a predetermined conclusion. She will attempt to flee the hold of the neutron star; she either will or will not succeed. Whatever that outcome, the penultimate decision is highly visible, and the textual material interposed between the statement of the problem and that solution is merely a lever for delay. It is quite clear what is going to happen; it is merely a matter of springing that conclusion, and in this sense the novel is not unlike traditional classic tragedy or its modern descendants such as *Death of a Salesman* or *Marat/Sade*, where suspense is not predicated so much upon what will happen to the principals as to how many mutually enriching levels of narrative irony can precede that end.

It should be clear by now, then, that the denouement of this novel has been obvious from the presentation of the problem. Lena, against all urgings and reasonable possibility, will essay to leave the hold of the neutron star through that power which *Skipstone* can give her. The reader, knowing this, may become restive, may have been running out of patience for some chapters before this. Why not get on with it? he might ask. Why not have her make the attempt, win or lose, wrap it up, but get out of this? What is being gained by holding back on discovery?

But to say this is to miss the point. I do not wish to accuse the reader; this is the simple basis of the matter. This novel is not about what happens to her—which is merely a function of astronomics after all—but why it has happened and what real effects this must have upon everyone, including the reader. The *whyness* of matters. The question not of consequence but of implication.

So it is clear that the satiric aspects of the scene with the comforters could have been milked for great and widening implication, and unless a skillful and controlling hand were kept upon the material, the novel could, at this point, be well on the way toward the truly farcical.

Consider this. Here is, after all, a background woven of the metaphysical and the hard sciences on a canvas of the inconceivably vast, yet before this construction is being enacted hastily and with a tint of the disreputable the same old comedy, the same folly, the same easy and dreadful juxtapositions of character which would fuel the dullest of well-made plays. Has the novel voyaged out to such inconceivable destination merely to bring the same old messages of human spite and mechanical pointlessness? Is this going to be a recapitulation of the same wearying human limitations which could occur in any split-level beside the intersection of the new interstate with Old Armonk Road, rubber toys in the small backyard, the crabgrass glinting under the haze of the suburban moon? This would be a legitimate question; it will not easily be defeated. The material would indeed have to be handled carefully and with an awareness of how easily it might descend to the riotous. Pain would have to be wrenched out of it; the reader would have to feel with the characters. Not only intellectual content but levels of the ambiguous would have to be woven through less *Galaxies* become merely an attack upon the technological, a curse against that absurdity. Nothing, surely, could be further from the intent of the novel. Yet the danger is there. Let it be acknowledged.

Even as the least talented comedian working in the dullest and dirtiest nightclub in the outskirts of Jamaica, Queens, New York, would know, great issues can be reduced to the scatological simply by particularization, by bringing them to the level of common, human necessity. Napoleon had to move his bowels; Hitler had itches; the Kennedys believed in Camelot and said prayers before bedtime (certain biographers informed us) but also had moments of false climax and sieges of pus. The sad stories of the death of kings might have had to do with constipation or embarrassing hemorrhage; the royal families of several nations have had a hereditary syphilis. Similarly, the novel must risk trivialization by bringing its material to the level of human necessity, and the scene with the cyborg, with its clanking, its religious (or antireligious) satire and even the whiff of a fart here or there, cosmological farts to be sure, might well furnish needed comic relief to what is, after all, a rather depressing construct.

In fact, in fact: why fight the issue? It would be best to accept and utilize the humor that can be found in various passages; to take one's relief where one can get it. There is no reason why the novel has to be negative; to the contrary. If it can find humor in *this*, the unstated message might be, well, then, it can find humor in anything. Matters cannot be quite that bad after all.

(Then, too, it could be easy to wring from the material the fact that, even surrounded by the cosmos and the palpable edge of the universe, man remains a corrupt and flatulent race; the fart will outweigh the metaphysical cry anytime at all. One remains what one must be regardless of circumstance. Could the reader settle for this and leave the novel go there?)

But, of course, there is ample material available to save from itself this scene with the cyborgs, to keep the novel on track and to make sure that at no point does the construction depart from its basic vision.

And that basic vision must be nothing less than the setting of the final chapters.

# 36

For it must be lush in physical depiction of the black galaxy, of the neutron star, of the altering effects that each will have had upon the perceived reality. There must be a heightened sense of the visual; surely it is this otherness which must be communicated, and therefore descriptive passages will not be scanted. Indeed, every time the plot seems to flag, when the dialogue becomes flat, the characters hysterical or the author unctuous, at every such point when the narrative drive appears to falter, *Galaxies* will drag itself over to the portholes to deep and wondering looks at the terrain of exploration.

And here is the source of the ultimate power, that which will excuse it from the many deficiencies inevitable with such a scheme. For the terrain is one which can be offered only in the broadest and most ambitious of science fiction, and every rhetorical trick, every typographical device, every nuance of language and memory which the author has in his scruffy, dusty bag of techniques sitting by the typewriter will be called upon to describe the appearance of the galaxy, the effects that the galaxy has upon all those who enter it.

Lena—who one must admit is a rather superficial character; there just is not all that much to her, although she is not devoid of sympathetic traits—will nonetheless be used to the limit of her expressive possibilities to work this through; nor will the writer, aware of another factor here, dismiss the dead, who also feel in this space and who can communicate this response.

Needless to say, this will be a rather bleak vision. There is no way to avoid that; the novel can hardly be said to be optimistic, for the effect the galaxy will have upon anyone trapped will be quite terrible. It results in a complete alteration of consciousness, and the hold which most of us have upon our vision of reality, our assessment of life, is already sufficiently tentative to make almost anything attacking it quite threatening. But with all of that bleakness, with all of the lush and rather prurient imagery which will be used to show how the effects act to destroy consciousness, the novel will not be completely hopeless. Not at all. In fact it will be possible for some to say (and some may even say it) that rather than being terrible the vision is somehow "poetic" here or "optimistic."

For, if the rhetorical effects are properly applied, if the writing shows power and control, then the construct will demonstrate, finally, that those concepts which we label "beauty" or "ugliness" or "good" or "evil" or "love" or "life" or "death" are little more than metaphors, poorly ascribed, semantically limited, refracted through the weak receptors which we possess to the utter diminution of what they really mean, and it will be suggested that, rather than showing us an alternate reality, the black galaxy may only be showing us our own but *extended*, opened up so that the novel may give us, as science fiction can in the rare times when it is good and as almost nothing else ever can, some glimpse of possibilities beyond ourselves, possibilities not truly compensated by word rates or the problems of categorization to a limited audience.

What is love? What is death? What is the meaning of all this anyway? The author does not want to start metaphysical disquisition at this or any other point. Sections of an author's novels written in his true voice are always the dullest and least affecting; the philosophical opinions of writers are of no use to anyone, the writers least of all. The good novelists can compose novels, all right, but even the best of them cannot think, and the "opinions" of a writer taken out of the mask of characterization or structure are always as banal as those of politicians. The ability to create character or assemble a set of narrative materials does not qualify the opinions of the author. If anything, they must be more suspect than those of an essayist: who, after all, is doing the talking? In what persona is the writer speaking now? So the reader will be spared, not only in this set of working notes, but also in the novel itself, laborious and mystical ramblings on the nature of things like "love" or "death" or "theme" or "religion" or "ultimate significances."

Who cares? Tolstoy went crazy, Mailer ran for mayor, Dos Passos looked for Communists, Sinclair Lewis went foursquare for Main Street, Kerouac ended hating children. Something happens to writers past the point of their creative options, something obscene, like the damages (not only of age) on the faces of prostitutes or the aspect of actors lumbering their way through retirement homes for grand old troupers. Considering that the best of them will end as fools, the best that a writer can do, it would seem, would be to cultivate a decent silence which will at least hold his folly to himself, and there are a few contemporary examples of this approach, which are worth emulating.

The reader, in any case, need not be concerned by this. The writer's silence is not immediate but will have to do only with the longer range; if the writer is to become silent, he will not do it in the midst of this novel which deserves a smashing climax and which will receive it. There is time, there is time: there is the rest of the writer's life, after all, in which to cultivate silence, and for the time being his obligations are clear: to follow smoothly if discursively through all of the issues raised here to an ending which will not deprive the reader of his expectation that there is some order and that the reeds of this narrative will not blow their way into silence, discord and white noise to conclude the wry and tentative harmonies suggested.

Interwoven as well will be the more human story of Lena's containment and suffering. She will, thus, be a "warm" and "sympathetic" character most identifiable to the reader so that he will be able to participate more fully in the abstract sections of the story. She will lead him there.

If Lena failed to come alive, if the reader could not feel sympathy for her plight and respond in a way which will enable him to find the outcome personally involving, this would be a cold, distant performance, brilliance in the way that the technically efficient can be, of course, but devoid of those qualities of pain which are worth more than technical briskness. "Pain" or "warmth" are by certain standards reserved to the catalog of merely commercial or sentimental literature, but if these qualities are not incorporated here, this novel will lose intrinsic value.

So characteriological touches for Lena will not be skimped. Consider her as she comes struggling to individuation: the reader should see her as an admirable person for all her faults, really remarkably courageous in the face of all her disasters, her seventy thousand years, her one thousand lives. Her own character emerges from all of them; her determination to seek and remain herself is touching. Throughout all of it she has held on to her own character and her goal and this is not unremarkable.

This accretion of sympathy can be managed through a bag of fictional techniques, some of them conventional, some more ambitious. Individuation through defining idiosyncrasy, for instance: tricks of speech, habits, mannerisms and so on. The kind of thing which could have been applied to the scene with the cyborgs if the writer had not had such an excess of integrity. Stammer or lisp, hitch in pace, a sudden characteristic stumble or aversion to odors as she limps across the cabin to check the portholes. Rhetorical devices peculiar to her, as in the instances of sex with John where her rhetoric becomes florid. Little physical signs, a large bosom or cast in the eye if nothing of greater originality occurs. Keep those devices modest and visible, however; science fiction is bizarre enough without increasing the distance of characters from the reader.

Any competent writer knows how to do this. So do the incompetent ones, sometimes better, which blurs distinctions further. But competent or incompetent, we all pretty much know what to do: set off one character against all the others in a scene by something visible, or at any rate easily grasped, so that the reader will be able to make mental pictures, hear distinct sounds. Feel that the character is a recognizable human being just as himself. The reader, that only true participant, that only character in a novel the reader himself must invent with only the code of language to help him on his way, needs all of the suggestions he can get. Individuation is not to be mocked nor is this to be scorned. Without it fiction is merely shadow play, disembodied ideas struggling through the haze, some glimpse of ruined forms gasping their way through the wasteland which is already of our time and which the reader has pursued fiction to avoid.

(Even with the cunning use of these devices, it is a miracle that fiction exists at all. Consider the code, consider the network, the levels of abstraction. Even a bad writer, an uneasy reader, is a kind of miracle. In writing or reading alike, one must completely reconstruct that which does not exist at all without participation.)

Still, science fiction, that glittering literature of ideas or at least pseudoideas, poses particular problems for all of us. In common, everyday fiction, the kind which our academic or *Redbook* writers alike write so bravely, we could give Lena her affecting stutter, dimple on the left breast, tremor in the right cheekbone, love of old houses, hatred of old houses, hatred of dimples, love of stutter, fear of noise, acceptance of flight, twitch of finger under stress and go no further. From these encoded signals, all would be able to infer their own state of mind. But in this difficult and highly abstract novel, because of the abstract nature of the theme, the way that the theme floods the very characterization and, in fact, can be said to overtake it, it will be necessary to do more than slash clumsy ribbons of paint at the archetypes on the shelf. One will have to find originalities of idiosyncrasy which in their suggestivity will approximate the black hole itself. If the situation, that is to say, is really crazy, then Lena will have to be really crazy, too, in order to convey it. Otherwise all will come off as grotesquerie instead of as a sharpened, careful assault upon the conditions which squeeze life into their shape rather than submitting to it. This will not be easy. It will tax the modest powers of invention available to me.

"I'm crazy," Lena might say staring through her hands, observing that fine translucence through which she can see the network of the ship itself, fine streaks of wire running through the metal like cobwebs, "I'm crazy; I would have to be crazy to remain here, even to be alive through all of this." The engines still maintaining the support systems give a confirmatory throb. "I've got to be mad," she says; "how else could this be?" She stumbles away, feeling her body extended to infinite dimensions, feeling herself as an extension that can overtake any part of the ship. Bigger than the black galaxy itself, she sends her persona to invade all of *Skipstone*, plants a betraying, informative kiss upon the dead in the hold. "Take that," she says, "take that if you think you're out of it. You fall deeper and deeper as do I; life and death have no meaning here. Do you see where all your dreams have gotten you, where your mad wills and inheritances have taken? You wanted to live again, and so you are, and, therefore, if I were you, I would choose death, but it's too late, too late for any of that now. You'll just have to take it as it is and make the best of it.

You're crazy, too," she might point out to the dead; "all of us are here, otherwise we could not possibly survive this."

A legitimate technique, this, turning the substance of the novel against what has seemed its first tension. Lena is not trying to remain sane but to be mad as efficaciously as possible, and the ironies here are workable. But enough, enough of that: the problems of the writer are not those of the reader. Even as the writer struggles to invent a novel, he must somehow entertain and induce that efficient briskness which is the key to diversion, particularly in so-called escape literature. The reader is not concerned with the author's fatigue, his almost constant series of complaints, his persistent horror of the act of writing, his domestic problems, car problems, financial problems, gray obsessions, light obsessions, slashes and dashes and smashes of fatigue which in the midst of his best efforts suddenly make him feel trivial and old. No, none of these factors can interest the reader whose attention through these complaints has already started to break up like patches of ice under sun. Soon it will vanish into little clots of damp, drying to bone. Why *this* book? the reader asks himself, now well into the fourth hour of his continental flight, staring through little clouds, a child's vision of heaven, toward a wing, wondering exactly when fire will burst from that wing and he will see his death sketched out against the sky, turning away from the window to look past sleeping businessmen and a fat woman knitting furious epitaphs between her hands, looking for a stewardess—more asepsis—with whom he can establish some contact. Why did I buy this one? the earnest and suffering reader wonders; why didn't I pick something to the left and right? *Sloggers of the Slime Planet* had a cover almost as attractive. Do I really want or need this? the reader thinks, shaking his head and moving his agonized shoulder blades several inches to and fro in a rabbit's gesture, trying to work out the stiffness and itching from the core of his back. Why did I take this flight? Couldn't I have taken one at night? Do I really have to see this person, these people in Los Angeles? Couldn't it have been let go for another six months? What is there to gain at this moment from reconciliation and why didn't I order the second complimentary Gibson, when several days ago the stewardess asked me if I would like it?

No, this will get me nowhere, the reader thinks; I am descending into futility; I must be positive-minded and forward-looking. *Galaxies* is confusing, but here are elements of tension, there are certain mind-broadening concepts, over here in the corner is the promise of a flaming and dramatic resolution; if I can hold on through all of this, I have enough faith in the author to know that I will not be cheated.

Still, he thinks, turning petulant and self-pitying the way that most of us do and no harm in it, self-pity being virtually the only emotion with which a sane person can confront life, still it is not fair. Here is a novel which seems to lurch in and out of its textual material like a drunk trying to find a line on the sidewalk or a jockey looking for an opening along the rail; it cannot possibly transport me from the more ominous and terrifying perspectives to be gained from looking at the wing tip. Where are all those college girls and divorcées? Where are those women with whom one is supposed to be able to establish contact during long flights or bus trips? Surely this cannot be my destiny entire. There has got to be more to this than there seems to be.

The writer has sympathy. Indeed, I can understand the problem here, can only assure in return that none of this is self-indulgent, that *Galaxies* tracks its purposes as relentlessly as the breathing of the reader's seatmates tracks and holds the beat of the jets in the nostrils. Bear with me and find not only resolution, but also excitement and adventure to exceed even what has gone heretofore. Science fiction is an adventurous format. Science fiction is a medium of wonder.

Lena will be individuated and thus become far more accessible. Her individuation will be accomplished in sections which will be interwoven with the more objective if surreal descriptions of the properties of the black galaxy. Although this meshing of personality and astrophysics will be dazzling and even verge upon tour de force, it will, in truth, be the easiest technical problem of the novel to solve. Two skills which fall well within my range—flat, deadpan, descriptive prose and highly charged sexual imagery—will effortlessly complement one another, giving an impression of more depth than may even be present. Technique can often supplant reason. Sometimes it may become meaning itself.

**38**

But let it be made clear again; this is not a novel but merely a set of notes for one. The novel itself remains unutterably beyond our time and hence outside of the devices of fiction. It moves beyond any considerations of normal space, can be glimpsed only in those empty little flickers of light which reveal the galaxies much as Lena cannot see the neutron star but only sense its effects, much as Lena can only infer the gravity, not gauge it. These notes are surely as close to the narrative as anyone of this time can get, because the novel cannot be written for almost two thousand years...but let us not become megalomaniacal in the pursuit of theme. These are merely notes. They are not definitive. The very language of the techniques necessary to write it will not be ours for two millennia.

Still, one does the best that one can under the situation presented. Little more can be asked of a writer. There will be long descriptive sections idiosyncratizing Lena and making her visible to the reader. She will talk to him by talking to herself; she will laugh, cry, mourn, express wonder at the dimensions of her situation, know moments of terror. She may (but then again she may not; we will see, it will be my decision) engage in streams of consciousness triggering flashbacks which will lend characterizational veracity. We will know more than what is necessary in order to accept her reality.

As these sections end, they will draw upon the conclusion that Lena has made her decision to leave the black galaxy by the dangerous means which are her only option. She will try to convert to FTL drive without acceleration. This decision has squirmed through her preconscious (not the author's; he has no opinion on the subject) and now is in the front of that part of her brain responsible for making rational evaluation. She does not know where she will emerge or when, just as the comforters have warned her, but she does know that this must be the way in which *Skipstone*'s tragedy and her own must end.

She prepares to set the controls for the plunge, her breath shallow and moist within her but laid against the rasp and controlled rhythm of her purpose. She knows that what she is doing is best for all of them here.

But before she can do it, she must tell them. She must tell those who will be most affected by this. She must make sure that they understand the situation and share her approach, that they accept the inevitability as she has.

She locks the controls, musing, and sets off to make confrontation with the dead.

# 39

For in a sense the dead have controlled everything; they are not the mere cargo but the creation of the voyage. If it were not for their presence, their generosity, their estates, their greed and terror, the FTL experiments would not have been at all financially feasible; if it were not for the lives transmuted now by the effects of the black galaxy to impinge upon Lena's consciousness, she might not be sentient at all. She might have died in the subjective time imposed by the gravity. It is only the cargo, then, that has kept her shielded against what would have otherwise been utter fragmentation; by using first one personality and then the next, the thousand, as interposition against the forces of the fall, she would have disintegrated. She knows this and knows that there has been a conscious element of use.

But she knows something else as well which is even more significant: the FTL experiments, Lena has come to understand (and with her the writer himself), the FTL experiments have always been shaped by the dead; in truth they fed upon the quality of death, and the Bureau, consciously or not, has shaped itself utterly around that cargo. There must have been some irony in that position, an irony that was built deeply into the projects, and that irony would be this: what was supposedly life-enforcing and expanding was sustained only by the presence of death. From the very beginning the experiments, rather than using the dead, have been their celebration. They have exalted it. That was what was really going on here from the start.

In the black galaxy, life and death have intermingled. But this is merely an extension, a concrete physical manifestation of what has been true from the beginning. Without the dead there is no life. Life has embraced the dead. All together they fall and the gravitation is their mortality, plunging them relentlessly toward the sun that will fold them through to another way of life.

Leaning over the console, then, she permits one of the dead to come forth and address her, no expectation in her bearing, merely the willingness to allow, finally, the dead to overtake her. What she does is without thought or even conscious intention, merely the extension of necessity.

She need make no formal gesture to summon the dead. They have been battering on her skull, screaming for seventy thousand years, and now, with a single, mental whisk, she has merely permitted all of those partitions to slide. Stricken and yet curiously unmoved, restless and yet strangely at peace (because she is doing she knows what she always should have done), Lena holds position while the dead stalks through all the corridors of her being, first prodding, then poking, inspecting and massaging areas of consciousness, then, this preliminary done, having satisfied itself with the fact that she is a proper arena, the dead begins to speak with her. She lets this happen because, from having no time at all, she has turned to all the time necessary, and however long it takes to talk with the dead, she will control the chronology.

When it is time to take *Skipstone* out, she will do so. She feels no urgency whatsoever. Doubt has been resolved. There is a kind of pitiless, bloodless joy to blending finally with what she has always known must happen.

"Just listen here," the dead says.

"I'm listening."

"Let me explain everything to you."

"No one can explain everything."

"With the dead all is known."

"All right," she says then, "all right."

"You believe that I can tell you everything or you would not have summoned me."

"That is not true," she says, "that is true."

Perhaps one should characterize this dead before moving further, individuate him in some way. It is not necessary to do this in order to make the full force of the dialogue apparent, but the dead, no less than the living, are entitled to characterization, and it is not intended here to slight him.

He was born—this is a male—in 3361, died in 3401, five hundred and one years ago. Cancer of the bone killed him at the age of forty. For some twenty-five generations, now, this dead has been embalmed, and yet despite all that has happened since, he submitted himself to the stasis of the machinery; despite all that has happened in the time intervening, not very much has happened at all. This is not a fluid society. Very few social and cultural changes can be said to have occurred in a millennium.

So certainly, brought to consciousness with the rest of the cargo when *Skipstone* hit the field, he has had ample time to pick up on any details which he might have missed through the period of stasis, and he has also been able to make certain linguistic adjustments, semantic reassessments which enable him to communicate with Lena spontaneously and in the vernacular of her day. His name, of course, does not matter; his name is *dead*, his characterization is formed by his condition. All, the memorial services remind us, all are the same in death: the wise man, the fool, the rich man in the palace and the poor man in his hovel, all of them, fallen asleep like a child over his toys, have let go of their earthly possessions and are now the same.

But for all of that, for all the leveling of death, it is a hard and unique characterization which would make this dead significantly different from any of the others. The personality will always reach for itself. Under any conditions short of crisis, we will strive for difference; the brutalizing effects of tyranny are that these effects permit the differences to be shut off...a secret known to tyrants.

"Listen here to me," he says again, "and I'll put the full and final truth of this to you."

"That's why you're here." She speaks in a rather dull and abstracted fashion, her glance frozen inward to confront the dead as if he were some aspect of herself. Is he? This is a theme which the novel cannot touch. "If I didn't understand what was happening here, you never would have been summoned."

"Nonsense," the other says briskly. "That's easy sophistry, and while it may work with those other fools, you're not going to manage it with me. I'm not like them at all. Remember, I've already passed over the edge. You're only going to get the truth from me. There's nothing else."

"What's the truth?"

"The truth is that you cannot possibly leave here."

"I'm going to try," she says.

"I didn't say that you couldn't *try*. You may well succeed in breaking from the field, your thinking is correct on that issue, there may be a means of exit. But what I'm saying is that you can't do it because it's only going to make things much worse."

"Impossible. Nothing could be worse."

"Not impossible but quite true. Better the death we know than the death that you want to give us. The one is eternal and we can dwell within it. The other is final and will cancel all possibility of time."

"The decision is made," Lena says. Her fingers clamp against one another; she adopts an earnestly penitential position. "It has been made and there will be no turning back from this."

"We are dead now. At least let this death continue. At least in the field of this galaxy where there is no time at all we have a kind of life or at least we have that nullity of which we have always dreamed. I wish I could tell you some of the things that we have learned together during these seventy thousand years of perceived time, but they would make no sense to you."

"How do you know?"

"There is no order."

"Everything is ordered," Lena says; "everything, ultimately, does make sense."

Her tone is so flat, so deprived of affect, that she might be dead herself. One must understand the degree to which she has reached an absolute communion with her cargo. She sees no disparity between her position and theirs. In a way she wishes that she did, because if she could see herself as different from the dead, she would not be faced with the need she feels to persuade the spokesman that she is right. But she is one of them, and what she does to them, then, she does to herself.

She knows that to share with the dead, to understand them, is to pass the last of all barriers. To understand that in the jaws of the universe biting down hard, biting down harder, more toward blankness, that aberration known as humanity is so slight as to make even discrimination between its living and dead components no more significant than the differentiation one might make between the halves of an amoeba in mitosis. Living and dead, they have been joined in this everlasting and terrible vault, and she wishes somehow that she could make the dead understand this, too.

But he would not. Not ever. The pain of the dead is even greater, she supposes, than the pain of the living, and their bitterness, too, must increase. So all that she can do now is to listen submissively although her heart itself would scream, and if she could embrace this man, this dead, this specter, this craziness, she would, only to hold him against the anguish...but here is an irrationality, she knows, of such dimension that even in these altered circumstances she would not try to explain it. Certain things can never be understood, can never be confronted, but must be put from all of us. In that is the beginning of implication.

She faces the dead, voyaging within her to find the part where it has spoken, still without face and says, "I know what you are going to say."

"Do you? Do you really? Then do you know that we have found resignation, and can you even understand what resignation would be to us?"

"Yes, I know that."

"Do you know what is meant by the peace that passeth all understanding? Do you grasp what I am trying to say to you for all of us?"

"Yes," she says, "I know of that. I know of the peace that passes understanding."

"Pass*eth*. It's Biblical."

"All right. Biblical. I seek it in my way, and that is why we must leave, for there is no peace here."

"It is perfect. There is perfect and complete peace."

"That is an illusion. You have suffered greatly, and you prefer what we have found to the possibility of more suffering. But there is no accommodation. There is no way in which this can be adjusted to. Time is infinite but our own capacities are not. We will fall and fall. Forever."

"Toward oblivion."

"No. Toward madness."

"This is already madness."

"No, oblivion," she says; "that is what you do not see. We would have lost control, we would be utterly mad, and yet for the rest of all time we would know this, and that is what I cannot bear and why we must leave. Whatever the risk."

"You cannot measure the risk."

"This is merely a transitional stage. It is not the last which has been planned for us. If we do not get out, things will become even more terrible."

"No, they would not. We have gone through the other end; we are already dead and know the difference."

"You do not know madness or what they have in store for us. You understand none of that. None of it."

"You have no right to say that. That is merely arrogance. Once dead we have passed through to the realization of all."

"No," she says. She would stake everything on this denial. "No, that is not so."

"Are *you* dead?"

"We are the same here."

"Yes, but have you died?"

"I don't know. Who can tell? I know what we have passed through together, and I have seen much more than death."

"No," the dead says, "you are terribly wrong there. You have misunderstood utterly. There are absolutes," he says; "damn it, damn you, there are absolutes after all," and then he seems able, at least momentarily, to say no more.

The speed of light is one hundred and eighty-six thousand miles a second, which would seem to be fast enough, and yet in astronomical terms, in terms of space exploration, it would be the Seventh Avenue local with brake trouble.

It takes, for instance, more than four years for light to travel from the nearest star, Proxima Centauri, to the Earth, about nine or ten times that for light to travel from Sirius, which we take to be virtually the nearest star with the possibility of a planetary system and conditions that might support our own kind of life. Just in the Milky Way, that corner of the galaxy occupied by Sol, thousands of years elapse in the passage of light from one side to the next. There are galaxies whose light we now see is the expression of energy emitted hundreds of thousands of years ago.

And far beyond the realm of sight or even the most powerful telescopy lie the pulsars, believed to be the waves of energy emitted by galaxies at such inconceivable distance that their light has not reached us, may not reach us for millennia, may never reach us at all, because by the time their light has traveled here, Sol itself may have died, and the Earth may be a burned pellet circling the ruined star. Or may have been absorbed in the final explosion.

Consider these two factors: the dimension of the universe and the impossibility of tracking it through any speeds up to the speed of light. The Bureau had to consider them in the early years of the fourth millennium, just as science-fiction writers of our own day had had to deal with them. It might have served the purposes of the Bureau if it had had access to these texts…but of course none of them existed.

(No records remained of that period toward the end of the second millennium. There was not a single scrap of evidence showing how the folk of that time had dealt with their problem, not even a sacred scroll embodying the words of the followers enshrined in some buried museum of artifacts. All of it had been destroyed much earlier, as if someone in the eras succeeding that millennium had made a unilateral decision that there should be no trace whatsoever of the past. Civilization appears to have been virtually reconstructed beginning around the year 2200; there is little bridge between that second era and all that preceded.

(Nor had there been such a museum, a collection of artifacts, would they have been closely observed. This is a notably phlegmatic and unsentimental age, without any sense of history or interest in pursuing a past deemed irrelevant. Human endeavor is cyclical, and there was a period in the 2500s when archaeology flourished: there was a stochastic frenzy and a desperate interest in finding how civilization had once destroyed itself through technology so that it would not happen again, and there had been a tyranny of researchers which had led to colorful and vicious episodes of political brutality, proving that historians and archaeologists were no less intrinsically violent than those who cared not of the past. But the 2500s are quaint now, have long passed into anonymity, and little traces of that civilization likewise remain. In the year 3902 there are virtually no archaeologists.)

That problem the Bureau faced was the development of a practical, faster-than-light drive.

The galaxy, let alone the universe, could not be colonized without it. It is impossible to conceive of any flight that could last hundreds or thousands of years without the descendants of the original crew having lost any sense of mission, any desire for completion, any understanding of origin, and, furthermore, there is no level of alienation as complete as to make competent people consent to spending the remainder of their lives in a ship moving at impossible but still finite speeds toward an unknown destination. People could not even be bred for this, although there were some rather horrid experiments conducted at mental institutions hundreds of years ago.

Accordingly, the Bureau researchers had to understand, man's tenuous efforts to populate or at least chart the universe which had moved at geometric rate through the conquest of Centaurus and even toward the initial hold on Sirius—thirty-six years to the hardy explorers of that time was just barely feasible, what with the enormous bonuses the Bureau paid as well as the parole from death sentences—would come to a complete stop. Science-fiction writers of this time, then, were not the only group that could not deal with that possibility. The Bureau writhed under it as well. How was it going to evolve a drive that would bring it the stars? How would it get around the chronological gap? What was the point in having a Bureau at all? What was the point in evolving interplanetary travel and sophisticated devices of colonization and exploration if they were cut off at a given point? The Bureau might have to dissolve. This was impossible, since in certain crucial senses, ways which the population did not entirely understand, the Bureau ran the world.

The work of Einstein had been buried with that of all his contemporaries, but his work was painfully reconstructed by physicists of the 3500s who worked independently, as if Einstein had never existed. Like him, they postulated at first that faster-than-light travel was impossible under all terms of conceptually grasped Euclidean physics. As speed approached that of light, these neo-Einsteinian theories of relativity held; mass and time would dwindle inversely so that a ship traveling right up to the speed of light (and never exactly at it, since it could only be approached, not met) would remain in static time at microscopic size. When it decelerated and reached its destination, the occupants would find that hundreds, perhaps thousands of years had passed while they had undergone only the relative time span of the trip. Thirty-six years to Sirius, then, only to find oneself utterly separate from the culture he had left!

Of course this would not matter on Sirius, but it would matter very much indeed in terms of obtaining contact with the culture from which you had left. Would it have kept proper records of your flight or would it have disappeared under another millennial frenzy?

During the course of the Bureau's cautious experimentation through the mid- to late thirties, it was found that this part, at least, of the relativity equation did not apply. Crews did not become microscopic nor did time pass at a shuddering and insurmountable rate outside of the space capsule. What the neo-Einsteinians had postulated just did not check out, to the relief, of course, of the Bureau.

But the other significant section of the relativity theory did appear to hold. Although a faster-than-light drive might have been theoretically possible under non-Euclidean physics, no one could make it practical. The speed of light could not be exceeded. And a ship walled in by that upper limit might as well not be traveling—in terms of cosmic exploration—at all.

It was then that the Bureau embarked upon its long, secret and dangerous experiments in search of a hyperdrive, one that would indeed exceed the speed of light. At the time of this novel, the bureaucracy, as the reader can well sense, had long since fallen into decadence, self-contempt, rigidified forms and custom, but it would do discredit to the brilliant and courageous researchers and voyagers of this early time who were responsible for the great days of an institution that for the last five hundred years had merely been moving on the inertial impact of those energies. The experiments went forward; they caused great loss of life and circumstance, but they can be said to have given man the universe. They opened up the possibility of the faster-than-light drive.

That drive was predicated upon tachyonic force: the conversion, that is, of the constituent ions of the ship to particles which assumed the qualities of faster-than-light atoms. These atoms are different in all of their properties from those of the "normal" universe, although they can be reconstituted. The atoms, in short, can change their condition.

That was the most brilliant insight of the Bureau researchers and voyagers in those early days...that they were able to change the literal constituent qualities of atoms so that a ship could slip in and out of the field of faster-than-light drive in some exact reclamation of its original form. There was less trouble in sending a ship into hyperspace than in getting it out in its original condition. That could only be accomplished by a trial-and-error process which was, to be sure, intermittently disastrous.

There were failures: experiments which resulted in hideous effects upon those returned in different form or no form at all, grotesques shambling from the converters, creatures which were of no universe we can name seen in the force fields shimmering before return, destroyed by the technicians before they could come out...and of these failures as much should be written as of the successes, for only through failure can humanity transcend itself. Success teaches nothing; failure presents limits, gives us the tragic sense without which understanding is impossible. Successes are composed of a thousand failures like the way the photos in newspapers reduce on inspection to myriad scattered dots, each expressionless, all comprising vision. And of the Bureau in those middle years of the fourth millennium, a great and grave instrument, something must be written and someday will because this is a history accessible to many.

The author may charge himself to the task. What is a body of work in our field without somewhere tucked in a future history? The idea of a future history may seem frivolous: after all, it might well be presumptuous to sketch a future when too few of us have any grasp whatsoever of the past, let alone the present, and if we cannot comprehend our future without a sense of history, then science fiction must be the least relevant of all branches of literature. And then again, assuming that we will never possess our history (the people of 3902 have utterly lost theirs), assuming that our history is being eradicated through event and in our culture has become almost instantaneous, certainly always contemptible...then if that is the case, perhaps the future can replace the past. By knowing where we thought we might go, we can reconstruct what we might have been. One will work as well as the other. Chronology is only a function of personality-in-culture. One may, scratching out didacticism where it can be found, take on a new kind of cunning.

So there might at some time be other works which will paint in some of the gaps only suggested here. The struggles of the Bureau to perfect the hyperdrive in the face of the pain, the losses, the ships that never returned and those which did in altered form and those few, gallant stragglers which by docking in the Antares system or transversing corners of the Milky Way proved that it was possible that the tachyons could hold matter as well as the tardyons and that the only barriers which held man to his limitations were self-erected.

There are stories here of schemes and wonder: the courage of the Bureau and many of those who, seeing what the Bureau would become when the struggles were over, did all they could to subvert it, but, losing, did away with themselves. There are the stories of the lost ships and the monsters within, some who sacrificed themselves willingly when they could have returned and exposed themselves to the world, brought about the end of the program in revulsion. Most of those stories would do more credit to the Bureau than what does exist here. But it would not be entirely fair to the Bureau to judge it by what it has become: not fair either to judge history either by the point that it has reached in 3902. There is much to be said, then, which can only be inferred here; there will be time, later on, to go back and to pick out, chiaroscuro fashion, notes toward a larger and more definitive series of novels which will explore the history of the Bureau from the days of origin until its bleak and somehow pathetic end in the year 4911 when its total membership had been reduced to four.

But not now, of course, not now: there is the instant situation with which to deal and that is certainly more than enough. Lena through *Skipstone* has not been testing the tachyonic drive—that has already been known and stabilized for several hundred years—but modification on the tachyons which would enable them to carry a much larger payload at the same speed, a payload, to be sure, mostly concerned with loading more of the dead aboard, getting greater cargo, greater remuneration. The more dead the more income the larger the payload and the more dead…or at least this is the circularity in which the Bureau—which I hope has been made clear by this time is a rather tragic institution—has gotten itself trapped.

At the beginning there were plans to carry larger crews on the FTL, having larger and more diversified colonization teams than had been true in the past, but early on, when the principle of financing pay-as-you-go through the dead had been evolved, it seemed to the Bureau that it would be better to outfit the ships with dead rather than living. This may show a certain dimness of thought, shortsightedness on its part, but then again the Bureau is decadent and running a decadent age. In 3619 it would have been inconceivable for someone as casually qualified as Lena Thomas to have been in solitary command of a piece of equipment as complex as *Skipstone*. There would have been a crew of at least a half-dozen and she would have been no more than fifth in seniority. But more living would have been here, fewer dead, and it is the dead who have made the program possible. One must leave metaphysical considerations out of this. Only spiritual reasoning, if that is the word, could apply, for in the Bureau's estimation the dead have become the living and the living merely dead space, using up resources that could be better assigned to several of the more economically stacked dead.

At ten point eight million miles per second, *Skipstone* has moved in free fall, searching the arms of the spiral galaxy until caught by the neutron star and sent with its dead into the pit that will end time. And in a way this is all the Bureau's fault, for the experiments themselves and for failing to take proper precautions, for not having anticipated the possibility of the black galaxy. But in another way it is not the fault of the Bureau at all.

It has nothing to do with the Bureau, has nothing to do with anything except preordination and the shaping hand of the author, because it was always destined—one can find this out for sure by correctly interpreting the prophecies contained in the Book of Daniel—for time to end in this seventh month of the year 3902, three thousand nine hundred and six years since the birth of the Saviour and a few more dozens of centuries past that from the second destruction of the temple which rendered the Jews forever a scattered people, wanderers and exiles like the FTL ship, probing the crevices of space for something which they could occupy. But there is little mysticism about the Judaic condition, something which cannot be said about what has happened to *Skipstone*.

# 42

"It would be apostasy to leave here," the dead says. All the time that the author has been laboring through his expository creaks and joints, the dead and Lena have still been trying to work things out, locked in their confrontation in *Skipstone* which will go utterly to resolution without extrinsic pressure because there is no time here. "You must stay. You owe that obligation not only to us, but also to yourself. In what form do you think you will be when you emerge? Have you opened that issue to your heart? Do you understand what you might become?"

"Yes," Lena says, "I have thought of that, I have thought of everything without you. And it does not matter. It does not matter what form I will take. Nothing matters."

"Everything matters. Everything affects everything else in an endless chain of consequence. I have made you; you are the product of all the dead, just as you in turn will be the product of those who will make us. Life does not exist in cubicles but only in terms of what it inhabits."

"I know that."

"There is an endless chain of consequence of which everyone is a link. You must accept that."

"I do," Lena says. She has entered a mystical, almost penitential frame of mind. Nothing can touch her. She feels easy; her joints seem to glide, she has an impression of herself as a physical being which she has not had in a long time. "I do understand. I am not stupid. Nor am I dead."

"Of course you aren't," the dead says rather vaguely. He seems to be discombobulated, but this may only be the shift of vapors in the hold, impossible to say. Confidence drains from him; he seems to take on a rather imploring tone as if he had realized that the right of decision had passed to Lena, which, of course, it has. "That has nothing to do with it. Who said that you were dead?"

Twitches of the pain which sent him into the vault, closed down the windows of his mortality, assault him then; he feels an old weakness which is composed not only of metaphysical spite but seems to occupy a physical plane. "Please," he says, "I don't know what you're talking about now. I really don't know what you want. How can you try to leave? Are you possessed? If you do, then it will surely destroy us all."

"So be it. We need destruction."

"It may even destroy time. Have you thought of that? You may shake the balance of the universe. You may end all time as we comprehend it. Have you thought of doing this? Would you end everything?"

"Let the universe take care of itself."

"What a selfish answer."

"What a *human* answer. Why do I have to think of the fate of the universe? That's only an excuse for the truth. The truth is what becomes of me."

"Is your vanity so great?"

"Great enough," she says, "great enough." Then she attempts to put everything which she has so perilously learned in terms so simple that even this obdurate dead can understand. "We are obligated to try. We must do the best we can for ourselves. If we do that, the universe will follow. We cannot be concerned with the universe; our concern is our own fate."

"Nonsense."

"We fell in, we must get out."

"Not we. Just you."

"All of us carry within ourselves the totality of humanity. We must reconstruct our history at every moment. Man must struggle, attempt to control the conditions that oppress him."

"Even if they cannot be controlled?"

"Only the dead believe that," she says, "but the living are not the dead and that is the difference, the belief that we can control. Isn't that the only difference between us? And even if it's only a passage from struggle to oblivion, that still is a kind of destiny. Isn't it?"

"You are a fool. You are saying that you know you will become the dead. We wait for you. All of your struggles are toward that end. But if you know the answer, if you know your fate, then what is the point of the struggle?"

"No point," she says. "That must be left in judgment out of the equation. Since we cannot understand death, it is of no matter what revelation it must hold. We must struggle as if death were merely a transitional stage."

"Bullshit," the dead man says. "You are a fool. Now you will destroy everything."

"But it's life."

"This is life?"

"It isn't death," she says, "and if we can't hold onto that difference then what, tell me, what is the meaning of any of this?"

And the music of the fall overwhelms her as the dead does not answer. *The dead does not answer.* There is nothing, at last, to say.

"I'm afraid," she had said to John at some point in her training, impossible to localize the time, but then she had always been afraid. She can admit that now; she had entered the Bureau in fear, and fear magnified had been all of growth that she knew. "I don't want to go. I don't like what they're doing to us here. It isn't right."

"It's merely your fear of the unknown," he said to her. Perhaps they were twined together in bed somewhere, perhaps they were having this discussion under the cool high glare of circuitry in some public place. It does not matter. He leaned forward, put his cheek against her, she felt the arching slab of his face as he spoke. "It's natural, it's normal to feel this way. Put it under the name of xenophobia. The atavism of the savage, the fear of that which he feels he cannot control. You can conquer it; you will be able to deal with it if you only will. All of that is to be expected and they have taken it into account."

"It isn't right," she said, "it isn't right. Can't I make you see that?"

"Right doesn't matter."

"They don't know what's going on there, and they're merely using us for experimentation." She shook against him; he touched her but was cold, cold now, his body shadows and clutching. She could not see his eyes. "But they won't let me stop now, will they?" she said. "That's for sure."

"No," he said, "no, there's no turning back, and you wouldn't want to anyway; this is where you should be, this is what you should be doing," and thought that he had lied, this was not normal; she was, in fact, at a dangerous point where she might go now in either direction. She might retreat into panic and refuse to take the *Skipstone* out and in that case what would the Bureau do? She may have no legal right of refusal, but it could hardly send a reluctant pilot. There have, in the past, been commanders who had refused, ultimately, to partake of the voyages, but none of them had taken hold of anything as significant as this, had had this large a cargo or that much of an investment in the voyage. "Don't worry about it," John said, feeling futile, and held her more tightly, reaching for some affectional basis (he hated himself for thinking in this way, but that was what the Bureau had delegated him to do), the aftermath of sex and its ruined fires like a damp wall crumbling between them but trying to force her by pressure into an accommodation which reason itself might not accomplish.

"Everything will be all right," he said. "The training goes satisfactorily, you are doing well, you should be without fear. All will work out for the best, and you will be glad, at the end, that you have done this."

"The dead," she said. "The dead." She held herself against him, her hands up and down the running surfaces of his body, and John, trembling underneath, felt the touch of those hands open him to a kind of darkness which he could not comprehend but which would penetrate him, he knew, to levels that he had never before touched, a pain which went to the very core of his relationship with the Bureau and which took him into areas he was simply not equipped to handle. (For all of his superficial intelligence and charm, he was really quite limited, and he has just enough intelligence to know this.) He pushed her away from him and said then, "I don't know what you're talking about," even though he did. "Please, Lena; you must stop this now.

It does nothing for us." Something like fear coiled within him. He had never before thought of the emotional significance of carrying the dead, vaulting a cargo of corpses at unspeakable speed. *What would it do to one, what did it really mean?* He did not want to think anymore of this.

"The dead," she said again, her eyes closed against the light of her vision, "that's the purpose of this mission; there is no other. To convey the dead, to carry them. Everything else, the tachyonic drive, the search for new galaxies, the colonization rationale are merely excuses. Why won't they tell us the truth? Everything is for the dead and what they have given us."

"No," John said, "not for the dead but the living," but he did not believe this, when all was finally at conclusion, he knew then as he always would that he was not a fool and what he said was so obviously untrue, so pointless and equivocating as against the simple power of her statement, that he could hardly take himself seriously much less the attempts that he made then to soothe and quiet her, holding her against him, talking to her deeply, intensely, trying to communicate through touch and tone what words would not bring.

"For the living," he said, "only for the living," and she said, "No, for the dead; that was the way that they always wanted it, to find a way to deal with the dead, and if they ever solved that problem then they would be committed to death," and at the end of this it would be only weariness which brought them together, not passion, their opposition welded, dead and living, living and dead, meshed over all the spaces of the pallet on which once again they entered one another because in this year 3902, just as today except more so, because of the decadence and rigid formulations of those times, sex was sought as a release from the tensions and pressures of the common existence, although it only led more often than not to frustration, doubt, misery and loss, this being one of the numerous ironies played upon the race by the conditions of its mortality.

Living and dead, dead and living, the scent of them flowing on the hard, brown surrounding husk of their union.

Eager to make his argument, eager for once to make the issues clear and without the masking of characterization, the author has been in such haste to hurl didacticism at the reader that intention may be too forthright. Expository material, individuating touches have been scrapped in these concluding sections; the dialogue has become florid. It need not, for example, have been so compressed; it might have been useful to have moved away from such philosophic or metaphysical intensity, to have described yet again the interior of the cabin, the appearance of the prostheses, the sensations of falling, the sound of the engines, the whispers of the dead. Also, one could have woven in detail the past life of the dead with whom she has had her final argument, certain details of his biography, rowdy and solemn by turns, to give him a warm, human aspect, the actual physical projection of him which she sees mentally, the way in which she reacts to this vision as contrasted to and compared with the way that she reached her lover/superior John. Once again the old equation between sex and death, so popular in modern literature, could have been a serviceable metaphor for the argument that passes between them.

Impatient for once, however, I have scrapped these details for the more abstract. Issues are more important than people in science fiction, and even that kind of science fiction which devotes relative attention to characterization or pain must, when confronted with the ultimate necessity to *keep things scientific*, move away from the matter of humanity. If you want to write about people, you had better stay away from this format; this is a truth taken to heart by everyone who has ever worked successfully within the form, and the author is no exception; he is involved with the effects here. The neutron star comes as close to a protagonist as this novel will ever have.

This is not to say that the intention all along was a disguised lecture in astrophysics and time. I am certainly no less interested in metaphor, description, idiosyncrasy, structure, than a writer of any routine literary bent...but the arguments of *Galaxies* can best be accomplished through letting the rags of didacticism flutter, however drably, in the breeze of dialogue. If this will alienate some readers, well then, again, it will be of attraction to others. Science-fiction readers have historically shown themselves more willing to settle for straight factual presentation and argument than the readers of any other class of popular literature.

Indeed, many of us modern-type science-fiction writers have been criticized for ignoring the intellectual interests of our readers, failing to provide them with a nourishing diet of ideas to complement the technical displays and characteriological evasions with which so much of the literature of the field has been recently concerned. That being so—of course it is so—I can hardly be criticized for having been so straightforward in these chapters. Indeed, I have taken the instructions of those critics to heart and, for once, am doing it their way. The argument is certainly the core of this novel, for if it is not, then there cannot, by any means, be an emotional effect.

No, the author busily wants this to be a freak show, one of his characteristic productions of sleazy wonders shown giggling and peeping back at the onlookers through the tent of purpose; he does not want this to be yet another display of idiosyncrasy but instead a solid and thoughtful attempt to limn out a future history arching toward the end of time, setting up the base pivot which has caused all of this to happen. The end of the universe cannot, should not, be done within the context of the freak show. A certain decorum is called for. Nothing should be done below the literary waist. One must not take liberties. One should not seek to titillate but to appeal to the intellectual faculties of the reader, for the reader must have respect for the writer if anything is to come through. We must not violate one another.

And if nothing else, the writer is confident that, having come to this point, the reader with him, he has at least gained the respect of the reader. He knows that the author's intentions are pure, that he will not, at the least, be violated. What after all is the writer but the reader's creation, helping him to construct collaboratively that ultimately satisfying novel which he seeks to leave the place where he has been? It is a long flight; the reader needs all the help available to get through this one. He can almost but not quite do it by himself.

And the author has been a deferential guide: slow, sincere, a little pedantic and inclined toward self-mockery, but he has revealed himself while asking no revelations in turn (and thereby foregoing catharsis) but merely the grim knowledge that, if it were not for this, the novel could not work at all. He is sure that his honesty will be rewarded. The reader will make allowances for any obscurities; he will go along at this stage. Because if those allowances are not made, you see, all of this has been pointless...much as if Lena is wrong in her determination and decision, then the novel itself must be without point.

"You see," she says almost conversationally, her emotion drained by the anguish of what she has said, what she has had to fight through to have reached that knowledge, "you see, I don't care about the dead. My concern is for the living among us."

"What living? Just yourself?"

"For all of us."

"If you care only for the living," the dead man says, winking one large, bleak eye in the center of the ruined forehead, this new form one with which she is comfortable, meeting and mocking her perception of him as utterly vile, "if you care for the living, then you must show some concern for the universe itself which contains all of the living."

"The universe is of the dead."

"Now that would be an alternative universe, one which you could not conceive, could not know of. The universe in which you live holds only life. And do you know what can happen if you try to come through it?"

"No. Of course not. Nor do you."

"But I am not seeking to do it. You have to have concern for what may happen."

"Ah, well," she says, "we will just find out. We will find out what happens because we will go through it."

"I will tell you," the dead says, "I will tell you what could happen. No one can be absolutely sure of this, but this is as close as one can come to true suggestion. By going through the center of the black hole, which is what will happen when you switch to tachyons without transition, you will rupture the seamless fabric of space and time themselves. Normal considerations which you hold do not apply. The effect of the tachyonic switch will be absolutely calamitous; you will fall through, and you will destroy space and time itself, the totality ripped."

"If I don't know that how can you?"

"Because there are layers of knowledge open to the dead which cannot be shared by the living. Everything will be destroyed."

"Why don't I hear from any other of the dead? Why just from you?"

"I am their spokesman."

"Who decided?"

"Through my voice you hear many voices. Through my voice you hear all voices. The explosion working against the implosion of the star may extend the funnel of gravitational forces to infinite proportion."

The dead pauses, blinks his eye, seems to investigate the images evoked by what he has just said. "All of the universe will fall through that hole," he says, "and all of time as well. Time will reconstruct itself but only in the abyss. You will never know what you have done, because you will never move past that point. Do you know what that means, then? You will relive this over and again. So you will never leave. Never. You will be in anguish forever, reenacting this constancy over and again."

Lena shakes her head. If she is jolted, she will not show it at any level which the dead can apprehend (although, she thinks, this is foolish because the dead can apprehend everything). "All right," she says, "that's terrible. But it still makes no difference." She will yield nothing to this creature. Nothing whatsoever. She will give no part of herself or feeling. The dead must be another of her tempters; the dead has become a fourth comforter in yet more cunning and outrageous guise. It is a plot. It is all a plot worked out by the Bureau to make her progressively confused and malleable. It never had her interests at heart. Now it does not want her to return and expose it. She must believe this. She must hold onto this, because if she does not, she has gone through all of this exactly nowhere and seventy thousand years have had no significance.

"You are lying," she says.

"I cannot lie by definition."

"And even if it's the truth, so what? So who cares? You do not even exist; there is no reality to you. I hear your voice, but it is merely hallucinative. It is another effect of the neutron star; it has made me irrational."

"You are irrational."

"I am responsible only to myself. The universe is merely an excuse, an extension of my own personality and the *Skipstone*'s struggle. It is not an issue. It never was. It's only an excuse for doing things that are terrible."

"*That* makes no sense."

"It does!" she says desperately. "It does! It isn't a rationalization, it isn't an excuse. I know that this is the truth, that you're just trying to confuse me with talk of the universe, space and time because of my own fear of leaving, of taking the risk. I've no need to listen to you. You aren't telling me the truth. You can't be!"

"But I am," he says. He has seen her hesitation, scented her pain and feels, as if old mysteries were moving the ruined blood again, his victory. He knows that if he can pursue the advantage opened here they will never leave this galaxy, because in the end he has proven the stronger. The dead are stronger than the living always, he thinks, because they are destination. "You are rationalizing," he says; "you will not confront the truth. You know it now as well as I do. You cannot avoid it."

"No."

"Yes. Yes! You can't be an utter solipsist, Lena, not here, not even under seventy thousand years of the lash. You aren't God, there is no God, not here."

"Yes, there is. There must be a God."

"If there was, He would not be here. This is dead space, this is null time. This is that from which the universe was created. This is before the beginning."

"That's evil to say. If there is a God, He would be everywhere, certainly here."

"Would He? Do you really believe that? This is the truth. You must measure this universe by yourself; that is the only faith that you can ever find, the only constancy that you will ever know. You can look for no one, nothing else."

The dead has said this triumphantly, his inner voice arching through a shout. He knows that he has won. She looks at him and he looks at Lena and in that confrontation, in the shade of his one, clouded eye as his glance passes through the dull illumination of the neutron star, she sees that they are close to a communion so terrible that it will become a weld, will be a true connection. If she listens to this dead for even another instant, she will collapse within those features as *Skipstone* has collapsed into the black hole, and she cannot bear this. It cannot be.

No, it cannot be; she must preserve herself at all costs. She must hold onto her individuation, the feeling that she is right, that she has at all costs won through to an epiphany worth the having and that the separation between the living and the dead is real, that it will hold and that there will be dignity in that situation. Life, she thinks, life is not death, because if that is so, there is no point in having struggled. If she believes that, she denies herself and all the becoming necessary for her to be here.

## 45

So she does not consider further. She will not think because to give thought is submission. Quickly she moves toward the controls, the levers of power which when hit will convert the ship instantly past the speed of light, and then in the explosions of many suns that might only be the illumination of the network of pain within her, she hides her head in her arms. She screams.

Screams not for herself but for the dead, not for the dead but for all the cargo, the lusterless, gelatinous forms lying in the hold, slipping like fish through the ocean of space: now she sees them, holds onto them in a sense of fusion unlike anything she has known before. They are not *the* but *her* dead, all of them, gliding in and out in a sleek possession harder and brighter than anything, almost as if all of them have been massed to plead with her.

"Oh, no," she says, for the pain is quite inexpressible, and she has been reduced to simple moans and murmurs. "Oh, no, it can't be. Something like this cannot be."

"Yes," the dead says, stronger now even though knowledge of his defeat has seeped through him sudden in the backwash of victory; he does not quite understand how this has happened to him, and yet loss seems to renew him as victory never would; he has the strength drawn from doom. "Yes, this is what has happened. This is the way that it will be."

"It's too terrible."

"All of us with you, Lena. All of us. No separation, just the complete binding."

"I never wanted it this way. I didn't want—"

"It could have been no other."

"Please—"

"Yes," she says, "yes."

They speak to one another now in the short, abbreviated barks of lovers, little stumps of words and thought. They might indeed be lovers intertwined on a bed rather than on the canopy of space. *Please. No. Yes. Willwont. Ahoh. Help. Now. Lossoh.* The murmurs of exchange pass between them like the darker and older coins of love. She finds herself too weary to continue and yet she must. She finds that she cannot go on and yet she continues. If she does not, then it has all been futile. She wants not only his acceptance—which acceptance he could never have denied—but his understanding. Can she make this clear to him? Can she communicate? "I want to live," she says, "that's all, live."

"All did. All do."

"I have a right to live."

"Not at the cost of time."

"At any cost. At any cost at all."

"Life should not only be an expression of selfishness."

"It must be. You're wrong. In order to persist, it has to be. Otherwise I would be dead. No one would have ever lived. Life itself would not exist."

"It is your decision, Lena." Centuries of anguish have flowed through him like water, just since she pushed the levers; now he has nothing left. He cannot continue the disputation. Whatever it is, it is over. "It was always your decision, if you wanted to do it. No one can change you. You can never be changed."

"No matter the cost."

"You have made it that way."

"Yes," she says, "yes. I have made it that way. I want it, I want eviction from this galaxy. I want the sun again, I want light, I want this, I want that, I want, I want—"

She stops. She throws back her head. And then she screams.

And the dead screams, too; it is not a cry of accomplishment or joy, but not of terror either; this must be understood; what comes out of this, what comes from the two of them, is the true natal cry suspended, as it were, in these moments of limbo. Life and expiration become fused here, their shrieks intertwine much as all the themes of the novel can be said at this point to blend, and if the work has been done well, the reader at this point should feel a real jolt of terror, terror of recognition, of course. Then in the womb of *Skipstone* they continue to scream in a rhythmic fashion, the shrieks entwined as the ship pours through the redeemed and climactic light.

# 46

We are upon the conclusion and that conclusion, obviously, is open-ended.

Cunningly it has been built into the construct from the very outset. It is a characteristic of a certain kind of well-structured fiction that it will lead toward a resolution which in retrospect may appear inevitable but which in fact is only one of a series of choices which could have been made and which, in the fact of its selection, has become the transmutative force of the work, has cast back little slices of light from which the novel, read once again, may acquire additional depth. The proper ending for the writer, then, is not so much constructed as *discovered*; it is a matter of working through the material consciously or subconsciously so that the ending is seen retrospectively as having been in place all along, not to be recognized until the point of its organic extension from the material.

This is not quite such a construction, alas; the ending could go any way at all, much as could *Skipstone*. It would be hard to write a tight resolution, an elegantly structured novel given the material here. With nothing less than all possibility as its field, how could *Galaxies* cleanly seize one from a set of alternatives as to make it appear that there were none other?

No, anything at all can happen here. The novel, many-leveled and certainly provocative in premise if not characterization, would yield to a number of endings. Only a few of them can be suggested here. Let them represent a much larger number.

Perhaps, then, Lena emerges once again into her own time and space. She finds that all of the events in the black galaxy have merely been a concealing sheath over the greater reality.

"I see," she would say as she flicked into normal space a hundred light years from Sirius, the breath of her anticipation cooling in her chest, all voices silenced, "I see now, I see what they wanted to do. It is not fair," she would say, her eyes filling with stunned wonder at the audacity of the Bureau, at its cruelty. It was all a test. "It cannot be this way; they cannot do this to us; we have more importance than they give us credit for having," and so on and so forth, the force of her discovery taking her almost all the way to madness and then back again as the ship on automatic settles toward its predetermined docking where the experimenters would swarm and pull from *Skipstone* every last scrap of data embedded on those tapes, the tapes a full recording of all the interesting events just as the Bureau had hoped in setting up its ultimate stress reaction as Lena herself, a muttering husk, is committed to the deepest, institutional abscess of the Bureau where for the next several years she might lie under the electrodes, being at last gutted. Not a happy conclusion, this, not happy at all, and yet one can see that she has gotten what she deserved all the time. The Bureau, having manipulated the conquest of space for more than a millennium, would hardly have allowed the ship to fall into a black galaxy: the only black galaxy that would exist would be one prepared by the simulators. So much for metaphysics. So much for the seriousness of the issues raised. It was all an experiment, and the decadent Bureau has decadently manipulated her, to say nothing of the reader, only to find out to what limits its technicians will sustain their humanity. Knowing those limits, they can then easily move past them.

That is one ending; another might see Lena emerging into an otherness. One moment she is being torn through the black galaxy, in the next she finds herself in a gray space where all of time, light, depth, possibility have been suspended. In emptiness the tachyons strain, trying to lift the ship beyond. In perfect nullity the thing that was Lena stands rooted to the plates of the ship, waiting for that moment of stasis to pass, but this will never happen.

No, it cannot: she has fallen through the pit of the universe in the one moment of leap and now toward a state of denial, of antiexistence. One can see denial in her finger, her eyebrows, the desperate attempt of what was once her mouth and is now a horror to form words of prayer…but in this void words cannot be formed nor thoughts. In perfect stasis she stays there forever. She has no sensation of time passing nor does she have the sensation of it being instantaneous. She is not dead nor is she alive. She does not succeed nor does she fail. Mindlessly, she and the ship are imploded within to hold the moment in which she pushed the cruel lever home.

Maybe a monument is erected to her in memory of this; maybe at another time she becomes an artifact to be glimpsed by fascinated tourists who pass in and out of hyperspace on their tours, circling the black galaxy at a time infinitely advanced when the gravitational effects can at last be exploited. All of the universe may someday be an amusement park; Lena would be an exhibit well worth the trouble. Galactic Wonderburgers would be nearby. This ending would be flooded with warm, individuating touches to augment its irony; it would deal with the imperishability of man, his ability to make junk out of any part of the cosmos. Nothing can defy his trivialization, but that trivialization becomes in itself a profundity; it is a comment which makes as much sense, if not more, than a deification. Why deify the unknown if it can be manipulated, controlled, packaged and sold? Idolatry need not blind the eye; it may seem to sharpen it, lift that which it reflects to celebration.

And there might be another ending, here a construction in which Lena does escape. She emerges into a vortex of fire and is grabbed by the thrashing heart of a star, winking instantaneously into death along with all of her dead; they muddle and mingle together in a star song of extinction. So much here, then, for celestial exploration, so much for the broken spirit of man. So there for all of you, so *there*. All of the pain, the struggle for acquisition, the explanation and metaphor for nothing. A burst of epiphany and then obliteration. All of them overwhelmed and yet unthinking.

But, of course, of course, there are many such alternatives, and all of these must be passed over in pursuit of the real and true, the absolute conclusion which has not yet been stated.

47

For, after all, not any ending will do. Not everything would fall into place, would be emotionally satisfying. The discovered ending which would be the truth is hard bought, but it is there, and I think that I have found it. The going has not been easy through any of this, and the climax has oozed rather than leaped from that canister of the unconscious to which it has been confined...but still, there it is, there it is now, and looking at it with mingled revulsion and awe, the author can do nothing but state it.

And it must be understood before that resolution is given that, just as these are merely a set of notes for a novel, so, similarly, the ending as conceived is just that, nothing more: a series of notes toward the conclusion. For the ending cannot be sculptured any more satisfactorily than the novel to which it is prefatory matter can be. It is simply too audacious, this, too broad, entirely too removed from the experience of even the most broad-minded of us. It can only be hinted, and perhaps circumvention is the way to get at this rather than using confrontation. What is there to say? What can be easily stated? If Lena's dilemma is immeasurably vast, then the way in which the novel comes to terms may simply be slight. Any outcome would seem trivial.

But, the resolution is there. It is viable, it is, in fact, inevitable. Emerging textually from the material, it has been hard bought, and perhaps one can see that it was, after all, implied from the very beginning, from the onset of these notes. The author has struggled, he has worked hard, he has done what he could to piece out this resolution. Give him, then, give him that ending.

The characters, too, deserve it.

# 48

For in the infinity of all time and all space, anything is possible if only once. Anything may happen if only at a given time, and as *Skipstone* trembles with the power of its transition, as time shifts and they are vomited from that black hole, Lena and her dead fall into infinity. They become bound to it. They scurry like the hand of a drunken painter over the vast canvas of all possibility, cleaving through the burlap of the galaxies.

Now here they are in the Antares Cluster, flickering like a bulb, the ship power shuddering as they plunge toward the dead star, and now here they are again momentarily at the heart of Sirius, the core heat a series of blows to the drowned metal; now yet again they move through some slip in time to find themselves in ancient Rome, possibly in an arena watching gladiators, brutish men with stupid faces reflecting pain, struggle in an abattoir, then moving in the air like some machine of prophecy watching another man haul wood up a high mountain....

And they do not know what they have seen, of course, certain myths being nonrecurring, traditions being reconstituted every few centuries, but even as they attempt to take in the significance of that, the ship moves again, shedding various levels of reality just as it sheds space and time, and they plunge a billion years across the flat, dead span of the universe, cling briefly to a hundred thousand habitable planets, and on each of them, infinity encompassing all, there is a mountain with a man carrying wooden bulk, and on each of them they see this, although memory is abolished along with context, and for each of them witness is as the first time. There is no history nor is there accumulation.

It is impossible to say how long this goes on or whether time can be said to apply to it at all. All that can be known is that *Skipstone* moves, and its occupants and author alike tremble on the verge of an epiphany and that epiphany is this: they cannot partake of the infinite; the equipment which receives this is so limited as to cancel consequence and we are after all merely human. We must reconstruct from all the pathways of the possible, then, that frail gestalt which is all that we can know. Lena, *Skipstone*, John, the prostheses, the dead themselves cannot become other than what they are but must only recapitulate themselves over and again. Trapped within the consciousness of the writer, the penitentiary of his being, much as the writer himself has been trapped within the *Skipstone* of his mortality, Lena and her dead emerge.

They emerge into a known sector of the universe.

And this is where they are.

# 49

They emerge in the year 1975, July 1975, in the town of Ridgefield Park, New Jersey, floating to the cobbled and bleak surfaces of that town in a haze which absorbs all matter and there, by the laws of energy conservation and probability, they come to inhabit the bodies of the fifteen thousand souls of that town. They merge with them, become part of their consciousness so that they cannot be distinguished, they assume not only the flesh but the persona, the jobs, the loves and lives and memories of the residents of this little town, and there they remain and there they will be. There they are; there they are now.

And now and now and yet and yet: dwelling, amidst the refineries, strolling on Main Street past the Rialto Theatre, queuing at the theater to see films at reduced prices, shopping in the supermarkets, pausing in the gas stations, pairing off and clutching one another, some of them, in the imploded stars of their beds at the very moment at which the author, that cosmic accident himself, writes this about them.

Yes, it seems unimaginable that they would come, Lena and the dead, from the heart of the black galaxy to reconstruct and tenant the town of Ridgefield Park, New Jersey...but there is something less imaginable which makes, finally, this difficult resolution just for all.

For how can this be? How can it be? That from all the Ridgefield Parks of our time we will assemble to build great engines which will take us to the stars...and some of the stars will bring death and others will bring life and then there are those which will bring us nothing at all but the engines will continue, they will go on forever.

And so, in a fashion, after our fashion, will we.

# AFTERWORD

Consider the story of the blind men who visited the elephant. Unable to see the elephant whole, each brought away a different tactile impression of the beast, and a different definition: the elephant consists of great, rough limbs resting on horny toes and extending to the top of the sky; the elephant is a ropy, muscular tentacle with suction at its distal end; the elephant is a scaly wing of flesh.

The totality of the elephant was, and remains, beyond comprehension. As does much else.

Barry Malzberg was born on July 24, 1939, in New York City, leaving the City for New Jersey in 1971. He has a wife and two daughters. He sold his first science fiction story to *Galaxy* magazine on or around January 11, 1967, and remembers it as the "worst, most dangerous event of my life."[1] He is the author of over seventy novels and over 150 short stories. Most of his works are in the field of science fiction. He is a large, morose man with an admitted fondness for chess. He has coedited at least seven anthologies. His novel *Beyond Apollo* won the John W. Campbell Award for best science fiction novel of 1972.

[1] LETTER FROM BARRY MALZBERG TO MARTA RANDALL, JANUARY 11, 1979.

The critic, magnifying glass held firmly before eye, finds nothing in this recital of facts to illuminate the writings of Barry Malzberg. There may be other facts lurking in the wings but they are not available to the critic, nor should they be. Biography in place of attention is an evasion, albeit a tempting one.

Galaxies is an expansion of a novelette, "A Galaxy Called Rome"; the novelette was written in 1974 and published in 1975 in The Magazine of Fantasy and Science Fiction. The novelette may be one of the best and most self-observant pieces of short fiction published in the genre. However, it is not the subject of consideration here; instead we concentrate on the novelette's larger, and more annoying, offspring.

Galaxies, like the novelette, was written in 1974 and published in 1975 by Pyramid Books, with a remarkably ugly pink cover and some of the most misleading cover blurbs ever to come out of a field noted for the mendacity of its advertisements. Print-run figures and sales figures are not immediately available, but it seems safe to assume that the book met with a silent and muddy death soon after its publication.

Galaxies is not a novel; it is, rather, notes toward a novel, as Malzberg makes abundantly clear on the first page of the book:

> The novel itself cannot be written…because it partakes of its time and that time is of the fortieth century…it could be perceived only through the idiom and devices of that era which, to be sure, will not exist for more than eighteen hundred years. (p. 257)

There is both blunt honesty and warning to this caveat. If science fiction should consist, as John W. Campbell once said, of the mainstream fiction of the future, then anything written now as science fiction is, on the face of it, wrong. We can no more write the mainstream fiction of the fortieth century than Virgil could write the mainstream fiction of today; to claim to do so would be to partake of the same self-satisfied folly that led certain Victorians to declare that science and technology, that culture and civilization, had reached their zenith, and that future history would roll along at exactly the same level as that enjoyed in the 1870s.

The startling difference between the 1870s and the 1970s, between a world of steam engines and a world of nuclear power, should be enough to convince the most optimistic science fiction practitioner that even to conceive of predicting the future is an act of hubris; we can, at best, make wild guesses. But even those guesses are expressed and rationalized in terms of our experience, our current language, our cultural expectations and desires. The barriers of our imagination are solidly woven into our sense and our senses; it could be argued that were we granted a glimpse of the distant future, we could not comprehend it.

Malzberg accepts this, states this, understands this, and proceeds to tell us a story of the future anyway, a story which, by his own admission, is one which we cannot perceive. In setting forth both caveat and story, Malzberg introduces a theme and a device which persists, in different guises, throughout *Galaxies*: believe everything, believe nothing. Your belief or disbelief is of concern only to yourself, but by the same token shapes the universe; your belief or disbelief is the result of your own processes of thought and rationalization, yet is also the result of careful manipulation by the author. You cannot know the foundations of your own convictions, but you may not live without convictions at all.

More simply stated, the thematic question of *Galaxies* is: "What is reality?"

And the answer, simply stated, is: "Reality is the elephant."

The device of writing a novel as notes toward fiction rather than as fiction itself, is one which allows for a great deal of latitude on the part of the writer. Having deliberately moved beyond the conventions of classical fiction, the writer can toss naked onto the page the bones and muscles which lie beneath a fictional work, and by so unmasking them, diminish them as barriers lying between the reader and what the writer is trying to say.

Malzberg, with no apologies, introduces himself into the text of *Galaxies* and speaks of his history, his desires, and his fears. The portrait he gives is not of a confident or happy man, and this assessment is one which he continues to hold. In a letter to this introducer, Malzberg reiterates and characterizes his own introduction to one edition of the book as "expressing my horror at the innocence and self-exposition of the book and pointing out that its author (thirty-five in the summer of 1974) could be clearly seen heading for plenty of trouble. (Which he found.) …[T]he man who wrote it is long (and thankfully) gone onto other *tsurus*…"[2] This is, certainly, a grim assessment of a man who, by the evidence of the book itself, was uneasily aware of the protruding elbows of the world, and half suspected that their existence was due as much to his own seeking them out as to their external reality. As for "innocence and self-exposition," it is unarguably true that *Galaxies* is 55,000 words of self-exposition, but what work of fiction, ultimately, is not? And if there is innocence expressed in the book, and Malzberg has gone beyond it, then a report on reality as currently perceived by the author of *Galaxies* is something best left to the midnight imagination.

Despite Malzberg's constant presence in the text of the book, despite the sincerity of his auctorial outcries, we are no more allowed to believe in Malzberg than we are allowed to believe in the concept of the book itself.

> Even this use of "author" as character is a device, then; it is an invented persona which is in certain ways a metaphor for the real writer and in other ways not; it is a thing of string and cheap baling wire which, if it is handled correctly, will give you the impression that you know me when all you know is what I wish to present. So there. (p. 261)

Nor are we allowed to forget this, for the writer is the most constantly present character in the book, forever sneaking his head into the fabric of the work to comment, explain, complain, mislead, direct, decry. But the conviction of his own belief, he instructs, is not to be believed. Believe everything, believe nothing: here is another face of the elephant, and not likely to be any more trustworthy than the rest.

Not content with disallowing the validity of story and of author, Malzberg proceeds to whittle away at the bastions of technique. Sprinkled throughout the book are the author's notes, pulled from his

---

[2] LETTER FROM BARRY MALZBERG TO MARTA RANDALL. DECEMBER 30, 1978.

own "bag of fictional techniques" (p. 368): bald comments on the mechanics of characterization, pacing, style; reminders to add a load of scenery here, a mass of individual crotchets there; here a gram of pathos, there a pound of action. Arguments about the validity of a certain method of pacing; avowals of his own integrity in refusing to use a particular technique which he has, in fact, used to effect not ten pages earlier. Malzberg in his persona of writer-as-character presents a wry vision of the author as some demented Wizard of Oz, huddled behind the paltry scrims of his verbiage, busy pulling levers and poking buttons, activating the Voice of Doom or the Lights of Wonder, keeping a cagey eye on the audience to make sure that his carefully charted effects are generating the proper response. Reminding us that what he is doing is not easy at all, and strutting the quality of *his* version of *angst* before the frowning ranks of his fictional peers:

> ...take *that* Barth, Barthelme, Roth or Oates! *Pace* Bellow and Malamud, and may your Guggenheims multiply, but what have any of you or those unnamed created to compare with this? *Angst*, this is the sign from which all self-pity once must have come. But the author ducks away, keeps his mind on business, modestly looks away from the audience and then down, transmuting (as he tries to except at very weary moments) his responses, histories, revulsion or envy to his characters. That is, after all, the more lasting and satisfying way to do this. (p. 360)

The techniques of fiction rest on the assumption that the endpoint of fiction is to create a seamless whole, a thing of smoothly joined surfaces in which the effectiveness of the technique is commensurate with the extent to which technique is, in the finished product, invisible. By laying the structure bare, by opening for inspection the joints and sockets, the baling wire, chewing gum, spit, and bent hairpins of the craft, Malzberg removes it, too, as a barrier between writer and reader. Technique, here, becomes another description of the elephant, and no more the elephant itself than the tree-trunk legs or bat-wing ears.

It is, of course, not fair for an author to explain the symbolism of his work, in his work. Malzberg pays no more attention to this rule than he has to any others, and cheerfully explicates the symbolism he intends to secrete in the fabric of the book which he is not, in fact, writing.

> ...the black galaxy itself some sort of ultimate vaginal symbol whose Freudian overcast would not be ignored in the imagery of the novel... (p. 283)

*Galaxies*, then, can no more be explored on its symbolic level than it can be explored on the level of fiction-as-biography. What Malzberg means to say in this book, he will say straightforwardly, without evasion. The essence of this elephant cannot be evaded by cloaking it in arcane terminology and stuffing it into the psychoanalyst's bestiary. The elephant is not a mass hallucination: the elephant is real.

Not content with defanging such time-honored barriers as auctorial biography, technique, symbolism, and the validity of fiction itself, Malzberg proceeds to hack away the other props of the critic's trade. Amid assurances that he does not care to contemplate, indeed is not interested in and finds distracting the cultural climate of the year 3902, he paints a group of worlds which is stable, bored, boring, and passionless; controlled by a Bureau which is greedy, homicidal, secretive, insensitive, and committed only to its own expansion. By Malzberg's own terms, though, it is not possible to understand this world; in its very commonness lies its alien nature. 3902 A.D. is not open to our comprehension, yet is given to us clear and terrifying.

A harassed psychiatrist once confided, *sotto voce*, that "if they're really out to get you, it's not paranoia." In the year 3902, Malzberg presents a world in which paranoia is not a rational response, for paranoia presupposes the non-existence of a threat, and is defined as a well-rationalized delusion of persecution. In 3902 A.D., persecution is not a delusion. But 3902 A.D. is in so many ways the counterpart of the last half of the twentieth century that we are left wondering whether the obviation of paranoia is not as true for our world as it is for those of *Galaxies*. Yet "the novel itself remains unutterably beyond our time and hence outside of the devices of fiction" (p. 376); in which case, to view *Galaxies* as a sociological investigation of our present world is both false (for we are dealing with a world incomprehensible to us) and true (for the incomprehensibility of this distant time is all too familiar.)

This report on the elephant cannot be dismissed as easily as its predecessors, for it begins to bridge the gap which Malzberg has firmly established between present and unknowable future. As the Bureau and its unhappy subjects are the background to Lena Thomas, pilot, so Ridgefield Park, New Jersey, is the background to Barry Malzberg, author. Both locations and constructs are fictitious, and the difference between them is one of magnitude rather than of kind.

Science fiction has, classically, rested its final case on technology. The exploration of the future, or, more precisely, the illusion of exploration of the future, has excused many sins of awkward characterization, lapses of technique, failures of plot and story. The broad back of technology has supported a multitude of auctorial failings, and Malzberg is the last to deny it. Indeed, technology itself becomes a part of the elephant:

> Science fiction, since its formal inception as a romantic subgenre...has best been known for its simple and melodramatic plots which demonstrate man's mastery (or later on, loss of control) of technology. The conventions of the genre then demand that the novel pivot upon the attempts of the crew to leave this entrapment and return to their planet of origin.
>
> This problem-solving pivot is not one which I might attempt, given my own devices.... Left to myself I would be more interested in showing how they set up light housekeeping...but this would not do for the purposes of the science-fiction novel.... Science fiction, then, is *technological fiction*; it is an attempt to relieve anxieties about the encroaching machinery by showing people how that machinery may be usefully applied. Science as benign instrumentation.

I have always had a certain awe for this kind of science fiction, and, although I cannot really do it well myself, wish that the genre had more of it. Unhappily, "hard" science fiction is largely a myth; there is almost no science in science fiction, and never has been. (pp. 265-268)

The author then proceeds to punctuate the book with long discussions of the technology, the "science" of black holes, black galaxies, neutron stars, tachyonic drives, and other such staples of nonscience, belying both his assurance of his own scientific incompetence (at least in terms of the genre) and his avowals of the absence of such "science" from the field. This can, of course, be considered a good example of the author covering his own lines of retreat, but Malzberg further complicates the issue by noting that the audience for such probably mythological "hard" science fiction is great, and further that:

My own decision has been made.... I would rather command an audience than not, to say nothing of publishers' advances.... No writer of integrity with a wife and two helpless children could do less.... (pp. 266-267)

This part of the elephant seems to have been explored by a quasi-honorable mahout with a cagey eye out for the main chance. Thus are integrity and technology both tucked into the same box.

One of the most recurrent, and strongly stated, aspects of Malzberg's fiction is a sense of the uselessness of human action. This aspect, and some others, ring through the fabric of *Galaxies*, cutting through points and counterpoints, through explosions of technique and explications of symbolism. Malzberg states these things baldly; symbolism, remember, has already been discarded.

Space is asepsis; life is an incomprehensibly small glitch in nothingness; matter itself is a delusion. The black galaxy into which Malzberg throws us is the only reality, and even our perceptions of it are suspect.

Existence as we know it may be an accidental offshoot, an interruption in the cycle controlled by the neutron star whose creation and expulsion are the true ordering force of the universe. (p. 300)

In the face of the assertion that both life and death, in that they relate to matter at all, are illusory and supremely unimportant, the "galaxies themselves…are merely interruptions in the lightless canvas of the universe" (p. 298), it becomes only reasonable that terrified incompetence is the keystone of humanity; all matter, including ourselves, is a mistake. The universe is neither a rational nor an irrational construction—rationality has nothing to do with the matter, and is only another of the illusory blocks we put up between ourselves and the knowledge that our supreme self-importance, our vanity, is absurd beyond the need for comprehension. Malzberg's characters are incapable of resolving their dilemmas because there is no resolution to be had. Our perception of "reality" is, in the final analysis, nothing more than a series of mental constructs accepted only on faith, and Malzberg reminds us, over and over, that nothing is to be taken on faith, and that we must manage

> …to understand that in the jaws of the universe biting down hard, biting down harder, more toward blankness, that aberration known as humanity is so slight as to make even discrimination between its living and dead components no more significant than the differentiation one might make between the halves of an amoeba in mitosis. (p. 383)

The utter bleakness of this vision is unbearable, blasphemous, unthinkable, and terrifying. There can be no competence because competence is irrelevant; there can be no order because order itself is illusory.

Lena Thomas, in her need to escape from the black galaxy, argues with the machines and the dead around her, and both ask her the same question: how can you make decisions which you claim are right for us, since you have never been one of us? Lena, insisting that she is indeed capable of making proper decisions, cannot articulate what is, after all, the correct answer: Lena can decide correctly for living and dead, for machine and flesh, because they are all, ultimately, identical.

Malzberg, with wry irony, calls this *angst* and invites his contemporaries to admire the extent of it.

And *angst*, too, is another part of the elephant.

There is, however, a resolution to *Galaxies*. This is, after all, a novel—or at least notes toward a novel, and the fictional priorities demand that a resolution be provided. Malzberg provides his fictional construct with four of them.

Lena emerges, after great pain, into her own and proper galaxy, to discover that the neutron star and all that befell her in its field were engineered by the simulators of the Bureau:

> It was all an experiment, and the decadent Bureau has decadently manipulated her, to say nothing of the reader, only to find out to what limits its technicians will sustain their humanity…. (p. 409)

But this resolution fails on a multitude of levels: it does not answer science fiction's need for a melodramatic plot with a point to it; it does not resolve the issue of humanity as a by-product of universal chaos; it is certainly an unsatisfying conclusion to a novel stated to be as deep and far-ranging as the one Malzberg has consistently refused to write.

The second resolution has Lena popping from the black galaxy into a state of nonexistence in which she remains forever frozen. This, of course, is no resolution at all.

In the third proposed ending, Lena and her ship emerge into the heart of a star and are immediately annihilated. When my son was much younger, he would interrupt bedtime stories to end them with the statement that "and then a bear ate them up and they lived happily ever after." This is, in a complicated novel, a wildly tempting, and utterly unacceptable, way to end a story. Malzberg knows this. So do we.

So much here, then, for celestial exploration, so much for the broken spirit of man. So there for all of you, so *there*. All of the pain, the struggle for acquisition, the explanation and metaphor for nothing. A burst of epiphany and then obliteration. (p. 410-411)

This is no way to treat an elephant.

For, after all, not any ending will do.... The discovered ending which would be the truth is hard bought.... But the resolution is there. It is viable, it is, in fact, inevitable. Emerging textually from the material, it has been hard bought, and perhaps one can see that it was, after all, implied from the very beginning, from the onset of these notes. The author has struggled, he has worked hard, he has done what he could to piece out this resolution. Give him, then, give him that ending.
The characters, too, deserve it. (p. 413)

The ending is, indeed, no better and no worse than we all deserve, and is, in truth, inevitable. For, flickering in time from the body of the neutron star, Lena and her ship of fools slide from the incomprehensibility of 3902 A.D. into the incomprehensibility of July, 1975, and the absurdity of Ridgefield Park, New Jersey, where they settle into the bodies of the inhabitants, to take on their duties among the hamburger stands, empty lots, and smog. Malzberg's true ending is the most futile, most absurd, most circular, and most terrifying resolution of all.

"The farther humanity voyages," Malzberg says, "the more it seems merely to confront itself" (p. 288).

What Malzberg has done in *Galaxies* is to give us a novel in which *nothing* is stable, in which any objective position is impossible, in which any mode of explication is rendered irrational, and in which we finally, like his characters, find ourselves floundering in a world in which consecutive thought and concrete action are seen to be nothing more than vague twitchings at the surface of what is slowly perceived to be a deeply chaotic and entirely uncontrollable reality. Malzberg is not content with telling us that the universe is a menacingly impersonal creation; he drops us in the middle of that impersonality, matching his characters' wild attempts at sanity with our own. We manipulate nothing, we are manipulated by nothing. We are futility, its expression, and its existence; all our constructs, including ourselves, are vanity and illusion.

Malzberg has seen the elephant, and it is us.

Marta Randall
Oakland, California

# EPILOGUE AGAIN

And here is *Galaxies* yet again, being prepared for publication. The novel was completed in the fall of 1974, (nearly) twenty-three wonderful years have come and (almost) gone and the work seems to have survived not only the state of science fiction which motivated its composition but science fiction itself. "A novel which is published again ten years after its first publication: that is a good book," Cyril Connolly wrote in *The Enemies of Promise*. Well, perhaps.

The novel was framed in the hope that it would function as its own afterword: the self-reflexive work which would not only anticipate but encompass any response. Silverberg's quoted review proved that this was not quite so and then Marta Randall's afterword and her elephant proved how abysmal my intention. So I wrote an afterword to her foreword which I thought would do the job. Defiant, Dann, Sargent and Zebrowski made my own position anomalous.

So here I go again, trying to have the last word but like father-son relations, this is probably dialogue which will not end, even unto the last tintinnabulation of doom.

What an interesting novel this is, anyway, at least to its author, filled with self-observance raised or lowered to a species of winsomeness. That lovely condition: here is Max Jamison, Wilfrid Sheed's critic of a protagonist in his deadly novel, observing himself as he does so infrequently from the outside. Here is the critic reflected in all of the mirrors, posturing, raised, alert, expanded, obscene, his face contorted, his teeth all arranged in a yowl of surmise. Under this posturing image the real, the ineluctable Max Jamison feels himself extinguished.

Here like poor, lecherous, squalling Max, is 1974's very own thirty-five-year-old Malzberg engaged in the most herculean of inner monologues, casting glances to the back of the room during glottal pauses. "Have you got that? Have you noticed me? Are there any big fans out there? Come up front and give me a great big kiss."

What a remarkable novel this is: of life and science fiction it may say nothing but of its thirty-five-year-old author it says as was meant nearly everything. BUT IT DOESN'T SAY WHAT THE AUTHOR THOUGHT HE WAS SAYING.

Good luck to it anyway, it truly meant well. It meant no harm. Cheers and kudos as well to the cast of *Star Trek: The Next Generation* as they too joyously scuttle toward our own true millennia.

Barry N. Malzberg
New Jersey
17 May, 1997

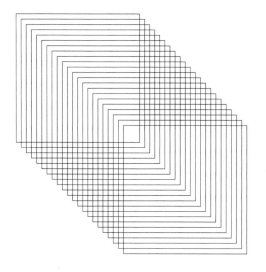

INTRODUCED BY
PAMELA SARGENT

# THE ENEMY
# STARS

### BY POUL ANDERSON

# INTRODUCTION

"The lessons of history aren't really hard to learn," Poul Anderson writes in his essay "Science Fiction and History" (1989); "the trouble is that hardly anyone wants to learn them." His deep and detailed knowledge of history is one of Anderson's strengths as a writer; the historical sense is present in almost everything he has written. One might also say that Anderson's view of history, and the lessons he has drawn from it, may be responsible for the ways in which some have viewed his work.

Poul Anderson has been described by many as a political conservative, and it is possible to see the sense of history in Anderson's work, and his belief that "the past gives us our only real clues to the future" (in "Science Fiction and History"), as evidence of his essential conservatism. The note of pessimism in his writing seems rooted in his belief that human beings have not yet created a "social order that does not carry the seeds of its own destruction." But Anderson also admits that "there will surely be developments unprecedented in history, unforeseen by us all"—hardly the sentiment of a rigid conservative.

Poul Anderson himself described his views this way: "If I had to call myself something, it would be either a conservative libertarian or a libertarian conservative. But I prefer to avoid labels. Basically, I feel that the concepts of liberty that were expressed in the eighteenth century by people like the Founding Fathers were actually the radically bold concepts from which people have been retreating ever since. And I don't believe that it's necessarily reactionary to say so." (In *Dream Makers Volume II*, interviews by Charles Platt, 1983.)

These views are worth mentioning here because they underlie much of Anderson's writing. He is not in the business of writing sermons, and has said himself that "I try not to preach in my fiction.... But we all inevitably stand on one or another philosophical platform and speak from it, and this is bound to show to some extent." One might disagree with Anderson's political stance or his views on various issues—I, a diehard leftist child of the Sixties, do so myself—but one cannot accuse him of holding them unthinkingly and reflexively or of being unwilling to listen to those who disagree. Anderson often presents his opinions by saying, as he did in a 1988 essay on the work of Rudyard Kipling: "Quite likely you'll find points of disagreement. That is as it should be." Anderson is not a dogmatist clinging to unchanging truths; he is willing to argue. But some readers, looking at his work through ideological lenses, can too quickly dismiss, undervalue, or misunderstand it. A feminist reader might feel that Anderson, especially in earlier works, portrays women as secondary characters in stories dominated by males, but other stories and novels feature strong and accomplished female characters. (Ingrid Lindgren in *Tau Zero*, perhaps the author's best-known novel, is only one memorable example.) Read enough Anderson novels and stories— which takes some time, because he is one of science fiction's most prolific authors—and you begin to see that he cannot be so easily contained by current political labels. Nor do any views which might inform or underlie his stories interfere with a reader's enjoyment, even a reader who might take issue with the author on various points.

The sheer volume of work that Anderson has produced may also account for his being undervalued in some quarters. He has certainly not been neglected; he has been a very popular writer for over four decades, and among his honors are three Nebula Awards and seven Hugo Awards. Still, Anderson's accomplishment is such that one could argue that he deserved even more awards than that. Novels such as the hard-science classic *Tau Zero* (1970), the elaborately inventive *There Will Be Time* (1972), the superb early novel *Brain Wave* (1954), the much-loved adventure *The High Crusade* (1960), and the exploration of the consequences of immortality in *The Boat of a Million Years* (1989), won no awards, much as they merited them. While science fiction writers such as Arthur C. Clarke, Isaac Asimov, Anne McCaffrey, Ursula K. Le Guin, Frank Herbert, and William Gibson have reached bestsellerdom and a large general audience, Poul Anderson has not yet broken through to such wide popularity. I say "not yet" because perhaps some wise publisher will soon see that Anderson has such potential, and promote the work of this soft-spoken and modest man more aggressively.

There is still time to do so. In 1971, science fiction writer and critic James Blish wrote about his colleague in the *Magazine of Fantasy and Science Fiction*:

> It's my opinion, which I suspect is widely shared, that Anderson is the only surviving writer of the Golden Age of *Astounding* who is still writing sf whose work has not gone steadily (or jerkily) downhill. But even this is a negative way of putting the matter. The positive side is that Poul Anderson the scientist, the technician, the stylist, the bard, the humanist and the humorist—a nonexhaustive list—is completely immune to any changes in fashion. He is, in short, an artist.

And the same is true of Anderson today, as he enters his seventies and continues to write. The worst of Anderson is always craftsmanlike, intelligent, and enjoyable reading; the best is, as Blish put it, "sufficiently spectacular to make fellow practitioners turn white with envy." Another of Anderson's fellow writers, Barry N. Malzberg, describes in a 1976 appreciation, "Recollecting Anderson," what it was like to discover the author and his work:

> I can still remember the joy with which I read "Sam Hall"…in the summer of 1953 when I was but fourteen years old and was not sure that anyone with my shaky grasp of

ninth-grade science would be permitted to be a science-fiction reader, much less writer…. Here was something that obviously made extrapolative and scientific sense: a rigorously imagined future society whose technology was obviously grasped, and yet the story—although it incorporated rather arcanely mythic elements—was *accessible*, structurally, characterologically, at the level of narrative pace that is perhaps almost all that a fourteen-year-old can grasp. In short, I found it a complete success. It was the first scientifically rigorous story that I had ever read with pleasure, and it marked Anderson…as a man to be attended to closely….

He brings to his kind of science fiction a reasonable narrative talent, a rigorous scientific background, a respect for the manner in which science and the human spirit may interact and, most importantly perhaps, a respect for the western literary tradition and for the reader.

Poul Anderson is also an extremely versatile writer, capable of writing in many genres. He has published mysteries (*Perish By the Sword*, 1959; *Murder in Black Letter*, 1960; *Murder Bound*, 1962), fantasy novels (*The Broken Sword*, 1954; *Three Hearts and Three Lions*, 1961), historical novels (the Last Viking trilogy, published in the early Eighties), has written poems, songs, and essays, and has translated prose and poetry into English from several Scandinavian languages. (Perhaps uniquely, in his story "Rokuru" [1991], he even wrote what he calls "a No play of the future.") He is also a master of realistic detail. One of his techniques, which he has mentioned frequently in speeches and essays, is to evoke at least three senses in each scene, in order to give the reader a feeling of living in the world depicted. To do this kind of thing well requires a body of knowledge, skills, and experiences, which Anderson has in abundance. (He can discourse intelligently about ships, sailing, physics, travel, military history, medieval Europe, and good food, among many other subjects.) Essays he has written on how to build a planet not only reveal the techniques he uses in creating his alien worlds, but also offer invaluable advice to writers.

The artistry and care he devotes to his creations ensure that his best work will survive even if new knowledge casts doubt on his assumptions. Back in the Seventies, I asked Poul Anderson for permission to reprint his classic story of biological change, "Call Me Joe" (1957), in my 1976 anthology *Bio-Futures*. He replied by saying that the picture of Jupiter presented in that story was so outdated by new discoveries that one could almost "hear the crinolines rustling." I happily reprinted "Call Me Joe" in spite of the author's reservations; the story has outlived the premises on which it was constructed, as has Ray Bradbury's Mars.

Another important quality of Anderson's work is his sense of tragedy. This isn't to say that he can't be funny; Anderson has written his share of comedic tales, among them the "Hoka" stories on which he collaborated with Gordon R. Dickson (collected in *Earthman's Burden* in 1957 and in *Hoka!* in 1983). Yet underlying much of his work is a sense of how pitiless the universe can be. James Blish has commented on this aspect of Anderson's writing:

> The sense of tragedy is…extremely rare in science fiction. To Poul Anderson it is a living entity. For him, it does not inhere in such commonplaces as the losses of old age, the deaths of lovers, the slaughters of war or Nature; as a physicist, he knows that the entropy gradient goes inexorably in only one direction, and he wastes no time sniveling about it. For Anderson, the tragic hero is…the man who is driven partly by circumstance, but mostly by his own conscience, to do the wrong thing for the right reason—and then has to live with the consequences.

This passage could be describing *The Enemy Stars*.

⚛

Poul Anderson was born in Bristol, Pennsylvania in 1926, of Danish parents. The family lived in Texas and Minnesota and eventually moved to Denmark, returning to the United States before the beginning of World War II. Anderson earned a degree in physics from the University of Minnesota in 1948, and his scientific training has greatly contributed to the verisimilitude of his stories. He married his wife, the former Karen Kruse, in 1953; Karen Anderson is herself an accomplished poet and writer with as many wide-ranging interests as her husband, and has collaborated with him, most notably on the four-volume fantasy *The King of Ys*, published in the late Eighties.

Poul Anderson began writing soon after leaving college and has been a freelance writer for nearly his entire adult life. (One thinks of a comment by V. S. Naipaul, another writer who has followed no other profession, in his book *A Turn in the South*: "...I had never wanted to be employed. I had always wanted to be a free man." The value Anderson places on freedom is reflected in his choice of occupation.) He published his first stories in the late Forties and his first novel, *Vault of the Ages*, in 1952. Since then, he has published over one hundred volumes of novels and short fiction. Among his shorter work are such treasures as "Sam Hall" (1953), "The Man Who Came Early" (1956), the Hugo Award winners "The Longest Voyage" (1960) and "No Truce With Kings" (1963), "Kyrie" (1968), the Nebula Award winners "The Queen of Air and Darkness" (1971) and "Goat Song" (1972), "The Saturn Game" (1980), which won both a Nebula and Hugo, and others too numerous to mention. (A comprehensive multivolume edition of Poul Anderson's short fiction is long overdue.)

*The Enemy Stars* (1959), which critic Sandra Miesel calls Anderson's "first philosophical SF novel," was originally published in *Astounding Science Fiction* in 1958 under the title "We Have Fed Our Sea," a title preferred by the author; it was drawn from a poem of Rudyard Kipling's, "The Song of the Dead," part of which is quoted at the end of the book.

The imagery of the sea is appropriate for this novel, which has some of the elements of a sea saga, among them men making a long, uncertain and dangerous voyage, their "shipwreck," and their desperate attempts to find their way home. (Indeed, two of the main characters are sailors and descendants of Earth's seagoing peoples.) Here, the sea is the sea of space, and the ship is the *Southern Cross*, an interstellar vessel that has been traveling outward from Earth for generations. Anderson brings his own inventive touches to this situation. No crew can survive aboard ship for the duration of such a long voyage; instead, shifts of crews are "beamed" to the *Southern Cross's* receiver room (the only way one can travel faster than light), where they tend to the ship before returning to Earth.

Anderson's central characters are four very different men who are to guide the *Southern Cross* to its destination. The *Southern Cross* crews are all men; the largely masculine world of the story is in keeping with much of Fifties science fiction, but given the grittiness of the tale and the apparent influence of the lore of the sea on the novel, this doesn't seem inappropriate. Those manning the *Southern Cross* are Terangi Maclaren, a gifted physicist but cynical playboy; the philosophical mathematician Seiichi Nakamura; the gravitics expert David Ryerson, a timid man still dominated by his father; and Chang Sverdlov, an earthy engineer who is secretly part of his planet's revolutionary movement. Tamara, the wife David Ryerson must leave behind on Earth with his hated father, is the only important female character in the novel, but she is crucial to the psychological development of the story and to its resolution. It is Tamara who speaks for those who do not understand why people have to take deadly risks to settle other worlds and push further into the unknown.

"There's no sense!" Tamara cries out near the end of the novel. "There's just dying and dying and dying—what for?—so that we can walk on still another planet, learn still another fact—what have we gained? What have we really done? And why?" *The Enemy Stars* is an attempt to answer that question. The mission the four main characters undertake quickly goes wrong; in their attempts to survive and find their way home, each man must become much more than he was.

This early work vividly expresses the outlook and beliefs that lie behind so much of Anderson's work, described this way by Sandra Miesel in her 1978 study *Against Time's Arrow: The High Crusade of Poul Anderson*:

> There is no substitute for sacrifice. Starfaring spacemen buy admiralty with their blood as their seagoing ancestors did in ages past. But Anderson believes that "our enterprise beyond the sky will keep alive that sense of bravery, wonder, and achievement without which man would hardly be himself."

Such sentiments may seem old-fashioned in these more ambiguous times, when acts of heroism are often seen as tainted by misplaced idealism, self-aggrandizement, adherence to outmoded values, or delusionary thinking. The dream of space exploration anticipated by Poul Anderson and others in the Fifties has, at least for now, become part of our past instead of our future. But people had such dreams once, and we can hope that they will again. *The Enemy Stars* is a stirring tale of the dream of space, and the price it may exact from those who dream it.

Pamela Sargent
Albany, New York
February, 1997

# THE ENEMY STARS

## BY POUL ANDERSON

They named her *Southern Cross* and launched her on the road whose end they would never see. Months afterward she was moving at half the speed of light; if there was to be enough reaction mass for deceleration and maneuver, the blast must be terminated. And so the long silence came. For four and a half centuries, the ship was to fall.

They manned her by turns, and dreamed other ships, and launched them, and saw how a few of the shortest journeys ended. Then they died.

And other men came after them. Wars flamed up and burned out, the howling peoples dwelt in smashed cities and kindled their fires with books. Conquerors followed, and conquerors of those, an empire killed its mother aborning, a religion called men to strange hilltops, a new race and a new state bestrode the Earth. But still the ships fell upward through night, and always there were men to stand watch upon them. Sometimes the men wore peaked caps and comets, sometimes steel helmets, sometimes decorous gray cowls, eventually blue berets with winged stars; but always they watched the ships, and more and more often as the decades passed they brought their craft to new harbors.

After ten generations, the *Southern Cross* was not quite halfway to her own goal, though she was the farthest from Earth of any human work. She was showing a little wear, here a scratch, there a patch, and not all the graffiti of bored and lonely men rubbed out by their successors. But those fields and particles which served her for eye, brain, nerve still swept heaven; each man at the end of his watch took a box of microplates with him as he made the hundred-light-year stride to Earth's Moon. Much of this was lost, or gathered dust, in the century when Earthmen were busy surviving. But there came a time when a patient electrically seeing machine ran through many such plates from many ships. And so it condemned certain people to death.

Sundown burned across great waters. Far to the west, the clouds banked tall above New Zealand threw hot gold into the sky. In that direction, the sea was too bright to look upon. Eastward it faded through green and royal blue to night, where the first stars trod forth and trembled. There was just enough wind to ruffle the surface, send wavelets lapping against the hull of the ketch, flow down the idle mainsail and stir the girl's loosened pale hair.

Terangi Maclaren pointed north. "The kelp beds are that way," he drawled. "Main source of the family income, y'know. They mutate, crossbreed, and get seaweed which furnishes all kind of useful products. It's beyond me, thank the honorable ancestors. Biochemistry is an organized mess. I'll stick to something simple, like the degenerate nucleus."

The girl giggled. "And if it isn't degenerate, will you make it so?" she asked.

She was a technic like himself, of course; he would never have let a common on his boat, since a few machines were, in effect, a sizable

THE ENEMY STARS

crew. Her rank was higher than his, so high that no one in her family worked productively—whereas Maclaren was one of the few in his who did not. She was of a carefully selected mutant Burmese strain, with amber skin, exquisite small features, and greenish-blond hair. Maclaren had been angling for weeks to get her alone like this. Not that General Feng, her drug-torpid null of a guardian, cared how much scandal she made, flying about the planet without so much as an amazon for chaperone. But she was more a creature of the Citadel and its hectic lights than of the sunset ocean.

Maclaren chuckled. "I wasn't swearing at the nucleus," he said. "Degeneracy is a state of matter under certain extreme conditions. Not too well understood, even after three hundred years of quantum theory. But I wander, and I would rather wonder. At you, naturally."

He padded barefoot across the deck and sat down by her. He was a tall man in his early thirties, slender, with wide shoulders and big hands, dark-haired and brown-skinned like all Oceanians; but there was an aquiline beak on the broad high-cheeked face, and some forgotten English ancestor looked out of hazel eyes. Like her, he wore merely an informal sarong and a few jewels.

"You're talking like a scholar, Terangi," she said. It was not a compliment. There was a growing element in the richest families who found Confucius, Plato, Einstein, and the other classics a thundering bore.

"Oh, but I am one," said Maclaren. "You'd be amazed how parched and snuffy I can get. Why, as a student—"

"But you were the amateur swimwrestling champion!" she protested.

"True. I could also drink any two men under the table and knew every dive on Earth and the Moon. However, d'you imagine my father—bless his dreary collection of old-fashioned virtues—would have subsidized me all these years if I didn't bring some credit to the family? It's kudos, having an astrophysicist for a son. Even if I am a rather expensive astrophysicist." He grinned through the gathering dusk. "Every so often, when I'd been on a particularly outrageous binge, he would threaten to cut my allowance off. Then I'd have no choice but to come up with a new observation or a brilliant new theory, or at least a book."

She snuggled a little closer. "Is that why you are going out to space now?" she asked.

"Well, no," said Maclaren. "That's purely my own idea. My notion of fun. I told you I was getting stuffy in my dotage."

"We haven't seen you very often in the Citadel, the last few years," she agreed. "And you were so busy when you did show."

"Politics, of a sort. The ship's course couldn't be changed without an order from a reluctant Exploration Authority, which meant bribing the right people, heading off the opposition, wheedling the Protector himself—d'you know, I discovered it was fun. I might even take up politics as a hobby, when I get back."

"How long will you be gone?" she asked.

"Can't say for certain, but probably just a month. That ought to furnish me with enough material for several years of study. Might dash back to the ship at odd moments for the rest of my life, of course. It'll take up permanent residence around that star."

"Couldn't you come home…every night?" she murmured.

"Don't tempt me," he groaned. "I can't. One month is the standard minimum watch on an interstellar vessel, barring emergencies. You see, every transmission uses up a Frank tube, which costs money."

"Well," she pouted, "if you think so much of an old dead star—"

"You don't understand, your gorgeousness. This is the first chance anyone has ever had, in more than two centuries of space travel, to net a close look at a truly burned-out star. There was even some argument whether the class existed. Is the universe old enough for any sun to have used up its nuclear *and* gravitational energy? By the ancestors, it's conceivable this one is left over from some previous cycle of creation!"

He felt a stiffening in her body, as if she resented his talk of what she neither understood nor cared about. And for a moment he resented her. She didn't really care about this boat either, or him, or anything except her own lovely shell…. Why was he wasting time in the old worn routines, when he should be studying and preparing— oh, hell, he knew precisely why.

And then her rigidity melted in a little shudder. He glanced at her, she was a shadow with a palely glowing mane, in the deep blue twilight. The last embers of sun were almost gone, and one star after another woke overhead, soon the sky would be crowded with their keenness.

Almost, she whispered: "Where is this spaceship, now?"

A bit startled, he pointed at the first tracings of the Southern Cross. "That way," he said. "She was originally bound for Alpha Crucis, and hasn't been diverted very far off that course. Since she's a good thirty parsecs out, we wouldn't notice the difference if we could see that far."

"But we can't. Not ever. The light would take a hundred years, and I...we would all be dead—No!"

He soothed her, a most pleasant proceeding which became still more pleasant as the night went on. And they were on his yacht, which had borne his love from the first day he took the tiller, in a calm sea, with wine and small sandwiches, and she even asked him to play his guitar and sing. But somehow it was not the episode he had awaited. He kept thinking of this or that preparation: what had he overlooked, what could he expect to find at the black sun? Perhaps he was indeed under the subtle tooth of age, or of maturity if you wanted a euphemism, or perhaps the Southern Cross burned disturbingly bright overhead.

# 2

Winter lay among the Outer Hebrides. Day was a sullen glimmer between two darknesses, often smothered in snow. When it did not fling itself upon the rocks and burst in freezing spume, the North Atlantic rolled in heavy and gnawing. There was no real horizon, leaden waves met leaden sky and misty leaden light hid the seam. "Here there is neither land nor water nor air, but a kind of mixture of them," wrote Pytheas.

The island was small. Once it had held a few fishermen, whose wives kept a sheep or two, but that was long ago. Now only one house remained, a stone cottage built centuries back and little changed. Down at the landing was a modern shelter for a sailboat, a family submarine and a battered aircar; but it was of gray plastic and fitted into the landscape like another boulder.

David Ryerson put down his own hired vehicle there, signaled the door to open, and rolled through. He had not been on Skula for half a decade: it touched him, in a way, how his hands remembered all the motions of steering into this place and how the dank interior was

THE ENEMY STARS

unaltered. As for his father—he bit back an inward fluttering, helped his bride from the car, and spread his cloak around them both as they stepped into the wind.

It howled in from the Pole, striking them so they reeled and Tamara's black locks broke free like torn banners. Ryerson thought he could almost hear the wind toning in the rock underfoot. Surely the blows of the sea did, crash after crash, through a bitter drift of flung scud. For a moment's primitive terror, he thought he heard his father's God, whom he had denied, roar in the deep. He fought his way to the cottage and laid numbed fingers on the anachronism of a corroded bronze knocker.

Magnus Ryerson opened the door and waved them in. "I'd not expected you yet," he said, which was as close as he would ever come to an apology. When he shut out the wind, there was a quietness which gaped.

This main room, brick-floored, whitewashed, irregular and solid, centered about a fireplace where peat burned low and blue. The chief concessions to the century were a radiglobe and a stunning close-up photograph of the Sirian binary. One did not count the pilot's manuals or the stones and skins and gods brought from beyond the sky; after all, any old sea captain would have kept his Bowditch and his souvenirs. The walls were lined with books as well as microspools. Most of the full-size volumes were antique, for little was printed in English these days.

Magnus Ryerson stood leaning on a cane of no Terrestrial wood. He was a huge man, two meters tall in his youth and not greatly stooped now, with breadth and thickness to match. His nose jutted craggily from a leather skin, shoulder-length white hair, breast-length white beard. Under tangled brows, the eyes were small and frost-blue. He wore the archaic local dress, a knitted sweater and canvas trousers. It came as a shock to realize after several minutes that his right hand was artificial.

"Well," he rumbled at last, in fluent Interhuman, "so this is the bride. Tamara Suwito Ryerson, eh? Welcome, girl." There was no great warmth in his tone.

She bent her face to folded hands. "I greet you most humbly, honorable father." She was Australian, a typical high-class common of that province, fine-boned, bronze-hued, with blue-black hair and oblique brown eyes; but her beauty was typical nowhere. She had dressed with becoming modesty in a long white gown and a hooded cloak, no ornaments save a wedding band with the Ryerson monogram on it.

Magnus looked away from her, to his son. "Professor's daughter, did you say?" he murmured in English.

"Professor of symbolics," said David. He made his answer a defiance by casting it in the Interhuman which his wife understood. "We—Tamara and I—met at his home. I needed a background in symbolics to understand my own specialty and—"

"You explain too much," said Magnus dryly. "Sit."

He lowered himself into a chair. After a moment, David followed. The son was just turned twenty years old, a slender boy of average height with light complexion, thin sharp features, yellow hair, and his father's blue eyes. He wore the tunic of a science graduate, with insignia of gravitics, self-consciously, but not so used to it that he would change for an ordinary civilian blouse.

Tamara made her way into the kitchen and began preparing tea. Magnus looked after her. "Well-trained, anyhow," he grunted in English. "So I suppose her family is at least heathen, and not any of these latter-day atheists. That's somewhat."

David felt the island years, alone with his widower father, return to roost heavy upon him. He stifled an anger and said, also in English: "I couldn't have made any better match. Even from some swinish practical standpoint. Not without marrying into a technic family, and—would you want me to do that? I'll gain technic rank on my own merits!"

"If you stay on Earth," said Magnus. "Who notices a colonial?"

"Who notices an Earthling, among ten billion others?" snapped David. "On a new planet—on Rama—a man can be himself. These stupid hereditary distinctions won't even matter."

"There is room enough right here," said Magnus. "As a boy you never used to complain Skula was crowded. On the contrary!"

"And I would settle down with some illiterate beefy-faced good Christian fishwife you picked for me and breed more servants for the Protectorate all my life!"

The words had come out before David thought. Now, in a kind of dismay, he waited for his father's reaction. This man had ordered him out into a winter gale, or supperless to bed, for fifteen years out of twenty. In theory the grown son was free of him, free of everyone save contractual overlords and whatever general had most recently seized the title of Protector. In practice it was not so easy. David knew with a chill that he would never have decided to emigrate without Tamara's unarrogant and unbendable will to stiffen his. He would probably never even have married her, without more than her father's consent, against the wish of his own—David gripped the worn arms of his chair.

Magnus sighed. He felt about after a pipe and tobacco pouch. "I would have preferred you to maintain residence on Earth," he said with a somehow shocking gentleness. "By the time the quarantine on Washington 5584 has been lifted, I'll be dead."

David locked his mouth. *You hoary old fraud,* he thought, *if you expect to hook me that way*—

"It's not as if you would be penned on one island all your days," said Magnus. "Why did I spend all I had saved to put my sons through the Academy? So they could be spacemen, as I was and my father and grandfather before me. Earth isn't a prison. The Earthman can go as far as the farthest ships have reached. It's the colonies are the hole. Once you go there to live, you never come back here."

"Is there so much to come back to?" said David. Then, after a minute, trying clumsily for reconciliation: "And father, I'm the last. Space ate them all. Radiation killed Tom, a meteor got Ned, Eric made a falling star all by himself, Ian just never returned from wherever it was. Don't you want to preserve our blood in me, at least?"

"So you mean to save your own life?"

"Now wait! You know how dangerous a new planet can be. That's the reason for putting the initial settlers under thirty years of absolute quarantine. If you think I—"

"No," said Magnus. "No, you're no coward, Davy, when it comes to physical things. When you deal with people, though...I don't know what you're like. You don't yourself. Are you running away from man, as you've been trying to run from the Lord God Jehovah? Not so many folk on Rama as on Earth; no need to work both with and against them, as on a ship—Well." He leaned forward, the pipe smoldering in his plastic hand. "I want you to be a spaceman, aye, of course. I cannot dictate your choice. But if you would at least try it, once only, so you could honestly come back and tell me you're not born for stars and, and openness and a sky all around you—Do you understand? I could let you go to your damned planet then. Not before. I would never know, otherwise, how much I had let you cheat yourself."

Silence fell between them. They heard the wind as it mourned under their eaves, and the remote snarling of the sea.

David said at last, slowly: "So that's why you…yes. Did you give my name to Technic Maclaren for that dark star expedition?"

Magnus nodded. "I heard from my friends in the Authority that Maclaren had gotten the *Cross* diverted from orbit. Some of them were mickle put out about it, too. After all, she was the first one sent directly toward a really remote goal, she is farther from Earth than any other ship has yet gotten, it was like breaking a tradition." He shrugged. "God knows when anyone will reach Alpha Crucis now. But I saw Maclaren is right. Alpha may be an interesting triple star, but a truly cold sun means a deal more to science. At any rate, I did pull a few wires. Maclaren needs a gravitics man to help him take his data. The post is yours if you wish it."

"I don't," said David. "How long would we be gone? A month, two months? A month from now I planned to be selecting my own estate on Rama."

"Also, you've only been wed a few weeks. Oh, yes. I understand. But you can be sent to Rama as soon as you get back; there'll be several waves of migration. You will have space pay plus exploratory bonus, some valuable experience, and," finished Magnus sardonically, "my blessing. Otherwise you can get out of my house this minute."

David hunched into his chair, as if facing an enemy. He heard Tamara move about, slow in the unfamiliar kitchen, surely more than a little frightened of this old barbarian. If he went to space, she would have to stay here, bound by a propriety which was one of the chains they had hoped to shed on Rama. It was a cheerless prospect for her, too.

And yet, thought David, the grim face before him had once turned skyward, on a spring night, telling him the names of the stars.

The other man, Ohara, was good, third-degree black. But finally his alertness wavered. He moved in unwarily, and Seiichi Nakamura threw him with a foot sweep that drew approving hisses from the audience. Seeing his chance, Nakamura pounced, got control of Ohara from the waist down by sitting on him, and applied a strangle. Ohara tried to break it, but starving lungs betrayed him. He slapped the mat when he was just short of unconsciousness. Nakamura released him and squatted, waiting. Presently Ohara rose. So did the winner. They retied their belts and bowed to each other. The abbot, who was refereeing, murmured a few words which ended the match. The contestants sat down, closed their eyes, and for a while the room held nothing but meditation.

Nakamura had progressed beyond enjoying victory for its own sake. He could still exult in the esthetics of a perfect maneuver; what a delightful toy the human body is, when you know how to throw eighty struggling kilos artistically through the air! But even that, he knew, was a spiritual weakness. Judo is more than a sport, it should be means to an end: ideally, a physical form of meditation upon the principles of Zen.

He wondered if he would ever attain that height. Rebelliously, he wondered if anyone ever had, in actual practice, for more than a few moments anyhow.... It was an unworthy thought. A wearer of the black belt in the fifth degree should at least have ceased inwardly barking at his betters. And now enough of all the personal. It was only his mind reflecting the tension of the contest, and tension was always the enemy. His mathematical training led him to visualize fields of force, and the human soul as a differential quantity $dX$ (where $X$ was a function of no one knew how many variables) which applied just enough vanishingly small increments of action so that the great fields slid over each other and—was this a desirable analog? He must discuss it with the abbot some time; it seemed too precise to reflect reality. For now he had better meditate upon one of the traditional paradoxes: consider the noise made by two hands clapping, and then the noise made by *one* hand clapping.

The abbot spoke another word. The several contestants on the mat bowed to him, rose, and went to the showers. The audience, yellow-robed monks and a motley group of townspeople, left their cushions and mingled cheerfully.

When Nakamura came out, his gi rolled under one arm, his short thickset body clad in plain gray coveralls, he saw the abbot talking to Diomed Umfando, chief of the local Protectorate garrison. He waited until they noticed him. Then he bowed and sucked in his breath respectfully.

"Ah," said the abbot. "A most admirable performance tonight."

"It was nothing, honorable sir," said Nakamura.

"What did you...yes. Indeed. You are leaving tomorrow, are you not?"

"Yes, master. On the *Southern Cross*, the expedition to the dark star. It is uncertain how long I shall be away." He laughed self-deprecatingly, as politeness required. "It is always possible that one does not return. May I humbly ask the honorable abbot that—"

"Of course," said the old man. "Your wife and children shall always be under our protection, and your sons will be educated here if no better place can be found for them." He smiled. "But who can doubt that the best pilot on Sarai will return as a conqueror?"

They exchanged ritual compliments. Nakamura went about saying goodbye to various other friends. As he came to the door, he saw the tall blue-clad form of Captain Umfando. He bowed.

"I am walking back into town now," said the officer, almost apologetically. "May I request the pleasure of your company?"

"If this unworthy person can offer even a moment's distraction to the noble captain."

They left together. The dojo was part of the Buddhist monastery, which stood two or three kilometers out of the town called Susa. A road went through grain fields, an empty road now, for the spectators were still drinking tea under the abbot's red roof. Nakamura and Umfando walked in silence for a while; the captain's bodyguard shouldered their rifles and followed unobtrusively.

Capella had long ago set. Its sixth planet, Il-Khan the giant, was near full phase, a vast golden shield blazoned with a hundred hues. Two other satellites, not much smaller than this Earth-sized Sarai on which humans dwelt, were visible. Only a few stars could shine through all that light, low in the purple sky; the fields lay drowned in amber radiance, Susa's lanterns looked feeble in the distance. Meteor trails crisscrossed heaven, as if someone wrote swift ideographs up there. On the left horizon, a sudden mountain range climbed until its peaks burned with snow. A moonbird was trilling, the fiddler insects answered, a small wind rustled in the grain. Otherwise only the scrunch of feet on gravel had voice.

"This is a lovely world," murmured Nakamura.

Captain Umfando shrugged. Wryness touched his ebony features. "I could wish it were more sociable."

"Believe me, sir, despite political differences, there is no ill-will toward you or your men personally—"

"Oh, come now," said the officer. "I am not that naïve. Sarai may begin by disliking us purely as soldiers and tax collectors for an Earth which will not let the ordinary colonist even visit it. But such feelings soon envelop the soldier himself. I've been jeered at, and mudballed by children, even out of uniform."

"It is most deplorable," said Nakamura in distress. "May I offer my apologies on behalf of my town?"

Umfando shrugged. "I'm not certain that an apology is in order. I didn't have to make a career of the Protector's army. And Earth does exploit the colonies. There are euphemisms and excuses, but exploitation is what it amounts to."

He thought for a moment, and asked with a near despair: "But what else can Earth do?"

Nakamura said nothing. They walked on in silence for a while.

Umfando said at last, "I wish to put a rude question." When the flat face beside him showed no reluctance, he plowed ahead. "Let us not waste time on modesty. You know you're one of the finest pilots in the Guild; any Capellan System pilot is—he has to be!—but you are the one they ask for when things get difficult. You've been on a dozen exploratory missions in new systems. It's not made you rich, but it has made you one of the most influential men on Sarai. Why do *you* treat me like a human being?"

Nakamura considered it gravely. "Well," he decided, "I cannot consider politics important enough to quarrel about."

"I see." A little embarrassed, Umfando changed the subject: "I can get you on a military transport to Batu tomorrow, if you wish. Drop you off at the 'caster station."

"Thank you, but I have already engaged passage on the regular intersatellite ferry."

"Uh…did you ask for the *Cross* berth?"

"No. I had served a few watches on her, of course, like everyone else. A good ship. A little outmoded now, perhaps, but well and honestly made. The Guild offered me the position, and since I had no other commitments, I accepted."

Guild offers were actually assignments for the lower ranks of spacemen, Umfando knew. A man of Nakamura's standing could have refused. But maybe the way you attained such prestige was by never refusing.

"Do you expect any trouble?" he asked.

"One is never certain. The great human mistake is to anticipate. The totally relaxed and unexpectant man is the one prepared for whatever may happen: he does not have to get out of an inappropriate posture before he can react."

"Ha! Maybe judo ought to be required for all pilots."

"No. I do not think the coerced mind ever really learns an art."

Nakamura saw his house ahead. It stood on the edge of town, half screened by Terrestrial bamboo. He had spent much time on the garden which surrounded it; many visitors were kind enough to call his garden beautiful. He sighed. A gracious house, a good and faithful wife, four promising children, health and achievement…what more could a man reasonably ask? He told himself that his remembrances of Kyoto were hazed, he had left Earth as a very young boy. Surely this serene and uncrowded Sarai offered more than poor tortured antheap Earth gave even to her overlords. And yet some mornings he woke up with the temple bells of Kyoto still chiming in his ears.

He stopped at the gate. "Will you honor my home for a cup of tea?" he asked.

"No, thanks," said Umfando, almost roughly. "You've a family to…to say goodbye to. I will see you when—"

Fire streaked across the sky. For an instant Il-Khan himself was lost in blue flame. The bolide struck somewhere among the mountains. A sheet of pure outraged energy flared above ragged peaks. Then smoke and dust swirled up like a devil, and moments afterward thunder came banging down through the valley.

Umfando whistled. "That was a monster!"

"A…yes…most unusual…yes, yes." Nakamura stammered something, somehow he bowed goodnight and somehow he kept from running along the path to his roof. But as he walked he began to shake.

It was only a meteorite, he told himself frantically. Only a meteorite. The space around a giant star, a close double, like Capella, and especially around its biggest planet, was certain to be full of cosmic junk. Billions of meteors hit Sarai every day. Hundreds of them got through to the surface. But Sarai was as big as Earth, he told himself. Sarai had oceans, deserts, uninhabited plains and forests…why, even on Sarai you were more likely to be killed by lightning than by a meteorite and—and—

*Oh, the jewel in the lotus!* he cried out. *I am afraid. I am afraid of the black sun.*

It was raining again, but no one on Krasna pays attention to that. They wear a few light nonabsorbent garments and welcome the rain on their bodies, a moment's relief from saturated hot air. The clouds thin overhead, so that the land glimmers with watery brightness, sometimes even the uppermost clouds break apart and Tau Ceti spears a blinding reddish shaft through smoke-blue masses and silvery rain.

Chang Sverdlov rode into Dynamogorsk with a hornbeast lashed behind his saddle. It had been a dangerous chase, through the tidal marshes and up over the bleak heights of Czar Nicholas IV Range, but he needed evidence to back his story, that he had only been going out to hunt. Mukerji, the chief intelligence officer of the Protectorate garrison, was getting suspicious, God rot his brain.

Two soldiers came along the elevated sidewalk. Rain drummed on their helmets and sluiced off the slung rifles. Earth soldiers went in armed pairs on a street like Trumpet Road: for a Krasnan swamp-rancher, fisher, miner, logger, trapper, brawling away his accumulated loneliness, with a skinful of vodka or rice wine, a fluff-headed *fille-de-joie* to impress, and a sullen suspicion that the dice had been loaded, was apt to unlimber his weapons when he saw a blueback.

Sverdlov contented himself with spitting at their boots, which were about level with his head. It went unnoticed in the downpour. And in the noise, and crowding, and blinking lights, with thunder above the city's gables. He clucked to his saurian and guided her toward the middle of the slough called Trumpet Road. Its excitement lifted his anger a bit. *I'll report in*, he told himself, *and go wheedle an advance from the Guild bank, and then make up six weeks of bushranging in a way the joyhouses will remember!*

He turned off on the Avenue of Tigers and stopped before a certain inn. Tethering his lizard and throwing the guard a coin, he entered the taproom. It was as full of men and racket as usual. He shouldered up to the bar. The landlord recognized him; Sverdlov was a very big and solid young man, bullet-headed, crop-haired, with a thick nose and small brown eyes in a pockmarked face. The landlord drew a mug of kvass, spiked it with vodka, and set it out. He nodded toward the ceiling. "I will tell her you are here," he said, and left.

Sverdlov leaned on the bar, one hand resting on a pistol butt, the other holding up his drink. *I could wish it really were one of the upstairs girls expecting me*, he thought. *Do we need all this melodrama of codes, countersigns, and cell organization?* He considered the seething of near-naked men in the room. A chess game, a card game, a dirty joke, an Indian wrestling match, a brag, a wheedle, an incipient fight: his own Krasnans! It hardly seemed possible that any of those ears could have been hired by the Protector, and yet...

The landlord came back. "She's here and ready for you," he grinned. A couple of nearby men guffawed coarsely. Sverdlov tossed off his drink, lit one of the cheap cigars he favored, and pushed through to the stairs.

At the end of a third-floor corridor he rapped on a door. A voice invited him in. The room beyond was small and drably furnished but its window looked down a straight street to the town's end and a sudden feathery splendor of rainbow trees. Lightning flimmered through the bright rain of Krasna. Sverdlov wondered scornfully if Earth had jungle and infinite promise on any doorstep.

He closed the door and nodded at the two men who sat waiting. He knew fat Li-Tsung; the gaunt Arabic-looking fellow was strange to him, and neither asked for an introduction.

Li-Tsung raised an eyebrow. Sverdlov said, "It is going well. They were having some new troubles—the aerospores were playing merry hell with the electrical insulation—but I think I worked out a solution. The Wetlanders are keeping our boys amply fed, and there is no indication anyone has betrayed them. Yet."

The thin man asked, "This is the clandestine bomb factory?"

"No," said Li-Tsung. "It is time you learned of these matters, especially when you are leaving the system today. This man has been helping direct something more important than small-arms manufacture. They are tooling up out there to make interplanetary missiles."

"What for?" answered the stranger. "Once the Fellowship has seized the mattercaster, it will be years before reinforcements can arrive from any other system. You'll have time enough to build heavy armament then." He glanced inquiringly at Sverdlov. Li-Tsung nodded. "In fact," said the thin man, "my division is trying to so organize things that there will be no closer Protectorate forces than Earth itself. Simultaneous revolution on a dozen planets. Then it would be at least two decades before spaceships could reach Tau Ceti."

"Ah," grunted Sverdlov. He lowered his hairy body into a chair. His cigar jabbed at the thin man. "Have you ever thought, the Earthlings are no fools? The mattercaster for the Tau Ceti System is up there on Moon Two. Sure. We seize it, or destroy it. But is it the *only* transceiver around?"

The thin man choked. Li-Tsung murmured, "This is not for the rank and file. There is enough awe of Earth already, to hold the people back. But in point of fact, the Protector is an idiot if there is not at least one asteroid in some unlikely orbit, with a heavy-duty 'caster mounted on it. We can expect the Navy in our skies within hours of the independence proclamation. We must be prepared to fight!"

"But—" said the thin man, "but this means it will take years more to make ready than I thought. I had hoped—"

"The Centaurians rebelled prematurely, forty years ago," said Li-Tsung. "Let us never forget the lesson. Do you want to be lobotomized?"

There was silence for a while. Rain hammered on the roof. Down in the street, a couple of rangers just in from the Uplands were organizing an impromptu saurian fight.

"Well," said Sverdlov at last. "I'd better not stay here."

"Oh, but you should," said Li-Tsung. "You are supposedly visiting a woman, do you remember?"

Sverdlov snorted impatience, but reached for the little chess set in his pouch. "Who'll play me a quick game, then?"

"Are the bright lights that attractive?" asked Li-Tsung.

Sverdlov spoke an obscenity. "I've spent nearly my whole leave chasing through the bush and up into the Czar," he said. "I'll be off to Thovo—or worse yet, to Krimchak or Cupra or the Belt, Thovo has a settlement at least—for weeks. Months perhaps! Let me relax a little first."

"As a matter of fact," said Li-Tsung, "your next berth has already been assigned, and it is not to any of those places. It is outsystem." In his public persona, he was a minor official in the local branch of the Astronautical Guild.

"What?" Sverdlov cursed for a steady minute. "You mean I'm to be locked up for a month on some stinking ship in the middle of interstellar space, and—"

"Calmly, please, calmly. You won't be standing a routine single-handed just-in-case watch. This will be rather more interesting. You will be on the XA463, the *Southern Cross*."

Sverdlov considered. He had taken his turn on the stellar vessels, but had no interest in them: they were a chore, one of the less desirable aspects of a spaceman's life. He had even been on duty when a new system was entered, but it had thrilled him not. Its planets turned out to be poisonous hells; he had finished his hitch and gone home before they even completed the transceiver station, the devil could drink his share of the dedication party.

"I don't know which of them that would be," he said.

"It is bound for Alpha Crucis. Or was. Several years ago, the photographs taken by its instruments were routinely robo-analyzed on Earth. There were discrepancies. Chiefly, some of the background stars were displaced, the Einstein effect of mass on light rays. A more careful study revealed there was a feeble source of long radio waves in that direction. They appear to be the dying gasp of a star."

Since Sverdlov's work involved him with the atomic nucleus, he could not help arguing: "I don't think so. The dying gasp, as you put it, would be gravitational potential energy, released as radiation when a star's own fires are all exhausted. But a thing so cold it only emits in the far radio frequencies...I'd say that was merely some kind of turbulence in what passes for an atmosphere. That the star isn't just dying, it's *dead.*"

"I don't know," shrugged Li-Tsung. "Perhaps no one does. This expedition will be to answer such questions. They gave up on Alpha Crucis for the time being and decelerated the ship toward this black star. It is arriving there now. The next personnel will take up an orbit and make the initial studies. You are the engineer."

Sverdlov drew heavily on his cigar. "Why me?" he protested. "I'm an interplanetary man. Except for those damned interstellar tours, I've never even been out of the Tau Ceti System."

"That may be one reason you were picked," said Li-Tsung. "The Guild does not like its men too provincial in outlook."

"Surely," sneered Sverdlov. "We colonials can travel anywhere we please, except to Earth. Only our goods go to Earth without special permission."

"You need not recruit us into the Fellowship of Independence," said the thin man in a parched voice.

Sverdlov clamped teeth together and got out through stiff lips: "There will be Earthlings aboard, won't there? It's asking for trouble, to put me on the same ship as an Earthling."

"You will be very polite and cooperative," said Li-Tsung sharply. "There are other reasons for your assignment. I cannot say much, but you can guess that we have sympathizers, even members, in the Guild...on a higher level than spacehand! It is possible that something of potential military value will be learned from the dark star. Who knows? Something about force fields or—Use your own imagination. It can do no harm to have a Fellowship man on the *Cross.* It may do some good. You will report to me when you return."

"Very well, very well," grumbled Sverdlov. "I can stand a month or two of Earthlings, I suppose."

"You will get your official orders soon," Li-Tsung told him. He glanced at his watch. "I think you can run along now; you have a reputation as a, hm-m, fast worker. Enjoy yourself."

"And don't get talking drunk," said the thin man.

Sverdlov paused in the doorway. "I don't," he said. "I wouldn't be alive now if I did."

The Authority booked first-class passages for all expeditionary personnel, which in the case of a hop up to the Moon meant a direct ferry traveling at one gee all the way. Standing by the observation window, an untasted drink in his hand, David Ryerson remarked: "You know, this is only the third time I've ever been off Earth. And the other two, we transshipped at Satellite and went free-fall most of the way."

"Sounds like fun," said Maclaren. "I must try it sometime."

"You…in your line of work…you must go to the Moon quite often," said Ryerson shyly.

Maclaren nodded. "Mount Ambarzumian Observatory, on Farside. Still a little dust and gas to bother us, of course, but I'll let the purists go out to Pluto Satellite and bring me back their plates."

"And…no. Forgive me." Ryerson shook his blond head.

"Go on." Maclaren, seated in a voluptuous formfit lounger, offered a box of cigarettes. He thought he knew Ryerson's type, serious, gifted, ambitious, but awe-smitten at the gimcrack fact of someone's hereditary technic rank. "Go ahead," he invited. "I don't embarrass easy."

"I was only wondering…who paid for all your trips…the observatory or—"

"Great ancestors! The observatory!" Maclaren threw back his head and laughed with the heartiness of a man who had never had to be very cautious. It rang above the low music and cultivated chatter; even the ecdysiast paused an instant on her stage.

"My dear old colleague," said Maclaren, "I not only pay my own freight, I am expected to contribute generously toward the expenses of the institution. At least," he added, "my father is. But where else would money for pure research come from? You can't tax it out of the lower commons, y'know. They haven't got it. The upper commons are already taxed to the limit, short of pushing them back down into the hand-to-mouth masses. And the Protectorate rests on a technic class serving but not paying. That's the theory, anyhow: in practice, of course, a lot of 'em do neither. But how else would you support abstract science, except by patronage? Thank the Powers for the human snob instinct, it keeps both research and art alive."

Ryerson looked alarmed, glanced about as if expecting momentary arrest, finally lowered himself to the edge of a chair and almost whispered: "Yes, sir, yes, I know, naturally. I was just not so…so familiar with the details of…financing."

"Eh? But how could you have missed learning? You trained to be a scientist, didn't you?"

Ryerson stared out at Earth, sprawling splendor across the constellations. "I set out to be a spaceman," he said, blushing. "But in the last couple of years I got more interested in gravitics, and had to concentrate too much on catching up in that field to…well…also, I was planning to emigrate, so I wasn't interested in—The colonies need trained men. The opportunities—"

*Pioneering is an unlimited chance to become the biggest frog, provided the puddle is small enough,* thought Maclaren. But he asked aloud, politely, "Where to?"

"Rama. The third planet of Washington 5584."

"Hm? Oh, yes. The new one, the GO dwarf. Uh, how far from here?"

"Ninety-seven light years. Rama has just passed the five-year survey test." Ryerson leaned forward, losing shyness in his enthusiasm. "Actually, sir, Rama is the most nearly terrestroid planet they have yet found. The biochemistry is so similar to Earth's that one can even eat some of the native plants. Oh, and there are climatic zones, oceans, forests, mountains, a single big moon—"

"And thirty years of isolation," said Maclaren. "Nothing connecting you to the universe but a voice."

Ryerson reddened again. "Does that matter so much?" he asked aggressively. "Are we losing a great deal by that?"

"I suppose not," said Maclaren. *Your lives, perhaps,* he thought. *Remember the Shadow Plague on New Kashmir? Or your children—there was the mutation virus on Gondwana. Five years is not long enough to learn a planet; the thirty-year quarantine is an arbitrary minimum. And, of course, there are the more obvious and spectacular things, which merely kill colonists without threatening the human race. Storms, quakes, morasses, volcanoes, meteorites. Cumulative poisoning. Wild animals. Unsuspected half-intelligent aborigines. Strangeness, loneliness, madness. It's no wonder the colonies which survive develop their own cultures. It's no wonder they come to think of Earth as a parasite on their own tedious heroisms. Of course, with ten billion people, and a great deal of once-arable country sterilized by radiation, Earth has little choice.*

*What I would like to know is, why does anyone emigrate in the first place? The lessons are ghastly enough; why do otherwise sensible people, like this boy, refuse to learn them?*

"Oh, well," he said aloud. He signaled the waiter. "Refuel us, chop-chop."

Ryerson looked in some awe at the chit which the other man thumbprinted. He could not suppress it: "Do you always travel first class to the moon?"

Maclaren put a fresh cigarette between his lips and touched his lighter-ring to the end. His smile cocked it at a wry angle. "I suppose," he answered, "I have always traveled first class through life."

The ferry made turnover without spilling a drink or a passenger and backed down onto Tycho Port. Maclaren adjusted without a thought to Lunar gravity, Ryerson turned a little green and swallowed a pill. But even in his momentary distress, Ryerson was bewildered at merely walking through a tube to a monorail station. Third-class passengers must submit to interminable official bullying: safety regulations, queues, assignment to hostel. Now, within minutes, he was again on soft cushions, staring through crystalline panes at the saw-toothed magnificence of mountains.

When the train got under way, he gripped his hands together, irrationally afraid. It took him a while to hunt down the reason: the ghost of his father's God, ranting at pride and sloth from the tomb which the son had erected.

"Let's eat," said Maclaren. "I chose this train with malice aforethought. It's slow enough so we can enjoy our meal en route, and the chef puts his heart into the oysters won-ton."

"I'm not...not hungry," stammered Ryerson.

Maclaren's dark, hooked face flashed a grin. "That's what cocktails and hors d'oeuvres are for, lad. Stuff yourself. If it's true what I've heard of deep space rations, we're in for a dreary month or two."

"You mean you've never been on an interstellar ship?"

"Of course not. Never been beyond the Moon in my life. Why should I do any such ridiculous thing?"

Maclaren's cloak swirled like fire as he led the way toward the diner. Beneath an iridescent white tunic, his legs showed muscular and hairless, down to the tooled-leather buskins; the slant of the beret on his head was pure insolence. Ryerson, trailing drably behind in spaceman's gray coveralls, felt bitterness. *What the hell have I been dragged away from Tamara for? Does this peacock know a mass from a scroll in the ground? He's hired himself a toy, is all, because for a while he's bored with wine and women...and Tamara is locked away on a rock with a self-righteous old beast who hates the sound of her name!*

As they sat down at their table, Maclaren went on, "But this is too good a chance to pass up. I found me a tame mathematician last year and sicced him onto the Schrödinger equation—Sugimoto's relativistic version, I mean; Yuen postulates too bloody much for my taste—anyhow, he worked it out for the quantities involved in a dark star, mass and gravitational intensities and cetera. His results make us both wonder if such a body doesn't go over to an entirely new stage of degeneracy at the core. One gigantic neutron? Well, maybe that's too fantastic. But consider—"

And while the monorail ran on toward Farside, Maclaren left the Interhuman language quite behind him. Ryerson could follow tensors, even when scribbled on a menu, but Maclaren had some new function, symbolized by a pneumatic female outline, that reduced to a generalized tensor under certain conditions. Ryerson stepped out on Farside, two hours later, with his brain rotating.

He had heard of the cyclopean installations which fill the whole of Yukawa Crater and spread out onto the plains beyond. Who has not? But all he saw on his first visit was a gigantic concourse, a long slideway tunnel, and a good many uniformed technicians. He made some timid mention of his disappointment to Maclaren. The New Zealander nodded: "Exactly. There's more romance, more sense of distance covered, and a devil of a lot better scenery, in an afternoon on the bay, than in a fifty-light-year leap. I say space travel is overrated. And it's a fact, I've heard, that spacemen themselves prefer the interplanetary runs. They take the dull interstellar watches as a matter of duty, by turns."

Here and there the tunnel branched off, signs indicating the way to Alpha Centauri Jump, Tau Ceti Jump, Epsilon Eridani Jump, all the long-colonized systems. Those were for passengers; freight went by other beams. There was no great bustle along any of the tubes. Comparatively few Earthlings had occasion to visit outsystem on business, still fewer could afford it for pleasure, and of course no colonial came here without a grudging okay. The Protector had trouble enough; he was not going to expose the mother planet and its restless billions to new ideas born under new skies, nor let any more colonials than he could help see first-hand what an inferior position they held. That was the real reason for the ban, every educated Terrestrial knew as much. The masses, being illiterate, swallowed a vague official excuse about trade policy.

The branches leading to Sirius Jump, Procyon Jump, and the other attained but uncolonizable systems, were almost deserted. Little came from such places—perhaps an occasional gem or exotic chemical. But relay stations had been established there, for 'casting to more useful planets.

Ryerson's heart leaped when he passed a newly activated sign: an arrow and WASHINGTON 5584 JUMP burning above. *That* tunnel would be filled, come next week!

He should have been in the line. And Tamara. Well, there would be later waves. His passage was already paid for, he had had no difficulty about transfering to another section.

To make conversation, he said through a tightness: "Where are the bulkheads?"

"Which ones?" asked Maclaren absently.

"Safety bulkheads. A receiver does fail once in a great while, you know. That's why the installations here are spread out so much, why every star has a separate 'caster. There's a vast amount of energy involved in each transmission—one reason why a 'casting is more expensive than transportation by spaceship. Even a small increment, undissipated, can melt a whole chamber."

"Oh, yes. That." Maclaren had let Ryerson get pompous about the obvious because it was plain he needed something to bolster himself. What itched the kid, anyhow? One should think that when the Authority offered a fledgling a post on an expedition as fundamental as this—Of course, it had upset Ryerson's plans of emigration. But not importantly. There was no danger he would find all the choice sites on Rama occupied if he came several weeks late: too few people had the fare as it was.

Maclaren said, "I see what you mean. Yes, the bulkheads are there, but recessed into the walls and camouflaged. You don't want to emphasize possible danger to the cash customers, eh? Some technic might get annoyed and make trouble."

"Some day," said Ryerson, "they'll reduce the energy margin needed; and they'll figure how to reproduce a Frank tube, rather than manufacture it. Record the pattern and recreate from a matter bank. Then anyone can afford to ride the beams. Interplanetary ships, even air and surface craft, will become obsolete."

Maclaren made no answer. He had sometimes thought, more or less idly, about the unrealized potentialities of mattercasting. Hard to say whether personal immortality would be a good thing or not. Not for the masses, surely! Too many of them as it was. But a select few, like Terangi Maclaren—or was it worth the trouble? Even given boats, chess, music, the No Drama, beautiful women and beautiful spectroscopes, life could get heavy.

As for matter transmission, the difficulty and hence the expense lay in the complexity of the signal. Consider an adult human. There are some $10^{14}$ cells in him, each an elaborate structure involving many proteins with molecular weights in the millions. You had to scan every one of those molecules—identify it structurally, ticket its momentary energy levels, and place it in proper spatiotemporal relationship to every other molecule—as nearly simultaneously as the laws of physics permitted. You couldn't take a man apart, or reassemble him, in more than a few microseconds; he wouldn't survive it. You couldn't even transmit a recognizable beefsteak in much less of a hurry.

So the scanning beam went through and through, like a blade of energy. It touched every atom in its path, was modified thereby, and flashed that modification onto the transmitter matrix. But such fury destroyed. The scanned object was reduced to gas, so quickly that only an oscilloscope could watch the process. The gas was sucked into the destructor chamber and atomically condensed in the matter bank; in time it would become an incoming passenger, or incoming freight. In a sense, the man had died.

If you could record the signal which entered the transmitter matrix, you could keep such a record indefinitely, recreate the man and his instantaneous memories, thoughts, habits, prejudices, hopes and loves and hates and horrors, a thousand years afterward. You could create a billion identical men. Or, more practically, a single handmade prototype could become a billion indistinguishable copies; nothing would be worth more than any handful of dirt. Or…superimpose the neurone trace-patterns, memories, of a lifetime, onto a recorded twenty-year-old body, be born again and live forever!

The signal was too complex, though. An unpromising research program went on. Perhaps in a few centuries they would find some trick which would enable them to record a man, or even a Frank tube. Meanwhile, transmission had to be simultaneous with scanning. The signal went out. Probably it would be relayed a few times. Eventually the desired receiving chamber got it. The receiver matrix, powered by dying atomic nuclei, flung gases together, formed higher elements, formed molecules and cells and dreams according to the signal, in microseconds. It was designed as an energy-consuming process, for obvious reasons: packing fraction energy was dissipated in gravitic and magnetic fields, to help shape the man (or the beefsteak, or the spaceship, or the colonial planet's produce). He left the receiving chamber and went about his business.

*A mono-isotopic element is a simple enough signal to record,* Maclaren reminded himself, *though even that requires a houseful of transistor elements. So this civilization can afford to be extravagant with metals—can use pure mercury as the raw material of a spaceship's blast, for instance. But we still eat our bread in the sweat of some commoner's brow.*

Not for the first time, but with no great indignation—life was too short for anything but amusement at the human race—Maclaren wondered if the recording problem really was as difficult as the physicists claimed. No government likes revolutions, and molecular duplication would revolutionize society beyond imagining. Just think how they had to guard the stations as it was, and stick them out here on the Moon...otherwise, even today, some fanatic could steal a tube of radium from a hospital and duplicate enough to sterilize a planet!

"Oh, well," he said, half aloud.

They reached the special exploratory section and entered an office. There was red tape to unsnarl. Ryerson let Maclaren handle it, and spent the time trying to understand that soon the pattern which was himself would be embodied in newly shaped atoms, a hundred light-years from Tamara. It wouldn't penetrate. It was only words.

Finally the papers were stamped. The transceivers to/from an interstellar spaceship could handle several hundred kilos at a time; Maclaren and Ryerson went together. They had a moment's wait because of locked safety switches on the *Southern Cross:* someone else was arriving or departing ahead of them.

"Watch that first step," said Maclaren. "It's a honey."

"What?" Ryerson blinked at him, uncomprehending.

The circuit closed. The pair felt no sensation, the process went too fast.

The scanner put its signal into the matrix. Inconceivable energies surged within a thermonuclear fire chamber; nothing controlled them, nothing could control them, but the force fields they themselves generated. Matter pulsed in and out of existence *qua* matter, from particle to gamma ray quantum and back. Since quanta have no rest mass, the pulsations disturbed the geometry of space according to the laws of Einsteinian mechanics. Gravitational waves laid hold of the tachyons which sprang into being, paired with tardyons, and formed them into a beam, and modulated it.

At hundreds of times the speed of light, the beam departed Luna, bearing the unimaginably complex signal which corresponded to two human beings. Distance attenuated it, but small, automated stations planted along the way relayed, and eventually refined its aim. After minutes, the tachyon pattern found and activated a matrix aboard the *Cross*.

Despite the pill inside him, Ryerson felt as if the bottom had dropped out of the world. He grabbed for a handhold. The after-image of the transmitter chamber yielded to the coils and banks of the receiver room on a spaceship. He hung weightless, a thousand billion billion kilometers from Earth.

Forward of the 'casting chambers, "above" them during acceleration, were fuel deck, gyros, and air-renewal plant. Then you passed through the observation deck, where instruments and laboratory equipment crowded together. A flimsy wall around the shaftway marked off the living quarters: folding bunks, galley, bath, table, benches, shelves, lockers, all crammed into a six-meter circle.

Seiichi Nakamura wrapped one leg casually around a stanchion, to keep himself from drifting in air currents, and made a ceremony out of leafing through the log book in his hands. It gave the others a chance to calm down, and the yellow-haired boy, David Ryerson, seemed to need it. The astrophysicist, Maclaren, achieved the unusual feat of lounging in free fall; he puffed an expensive Earthside cigarette and wrinkled his patrician nose at the pervading smell of an old ship, two hundred years of cooking and sweat and machine oil. The big, ugly young engineer, Sverdlov, merely looked sullen. Nakamura had never met any of them before.

"Well, gentlemen," he said at last. "Pardon me, I had to check the data recorded by the last pilot. Now I know approximately where we are at." He laughed with polite self-deprecation. "Of course you are all familiar with the articles. The pilot is captain. His duty is to guide the ship where the chief scientist—Dr. Maclaren-san in this case— wishes, within the limits of safety as determined by his own judgment. In case of my death or disability, command devolves upon the engineer, ah, Sverdlov-san, and you are to return home as soon as practicable. Yes-s-s. But I am sure we will all have a most pleasant and instructive expedition together."

He felt the banality of his words. It was the law, and a wise one, that authority be defined at once if there were non-Guild personnel aboard. Some pilots contented themselves with reading the regulations aloud, but it had always seemed an unnecessarily cold procedure to Nakamura. Only…he saw a sick bewilderment in Ryerson's eyes, supercilious humor in Maclaren's, angry impatience in Sverdlov's…his attempt at friendliness had gone flat.

"We do not operate so formally," he went on in a lame fashion. "We shall post a schedule of housekeeping duties and help each other, yes? Well. That is for later. Now as to the star, we have some approximate data and estimates taken by previous watches. It appears to have about four times the mass of Sol; its radius is hardly more than twice Earth's, possibly less; it emits detectably only in the lower radio frequencies, and even that is feeble. I have here a quick reading of the spectrum which may interest you, Dr. Maclaren."

The big dark man reached out for it. His brows went up. "Now this," he said, "is the weirdest collection of wavelengths I ever saw." He flickered experienced eyes along the column of numbers. "Seems to be a lot of triplets, but the lines appear so broad, judging from the probable errors given, that I can't be sure without more careful—hm-m." Glancing back at Nakamura: "Just where are we with relation to the star?"

"Approximately two million kilometers from the center of its mass. We are being drawn toward it, of course, since an orbit has not yet been established, but have enough radial velocity of our own to—"

"Never mind." The sophistication dropped from Maclaren like a tunic. He said with a boy's eagerness, "I would like to get as near the star as possible. How close do you think you can put us?"

THE ENEMY STARS

Nakamura smiled. He had a feeling Maclaren could prove likeable. "Too close isn't prudent. There would be meteors."

"Not around this one!" exclaimed Maclaren. "If physical theory is anything but mescaline dreams, a dead star is the clinker of a supernova. Any matter orbiting in its neighborhood became incandescent gas long ago."

"Atmosphere?" asked Nakamura dubiously. "Since we have nothing to see by, except starlight, we could hit its air."

"Hm. Yes. I suppose it would have some. But not very deep: too compressed to be deep. In fact, the radio photosphere, from which the previous watches estimated the star's diameter, must be nearly identical with the fringes of atmosphere."

"It would also take a great deal of reaction mass to pull us back out of its attraction, if we got too close," said Nakamura. He unclipped the specialized slide rule at his belt and made a few quick computations. "In fact, this vessel cannot escape from a distance much less than three-quarters million kilometers, if there is to be reasonable amount of mass left for maneuvering around afterward. And I am sure you wish to explore regions farther from the star, yes-s-s? However, I am willing to go that close."

Maclaren smiled. "Good enough. How long to arrive?"

"I estimate three hours, including time to establish the orbit." Nakamura looked around at their faces. "If everyone is prepared to go on duty, it is best we get into the desired path at once."

"Not even a cup of tea first?" grumbled Sverdlov.

Nakamura nodded at Maclaren and Ryerson. "You gentlemen will please prepare tea and sandwiches, and take them to the engineer and myself in about ninety minutes."

"Now, wait!" protested Maclaren. "We've hardly arrived. I haven't even looked at my instruments. I have to set up—"

"In ninety minutes, if you will be so kind. Very well, let us assume our posts."

Nakamura turned from Maclaren's suddenly mutinous look and Sverdlov's broad grin. He entered the shaftway and pulled himself along it by the rungs. Through the transparent plastic he saw the observation deck fall behind. The boat deck was next, heavy storage levels followed, and then he was forward, into the main turret.

It was a clear plastic bubble, unshuttered now when the sole outside illumination was a wintry blaze of stars. Floating toward the controls, Nakamura grew aware of the silence. So quiet. So uncountably many stars. The constellations were noticeably distorted, some altogether foreign. He searched a crystal darkness for Capella, but the bulge of the ship hid it from him. No use looking for Sol without a telescope, here on the lonely edge of the known.

Fear of raw emptiness lay tightly coiled within him. He smothered it by routine: strapped himself before the console, checked the instruments one by one, spoke with Sverdlov down the length of the ship. His fingers chattered out a computation on a set of keys, he fed the tape to the robot, he felt a faint tug as the gyros woke up, swiveling the vessel into position for blast. Even now, at the end of acceleration to half light-speed and deceleration to a few hundred kilometers per second, the *Cross* bore several tons of reaction-mass mercury. The total mass, including hull, equipment, and payload, was a bit over the kiloton. Accordingly, her massive gyroscopes needed half an hour to turn her completely around.

Waiting, he studied the viewscreens. Since he must back down on his goal, what they showed him was more important than what his eyes saw through this turret in the nose. He could not make out the black sun. *Well, what do you expect?* he asked himself angrily. *It must be occulting a few stars, but there are too many.* "Dr. Maclaren," he said into the intercom, "can you give me a radio directional on the target, as a check?"

"Aye, aye." A surly answer. Maclaren resented having to put his toys to work. He would rather have been taking spectra, reading ionoscopes, gulping gas and dust samples from outside into his analyzers, every centimeter of the way. Well, he would just have to get those data when they receded from the star again.

Nakamura's eyes strayed down the ship herself, as shown in the viewscreens. *Old,* he thought. *The very nation which built her has ceased to exist. But good work. A man's work outlives his hands. Though what remains of the little ivory figures my father carved to ornament our house? What chance did my brother have to create, before he shriveled in my arms? No!* He shut off the thought, like a surgeon clamping a vein, and refreshed his memory of the *Cygnus* class.

This hull was a sphere of reinforced self-sealing plastic, fifty meters across, its outside smoothness broken by hatches, ports, airlocks, and the like. The various decks sliced it in parallel planes. Aft, diametrically opposite this turret, the hull opened on the fire chamber. And thence ran two thin metal skeletons, thirty meters apart, a hundred meters long, like radio masts or ancient oil derricks. They comprised two series of rings, a couple of centimeters in diameter, with auxiliary wiring and a spidery framework holding it all together—the ion accelerators, built into and supported by the gravitic transceiver web.

"A ten-second test blast, if you please, Engineer Sverdlov," said Nakamura.

The instruments showed him a certain unbalance in the distribution of mass within the hull. Yussuf bin Suleiman, who had just finished watch aboard the ship and gone back to Earth, was sloppy about...no, it was unjust to think so...say that he had his own style of piloting. Nakamura set the pumps to work. Mercury ran from the fuel deck to the trim tanks.

By then the ship was pointed correctly and it was time to start decelerating again. "Stand by for blast.... Report...I shall want one-point-five-seven standard gees for—" Nakamura reeled it off almost automatically.

It rumbled in the ship. Weight came, like a sudden fist in the belly. Nakamura held his body relaxed in harness; only his eyes moved, now and then a finger touched a control. The secret of judo, of life, was to hold every part of the organism at ease except those precise tissues needed for the moment's task. Why was it so damnably difficult to put into practice?

Mercury fed through pipes and pumps, past Sverdlov's control board, past the radiation wall, into the expansion chamber and through the ionizer and so as a spray past the sunlike heart of a thermonuclear plasma. Briefly, each atom endured a rage of mesons. It broke down, gave up its mass as pure energy, which at once became proton-antiproton pairs. Magnetic fields separated them as they were born: positive and negative particles fled down the linear accelerators. The plasma, converting the death of matter directly into electricity, charged each ring at a successively higher potential. When the particles emerged from the last ring, they were traveling at three-fourths the speed of light.

At such an exhaust velocity, no great mass had to be discharged. Nor was the twin stream visible; it was too efficient. Sensitive instruments might have detected a pale gamma-colored splotch, very far behind the ship, as a few opposite charges finally converged on each other, but that effect was of no importance.

The process was energy-eating. It had to be. Otherwise surplus heat would have vaporized the ship. The plasma furnished energy to spare. The process was a good deal more complex than a few words can describe, and yet less so than an engineer accustomed to more primitive branches of his art might imagine.

Nakamura gave himself up to the instruments. Their readings checked out with his running computation. The *Cross* was approaching the black star in a complex spiral curve, the resultant of several velocities and two accelerating vectors, which would become a nearly circular orbit 750,000 kilometers out.

He started to awareness of time when young Ryerson came up the shaftway rungs. "Oh," he exclaimed.

"Tea, sir," said the boy shyly.

"Thank you. Ah...set it down there, please...the regulations forbid entering this turret during blast without inquiring of the—No, no. Please!" Nakamura waved a hand, laughing. "You did not know. There is no harm done."

He saw Ryerson, stooped under one and a half gravities, lift a heavy head to the foreign stars. The Milky Way formed a cold halo about his tangled hair. Nakamura asked gently, "This is your first time in extrasolar space, yes?"

"Y-yes, sir." Ryerson licked his lips. The blue eyes were somehow hazy, unable to focus closer than the nebulae.

"Do not—" Nakamura paused. He had been about to say, "Do not be afraid," but it might hurt. He felt after words. "Space is a good place to meditate," he said. "I use the wrong word, of course. 'Meditation,' in Zen, consists more of an attempt at identification with the universe than verbalized thinking. What I mean to say," he floundered, "is this. Some people feel themselves so helplessly small out here that they become frightened. Others, remembering that home is no more than a step away through the transmitter, become careless and arrogant, the cosmos merely a set of meaningless numbers to them. Both attitudes are wrong, and have killed men. But if you think of yourself as being a *part* of everything else—integral—the same forces in you which shaped the suns—do you see?"

"'The heavens declare the glory of God,'" whispered Ryerson, "'and the firmament showeth His handiwork.'...It is a terrible thing to fall into the hands of the living God."

He had not been listening and Nakamura did not understand English. The pilot sighed. "I think you had best return to the observation deck," he said. "Dr. Maclaren may have need of you."

Ryerson nodded mutely and went back down the shaft.

*I preach a good theory,* Nakamura told himself. *Why can I not practice it? Because a stone fell from heaven onto Sarai, and suddenly father and mother and sister and house were not. Because Hideki died in my arms, after the universe had casually tortured him. Because I shall never see Kyoto again, where every morning was full of cool bells. Because I am a slave of myself.*

*And yet,* he thought, *sometimes I have achieved peace. And only in space.*

Now he saw the dead sun through a viewscreen, when his ship swung so that it transited the Milky Way. It was a tiny blackness. The next time around, it had grown. He wondered if it was indeed blacker than the sky. Nonsense. It should reflect starlight, should it not? But what color was metallic hydrogen? What gases overlay the metal? Space, especially here, was not absolutely black: there was a certain thin but measurable nebular cloud around the star. So conceivably the star might be blacker than the sky.

"I must ask Maclaren," he murmured to himself. "He can measure it, very simply, and tell me. Meditation upon the concept of blacker than total blackness is not helpful, it seems." That brought him a wry humor, which untensed his muscles. He grew aware of weariness. It should not have been; he had only been sitting here and pressing controls. He poured a cup of scalding tea and drank noisily and gratefully.

Down and down. Nakamura fell into an almost detached state. Now the star was close, not much smaller than the Moon seen from Earth.

It grew rapidly, and crawled still more rapidly around the circle of the viewscreens. Now it was as big as Batu, at closest approach to Sarai. Now it was bigger. The rhythms entered Nakamura's blood. Dimly, he felt himself become one with the ship, the fields, the immense interplay of forces. And this was why he went again and yet again into space. He touched the manual controls, assisting the robots, correcting, revising, in a pattern of unformulated but bodily known harmonies, a dance, a dream, yielding, controlling, unselfness, Nirvana, peace and wholeness....

Fire!

The shock rammed Nakamura's spine against his skull. He felt his teeth clashed together. Blood from a bitten tongue welled in his mouth. Thunder roared between the walls.

He stared into the screens, clawing for comprehension. The ship was a million or so kilometers out. The black star was not quite one degree wide, snipped out of an unnamed alien constellation. The far end of the ion accelerator system was white hot. Even as Nakamura watched, the framework curled up, writhed like fingers in agony, and vaporized.

*"What's going on?"* Horror bawled from the engine room.

The thrust fell off and weight dropped sickeningly. Nakamura saw hell eat along the accelerators. He jerked his eyes around to the primary megammeter. Its needle sank down a tale of numbers. The four outermost rings were already destroyed. Even as he watched, the next one shriveled.

It could not be felt, but he knew how the star's vast hand clamped on the ship and reeled her inward.

Metal whiffed into space. Underloaded, the nuclear system howled its anger. Echoes banged between shivering decks.

"Cut!" cried Nakamura. His hand slapped the pilot's master switch.

The silence that fell, and the no-weight, were like death.

Someone's voice gabbled from the observation deck. Automatically, Nakamura chopped that interference out of the intercom circuit.

"Engineer Sverdlov," he called. "What happened? Do you know what is wrong?"

"No. No." A groan. But at least the man lived. "Somehow the—

the ion streams...seem to have...gotten diverted. The focusing fields went awry. The blast struck the rings—but it couldn't happen!"

Nakamura hung on to his harness with all ten fingers. *I will not scream*, he shouted. *I will not scream.*

"The 'caster web seems to be gone too," said a rusty machine using his throat. His brother's dead face swam among the stars, just outside the turret, and mouthed at him.

"Aye." Sverdlov must be hunched over his own viewscreens. After a while that tingled, he said harshly: "Not yet beyond repair. All ships carry a few replacement parts, in case of meteors or—We can repair the web and transmit ourselves out of here."

"How long to do that job? Quickly!"

"How should I know?" A dragon snarl. Then: "I'd have to go out and take a closer look. The damaged sections will have to be cut away. It'll probably be necessary to machine some fittings. With luck, we can do it in several hours."

Nakamura paused. He worked his hands together, strength opposing strength; he drew slow breaths, rolled his head to loosen the neck muscles, finally closed his eyes and contemplated peace for as long as needful. And a measure of peace came. The death of this little ego was not so terrible after all, provided said ego refrained from wishing to hold Baby-san in its arms just one more time.

Almost absently, he punched the keys of the general computer. It was no surprise to see his guess verified.

"Are you there?" called Sverdlov, as if across centuries. "Are you there, pilot?"

"Yes. I beg your pardon. Several hours to repair the web, did you say? By that time, drifting free, we will have crashed on the star."

"What? But we're *in* orbit! Eccentric, maybe but—"

"It is too narrow. We still have too much inward radial velocity. If the star were a single point, we would be in no danger; but it has volume. As nearly as I can determine—though there are so many uncertainties—our present orbit intersects the star. I think I can put us into a safe path before the whatever-it-is force has quite destroyed the accelerators. Yes."

"But you'll burn them up! And the web! We'll damage the web beyond repair!"

"Perhaps something can be improvised, once we are in orbit. But if we continue simply falling, we are dead men."

"No!" Almost, Sverdlov shrieked. "Listen, maybe we can repair the web in time. Maybe we'll only need a couple of hours for the job. There's a chance. But caught in an orbit, with the web melted or vaporized…do you know how to build one from raw metal? I don't!"

"We have a gravitics specialist aboard. If anyone can fashion us a new transmitter, he can."

"And if he can't, we're trapped out here! To starve! Better to crash and be done!"

Nakamura's hands began to dance over the keyboard. He demanded data of the instruments, calculations of the computers, and nothing of the autopilot. For no machine could help steer a vessel whose thrust-engine was being unpredictably devoured. This would be a manual task.

"I am the captain," he said, as mildly as possible.

"Not anymore!"

Nakamura slapped his master switch. "You have just been cut out of the control circuits," he said. "Please remain at your post." He opened the intercom to the observation deck. "Will the two honorable scientists be so kind as to stop the engineer from interfering with the pilot?"

**7**

For a moment, the rage in Chang Sverdlov was such that blackness flapped before his eyes.

When he regained himself, he found the viewscreens still painted with ruin. Starlight lay wan along the frail network of the transceiver web and the two sets of rings which it held together. At the far end the metal glowed red. A few globs of spattered stuff orbited like lunatic fireflies. Beyond the twisted burned-off end of the system, light-years dropped away to the cold blue glitter of a thousand crowding stars. The dead sun was just discernible, a flattened darkness. It seemed to be swelling visibly. Whether that was a real effect or not, Sverdlov felt the dread of falling, the no-weight horrors, like a lump in his belly.

He hadn't been afraid of null-gee since he was a child. In his cadet days, he had invented more pranks involving free fall than any two other boys. But he had never been cut off from home in this fashion. Krasna had never been more than an interplanetary flight or an interstellar Jump away.

And that cookbook pilot would starve out here to save his worthless ship?

Sverdlov unbuckled his harness. He kicked himself across the little control room, twisted among the pipes and wheels and dials of the fuel-feed section like a swimming fish, and came to the tool rack. He chose a long wrench and arrowed for the shaftway. His fury had chilled into resolution: *I don't want to kill him, but he'll have to be made to see reason. And quickly, or we really will crash!*

He was rounding the transmitter chamber when deceleration resumed. He had been going up by the usual process, grab a rung ahead of you and whip your weightless body beyond. Suddenly two Terrestrial gravities snatched him.

He closed fingers about one of the bars. His left arm straightened, with a hundred and ninety kilos behind. The hand tore loose. He let go the wrench and caught with his right arm, jamming it between a rung and the shaft wall. The impact smashed across his biceps. Then his left hand clawed fast and he hung. He heard the wrench skid past the gyro housing, hit a straight drop-off, and clang on the after radiation shield.

Gasping, he found a lower rung with his feet and sagged for a minute. The right arm was numb, until the pain woke in it. He flexed the fingers. Nothing broken.

But he was supposed to be in harness. Nakamura's calculations might demand spurts of ten or fifteen gravities, if the accelerators could still put out that much. The fear of being smeared across a bulkhead jolted into Sverdlov. He scrambled over the rungs. It was nightmarishly like climbing through glue. After a thousand years he burst into the living quarters.

Maclaren sat up in one of the bunks. "No further, please," he said.

The deceleration climbed a notch. Sverdlov's weight was iron on his shoulders. He started back into the shaft. "No!" cried Ryerson. But it was Maclaren who flung off bunk harness and climbed to the deck. The brown face gleamed wet, but Maclaren smiled and said: "Didn't you hear me?"

Sverdlov grunted and re-entered the shaft, both feet on a rung. *I can make it up to the bubble and get my hands on Nakamura's throat.* Maclaren stood for a gauging instant, as Sverdlov's foot crept toward the next rung. Finally the physicist added with a sneer in the tone: "When a technic says sit, you squat...colonial."

Sverdlov halted. "What was that?" he asked slowly.

"I can haul you out of there if I must, you backwoods pig," said Maclaren, "but I'd rather you came to me."

Sverdlov wondered, with an odd quick sadness, why he responded. Did an Earthling's yap make so much difference? He decided that Maclaren would probably make good on that promise to follow him up the shaft, and under this weight a fight on the rungs could kill them both. Therefore—Sverdlov's brain seemed as heavy as his bones. He climbed back and stood slumping on the observation deck. "Well?" he said.

Maclaren folded his arms. "Better get into a bunk," he advised.

Sverdlov lumbered toward him. In a shimmery wisp of tunic, the Earthling looked muscular enough, but he probably massed ten kilos less, and lacked several centimeters of the Krasnan's height and reach. A few swift blows would disable him, and it might still not be too late to stop Nakamura.

"Put up your fists," said Sverdlov hoarsely.

Maclaren unfolded his arms. A sleepy smile crossed his face. Sverdlov came in, swinging at the eagle beak. Maclaren's head moved aside. His hands came up, took Sverdlov's arm, and applied a cruel leverage. Sverdlov gasped, broke free by sheer strength, and threw a blow to the ribs. Maclaren stopped that fist with an edge-on chop at the wrist behind it; almost, Sverdlov thought he felt the bones crack. They stood toe to toe. Sverdlov drew back the other fist. Maclaren punched him in the groin. The Krasnan doubled over in a jag of anguish. Maclaren rabbit-punched him. Sverdlov went to one knee. Maclaren kicked him in the solar plexus. Sverdlov fell over and struck the floor with three gravities to help.

Through a wobbling, ringing darkness, he heard the Earthling: "Help me with this beef, Dave." And he felt himself dragged across the floor, somehow manhandled into a bunk and harnessed.

His mind returned. Pain stabbed and flickered through him. He struggled to sit up. "That was an Earthman way to fight," he pushed out through a swelling mouth.

"I don't enjoy fighting," said Maclaren from his own bunk, "so I got it over with as soon as possible."

"You—" The Krasnan lifted grotesquely heavy hands and fumbled with his harness. "I'm going to the control turret. If you try to stop me this time—"

"You're already too late, brother Sverdlov," said Maclaren coolly. "Whatever you were setting out to forestall has gone irrevocably far toward happening."

The words were a physical blow.

"It's...yes," said the engineer. "I'm too late." The shout burst from him: "We're all too late, now!"

"Ease back," said Maclaren. "Frankly, your behavior doesn't give me much confidence in your judgment about anything."

It rumbled through the ship. That shouldn't be, thought Sverdlov's training; even full blast ought to be nearly noiseless, and this was only fractional. Sweat prickled his skin. For the first time in a violent life, he totally realized that he could die.

"I'm sorry for what I called you," said Maclaren. "I had to stop you, but now I apologize."

Sverdlov made no answer. He stared up at a blank ceiling. Oddly, his first emotion, as rage ebbed, was an overwhelming sorrow. Now he would never see Krasna made free.

Silence and no-weight were dreamlike. For a reason obscure to himself, Maclaren had dimmed the fluoros around the observation deck, so that twilight filled it and the scientific apparatus crouched in racks and on benches seemed to be a herd of long-necked monsters. Thus there was nothing to drown the steely brilliance of the stars, when you looked out an unshuttered port.

*The* star hurtled across his field of view. Her eccentric orbit took the *Cross* around it in thirty-seven minutes. Here, at closest approach, they were only half a million kilometers away. The thing had the visual diameter of three full Moons. It was curiously vague of outline: a central absolute blackness, fading toward deep gray near the edges where starlight caught an atmosphere more savagely compressed than Earth's ocean abyss. Through the telescope, there seemed to be changeable streaks and mottlings, bands, spots, a hint of color too faint for the eye to tell...as if the ghosts of burned-out fires still walked.

*Quite oblate,* Maclaren reminded himself. *That would have given us a hint, if we'd known. Or the radio spectrum; now I realize, when it's too late, that the lines really are triplets, and their broadening is Doppler shift.*

The silence was smothering.

Nakamura drifted in. He poised himself in the air and waited quietly.

"Well?" said Maclaren.

"Sverdlov is still outside, looking at the accelerators and web," said Nakamura. "He will not admit there is no hope."

"Neither will I," said Maclaren.

"Virtually the whole system is destroyed. Fifty meters of it have vanished. The rest is fused, twisted, short-circuited...a miracle it continued to give some feeble kind of blast, so I could at least find an orbit." Nakamura laughed. Maclaren thought that that high-pitched, apologetic giggle was going to be hard to live with, if one hadn't been raised among such symbols. "We carry a few spare parts, but not that many."

"Perhaps we can make some," said Maclaren.

"Perhaps," said Nakamura. "But of course the accelerators are of no importance in themselves, the reconstruction of the web is the only way to get home.... What has the young man Ryerson to say about that?"

"Don't know. I sent him off to check the manifest and then look over the stuff the ship actually carries. He's been gone a long time, but—"

"I understand," said Nakamura. "It is not easy to face a death sentence when one is young."

Maclaren nodded absently and returned his gaze to the scribbled data sheets in one hand. After a moment, Nakamura cleared his throat and said awkwardly: "Ah...I beg your pardon...about the affair of Engineer Sverdlov—"

"Well?" Maclaren didn't glance up from the figures. He had a lot of composure of his own to win back. *The fact is,* he thought through a hammerbeat in his temples, *I am the man afraid. Now that there is nothing I can do, only a cold waiting until word is given me whether I can live or must die...I find that Terangi Maclaren is a coward.*

Sickness was a doubled fist inside his gullet.

"I am not certain what, er, happened," stumbled Nakamura, "and I do not wish to know. If you will be so kind…I hope you were not unduly inconvenienced—"

"No. It's all right."

"If we could tacitly ignore it. As I think he has tried to do. Even the best men have a breaking point."

*I always knew that there must one day be an end to white sails above green water, and to wine, and No masks, and a woman's laughter. I had not expected it yet.*

"After all," said Nakamura, "we must work together now."

"Yes." *I had not expected it a light-century from the home of my fathers. My life was spent in having fun, and now I find that the black star has no interest at all in amusing me.*

"Do you know yet what happened?" asked Nakamura. "I would not press you for an answer, but—"

"Oh, yes," said Maclaren. "I know."

Beneath a scrapheap of songs and keels, loves and jokes and victories, which mattered no longer but would not leave him, Maclaren found his brain working with a startling dry clarity. "I'm not sure how much we can admit to the others," he said. "Because this could have been averted, if we'd proceeded with more caution."

"I wondered a little at the time." Nakamura laughed again. "But who would look for danger around a—a corpse?"

"Broadened spectrum lines mean a quickly rotating star," said Maclaren. "Since the ship was not approaching the equatorial plane, we missed the full Doppler effect, but we might have stopped to think. And tripled lines mean a Zeeman splitting."

"Ah." Nakamura sucked in a hiss of air. "Magnetism?"

"The most powerful bloody magnetic field ever noticed around any heavenly body," said Maclaren. "Judging from the readings I get here, the polar field is…oh, I can't say yet. Five, six, seven thousand gauss—somewhere on that order of magnitude. Fantastic! Sol's field is only fifty-three gauss. They don't ever go much above two thousand. Except here."

He rubbed his chin. "Blackett effect," he went on. The steadiness of his words was a faintly pleasing surprise to him. "Magnetic field is directly related to angular velocity. The reason no live sun has a field like this dead thing here is that it would have to rotate too fast.

Couldn't take the strain; it would go whoomp and scatter pieces of star from hell to tiffin." An odd, perverse comfort in speaking lightly: a lie to oneself, persuading the subconscious mind that its companions were not doomed men and a black sun, but an amorous girl waiting for the next jest in a Citadel tavern. "As this star collapsed on itself, after burning out, it had to spin faster, d'you see? Conservation of angular momentum. It seems to have had an unusual amount to start with, of course, but the rotational speed is chiefly a result of its degenerate state. And that same super-density allows it to twirl with such indecent haste. You might say the bursting strength is immensely greater."

"Yes," said Nakamura. "I see."

"I've been making some estimates," said Maclaren. "It didn't actually take a very strong field to wreck us. We could easily have been protected against it. Any ion-drive craft going close to a planet is—a counter-magnetic circuit with a feedback loop—elementary. But naturally, these big ships were not meant to land anywhere. They would certainly never approach a live sun this close, and the possibility of this black dwarf having such a vicious magnetism—well, no one ever thought of it."

He shrugged. "Figure it out yourself, Captain Nakamura. The old H, e, v formula. A proton traveling at three-fourths $c$ down a hundred-meter tube is deflected one centimeter by a field of seven one-hundredths gauss. We entered such a field at a million kilometers out, more or less. A tenuous but extremely energetic stream of ionized gas hit the outermost accelerator ring. I make the temperature equivalent of that velocity to be something like three million million degrees Absolute, if I remember the value of the gas constant correctly. The closer to the star we got, the stronger the field we were in, so the farther up the ions struck.

"Of course," finished Maclaren in a tired voice, "all these quantities are just estimates, using simple algebra. Since we slanted across the magnetic field, you'd need a vectorial differential equation to describe exactly what happened. You might find occasion to change my figures by a factor of five or six. But I think I have the general idea."

"Yes-s-s," said Nakamura, "I think you do."

They hung side by side in dimness and looked out at the eye-hurting bright stars.

"Do you know," said Maclaren, "there is one sin which is punished with unfailing certainty, and must therefore be the deadliest sin in all time. Stupidity."

"I am not so sure." Nakamura's reply jarred him a little, by its sober literal-mindedness. "I have known many—well, shall I call them unintellectual?—people who lived happy and useful lives."

"I wasn't referring to that kind of stupidity." Maclaren went through the motions of a chuckle. "I meant our own kind. Yours and mine. We bear the guilt, you know. We should have stopped and thought the situation over before rushing in. I did want to approach more slowly, measuring as we went, and you overruled me."

"I am ashamed," said Nakamura. He bent his face toward his hands.

"No, let me finish. I should have come here with a well-thought-out program in mind. I gave you no valid reasons *not* to establish a close-in orbit at once. My only grumble was that you wouldn't allow me time to take observations as we went toward the star. You were perfectly justified, on the basis of the information available to you— Oh, the devils take it! I bring this up only so you'll know what topics to avoid with our shipmates—who must also bear some of the blame for not thinking—because we can't afford quarrels." Maclaren felt his cheeks crease in a sort of grin. "I have no interest in the guilt question anyway. My problem is strictly pragmatic: I want out of here!"

Ryerson emerged from the living-quarter screen. Maclaren saw him first as a shadow. Then the young face came so near that he could see the eyes unnaturally bright and the lips shaking.

"What have you found, Dave?" The question ripped from him before he thought.

Ryerson looked away from them both. Thickly: "We can't do it. There aren't enough replacement parts to make a f-f-functioning...a web—we can't."

"I knew that," said Nakamura. "Of course. But we have instruments and machine tools. There is bar metal in the hold, which we can shape to our needs. The only problem is—"

"Is where to get four kilos of pure germanium!" Ryerson screamed it. The walls sneered at him with echoes. "Down on that star, maybe?"

Square and inhuman in a spacesuit, Sverdlov led the way through the engine-room airlock. When Ryerson, following, stepped forth onto the ship's hull, there was a moment outside existence.

He snatched for his breath. Alien suns went streaming past his head. Otherwise he knew only blackness, touched by meaningless dull splashes. He clawed after anything real. The motion tore him loose and he went spinning outward toward the dead star. But he felt it just as a tide of nausea; his ears roared at him, the scrambled darks and gleams made a wheel with himself crucified at the hub. He was never sure if he screamed.

The lifeline jerked him to a halt. He rebounded, more slowly. Sverdlov's sardonic voice struck his earphones: "Don't be so jumpy next time, Earthling," and there was a sense of direction as the Krasnan began to reel him in.

Suddenly Ryerson made out a pattern. The circle of shadow before him was the hull. The metallic shimmers projecting from it…oh, yes, one of the auxiliary tank attachments. The mass-ratio needed to reach one-half *c* with an exhaust velocity of three-fourths *c* is 4.35—relativistic formulas apply rather than the simple Newtonian exponential—and this must be squared for deceleration. The *Cross* had left Sol with a tank of mercury on either side, feeding into the fuel deck. Much later, the empty containers had been knocked down into parts of the aircraft now stowed inboard.

Ryerson pulled his mind back from the snugness of engineering data. Beyond the hull, and around it, behind him, for X billion light-years on all sides, lay the stars. The nearer ones flashed and glittered and stabbed his eyes, uncountably many. The outlines they scrawled were not those Ryerson remembered from Earth: even the recognizable constellations, like Sagittarius, were distorted, and he felt that as a somehow ghastly thing, as if it were his wife's face which had melted and run. The farther stars blended into the Milky Way, a single clotted swoop around the sky, the coldest color in all reality. And yet farther away, beyond a million light-years, you could see more suns—a few billions at a time, formed into the tiny blue-white coils of other galaxies.

Impact jarred Ryerson's feet. He stood erect, his bootsoles holding him by a weak stickiness to the plastic hull. There was just enough rotation to make the sky move slowly past his gaze. It created a dim sense of hanging head down; he thought of ghosts come back to the world like squeaking bats. His eyes sought Sverdlov's vague, armored shape. It was so solid and ugly a form that he could have wept his gratitude.

"All right," grunted the Krasnan. "Let's go."

They moved precariously around the curve of the ship. The long thin frame-sections lashed across their backs vibrated to their cautious footfalls. When they reached the lattice jutting from the stern, Sverdlov halted. "Show you a trick," he said. "Light doesn't diffuse in vacuum, makes it hard to see an object in the round, so—" He squeezed a small plastic bag with one gauntleted hand. His flashbeam snapped on, to glow through a fine mist in front of him. "It's a heavy organic liquid. Forms droplets which hang around for hours before dissipating. Now, what d'you think of the transceiver web?"

Ryerson stooped awkwardly, scrambled about peering for several minutes, and finally answered: "It bears out what you reported. I think all this can be repaired. But we'll have to take most of the parts inboard, perhaps melt them down—re-machine them, at least. And we'll need wholly new sections to replace what boiled away. Have we enough bar metal for that?"

"Guess so. Then what?"

"Then—" Ryerson felt sweat form beneath his armpits and break off in little globs. "You understand I am a graviticist, not a mattercasting engineer. A physicist would not be the best possible man to design a bridge; likewise, there's much I'll have to teach myself, to carry this out. But I can use the operating manual, and calculate a lot of quantities afresh, and...well...I think I could recreate a functioning web. The tuning will be strictly cut-and-try: you have to have exact resonance to get any effect at all, and the handbook assumes that such components as the distortion oscillator will have precise, standardized dimensions and crystal structure. Since they won't—we haven't the facilities to control it, even if I could remember what the quantities are—well, once we've rebuilt what looks like a workable web, I'll have to try out different combinations of settings, perhaps for weeks, until...well, Sol or Centauri or...or any of the stations, even another spaceship...resonates—"

"Are you related to a Professor Broussard of Lomonosov Academy?" interrupted the other man.

"Why, no. What—"

"You lecture just like he used to. I am not interested in the theory and practice of mattercasting. I want to know, can we get home?"

Ryerson clenched a fist. He was glad that helmets and darkness hid their two faces. "Yes," he said. "If all goes well. And if we can find four kilos of germanium."

"What do you want that for?"

"Do you see those thick junction points in the web? They are, uh, you might call them giant transistors. Half the lattice is gone: there, the germanium was simply whiffed away. I do know the crystallo-chemical structure involved. And we can get the other elements needed by cannibalizing, and there is an alloying unit aboard which could be adapted to manufacture the transistors themselves. But we don't have four spare kilos of germanium aboard."

Sverdlov's tone grew heavy with skepticism: "And that balloonhead Maclaren means to find a planet? And mine the stuff?"

"I don't know—" Ryerson wet his lips. "I don't know what else we can do."

"But this star went supernova!"

"It was a big star. It would have had many planets. Some of the outermost ones—if they were large to start with—may have survived."

"Ha! And you'd hunt around on a lump of fused nickel-iron, without even a sun in the sky, for germanium ore?"

"We have an isotope separator. It could be adapted to—I haven't figured it out yet, but—for God's sake!" Ryerson found himself screaming. "What else can we do?"

"Shut up!" rasped Sverdlov. "When I want my earphones broken I'll use a hammer."

He stood in a swirl of golden fog, and the gray-rimmed black eye of the dead star marched behind him. Ryerson crouched back, hooked into the framework and waiting. At last Sverdlov said: "It's one long string of ifs. But a transistor doesn't do anything a vacuum tube can't." He barked a laugh. "And we've got all the vacuum we'll ever want. Why not design and make the equivalent electronic elements? Ought to be a lot easier than—repairing the accelerators, and scouring space for a planet."

"Design them?" cried Ryerson. "And test them, and redesign them, and—do you realize that on half rations we have not quite six months' food supply?"

"I do," said Sverdlov. "I feel it in my belly right now." He muttered a few obscenities. "All right, then. I'll go along with the plan. Though if that clotbrain of a Nakamura hadn't—"

"He did the only thing possible! Did you *want* to crash us?"

"There are worse chances to take," said Sverdlov. "Now what have we got, but six months of beating our hearts out and then another month or two to die?" He made a harsh noise in the radiophone, as if wanting to spit. "I've met Sarai settlers before. They're worse than Earthlings for cowardice, and nearly as stupid."

"Now, wait—" began Ryerson. "Wait, let's not quarrel—"

"Afraid of what might happen?" jeered Sverdlov. "You don't know your friend Maclaren's dirty-fighting tricks, do you?"

The ship whirled through a darkness that grew noisy with Ryerson's uneven breathing. He raised his hands against the bulky robot shape confronting him. "Please," he stammered. "Now wait, wait, Engineer Sverdlov." Tears stung his eyes. "We're all in this together, you know."

"I wondered just when you'd be coming up with that cliché," snorted the Krasnan. "Having decided it would be oh, so amusing to tell your society friends how you spent maybe a whole month in deep space, you got me yanked off the job I really want to do, and tossed me into a situation you'd never once stopped to think about, and wrecked us all—and now you tell me, 'We're all in this together'!" Suddenly he roared his words: "You mangy son of a muck-eating cockroach, I'll get you back—not for your sake, nor for your wife's, because if she's an Earthling I know how she'll be spending the time you're gone—but for my own planet, d'you hear? They need me there!"

It grew very still. Ryerson felt how his heartbeat dropped down to normal, and then still further, until he could no longer hear his own pulse. His hands felt chilly and his face numb. A far and terrified part of him thought, *So this is how it feels, when the God of Hosts lays His hand upon a man*, but he stared past Sverdlov, into the relentless white blaze of the stars, and said in a flat voice: "That will do. I've heard the story of the poor oppressed colonies before now. I think you yourself are proof that the Protectorate is better than you deserve. As for me, I never saw a milli of this supposed extortion from other planets: my father worked his way up from midshipman to captain, my brothers and I went through the Academy on merit, as citizens of the poorest and most overcrowded world in the universe. Do you imagine you know what competition is? Why, you blowhard clodhopper, you wouldn't last a week on Earth. As a matter of fact, I myself had grown tired of the struggle. If it weren't for this wretched expedition, my wife and I would have started for a new colony next week. Now you make me wonder if it's wise. Are all colonials like you—just barely brave enough to slander an old man and a woman when they're a safe hundred light-years away?"

Sverdlov did not move. The slow spin of the *Cross* brought the black star into Ryerson's view again. It seemed bigger, as the ship swooped toward periastron. He had a horrible sense of falling into it. *Thou, God, watchest me, with the cold ashen eye of wrath.* The silence was like a membrane stretched close to ripping.

Finally, very slow, the bass voice came. "Are you prepared to back up those words, Earthling?"

"Right after we finish here!" shouted Ryerson.

"Oh." A moment longer. Then: "Forget it. Maybe I did speak out of turn. I've never known an Earth man who wasn't...an enemy of some kind."

"Did you ever try to know them?"

"Forget it, I said. I'll get you home. I might even come around one day and say hello, on your new planet. Now let's get busy here. Our first job is to start the accelerators operating again."

The weakness which poured through David Ryerson was such that he wondered if he would have fallen under gravity. *Oh, Tamara,* he thought, *be with me now.* He remembered how they had camped on a California beach...had it all to themselves, no one lived in the deserts eastward...and the gulls had swarmed around begging bread until both of them were helpless with laughter. Now why should he suddenly remember that, out of all the times they had had?

# 10

When the mind gave up and the mathematics became a blur, there was work for Maclaren's hands. Sverdlov, and Ryerson under him, did the machine-tool jobs; Nakamura's small fingers showed such delicacy that he was set to drawing wire and polishing control-ring surfaces. Maclaren was left with the least-skilled assignment, least urgent because he was always far ahead of the consumption of his product: melting, separating, and re-alloying the fused salvage from ion accelerators and transceiver web.

But it was tricky in null-gee. There could not be any significant spin on the ship or assembly, out on the lattice, would have become too complicated for so small a gang of workers. Coriolis force would have created serious problems even for the inboard jobs. On the other hand, weightless melt had foul habits. Maclaren's left arm was still bandaged, the burn on his forehead still a crimson gouge.

It didn't seem to matter. When he looked in a mirror, he hardly recognized his face. There hadn't been much physical change yet, but the expression was a stranger's. And his life had narrowed to these past weeks; behind them lay only a dream. In moments when there was nothing else to do he might still play a quick chess game with Sverdlov, argue the merits of No versus Kabuki with Nakamura, or shock young Ryerson with a well-chosen dirty limerick. But thinking back, he saw how such times had become more and more sparse. He had quit trying to make iron rations palatable, when his turn in the galley came up; he had not sung a ballad for hundreds of the *Cross's* black-sun years. He shaved by the clock and hung on to fastidiousness of dress as pure ritual, the way Nakamura contemplated his paradoxes or Ryerson quoted his Bible or Sverdlov thumbed through his nude photographs of past mistresses. It was a way of telling yourself, *I am still alive*.

There came a moment when Maclaren asked himself what he was doing other than going through the motions of survival. That was a bad question.

"You see," he told his mirror twin, "it suggests a further inquiry: Why? And that's the problem we've been dodging all our mutual days."

He stowed his electric razor, adjusted his tunic, and pushed out of the tiny bathroom. The living section was deserted, as it had been most of the time. Not only were they all too busy to sit around, but it was too narrow.

Outside its wall, he moved through the comfort of his instruments. He admitted frankly that his project of learning as much as possible of the star was three-quarters selfish. It was not really very probable that exact knowledge of its atmospheric composition would be of any use to their escape. But it offered him a chance, for minutes at a time, to forget where he was. Of course, he did not admit the fact to anyone but himself. And he wondered a little what reticences the other men had.

This time he was not alone. Nakamura hovered at an observation port. The pilot's body was outlined with unwavering diamond stars. But as the dead sun swung by, Maclaren saw him grow tense and bring a hand toward his eyes, as if to cover them.

He drifted soundlessly behind Nakamura. "Boo," he said.

The other whirled around in air, gasping. As the thresh of arms and legs died away, Maclaren looked upon terror.

"I'm sorry!" he exclaimed. "I didn't think I'd startle you."

"I...it is nothing." Nakamura's brown gaze held some obscure beggary. "I should not have—it is nothing."

"Did you want anything of me?" Maclaren offered one of his last cigarettes. Nakamura accepted it blindly, without even saying thanks. *Something is very wrong with this lad,* thought Maclaren. Fear drained in through the glittering viewport. *And he's the only pilot we've got.*

"No. I had—I was resting a few moments. One cannot do precision work when...tired...yes-s-s." Nakamura's hunger-gaunted cheeks caved in with the violence of his sucking on the tobacco. A little crown of sweat-beads danced around his head.

"Oh, you're not bothering me." Maclaren crossed his legs and leaned back on the air. "As a matter of fact, I'm glad of your company. I need someone to talk with."

Nakamura laughed his meaningless laugh. "We should look to you for help, rather than you to us," he said. "You are the least changed of us all."

"Oh? I thought I was the most affected. Sverdlov hankers for his women and his alcohol and his politics. Ryerson wants back to his shiny new wife and his shiny new planet. You're the local rock of ages. But me—" Maclaren shrugged. "I've nothing to anchor me."

"You have grown quieter, yes." The cigarette in Nakamura's hand quivered a little, but his words came steadily now.

"I have begun to wonder about things." Maclaren scowled at the black sun. By treating it as a scientific problem, he had held at arm's length the obsession he had seen eating at Ryerson—who grew silent and large-eyed and reverted to the iron religion he had once been shaking off—and at Sverdlov, who waxed bitterly profane. So far, Maclaren had not begun thinking of the star as a half-alive malignancy. But it would be all too easy to start.

"One does, sooner or later." Nakamura's tone held no great interest. He was still wrapped up in his private horror, and that was what Maclaren wanted to get him out of.

"But I don't wonder efficiently. I find myself going blank, when all I'm really doing is routine stuff and I could just as well be thinking at my problems."

"Thought is a technique, to be learned," said Nakamura, "just as the uses of the body—" He broke off. "I have no right to teach. I have failed my own masters."

"I'd say you were doing very well. I've envied you your faith. You have an answer."

"Zen does not offer any cut-and-dried answers to problems. In fact, it tries to avoid all theory. No human system can comprehend the infinite real universe."

"I know."

"And that is my failure," whispered Nakamura. "I look for an explanation. I do not want merely to be. No, that is not enough…out here, I find that I want to be justified."

Maclaren stared into the cruelty of heaven. "I'll tell you something," he said. "I'm scared spitless."

"What? But I thought—"

"Oh, I have enough flip retorts to camouflage it. But I'm as much afraid to die, I'm struggling as frantically and with as little dignity, as any trapped rat. And I'm slowly coming to see why, too. It's because I haven't got anything but my own life—my own minute meaningless life of much learning and no understanding, much doing and no accomplishing, many acquaintances and no friends—it shouldn't be worth the trouble of salvaging, should it? And yet I'm unable to see any more in the entire universe than just that: a lot of scurrying small accidents of organic chemistry, on a lot of flyspeck planets. If things made even a little sense, if I could see there was anything at all more important than this bunch of mucous membranes labeled Terangi Maclaren…why, then there'd be no reason to fear my own termination. The things that mattered would go on."

Nakamura smoked in silence for a while. Maclaren finished his own cigarette in quick nervous puffs, fought temptation, swore to himself and lit another.

"I didn't mean to turn you into a weeping post," he said. And he thought: *The hell I didn't. I fed you your psychological medicine right on schedule. Though perhaps I did make the dose larger than planned.*

"I am unworthy," said Nakamura. "But it is an honor." He stared outward, side by side with the other man. "I try to reassure myself with the thought that there must be beings more highly developed than us," he said.

"Are you sure?" answered Maclaren, welcoming the chance to be impersonal. "We've never found any that were even comparable to us. In the brains department, at least. I'll admit the Van Maanen's abos are more beautiful, and the Old Thothians more reliable and sweet-tempered."

"How much do we know of the galaxy?"

"Um-m-m...yes."

"I have lived in the hope of encountering a truly great race. Even if they are not like gods—they will have their own wise men. They will not look at the world just as we do. From each other, two such peoples could learn the unimaginable, just as the high epochs of Earth's history came when different peoples interflowed. Yes-s-s. But this would be so much more, because the difference is greater. Less conflict. What reason would there be for it? More to offer, a billion years of separate experience as life-forms."

"I can tell you this much," said Maclaren, "the Protectorate would not like it. Our present civilization couldn't survive such a transfusion of ideas."

"Is our civilization anything so great?" asked Nakamura with an unwonted scornfulness.

"No. I suppose not."

"We have a number of technical tricks. Doubtless we could learn more from such aliens as I am thinking of. But what we would really learn that mattered—for this era of human history lacks one—would be a philosophy."

"I thought you didn't believe in philosophies."

"I used a wrong word. I meant a *do*—a way. A way of...an attitude? That is what life is for, that is your 'Why'—it is not a mechanical cause-and-effect thing, it is the spirit in which we live."

Nakamura laughed again. "But hear the child correcting the master! I, who cannot even follow the known precepts of Zen, ask for help from the unknown! Were it offered me, I would doubtless crawl into the nearest worm-hole."

And suddenly the horror flared up again. He grabbed Maclaren's arm. It sent them both twisting around, so that their outraged senses of balance made the stars whirl in their skulls. Maclaren felt Nakamura's grip like ice on his bare skin.

"I am afraid!" choked the pilot. "Help me! I am afraid!"

They regained their floating positions. Nakamura let go and took a fresh cigarette with shaking fingers. The silence grew thick.

Maclaren said at last, not looking toward the Saraian: "Why not tell me the reason? It might relieve you a bit."

Nakamura drew a breath. "I have always been afraid of space," he said. "And yet called to it also. Can you understand?"

"Yes. I think I know."

"It has—" Nakamura giggled—"unsettled me. All my life. First, as a child I was taken from my home on Earth, across space. And now, of course, I can never come back."

"I have some pull in the Citadel. A visa could be arranged."

"You are very kind. I am not sure whether it would help. Kyoto cannot be as I remember it. If it has not changed, surely I have, yes-s-s? But please let me continue. After a few years on Sarai, there was a meteor-fall which killed all my family except my brother. A stone from space, do you see? We did not think of it that way, then. The monastery raised us. We got scholarships to an astronautical academy. We made a voyage together as cadets. Have you heard of the *Firdawzi* disaster?"

"No, I'm afraid not." Maclaren poured smoke from his mouth, as a veil against the cosmos.

"Capella is a GO star like Sol, but a giant. The *Firdawzi* had been long at the innermost planet of the system, a remote-controlled survey trip. The radiations caused a metal fatigue. No one suspected. On our cruise, the ship suddenly failed. The pilot barely got us into an orbit, after we had fallen a long way toward Capella. There we had to wait until rescue came. Many died from the heat. My brother was one of them."

Stillness hummed.

"I see," said Maclaren at last.

"Since then I have been afraid of space. It rises into my consciousness from time to time." Maclaren stole a glance at Nakamura. The little man was lotus-postured in midair, save that he stared at his hands and they twisted together. Wretchedness overrode his voice. "And yet I could not stop my work either. Because out in space I often seem to come closer to...oneness...that which we all seek, what you have called understanding. But here, caught in this orbit about this star, the oneness is gone and the fear has grown and grown until I am afraid I will have to scream."

"It might help," said Maclaren.

Nakamura looked up. He tried to smile. "What do you think?" he asked.

Maclaren blew a meditative cloud of smoke. Now he would have to pick his words with care—and no background or training in the giving of succor—or lose the only man who could pull this ship free. Or lose Nakamura: that aspect of it seemed, all at once, more important.

"I wonder," he murmured, "even in an absolutely free society, if any such thing could exist—I wonder if every man isn't afraid of his bride."

"What?" Nakamura's lids snapped apart in startlement.

"And needs her at the same time," said Maclaren. "I might even extend it beyond sex. Perhaps fear is a necessary part of anything that matters. Could Bach have loved his God so magnificently without being inwardly afraid of Him? I don't know."

He stubbed out his cigarette. "I suggest you meditate upon this," he said lightly. "And on the further fact, which may be a little too obvious for you to have seen, that this is not Capella."

Then he waited.

Nakamura made a gesture with his body. Only afterward, thinking about it, did Maclaren realize it was a free-fall prostration. "Thank you," he said.

"I should thank you," said Maclaren, quite honestly. "You gave me a leg up too, y'know."

Nakamura departed for the machine shop.

Maclaren hung at the viewport a while longer. The rasp of a pocket lighter brought his head around.

Chang Sverdlov entered from the living section. The cigar in his mouth was held at a somehow resentful angle.

"Well," said Maclaren, "how long were you listening?"

"Long enough," grunted the engineer.

He blew cheap, atrocious smoke until his pocked face was lost in it. "So," he asked, "aren't you going to get mad at me?"

"If it serves a purpose," said Maclaren.

"Uh!" Sverdlov fumed away for a minute longer. "Maybe I had that coming," he said.

"Quite probably. But how are the repairs progressing outside?"

"All right. Look here," Sverdlov blurted, "do me a favor, will you? If you can. Don't admit to Ryerson, or me, that you're human—that you're just as scared and confused as the rest of us. Don't admit it to Nakamura, even. You didn't, you know, so far—not really. We need a—a—a damned cocky dude of a born-and-bred technic—to get us through!"

He whirled back into the quarters. Maclaren heard him dive, almost fleeing aft along the shaftway.

Nakamura noted in the log, which he had religiously maintained, the precise moment when the *Cross* blasted from the dead star. The others had not even tried to keep track of days. There were none out here. There was not even time, in any meaningful sense of the word—only existence, with an unreal impression of sunlight and leaves and women before existence began, like an inverted prenatal memory.

The initial minutes of blast were no more veritable. They took their posts and stared without any sense of victory at their instruments. Nakamura in the control turret, Maclaren on the observation deck feeding him data, Sverdlov and Ryerson watchful in the engine room, felt themselves merely doing another task in an infinite succession.

Sverdlov was the first who broke from his cold womb and knew himself alive. After an hour of poring over his dials and viewscreens, through eyes bulged by two gravities, he ran a hand across the bristles on his jaw. "Holy fecal matter," he whispered. "The canine-descended thing is hanging together."

And perhaps only Ryerson, who had worked outside with him for weeks of hours, could understand.

The lattice jutting from the sphere had a crude, unfinished look. And indeed little had been done toward restoring the transceiver web; time enough for that while they hunted a planet. Sverdlov had simply installed a framework to support his re-fashioned accelerator rings, antimagnetic shielding circuits, and incidental wires, tubes, grids, capacitors, transformers.... He had tested with a milliampere of ion current, cursed, readjusted, tested again, nodded, asked for a full amp, made obscene comments, readjusted, retested, and wondered if he could have done it without Ryerson. It was not so much that he needed the extra hands, but the boy had been impossibly patient. When Sverdlov could take no more electronic misbehavior, and went back into the ship and got a sledge and pounded at an iron bar for lack of human skulls to break, Ryerson had stayed outside trying a fresh hookup.

Once, when they were alone among galaxies, Sverdlov asked him about it. "Aren't you human, kid? Don't you ever want to throw a rheostat across the room?"

Ryerson's tone came gnat-like in his earphones, almost lost in an endless crackling of cosmic noise. "It doesn't do any good. My father taught me that much. We sailed a lot at home."

"So?"

"The sea never forgives you."

Sverdlov glanced at the other, couldn't find him in the tricky patching of highlight and blackness, and suddenly confronted Polaris. It was like being stabbed. How many men, he thought with a gasp, had followed the icy North Star to their weird?

"Of course," Ryerson admitted humbly, "it's not so easy to get along with people."

And the lattice grew. And finally it tested sound, and Sverdlov told Nakamura they could depart.

The engine which had accelerated the *Cross* to half light speed could not lift her straight away from this sun. Nor could her men have endured a couple of hundred gravities, even for a short time. She moved out at two gees, her gyros holding the blast toward the mass she was escaping, so that her elliptical orbit became a spiral. It would take hours to reach a point where the gravitational field had dropped so far that a hyperbolic path would be practicable.

Sverdlov crouched in his harness, glaring at screens and indicators. The bloody damned dead cinder wasn't going to let them escape this easily! He had stared too long at its ashen face to imagine that. There would be some new trick, and he would have to be ready. God, he was thirsty! The ship did have a water-regenerating unit, merely because astronautical regulations at the time she was built insisted on it. Odd, owing your life to some bureaucrat with two hundred years' dust on his own filing cabinets. But the regenerator was inadequate and hadn't been used in all that time. No need for it: waste material went into the matter bank, and was reborn as water or food or anything else, according to a signal sent from the Lunar station with every change of watch.

But there were no more signals coming to the *Cross*. Food, once eaten, was gone for good. Recycled water was little more than enough to maintain life. *Fire and thunder!* thought Sverdlov. *I can smell myself two kilometers away. I might not sell out the Fellowship for a bottle of beer, but the Protector had better not offer me a case.*

A soft *brroom-brroom-brroom* pervaded his awareness; the engine talked to itself. Too loud, somehow. The instruments read okay, but Sverdlov did not think an engine with a good destiny would make so much noise. He glanced back at the viewscreens. The black sun was scarcely visible. It couldn't be seen at all unless you knew just where to look. The haywired ugliness of the ion drive made a cage for stars. The faintest blue glow wavered down the rings. Shouldn't, of course. Inefficiency. St. Elmo's fire danced near the after end of the assembly. "Engine room to pilot. How are we making out?"

"Satisfactory." Nakamura's voice sounded thin. It must be a strain, yes, he was doing a hundred things manually for which the ship lacked robots. But who could have anticipated—?

Sverdlov narrowed his eyes. "Take a look at the tail of this rig, Dave," he said. "The rear negatron ring. See anything?"

"Well…" The boy's eyes, dark-rimmed and bloodshot, went heavily after Sverdlov's pointing finger. "Electrostatic discharge, that blue light—"

"See anything else?" Sverdlov glanced uneasily at the megammeters. He did not have a steady current going down the accelerators, it fluctuated continually by several percent. But was the needle for the negatron side creeping ever so slowly downward?

"No. No, I can't."

"Should'a put a thermocouple in every ring. Might be a very weak deflection of ions, chewing at the endmost till all at once its focusing goes blooey and we're in trouble."

"But we tested every single—And the star's magnetic field is attenuating with every centimeter we advance."

"Vibration, my cub-shaped friend. It'd be easy to shake one of those jury-rigged magnetic coils just enough out of alignment to—*Hold it!*"

The terminal starboard coil glowed red. Blue electric fire squirted forth and ran up the lattice. The negative megammeter dropped ten points and Sverdlov felt a little surge as the ship wallowed to one side from an unbalanced thrust.

"Engine room stopping blast!" he roared. His hand had already gone crashing onto the main lever.

The noise whined away to a mumble. He felt himself pitched off a cliff as high as eternity.

"What's the trouble?" barked Maclaren's voice.

Sverdlov relieved himself of a few unrepeatable remarks. "Something's gone sour out there. The last negatron accelerator began to glow and the current to drop. Didn't you feel us yaw?"

"Oh, Lord, have mercy," groaned Ryerson. He looked physically sick. "Not again."

"Ah, it needn't be so bad," said Sverdlov. "Me, I'm surprised the mucking thing held together this long. You can't do much with baling wire and spit, you know." Inwardly, he struggled with a wish to beat somebody's face.

"I presume we are in a stable orbit," said Nakamura. "But I would feel a good deal easier if the repair can be made soon. Do you want any help?"

"No. Dave and I can handle it. Stand by to give us a test blast."

Sverdlov and Ryerson got into their spacesuits. "I swear this smells fouler every day," said the Krasnan. "I didn't believe I could be such a filth generator." He slapped down his helmet and added into the radio: "So much for man the glorious star-conqueror."

"No," said Ryerson.

"What?"

"The stinks are only the body. That isn't important. What counts is the soul inside."

Sverdlov cocked his bullet head and stared at the other armored shape. "Do you actually believe that guff?"

"I'm sorry, I didn't mean to preach or—"

"Never mind. I don't feel like arguing either."

Sverdlov laughed roughly. "I'll give you just one thing to mull over, though. If the body's such a valueless piece of pork, and we'll all meet each other in the sweet bye and bye, and so on, why're you busting every gut you own to get back to your wife?"

He heard an outraged breath in his earphones. For a moment he felt he had failed somehow. There was no room here for quarrels. *Ah, shaft it*, he told himself. *If an Earthling don't like to listen to a colonial, he can jing-bangle well stay out of space.*

They gathered tools and instruments in a silence that smoldered. When they left the airlock, they had the usual trouble in seeing. Then their pupils expanded and their minds switched over to the alien gestalt. A raw blaze leaped forth and struck them.

Feeling his way aft along the lattice, Sverdlov sensed his anger bleeding away. The boy was right—it did no good to curse dead matter. Save your rage for those who needed it, tyrants and knaves and their sycophants. And you might even wonder (it was horrible to think) if they were worth it either. He stood with ten thousand bitter suns around him but none were Sol or Tau Ceti. O Polaris, death's lodestar, are we as little as all that?

He reached the end of the framework, clipped his lifeline on, and squirted a light-diffusing fog at the ring. Not too close, he didn't want it to interfere with his ion stream, but it gave him three-dimensional illumination. He let his body float out behind while he pulled himself squinting-close to the accelerator.

"Hm, yes, it's been pitted," he said. "Naturally it would be the negatron side which went wrong. Protons do a lot less harm, striking terrene matter. Hand me that counter, will you?"

Ryerson, wordless and faceless, gave him the instrument. Sverdlov checked for radioactivity. "Not enough to matter," he decided. "We won't have to replace this ring, we stopped the process in time. By readjusting the magnetic coils we can compensate for the change in the electric focusing field caused by its gnawed-up shape. I hope."

Ryerson said nothing. *Good grief,* thought Sverdlov, *did I offend him that much?* Hitherto they had talked a little when working outside, not real conversation but a trivial remark now and then, a grunt for response…just enough to drown out the hissing of the stars.

"Hello, pilot. Give me a microamp. One-second duration."

Sverdlov moved out of the way. Even a millionth of an ampere blast should be avoided, if it was an antiproton current.

Electric sparks crawled like ivy over the bones of the accelerator. Sverdlov, studying the instruments he had planted along the ion path, nodded. "What's the potentiometer say, Dave?" he asked. "If it's saying anything fit to print, I mean."

"Standard," snapped Ryerson.

*Maybe I should apologize*, thought Sverdlov. And then, in a geyser: *Judas, no! If he's so thin-skinned as all that, he can rot before I do.*

The stars swarmed just out of reach. Sometimes changes in the eyeball made them seem to move. Like flies. A million burning flies. Sverdlov swatted, unthinkingly, and snarled to himself.

After a while it occurred to him that Ryerson's nerves must also be rubbed pretty thin. You shouldn't expect the kid to act absolutely sensibly. *I lost my own head at the very start of this affair*, thought Sverdlov. The memory thickened his temples with blood. He began unbolting the Number One magnetic coil as if it were an enemy to emasculate.

"Okay, gimme another microamp one-second test."

"Try shifting Number Two a few centimeters forward," said Ryerson.

"You crazy?" snorted Sverdlov. *Yes, I suppose we're all a bit crazy by now.* "Look, if the deflected stream strikes here, you'll want to bend it down like so and—

"Never mind." Ryerson could not be seen to move, in the bulk of his armor, but Sverdlov imagined him turning away with a contemptuous shrug. It took several minutes of tinkering for the Krasnan to realize that the Earthling had visualized the interplay of forces correctly.

He swallowed. "You were right," he emitted.

"Well, let's get it reassembled," said Ryerson coldly.

*Very good, Earth snob, sir.* Sverdlov attacked the coils for several more minutes. "Test blast." Not quite. Try another setting. "Test blast. Repeat." That seemed to be it. "Give me a milliamp this time….A full amp…hm-m." The current had flowed too short a time to heat the ring, but needles wavered wildly.

"We're still getting some deflection," said Sverdlov. "Matter of velocity distribution. A certain small percentage of the particles have abnormal velocities and—" He realized he was crouched under Ryerson's hidden eyes babbling the obvious. "I'll try sliding this one a wee bit more aside. Gimme that vernier wrench….So. One amp test blast, please."

There was no further response from the instruments. Ryerson let out a whistling sigh. "We seem to have done it," he said.

*We?* thought Sverdlov. *Well, you handed me a few tools!*

Aloud: "We won't know for sure till full thrust is applied."

"Of course." Ryerson spoke hesitantly. Sverdlov recognized the tone, it was trying to be warm. Ryerson was over his fit of temper.

Well, I'm not!

"There isn't anything to be done about that except to try it and see, is there?" went on the Earthling.

"And if we still get significant deflection, drag on our suits and crawl back here—maybe a dozen times? No!"

"Why, that was how we did it before."

"I'm getting awfully hungry," said Sverdlov. Suddenly it flared out of him. "I'm sick of it! I'm sick of being cooped up in my own stink, and yours, I'm sick of the same stupid faces and the same stupid remarks, yes, the same stars even! I've had enough! Get on back inside. I'll stay here and watch under acceleration. If anything goes wrong, I'll be right on the spot to fix it."

"But—"

Nakamura's voice crackled above the mutter of stars. "What are you thinking of, Engineer Sverdlov? Two gravities would pull you off the ship! And we're not maneuverable enough to rescue you."

"This lifeline is tested for two thousand kilos," said the Krasnan. "It's standard procedure to make direct high-acceleration checks on the blast."

"By automatic instruments."

"Which we haven't got. Do you *know* the system is fully adjusted? Are you so sure there isn't some small cumulative effect, so the thing will quit on you one day when you need it the most?"

Maclaren's tone joined in, dry and somehow remote: "This is a curious time to think about that."

"I am the engineer," said Sverdlov stiffly. "Read the ship's articles again."

"Well," said Nakamura. "Well, but—"

"It would save time," said Ryerson. "Maybe even a few days' worth of time, if the coils really are badly maladjusted."

"Thanks, Dave," said Sverdlov clumsily.

"Well," said Nakamura, "you have the authority, of course. But I ask you again—"

"All I ask of *you* is two gravities' worth of oof for a few seconds," interrupted Sverdlov. "When I'm satisfied this ring will function properly, so we won't have to be forever making stops like this, I'll come inside."

He hooked his legs about the framework and began resetting the instruments clamped onto it. "Get on back, Dave," he said.

"Why...I thought I would—"

"No need to."

"But there is! You can't read every dial simultaneously, and if there's work to be done you'll need help."

"I'll call you if I want you. Give me your tool belt." Sverdlov took it from reluctant hands and buckled it around himself. "There is a certain amount of hazard involved, Dave. If I should be unlucky, you're the closest approximation to an engineer the ship will have. She can't spare both of us."

"But why take any risk at all?"

"Because I'm sick of being here! Because I've got to fight back at that damned black coal or start howling! Now get inside!"

As he watched the other blocky shape depart him, Sverdlov thought: I am actually not being very rational, am I now? But who could expect it, a hundred light-years from the sun?

As he made ready, he puzzled over what had driven him. There was the need to wrestle something tangible; and surely to balance on this skeleton of metal, under twice his normal weight, was a challenge. Beyond that, less important really, was the logic of it: the reasons he had given were sound enough as far as they went, and you could starve to death while proceeding at the pace of caution.

And below it all, he thought, was a dark wish he did not understand. Li-Tsung of Krasna would have told him to live at all costs, sacrifice all the others, to save himself for his planet and the Fellowship. But there were limits. You didn't have to accept Dave's Calvinism— though its unmerciful God seemed very near this dead star—to swallow the truth that some things were more important than survival. Than even the survival of a cause.

*Maybe I'm trying to find out what those things are*, he thought confusedly.

He crawled "up" till his feet were braced on a cross-member, with the terminal accelerator ring by his right ankle but the electroprober dial conveniently near his faceplate. His right hand gripped a vernier wrench, his left drew taut the lifeline. "Stand by for blast," he said into his radio. "Build up to two gees over a one-minute period, then hold it till I say cut."

Nothing happened for a while except the crawling of the constellations as gyros brought the ship around. Good boy, Seiichi! He'd get some escape distance out of even a test blast. "Stand by," it said in Sverdlov's earphones. And his weight came back to him, until he felt an exultant straining in the muscles of shoulder and arm and leg and belly; until his heart thudded loud enough to drown out the thin crackling talk of the stars.

The hull was above him now, a giant sphere upheld on twin derricks. Down the middle of each derrick guttered a ghostly blue light, and sparks writhed and fountained at junction points. The constellations shone chill through the electric discharge.

*Inefficient*, thought Sverdlov. *The result of reconstruction without adequate instruments. But it's pretty. Like festival fireworks.* He remembered a pyrotechnic display once, when he was small. His mother had taken him. They sat on a hired catamaran and watched wonder explode softly above the lake.

"Uh," grunted Sverdlov. He narrowed his eyes to peer at the detector dial. There certainly was a significant deflection yet, when whole grams of matter were being thrown out every second. It didn't heat up the ring very much, maybe not enough to notice; but negatrons plowed through terrene electron shells, into terrene nuclei, and atoms were destroyed. Presently there would be crystal deformation, fatigue, ultimate failure. He reported his findings and added with a sense of earned boasting: "I was right. This had to be done."

"I shall halt blast, then. Stand by."

Weightlessness came back. Sverdlov reached out delicately with his wrench, nipped a coil nut, and loosened the bolt. He shifted the coil itself backward. "I'll have this fixed in a minute. There! Now give me three gees for about thirty seconds, just to make sure."

"Three? Are you certain you—"

"I am. Fire!"

It came to Sverdlov that this was another way a man might serve his planet: just by being the right kind of man. Maybe a better way than planning the extinction of people who happened to live somewhere else. *Oh, come off it,* he told himself, *next thing you'll be teaching a Humane League kindergarten.*

The force on him climbed, and his muscles rejoiced in it.

At three gees there was no deflection against the ring...or was there? He peered closer. His right hand, weighted by the tool it still bore, slipped from the member on which it had been leaning. Sverdlov was thrown off balance. He flung both arms wide, instinctively trying not to fall. His right went between the field coils and into the negatron stream.

Fire spouted.

Nakamura cut the drive. Sverdlov hung free, staring by starlight at his arm. The blast had sliced it across as cleanly as an industrial torch. Blood and water vapor rushed out and froze in a small cloud, pale among the nebulae.

There was no pain. Not yet. But his eardrums popped as pressure fell. "Engine room!" he snapped. A part of him stood aside and marveled at his own mind. What a survival machine, when the need came! "Emergency! Drop total accelerator voltage to one thousand. Give me about ten amps down the tube. Quick!"

He felt no weight, such a blast didn't exert enough push on the hull to move it appreciably. He thrust his arm back into the ion stream. Pain did come now, but in his head, as the eardrums ruptured. One minute more and he would have the bends. The gas of antiprotons roared without noise around the stump of his wrist. Steel melted.

Sverdlov prodded with a hacksaw gripped in his left hand, trying to seal the spacesuit arm shut.

He seemed far away from everything. Night ate at his brain. He asked himself once in wonderment: "Was I planning to do this to other men?"

When he thought the sleeve was sealed, he withdrew it. "Cut blast," he whispered. "Come and get me." His airtanks fed him oxygen, pressure climbed again inside the suit. It was good to float at the end of a lifeline, breathing. Until he began to strangle on his own blood. Then he gave up and accepted the gift of darkness.

# 12

Now, about winter solstice, day was a pale glimmer, low in the south among steel-colored clouds. Tamara had been walking since the first light sneaked across the ocean, and already the sun was close to setting. She wondered if space itself could be blacker than this land. At least you saw the stars in space. On Skula you huddled indoors against the wind, and the sky was a blind whirl of snow.

A few dry flakes gusted as she came down off the moor to the beach. But they carried no warmth with them, there was not going to be a snowfall tonight. The wind streaked in from a thousand kilometers of Atlantic and icebergs. She felt the cold snap its teeth together around her; a hooded cloak was small protection. But she *would* not go back to the house. Not till day had drained from the world and it would be unsafe to remain outdoors.

She said to herself, drearily: *I would stay here even then, except it might harm the child, and the old man would come looking for me. David, help me, I don't know which would be worse!*

There was a twisted pleasure in being so honest with herself. By all the conventions, she should be thinking only of David's unborn baby, herself no more than its vessel. But it was not real to her...not yet...so far it was only sickness in the mornings and bad dreams at night. The reality was Magnus Ryerson, animal-like hairiness and a hoarse grumble at her for not doing the housework his way and incomprehensible readings aloud—his island and his sea and his bloody damned language lessons!

Tamara found herself voicing the curses. "Bloody damned English! Bloody damned English! You can take your language and you know what you can do with it!" She had heard the expression now and then—overheard it, rather, as a small girl peeping through doors while men talked—some of the coarser sort used such phrases, fish ranchers or coral miners or cattle guards. She was not sure what it was everybody knew could be done with it. Tear it into little bits, probably, and fling it on the wind, into the ugly Northern ocean.

For a moment her hands clawed together. If she could so destroy Magnus Ryerson!

She fought for decorum. She was a lady. Not a technic, but still a professor's daughter; she could read and write, she had learned to dance and play the flute, pour tea and embroider a dress and converse with learned men so they were not too bored while waiting for her father...the arts of graciousness. Her father would call it contrasocial, to hate her husband's father. This was her family now.

But.

Her boots picked a way down the hillside, through snow and heather bushes, until she came out on a beach of stones. The sea came directly in here, smashing at heaped boulders with a violence that shivered through the ground. She saw how the combers exploded where they struck. Spindrift stung her skin. Beyond the rocks was only a gray waste of galloping white-bearded waves, and the wind keening down from the Pole. It rolled and boomed and whistled out there.

She remembered a living greenish blue of southern waters, how they murmured up to the foot of palm trees under infinitely tall skies.

She remembered David saying wryly: "My people were Northerners as far back as we can trace it—Picts, Norse, Scots, sailors and crofters on the Atlantic edge—that must be why so many of them have become spacemen in the last several generations. To get away!"

And then, touching her hair with his lips: "But I've found what all of them were really looking for."

It was hard to imagine that David's warmth and tenderness and laughter had arisen in this tomb of a country. She had always thought of the religion which so troubled him (he first came to know her through her father; professor and student had sat up many nights under Australian stars while David groped for a God not all iron and hellfire) as an alien stamp, as if the legendary Other Race Out There had once branded him. The obscurity of the sect had aided her: Christians were not uncommon even today, but she had vaguely imagined a Protestant was some kind of Moslem.

Now she saw that Skula's dwellers and Skula's God had come from Skula iself, with winter seas in their veins. David had not been struggling toward normality; he had been reshaping himself into something which—down underneath—Magnus Ryerson thought was not human. Suddenly, almost blindingly, Tamara remembered a few weeks ago, one night when the old man had set her a ballad to translate. "Our folk have sung it for many hundreds of years," he said—and how he had looked at her under his heavy brows.

"He hath taken off cross and iron helm,
He hath bound his good horse to a limb,
He hath not spoken Jesu name
Since the Faerie Queen did first kiss him."

Tamara struck a fist into one palm. The wind caught her cloak and peeled it from her, so that it flapped at her shoulders like black wings. She pulled it back around her, shuddering.

The sun was a red sliver on the world's rim. Darkness would come in minutes, so thick you could freeze to death fumbling your way home. Tamara began to walk, quickly, hoping to find a decision. She had not come out today just because the house was unendurable. But her mind had been stiff, as if rusted. She still didn't know what to do.

*Or rather*, she thought, *I do know, but haven't saved up enough courage.*

When she reached the house, the air was already so murky she could almost not make out whitewashed walls and steep snow-streaked roof.

A few yellow gleams of light came through cracks in the shutters. She paused at the door. To go in—! But there was no choice. She twisted the knob and stepped through. The wind and the sea-growl came in with her.

"Close the door," said Magnus. "Close the door, you little fool."

She shut out all but a mumble and whine under the eaves, hung her cloak on a peg and faced around. Magnus Ryerson sat in his worn leather chair with a worn leather-bound book in his hands. As always, as always! How could you tell one day from the next in this den? The radiglobe was turned low, so that he was mostly shadow, with an icicle gleam of eyes and a dirty-white cataract of beard. A peat fire sputtered forlornly, trying to warm a teakettle on the hob.

Ryerson put the book down on his lap, knocked out his archaic pipe (it had made the air foul in here) and asked roughly: "Where have you been all day, girl? I was about to go look for you. You could turn an ankle and die of exposure, alone on the ring."

"I didn't," said Tamara. She exchanged her boots for zori and moved toward the kitchen.

"Wait!" said Magnus. "Will you never learn? I want my high tea at just 1630 hours.... Now. You must be more careful, lass. You're carrying the last of the Ryersons."

Tamara stopped. There was a downward slant to the ancient brick floor, she felt vaguely how her body braced itself. More nearly she felt how her chilled skin, which had begun to tingle as it warmed, grew numb again.

"Besides David," she said.

"If he is alive. Do you still believe it, after all these weeks?" Magnus began scraping out his pipe. He did not look at her.

"I don't believe he is dead," she answered.

"The Lunar crew couldn't establish gray-beam contact. Even if he is still alive, he'll die of old age before that ship reaches any star where men have an outpost. No, say rather he'll starve!"

"If he could repair whatever went wrong—"

The muffled surf-drums outside rolled up to a crescendo. Magnus tightened his mouth. "That is one way to destroy yourself...hoping," he said. "You must accept the worst, because there is always more of the worst than the best in this universe."

She glanced at the black book he called a Bible, heavy on one of the crowded shelves. "Do your holy writings claim that?" she asked. Her voice came out as a stranger's croak.

"Aye. So does the second law of thermodynamics." Magnus knocked his pipe against the ashtray. It was an unexpectedly loud noise above the wind.

"And you...and you...won't even let me put up his picture," she whispered.

"It's in the album, with my other dead sons. I'll not have it on the wall for you to blubber at. Our part is to take what God sends us and still hold ourselves up on both feet."

"Do you know—" Tamara stared at him with a slowly rising sense of horror. "Do you know, I cannot remember just what he looked like?"

She had had some obscure hope of provoking his rage. But the shaggy-sweatered broad shoulders merely lifted, a little shrug. "Aye, that's common enough. You've the words, blond hair and blue eyes and so on, but they make not any real image. Well, you didn't know him so very long, after all."

*You are telling me I am a foreigner*, she thought. *An interloper who stole what didn't belong to me.*

"There's time to review a little English grammar before tea," said the old man. "You've been terrible with the irregular verbs."

He put his book on the table—she recognized the title, Kipling's poems, whoever Kipling had been—and pointed at a shelf. "Fetch the text and sit down."

Something flared in the girl. She doubled her fists. "No."

"What?" The leather face turned in search of her.

"I am not going to study any more English."

"No—" Magnus peered as if she were a specimen from another planet. "Don't you feel well?"

She bit off the words, one after another: "I have better ways to spend my time than learning a dead language."

"Dead?" cried the man. She felt his rage lift in the air between them. "The language of fifty million—"

"Fifty million ignorant provincials, on exhausted lands between bombed-out cities," she said. "You can't step outside the British Isles or a few pockets on the North American coast and have it understood. You can't read a single modern author or scientist or…or anybody…in English. I say it's dead! A walking corpse!"

"Your own husband's language!" he bawled at her, half rising.

"Do you think he ever spoke it to anyone but you, once he'd…he'd escaped?" she flung back. "Did you believe…if David ever returns from that ship you made him go on…and we go to Rama—did you imagine we'd speak the language of a dying race? On a new world?"

She felt the tears as they whipped down her face, she gulped after breath amidst terror. The old man was so hairy, so huge. When he stood up, the single radiglobe and the wan firelight threw his shadow across her and choked a whole corner of the room with it. His head bristled against the ceiling.

"So now your husband's race is dying," he said like a gun. "Why did you marry him, if he was that effete?"

"*He* isn't!" she called out. The walls wobbled around her. "You are! Sitting here in your dreams of the past, when your people ruled Earth— a past we're well out of! David was going where…where the future is!"

"I see." Magnus Ryerson turned half away from her. He jammed both fists into his pockets, looked down at the floor and rumbled his words to someone else—not her.

"I know. You're like the others, brought up to hate the West because it was once your master. Your teacher. The white man owned this planet a few centuries ago. Our sins then will follow us for the next thousand years…till your people fail in their turn, and the ones you raised up take revenge for the help they got. Well, I'm not going to apologize for my ancestors. I'm proud of them. We were no more vicious than any other men, and we gave…even on the deathbed of our civilization, we gave you the stars."

His voice rose until it roared. "And we're not dead yet! Do you think this miserable Protectorate is a society? It isn't! It's not even a decent barbarism. It's a glorified garrison. It's the one worshiping the status quo and afraid to look futureward. I went to space because my people once went to sea. I gave my sons to space, and you'll give yours to space, because that's where the next civilization will be! And you'll learn the history and the language of our people—your people—by God, you'll learn what it *means* to be one of us!"

His words rang away into emptiness. For a while only the wind and a few tiny flames had voice. Down on the strand, the sea worried the island like a terrier with a rat.

Tamara said finally: "I already know what it means. It cost me David, but I know."

He faced her again, lowered his head and stared as if at an enemy.

"You murdered him," she said, not loudly. "You sent him to a dead sun to die. Because you—"

"You're overwrought," he broke in with tight-held anger. "I urged him to try just one space expedition. And this one was important. It could have meant a deal to science. He would have been proud afterward, whatever he did for a career, to say, 'I was on the *Cross*.'"

"So he should die for his pride?" she said. "It's as senseless a reason as the real one. But I'll tell you why you really made him go...and if you deny you forced him, I'll say you lie! You couldn't stand the idea that one child of yours had broken away—had penetrated this obscene farce of space exploration, covering distance for its own sake, as if there were some virtue in a large number of kilometers. David was going to live as nature meant him to live, on a living soil, with untanked air to breathe and with mountains to walk on instead of a spinning coffin...and his children would too...we would have been happy! And that was what you couldn't stand to have happen!"

Magnus grinned without humor. "There's a lot of meaningless noise for a symbolics professor's daughter to make," he said. "To begin at the end, what proof have you we were meant to be happy?"

"What proof have you we were meant to jump across light-years?" she cried. "It's another way of running from yourself—no more. It's not even a practical thing. If the ships only looked for planets to colonize, I could understand. But...the *Cross* herself was aimed for three giants! She was diverted to a black clinker! And now David is dead...for what? Scientific curiosity? You're not a research scientist, neither was he, and you know it. Wealth? He wasn't being paid more than he could earn on Earth. Glory? Few enough people on Earth care about exploration; not many more on Rama; he, not at all. Adventure? You can have more adventure in an hour's walk through a forest than in a year on a spaceship. I say you murdered your son because you saw him becoming sane!"

"Now that's enough," growled Magnus. He took a step toward her. "I've heard enough out of you. In my own house. And I never did hold with this newfangled notion of letting a woman yap—"

"Stand back!" she yelled. "I'm not your wife!"

He halted. The lines in his face grew suddenly blurred. He raised his artificial hand as if against a blow.

"You're my son's wife," he said, quite gently. "You're a Ryerson too…now."

"Not if this is what it means." She had found the resolution she sought. She went to the wall and took her cloak off its peg. "You'll lend me your aircar for a hop to Stornoway, I trust. I will send it back on autopilot and get transport for myself from there."

"But where are you going?" His voice was like a hurt child's.

"I don't know," she snapped. "To some place with a bearable climate. David's salary is payable to me till he's declared dead, and then there will be a pension. When I've waited long enough to be sure he won't come back, I'm going to Rama."

"But, lass—propriety—"

"Propriety be damned. I'd rather have David's child, alive."

She slipped her boots back on, took a flashlight from the cupboard, and went out the door. As she opened it, the wind came straight in and hit Magnus across the face.

"In the land of Chinchanchou,
Where the winds blow tender
From a sea like purple wine
Foaming to defend her,
Lives a princess beautiful
(May the gods amend her!)
Little known for virtue, but
Of most female gender."

As he came around the gyro housing and pulled himself forward to the observation deck, David Ryerson heard the guitar skitter through half a dozen chords and Maclaren's voice come bounding in its wake. He sighed, pushed the lank yellow hair back out of his eyes, and braced himself.

Maclaren floated in the living section. It was almost an insult to see him somehow clean all over, in a white tunic, when each man was allowed a daily spongeful of water for such purposes. And half rations had only leaned the New Zealander down, put angles in his smooth brown countenance; he didn't have bones jutting up under a stretched skin like Ryerson, or a flushed complexion and recurring toothache like Nakamura. It wasn't fair!

"Oh, hullo, Dave." Maclaren continued tickling his strings, but quietly. "How does the web progress?"

"I'm done."

"Hm?"

"I just clinched the last bolt and spotwelded the last connection. There's not a thing left except to find that germanium, make the transistors, and adjust the units." Ryerson hooked an arm around a stanchion and drifted free, staring out of sunken eyes toward emptiness. "God help me," he murmured, "what am I going to do now?"

"Wait," said Maclaren. "We can't do much except wait." He regarded the younger man for a while. "Frankly, both Seiichi and I found excuses not to help you, did less out there than we might have, for just that reason. I've been afraid you would finish the job before we found our planet."

Ryerson started. Redness crept into his chalky face. "Why, of all the—" His anger collapsed. "I see. All right."

"These weeks since we escaped have been an unparalleled chance to practice my music," remarked Maclaren. "I've even been composing Listen.

"In their golden-masted ships
Princes come a-wooing
Over darkling spindrift roads
Where the gales are brewing.
Lusty tales have drawn them thence,
Much to their undoing:
When they seek the lady's hand
*She gives them the—*"

"Will you stop that?" screamed Ryerson.

"As you like," said Maclaren mildly. He put the guitar back into its case. "I'd be glad to teach you," he offered.

"No."

"Care for a game of chess?"

"No."

"I wish to all the hells I'd been more of an intellectual," said Maclaren. "I never was, you know. I was a playboy, even in science. Now…I wish I'd brought a few hundred books with me. When I get back, I'm going to read them." His smile faded. "I think I might begin to understand them."

"When we get back?" Ryerson's thin frame doubled in mid-air as if for a leap. "*If* we get back, you mean!"

Nakamura entered. He had a sheaf of scribbled papers in one hand. His face was carefully blank. "I have completed the calculations on our latest data," he said.

Ryerson shuddered. "What have you found?" he cried. "For God's sake, what have you found?"

"Negative."

"Lord God of Israel," groaned Ryerson. "Negative again."

"That pretty well covers this orbit, then," said Maclaren calmly. "I've got the elements of the next one computed—somewhere." He went out among the instruments.

A muscle in Ryerson's cheek began to jump of itself. He looked at Nakamura for a long time. "Isn't there anything else we can do?" he asked. "The telescopes, the—Do we just have to sit?"

"We are circling a dead sun," the pilot reminded him. "There is only feeble starlight to see by. A very powerful instrument might photograph a planet, but not the telescopes we have. Not at any distance greater than we could find them gravitationally. S-s-so."

"We could make a big telescope!" exclaimed Ryerson. "We have glass, and…and silver and—"

"I've thought of that." Maclaren's tones drifted back from the observation section. "You're welcome to amuse yourself with it, but we'd starve long before a suitable mirror could be ground with the equipment here."

"But—Maclaren, space is so big! We could hunt for a million years and never find a planet if we can't…can't see them!"

"We're not working quite at random." Maclaren reappeared with a punched tape. "Perhaps you've forgotten the principle on which we are searching. We establish ourselves in an orbit about the star, follow it for a while, check our position repeatedly, and compute whether the path has been significantly perturbed. If it has been, that's due to a planet somewhere, and we can do a Leverrier to find that planet. If not—if we're too far away—we quarter to another arc of the same path and try again. Having exhausted a whole circumference thus, we move outward and try a bigger circle."

"Shut up!" rasped Ryerson. "I know it! I'm not a schoolboy, damn you! But we're *guessing!*"

"Not quite," said Maclaren. "You were occupied with the web when I worked out the secondary principle...yes, come to think of it, you never did ask me before. Let me explain. You see, by extrapolating from data on known stellar types, I know approximately what this star was like in its palmy days. From this, planetary-formation theory gives me the scale of its one-time system. For instance, its planets must have been more or less in the equatorial plane; such quantities as mass, angular momentum, and magnetic field determine the Bode's Law constants; to the extent that all this is known, I can draw an orbital map.

"Well, then the star went supernova. Its closer planets were whiffed into gas. The outermost giants would have survived, though badly damaged. But the semimajor axes of their orbits were so tremendous— theoretically, planets could have formed as much as a light-year from this star—that even a small percentage of error in the data makes my result uncertain by Astronomical Units. Another factor: the explosion filled this space with gas. We're actually inside a nonluminous nebula. That would shorten the orbits of the remaining planets; in the course of millions of years they've spiraled far inward. In one way that helps us: we've an area to search which is not hopelessly huge. But on the other hand, just how long has it been since the accident? What's the density distribution of the nebula now, and what was it back then? I've taken some readings and made some estimates. All very crude, but—" Maclaren shrugged—"what else can we do? The successive orbits we have been trying are, more or less, those I have calculated for the surviving planets as of today. And, of course, intermediate radii to make sure that we will be measurably perturbed no matter where those planets actually are. It's just a matter of getting close enough to one of them."

"If our food lasts," groaned Ryerson. "And we have to eat while we finish the web, too. Don't forget that."

"We're going to have to reorganize our schedules," said Maclaren thoughtfully. "Hitherto we've found things to keep us occupied. Now we must wait, and not go crazy waiting." He grinned. "I hereby declare the *Southern Cross* dirty-limerick contest open and offer a prize of—"

"Yes," said Ryerson. "Great sport. Fun and games, with Chang Sverdlov's frozen corpse listening in!"

Silence clapped down. They heard the air mumble in the ventilators.

"What else can we do with our poor friend?" asked Nakamura softly. "Send him on a test rocket into the black sun? He deserved better of us. Yes-s-s? Let his own people bury him."

"Bury a copy of him!" shrieked Ryerson. "Of all the senseless—"

"Please," said Nakamura. He tried to smile. "After all…it is no trouble to us, and it will comfort his friends at home, maybe yes? After all, speaking in terms of atoms, we do not even wish to send ourselves back. Only copies." He laughed.

"Will you stop that giggling!"

"Please." Nakamura pushed himself away, lifting astonished hands. "Please, if I have offended you, I am so sorry."

"So sorry! So sorry! Get out of here! Get out, both of you! I've seen more of you than I can stand!"

Nakamura started to leave, still bobbing his head, smiling and hissing in the shaftway. Maclaren launched himself between the other two. He snapped a hand onto either wrist.

"That will do!" They grew suddenly aware, it was shocking, how the eyes turned green in his dark hooked face. His words fell like axes. "Dave, you're a baby, screaming for mother to come change you. Seiichi, you think it's enough to make polite noises at the rest of the world. If you ever want to see sunlight again, you'll both have to mend your ideas." He shook them a little. "Dave, you'll keep yourself clean. Seiichi, you'll dress for dinner and talk with us. Both of you will stop feeling sorry for yourselves and start working to survive. And the next step is to become civilized again. We haven't got the size or the time or the force to beat that star: nothing but manhood. Now go off and start practicing how to be men!"

They said nothing, only stared at him for a few moments and then departed in opposite directions. Maclaren found himself gazing stupidly at his guitar case. *I'd better put that away till it's requested,* he thought. *If ever. I didn't stop to think, my own habits might possibly be hard to live with.*

After a long time: *Seems I'm the captain now, in fact if not in name. But how did it happen? What have I done, what have I got?* Presently, with an inward twisting: *It must be I've less to lose. I can be more objective because I've no wife, no children, no cause, no God. It's easy for a hollow man to remain calm.*

He covered his eyes, as if to deny he floated among a million unpitying stars. But he couldn't hunch up that way for long. Someone might come back, and the captain mustn't be seen afraid.

Not afraid of death. Of life.

**14**

Seen from a view turret on the observation deck, the planet looked eerily like its parent star which had murdered it. Ryerson crouched in darkness, staring out to darkness. Against strewn constellations there lay a gigantic black outline with wan streaks and edgings of gray. As he watched, Ryerson saw it march across the Milky Way and out of his sight. But it was the *Cross* which moved, he thought, circling her hope in fear.

*I stand on Mount Nebo,* he thought, *and down there is my Promised Land.*

Irrationally—but the months had made them all odd, silent introverts, Trappists because meaningful conversation was too rare and precious to spill without due heed—he reached into his breast pocket. He took forth Tamara's picture and held it close to him. Sometimes he woke up breathing the fragrance of her hair. *Have a look,* he told her. *We found it.* In a heathen adoration: *You are my luck, Tamara. You found it.*

As the black planet came back into sight, monstrously swallowing suns (it was only a thousand or so kilometers away), Ryerson turned his wife's image outward so she could see what they had gained.

"Are you there, Dave?"

Maclaren's voice came from around the cylinder of the living section. It had grown much lower in this time of search. Often you could scarcely hear Maclaren when he spoke. And the New Zealander, once in the best condition of them all, had lately gotten thinner than the other two, until his eyes stared from caves. But then, thought Ryerson, each man aboard had had to come to terms with himself, one way or another, and there had been a price. In his own case, he had paid with youth.

"Coming." Ryerson pulled himself around the deck, between the instruments. Maclaren was at his little desk, with a clipboard full of scrawled paper in one hand. Nakamura had just joined him. The Saraian had gone wholly behind a mask, more and more a polite unobtrusive robot. Ryerson wondered whether serenity now lay within the man, or the loneliest circle of hell, or both.

"I've got the data pretty well computed," said Maclaren.

Ryerson and Nakamura waited. There had been curiously little exultation when the planet finally revealed itself. *I*, thought Ryerson, *have become a plodder. Nothing is quite real out here—there is only a succession of motions, in my body and my brain—but I can celebrate no victory, because there is none, until the final and sole victory: Tamara.*

But I wonder why Terangi and Seiichi didn't cheer?

Maclaren ruffled through his papers. "It has a smaller mass and radius than Earth," he said, "but a considerably higher density suggesting it's mostly nickel-iron. No satellite, of course. And, even though the surface gravity is a bit more than Earth's, no atmosphere. Seems to be bare rock down there...or metal, I imagine. Solid, anyhow."

"How large was it once?" murmured Nakamura.

Maclaren shrugged. "That would be pure guesswork," he said. "I don't know which planet of the original system this is. One or two of the survivors may have crashed on the primary by now, you see. My personal guess, though, is that it was the 61 Cygni C type—more massive than Jupiter, though of less bulk because of core degeneracy. It had an extremely big orbit. Even so, the supernova boiled away all its hydrogen and probably some of the heavier elements too. But that took time, and the planet still had this much mass left when the star decayed into a white dwarf. Of course, with the pressure of the outer layers removed, the core reverted to normal density, which must have been a pretty spectacular catastrophe in itself. Since then, the residual stellar gases have been making the planet spiral slowly inward, for hundreds of megayears. And now—"

"Now we found it," said Ryerson. "With three weeks' food supply to spare."

"And the germanium still to get," said Maclaren.

Nakamura drew a breath. His eyes went to the deck "beneath" his feet. Far aft was a storage compartment which had been left open to the bitterness of space; and a dead man, lashed to a stanchion.

"Had there been four of us," he said, "we would have consumed our supplies already and be starving. I am most humbly grateful to Engineer Sverdlov."

Maclaren's tone was dry. "He didn't die for that reason."

"No. But has he given us less, merely because it was an accident?"

They floated a while in stillness. Then Maclaren shook himself and said: "We're wasting time. This ship was never intended to land on a planet. Since I've already informed you any world we found might very likely use vacuum for sky, and you didn't object, I assume the aircraft can make a landing."

Nakamura crossed his legs and rested impassively, hands folded on his lap. "How familiar are you with the standard exploratory technique?" he inquired.

"Not very," confessed Maclaren. "I gather that aircraft are preferred for reasons of mass economy."

"And even more for maneuverability. A nuclear-powered vessel, using wings and turbojets, can rise high into an atmosphere, above the worst air resistance, without having to expend the reaction mass of a rocket. Likewise it can land more easily and safely in the first place. The aircraft which we carry, dismantled, are intended to leave their orbiting mother ship with a short rocket burst, slip into the atmosphere of a new planet, and descend. The return is more difficult, of course, but they get into the stratosphere before applying the non-ionic rocket drive. This in turn takes them into space proper, where their ion accelerators will work. Naturally, the cabins being sealed, any kind of atmosphere will serve them.

"Now, this is for exploration purposes. But these auxiliary craft are also capable of landing on rockets alone. When the time has come to establish a beam-relay station, some airless, lifeless satellite is chosen, to avoid the necessity of quarantine. The craft shuttle back and forth, carrying the ship's dismantled transceiver. This is reassembled on the surface. Thereby the satellite's own mass becomes available to the matter bank, and any amount of material can be reconstructed according to the signals from the home station. The first things sent through are usually the parts for a much larger transceiver station, which can handle many tons of mass at a time."

"Well, good," said Maclaren. "That was more or less what I thought. Let's land and—oh, oh."

Ryerson felt a smile tugging his lips, though it was not a happy one. "You see?" he murmured.

Maclaren regarded him closely. "You don't seem too discouraged," he said. "There must be an answer."

Ryerson nodded. "I've already spoken with Seiichi about it, while you were busy determining the exact characteristics of the planet. It's not going to be fun, but—Well, let him tell you."

Maclaren said slowly: "I had hoped, it was at least possible, that any planet we found would have a surviving satellite, small enough to land the whole ship on, or lay alongside if you want to consider it that way. It would have been the best thing for us. But I'm sure now that this lump has no companion of any kind. So we'll have to get our germanium down there."

"Which we could also have done, had we been fortunate enough to locate the planet sooner," Nakamura told him. "We can take aircraft down to the surface even now. But we would have to transship all the mining and separating equipment, establish a working space and an airdome—It is too much work for three men to do before our three weeks of supplies are eaten up; and then the actual mining would still remain."

Maclaren nodded. "I should have thought of this myself," he said. "I wonder how sane and sensible we are—how can we measure rationality, when we are all the human race we know for tens of light-years?—Well. So I didn't think and you didn't talk. Nevertheless, I gather there's a way out of our dilemma."

"Yes," the pilot said. "A riskful way, but any other is certain death. We can take the ship down, and use her for our ready-made workshop and airdome."

"The *Cross*? But—well, of course the gravitation here is no problem to her, nor the magnetism now that the drive is shielded…but we can't make a tail landing, we'd crumple the web, and—hell's clanging bells, she can't land at all! She's not designed for it! Not maneuverable enough, why, it takes half an hour just to swing her clear around on gyros."

Nakamura said calmly, "I have made calculations for some time now, preparing for this eventuality. There was nothing we could do before knowing what we would actually find, but I do have some plans drawn up. We have six knocked-down auxiliary craft. Yes? It will not take long to assemble their non-ionic rocket drives, which are very simple devices, clamp these to the outside hull, and run their control systems through the ship's console. I think if we all work hard we can have it assembled, tested, and functioning in two or three days. Each pair of rockets should be so mounted as to form a couple which will rotate the ship around one of the three orthogonal space axes. No? Thus the spaceship will become most highly responsive to piloting. Furthermore, we shall cut up the aircraft hulls, as well as whatever else we may need and can spare for this purpose, such as interior fittings. From this, we shall construct a tripod enclosing and protecting the stern assembly. It will be clumsy and unbalanced, of course—but I trust my poor maneuverings can compensate for that—and it will be comparatively weak—but with the help of radar and our powerful ion-blast, the ship can be landed very gently."

"Hm-m." Maclaren rubbed his chin. His eyes flickered between the other two faces. "It shouldn't be hard to fix those rocket motors in place, as you say. But a tripod more than a hundred meters long, for a thing as massive as this ship—I don't know. If nothing else, how about the servos for it?"

"Please." Nakamura waved his words aside. "I realize we have not time to do this properly. My plan does not envision anything with self-adjusting legs. A simple, rigid structure must suffice. We can use the radar to select a nearly level landing place."

"All places are, down there," said Maclaren. "That iron was boiling once, and nothing has weathered it since. Of course, there are doubtless minor irregularities, which would topple us on our tripod—with a thousand tons of mass to hit the ground!"

Nakamura's eyes drooped. "It will be necessary for me to react quickly," he said. "That is the risk we take."

When the ship was prepared, they met once on the observation deck, to put on their spacesuits. The hull might be cracked in landing. Maclaren and Ryerson would be down at the engine controls, Nakamura in the pilot's turret, strapped into acceleration harness with only their hands left free.

Nakamura's gaze sought Maclaren's. "We may not meet again," he said.

"Possible," said Maclaren.

The small, compact body held steady, but Nakamura's face thawed. He had suddenly, after all the time which was gone, taken on an expression; and it was gentle.

"Since this may be my last chance," he said, "I would like to thank you."

"Whatever for?"

"I am not afraid anymore."

"Don't thank me," said Maclaren, embarrassed. "Something like that, a chap does for himself, y'know."

"You earned me the time for it, at least." Nakamura made a weightless bow. "*Sensei*, give me your blessing."

Maclaren said, with a degree of bewilderment: "Look here, everybody else has had more skill, contributed more, than I. I've told you a few things about the star and the planet, but you—Dave, at least—could have figured it out with slightly more difficulty. I'd never have known how to reconstruct a drive or a web, though; and I'd never be able to land this ship."

"I was not speaking of material survival," said Nakamura. A smile played over his mouth. "Still, do you remember how disorganized and noisy we were at first, and how we have grown so quiet since and work together so well? It is your doing. The highest interhuman art is to make it possible for others to use *their* arts." Then, seriously: "The next stage of achievement, though, lies within a man. You have taught me. Knowingly or not, Terangi-san, you have taught me. I would give much to be sure you will...have the chance...to teach yourself."

Ryerson appeared from the lockers. "Here they are," he said. "Tin suits all around."

Maclaren donned his armor and went aft. *I wonder how much Seiichi knows. Does he know that I've stopped making a fuss about things, that I didn't exult when we found this planet, not from stoicism but merely because I have been afraid to hope?*

I wouldn't even know what to hope for. All this struggle, just to get back to Earth and resume having fun? No, that's too grotesque.

"We should have issued the day's chow before going down," said Ryerson. "Might not be in any shape to eat it at the other end."

"Who's got an appetite under present circumstances?" said Maclaren. "So postponing dinner is one way of stretching out the rations a few more hours."

"Seventeen days' worth, now."

"We can keep going, foodless, for a while longer."

"We'll have to," said Ryerson. He wet his lips. "We won't mine our metal, and gasify it, and separate out the fractional percent of germanium, and make those transistors, and tune the circuits, in any seventeen days."

Maclaren grimaced. "Starvation, or the canned willy we've been afflicted with. Frankly, I don't think there's much difference."

Hastily, he grinned at Ryerson, so the boy would know it for a jest. Grumbling was not allowed any more; they didn't dare. And the positive side of conversation, the dreaming aloud of "when we get home," had long since worn thin. Dinner-table conversation had been a ritual they needed for a while, but in a sense they had outgrown it. Now a man was driven into his own soul. *And that's what Seiichi meant,* thought Maclaren. *Only, I haven't found anything in myself. Or, no. I have. But I don't know what. It's too dark to see.*

He strapped himself in and began checking instruments.

"Pilot to engine room. Read off!"

"Engine room to pilot. Plus voltage clear. Minus voltage clear. Mercury flow standard..."

The ship came to life.

And she moved down. Her blast slowed her in orbit, she spiraled, a featureless planet of black steel called her to itself. The path was cautious. There must be allowance for rotation; there must not be too quick a change of velocity, lest the ponderous sphere go wobbling out of control. Again and again the auxiliary motors blasted, spinning her, guiding her. The ion-drive was not loud, but the rockets roared on the hull like hammers.

And down. And down.

Only afterward, reconstructing confused memories, did Maclaren know what had happened; and he was never altogether sure. The *Cross* backed onto an iron plain. Her tripod touched, on one foot, on two. The surface was not quite level. She began to topple. Nakamura lifted her with a skill that blended main drive and auxiliaries into one smooth surge—such skill as only an utterly relaxed man could achieve, responding to the immense shifting forces as a part thereof. He rose a few hundred meters, changed position relative to the ground, and tried again. The tripod struck on two points once more. The ship toppled again. The third leg went off a small bluff, no more than a congealed ripple in the iron. It hit ground hard enough to buckle.

Nakamura raised ship barely in time. For an instant he poised in the sky on a single leg of flame, keeping his balance with snorts of rocket thrust. The bottom of the *Cross's* stern assembly was not many meters above ground.

Suddenly he killed the ion drive. Even as the ship fell, he spun her clear around on the rotator jets. The *Cross* struck nose first. The pilot's turret smashed, the bow caved in, automatic bulkheads slammed shut to save the air that whistled out. That was a great mass, and it struck hard. The sphere was crushed flat for meters aft of the bow. With her drive and her unharmed transceiver web aimed at the sky, the ship rested like Columbus's egg.

And the stars glittered down upon her.

Afterward Maclaren wondered: Nakamura might well have decided days beforehand that he would probably never be able to land any other way. Or he might have considered that his rations would last two men an extra week. Or perhaps, simply, he found his dark bride.

The planet spun quickly about its axis, once in less than ten hours. There went never a day across its iron plains, but hunger and the stars counted time. There was no wind, no rain, no sea, but a man's radio hissed with the thin dry talk of the stars.

When he stood at the pit's edge and looked upward, Maclaren saw the sky sharp and black and of an absolute cold. It had a somehow three-dimensional effect; theory said all those crowding suns, blue-white or frosty gold or pale heatless red, were alike at optical infinity, but the mind sensed remoteness beyond remoteness, and whimpered. Nor was the ground underfoot a comfort, for it was almost as dark; starlit vision reached a few meters and was gulped down. A chopped-off Milky Way and a rising constellation (the one Maclaren had privately named Risus, the Sneer) told him that a horizon existed, but his animal instincts did not believe it.

He sighed, slapped a glare filter across his faceplate, and began cutting. The atomic hydrogen torch was lurid enough to look upon, but it jostled the stars out of his eyes. He cut rapidly, ten-kilo slabs which he kicked down into the pit so they wouldn't fuse tight again. The hole itself had originally been blasted, but the *Cross* didn't carry enough explosive for him to mine all his ore that way.

Ore, he reflected, was a joke. How would two men on foot prospect a sterilized world sealed into vacuum a hundred million years ago? And there would have been little point in it. This planet had boiled once, at least on the surface; and even the metallic core had been heated and churned, quite probably to melting, when crushed atoms expanded to normal dimensions. The entire globe must be nearly uniform, one alloy lump. You took any piece, crushed it, gasified it, ionized it, put it through the electromagnetic isotope separator, and drew forth as much (or, rather, as minutely little) germanium as any other piece would have given you. From the known rate of extraction by such methods you could calculate when you would have four kilograms. The date lay weeks away.

Maclaren finished cutting, shut off his torch and hung it on its generator, and climbed into the bucket of the crane at the pit's edge. His flashbeam threw puddles of light on its walls as he was lowered. At the bottom he moved painfully about, loaded the bucket, and rode back to the surface. A small electric truck waited, he spilled the bucket into its box. And then it was to do again, and still again, until he had a full load.

Thank God and her dead designers, the *Cross* was well equipped for work on airless surfaces, she carried machines to dig and build and transport. But, of course, she had to. It was her main purpose, to establish a new transceiver station on a new moon; everything else could then come straight from the Solar System.

It had been her purpose.

Before heaven, it still was.

Maclaren climbed wearily onto the truck seat. He and his spacesuit had a fourth again their Earthweight here. His headlights picked out a line of paint leading toward the ship. It had been necessary to blast the pit some distance away, for fear of what ground vibrations might do to the web or the isotope separator. But then a trail had to be blazed, for nature had given no landmarks for guide, this ground was as bare as a skull.

Existence was like lead in Maclaren's bones.

After a while he made out the *Cross*, a flattened sphere crowned with a skeleton and the Orion nebula. It was no fun having everything upside down within her; a whole day had gone merely to reinstall the essential items. *Well, Seiichi, you did what seemed best, and your broken body lies honored with Chang Sverdlov's, on the wide plains of iron.*

Floodlights glared under the ship. Ryerson was just finishing the previous load, reducing stone to pebbles and thence to dust. Good timing. Maclaren halted his truck and climbed down. Ryerson turned toward him. The undiffused glow reached through his faceplate and picked a sunken, bearded face out of night, little more than nose and cheekbone and bristling jaw. In his unhuman armor, beneath that cavernous sky, he might have been a troll. *Or I might*, thought Maclaren. *Humanity is far from us. We have stopped bathing, shaving, dressing, cooking...pretending; we work till our brains go blank, and then work some more, and crawl up the ladder into the ship for a few hours' uneasy sleep, and are awakened by the clock, and fool our shriveled bellies with a liter of tea, and put a lump of food in our mouths and go out. For our time has grown thin.*

"Hello, Nibelung," said Ryerson.

Maclaren started. "Are you getting to be a telepath?"

"It's possible," said Ryerson. His voice had become a harsh whisper. His glance searched darkness. "Anything is possible here."

"After we put this load through," said Maclaren, evading the other thought, "we'd better move the slag out of the ship. That ninety-nine-plus percent of material we don't use piles up fast."

"M-hm." Ryerson clumped heavily to the truck and began unloading. "And then out once more, cutting and loading and grinding and—merciful God, but I'm tired! Do you really imagine we can keep on doing heavy manual work like this, after the last food has been eaten?"

"We'll have to," said Maclaren. "And, of course, there is always—" He picked up a rock. Dizziness whirled through him. He dropped the stone and sank to his knees on the ground.

"Terangi!" Ryerson's voice seemed to come from some Delphic deep, through mists. "Terangi, what's wrong?"

"Nothing," mumbled Maclaren. He pushed at the other man's

groping arms. "Lea' me be...all right in a minute...." He relaxed against the stiffness of armor and let his weakness go through him in tides.

After a while, some strength returned. He looked up. Ryerson was just feeding the last rocks into the crusher. The machine ate them with a growl that Maclaren felt through the planet and his body. It vibrated his teeth together.

"I'm sorry, Dave," he said.

" 'S all right. You should go up and bunk for a while."

"Just a spell. Maybe we shouldn't have cut our rations as short as we have."

"You do seem to've been losing weight even faster than me," said Ryerson. "Maybe you ought to have an extra ration."

"Nah. It's metabolic inefficiency, brought on by well-spent years of wine, women, and off-key song."

Ryerson sat down beside him. "I'm a bit short of breath myself. Let's both take a break while the stuff goes through the crusher."

"Well," said Maclaren, "if your tailbone insulators can stand it, I suppose mine can."

They remained in silence for a while. The machine rumbled in their flesh and the stars muttered in their heads.

"How long do you think it will take to prepare the web?" asked Maclaren. "I mean, what's your latest estimate?"

"Hitherto I've underestimated the time for everything," said Ryerson. "Now, I just don't know. First we'll have to get our germanium. Then, to make the units...I don't know. Two weeks, three? And then, once all the circuits are functioning, they'll have to be tuned. Mostly by guesswork, since I don't really know the critical constants. That will take x time, depending on how lucky we are."

"We'll open the last can of food soon," said Maclaren. In itself it was a totally useless reminder, but it was leading up to something they had both avoided.

Ryerson continued to squirm: "They say tobacco helps kill appetite."

"It does," said Maclaren, "but I smoked the last butts months ago. Now I've even lost the addiction. Though of course I'll happily rebuild same the moment we strike Earth."

"When we come home…" Ryerson's voice drifted off like a murmur in sleep. "We haven't talked about our plans for a long time."

"It got to be too predictable, what every man would say."

"Yes. But is it now? I mean, do you still want to take that sailboat cruise around Earth, with…er…a female crew and a cargo of champagne?"

"I don't know," said Maclaren, faintly surprised to realize it. "I hadn't thought…. Do you remember once in space, we talked about our respective sailing experiences, and you told me the sea is the most inhuman thing on our planet?"

"Mm-m-m—yes. Of course, my sea was the North Atlantic. You might have had different impressions."

"I did. Still, Dave, it has stuck in my mind, and I see now you are right. Any ocean is, is too—big, old, blind for us—too beautiful." He sought the billion suns of the Milky Way. "Even this black ocean we're wrecked in."

"That's odd," said Ryerson. "I thought it was your influence making me think more and more of the sea as a—not a friend, I suppose. But hope and life and, oh, I don't know. I only know I'd like to take that cruise with you."

"By all means," said Maclaren. "I didn't mean I'd become afraid of the water, just that I've looked a little deeper into it. Maybe into everything. Hard to tell, but I've had a feeling now and then, out here, of what Seiichi used to call insight."

"One does learn something in space," agreed Ryerson. "I began to, myself, once I'd decided that God hadn't cast me out here and God wasn't going to bring me back, it wasn't His part—Oh, about that cruise. I'd want to take my wife, but she'd understand about your, uh, companions."

"Surely," said Maclaren. "I'd expect that. You've told me so much about her, I feel like a family friend." *I feel as if I loved her.*

"Come around and be avuncular when we've settled—Damn, I forgot the quarantine. Well, come see our home on Rama in thirty years!"

Maclaren: *No, no, I am being foolish. The sky has crushed me back toward child. Because she has gallant eyes and hair like a dark flower it does not mean she is the one possible woman to fulfill that need I have tried for most of my life to drown out. It is only that she is the first woman since my mother's death whom I realize is a human being.*

*And for that, Tamara, I have been slipping three-fourths of my ration back into the common share, so your man may innocently take half of that for his. It is little enough I can do, to repay what you who I never saw gave to me.*

"Terangi! You're all right, aren't you?"

"Oh. Oh, yes, of course." Maclaren blinked at the other armored shape, shadowy beside him. "Sorry, old chap. My mind wandered off on some or other daisy-plucking expedition."

"It's an odd thing," said Ryerson. "I find myself thinking more and more frivolously. As this cruise of yours, for instance. I really mean to join you, if you're still willing, and we'll take that champagne along and stop at every sunny island and loaf about and have a hell of a good time. I wouldn't have expected this...what has happened...to change me in that direction. Would you?"

"Why, no," said Maclaren. "Uh, I thought actually you—"

"I know. Because God seemed to be scourging me, I believed the whole creation must lie under His wrath. And yet, well, I have been on the other side of Doomsday. Here, in nightmare land. And somehow, oh, I don't know, but the same God who kindled that nova saw equally fit to...to make wine for the wedding at Cana."

Maclaren wondered if the boy would regret so much self-revelation later. Perhaps not if it had been mutual. So he answered with care, "Oddly enough, or maybe not so oddly, my thinking has drifted in the other direction. I could never see any real reason to stay alive, except that it was more fun than being dead. Now I couldn't begin to list all the reasons. To raise kids into the world, and learn something about the universe, and not compromise with some crowned bastard's version of justice, and...I'm afraid I'm not a convert or anything. I still see the same blind cosmos governed by the same blind laws. But suddenly it matters. It matters terribly, and means something. What, I haven't figured out yet. I probably never will. But I have a reason for living, or for dying if need be. Maybe that's the whole purpose of life: purpose itself. I can't say. But I expect to enjoy the world a lot more."

Ryerson said in a thoughtful tone: "I believe we've learned to take life seriously. Both of us."

The grinder chuted its last dust into the receptacle. The gasifier was inboard; and the cold, not far from absolute zero, was penetrating the suit insulators. Ryerson got up. Shadows lapped his feet. "Of course," he said, his voice suddenly cracked, "that doesn't help us a great deal if we starve to death out here."

Maclaren rose with him. The floodlamps ridged both their faces against the huge hollow dark. Maclaren caught Ryerson's eyes with his own. For a moment they struggled, not moving under the constellations, but sweat sprang out upon Ryerson's forehead.

"You realize," said Maclaren, "that we actually can eat for quite a while longer. I'd say, at a guess, two more months."

"No," whispered Ryerson. "No, I won't."

"You will," Maclaren told him.

He stood there another minute, to make certain of his victory, which he meant as a gift to Tamara. Then he turned on his heel and walked over to the machine. "Come on," he said, "let's get to work."

# 16

Maclaren woke up of himself. For a moment he did not remember where he was. He had been in some place of trees, where water flashed bright beneath a hill. Someone had been with him, but her name and face would not come back. There was a lingering warmth on his lips.

He blinked at the table fastened to the ceiling. He was lying on a mattress—

Yes. The *Southern Cross*, a chilly knowledge. But why had he wakened early? Sleep was the last hiding place left to him and Dave. They stood watch and watch at the web controls, and came back to their upside-down bunkroom and ate sleep. Life had shrunken to that.

Maclaren yawned and rolled over. The alarm clock caught his eye. Had the stupid thing stopped? He looked at the second hand for a while, decided that it was indeed moving. But then he had slept for— holy shark-toothed sea gods—for thirteen hours!

He sat up with a gasp. Bloodlessness went through his head. He clung to his blankets and waited for strength to come back. How long a time had it been, while his tissues consumed themselves for lack of

THE ENEMY STARS

all other nourishment? He had stopped counting hours. But the ribs and joints stuck out on him so he sometimes listened for a rattle when he walked. Had it been a month? At least it was a time spent inboard, with little physical exertion; that fact alone had kept him alive.

Slowly, like a sick creature, he climbed to his feet. If Dave hadn't called him, Dave might have passed out, or died, or proven to have been only a starving man's whim. *With a host of furious fancies*— Maclaren shambled across to the shaftway. The transceiver rooms were aft of the gyros, they had been meant to be "down" with respect to the observation deck whenever there was acceleration and now they were up above. Fortunately, the ship had been designed in the knowledge she would be in free fall most of her life. Maclaren gripped a rung with both hands. *I could use a little free fall right now,* he reflected through the dizziness. He put one foot on the next rung, used that leg and both hands to pull the next foot up beside it; now, repeat; once more; one for Father and one for Mother and one for Nurse and one for the cat and so it goes until here we are, shaking with exhaustion.

Ryerson sat at the control panel outside the receiving and transmitting chambers. It had been necessary to spotweld a chair, with attached ladder, to the wall and, of course, learn how to operate an upside-down control panel. The face that turned toward Maclaren was bleached and hairy and caved-in; but the voice seemed almost cheerful: "So you're awake."

"The alarm didn't call me," said Maclaren. He panted for air. "Why didn't you come rouse me?"

"Because I turned off the alarm in the first place."

"What?" Maclaren sat down on what had been the ceiling and stared upward.

"You'll fall apart if you don't get more rest," said Ryerson. "You've been in worse shape than me for weeks, even before the…the food gave out. I can sit here and twiddle knobs without having to break off every eight hours."

"Well, maybe." Maclaren felt too tired to argue.

"Any luck?" he asked after a while.

"Not yet. I'm trying a new sequence now. Don't worry, we're bound to hit resonance soon."

Maclaren considered the problem for a while. Lately his mind seemed to have lost as much ability to hold things as his fingers. Painfully, he reconstructed the theory and practice of gravitic mattercasting. Everything followed with simple logic from the fact that it was possible at all.

The signals necessarily used a pulse code, with amplitude and duration as the variables; there were tricky ways to include a little more information through the number of pulses per millisecond, if you set an upper limit to the duration of each. It all took place so rapidly that engineers could speak in wave terms without too gross an approximation. Each transceiver identified itself by a "carrier" pattern, of which the actual mattercasting signal was a modulation. The process only took place if contact had been established; that is, if the transmitter was emitting the carrier pattern of a functioning receiver: the "resonance" or "awareness" effect which beat the inverse-square law, a development of Einstein's great truth that the entire cosmos is shaped by what momentarily happens to each of its material parts.

The 'caster itself, by the very act of scanning, generated the signals which recreated the object transmitted. But first the 'caster must be tuned in on the desired receiving station. The manual aboard ship gave the call pattern of every established transceiver: but, naturally, gave it in terms of the standardized and tested web originally built into the ship. Thus, to reach Sol, the book said, blend its pattern with that of Rashid's Star, the initial relay station in this particular case. Your signal will be automatically bucked on, through several worlds, till it reaches Earth's Moon. Here are the respective voltages, oscillator frequencies, etc., involved; add them up and use the resultant.

Ryerson's handmade web was not standardized. He could put a known pattern into it, electronically, but the gravities would emit an unknown one, the call signal of a station not to be built for the next thousand years. He lacked instruments to measure the relationship, so he could not recalculate the appropriate settings. It was cut and try, with a literal infinity of choices and only a few jackleg estimates to rule out some of the possibilities.

Maclaren sighed. A long time had passed while he sat thinking. Or so his watch claimed. He hadn't noticed it go by, himself.

THE ENEMY STARS

"You know something, Dave?" he said.

"Hm?" Ryerson turned a knob, slid a vernier one notch, and punched along a row of buttons.

"We are out on the far edge of no place. I forget how far to the nearest station, but a devil of a long ways. This haywire rig of ours may not have the power to reach it."

"I knew that all the time," said Ryerson. He slapped the main switch. Needles wavered on dials, oscilloscope tracings glowed elfhill green, it whined in the air. "I think our apparatus is husky enough, though. Remember, this ship has left Sol farther behind than any other ever did. They knew she would—a straight-line course would just naturally outrun the three-dimensional expansion of our territory—so they built the transceiver with capacity to spare. Even in its present battered state, it might reach Sol directly, if conditions were just right."

"Think we will? That would be fun."

Ryerson shrugged. "I doubt it, frankly. Just on a statistical basis. There are so many other stations by now—*Hey!*"

Maclaren found himself on his feet, shaking. "What is it?" he got out. "What is it? For the love of heaven, Dave, what is it?"

Ryerson's mouth opened and closed, but no sounds emerged. He pointed with one bony arm. It shook.

Below him (it was meant to be above, like a star) a light glowed red.

"Contact," said Maclaren.

The word echoed through his skull as if spoken by a creator, across a universe still black and empty.

Ryerson began to weep, silently, his lips working. "Tamara," he said. "Tamara, I'm coming home."

Maclaren thought: *If Chang and Seiichi had been by me now, what a high and proud moment.*

"Go on, Terangi," chattered Ryerson. His hands shook so he could not touch the controls. "Go on through."

Maclaren did not really understand it. Not yet. It was too swift a breaking. But the wariness of a race which had evolved among snakes and war spoke for him:

"Wait, Dave. Wait a minute. Just to be certain. Put a signal through.

A teletype, I mean; we've no voice microphone, have we? You can do it right at that keyboard."

"What for?" screamed Ryerson. "What for? If you won't go through, I will!"

"Just wait, is all." Suddenly Maclaren was begging. All the craziness of months between stars that burned his eyes woke up; he felt in a dim way that man must live under conditions and walk in awe, but this is one of the prides in being a man. He raised powerless hands and cried—it was not much above a whisper—"There could be some distortion, you know. Accidents do happen, once in a great while, and this web was made by hand, half of it from memory....Send a message. Ask for a test transmission back to us. It won't take long and...My God, Dave, what kind of thing could you send home to Tamara if the signal was wrong?"

Ryerson's chin quivered in its beard, but he punched the typer keys with hard angry strokes. Maclaren sat back down, breathing quickly and shallowly. So it was to become real after all. So he would again walk beneath the tall summer clouds of Earth.

*No,* he thought. *I never will. Terangi Maclaren died in an orbit around the black sun, and on the steel planet where it is always winter. The I that am may go home, but never the I that was.*

Ryerson bent over so he could look into the screen which gave him an image of the receiving chamber.

Maclaren waited. A long while passed.

"Nothing," said Ryerson. "They haven't sent a thing."

Maclaren could still not talk.

"A colonial station, of course," said Ryerson. "Probably one of the outpost jobs with two men for a staff...or, Lord, another spaceship. Yes, that's likeliest, we're in touch with an interstellar. Only one man on watch and—"

"And there should be a bell to call him, shouldn't there?" asked Maclaren, very slowly.

"You know how they get on the long haul," said Ryerson. He smote his chair arm with a fist that was all knobs. "The man is sleeping too hard to hear a thing. Or—"

"Wait," said Maclaren. "We've waited long enough. We can afford a few more minutes, to make certain."

Ryerson blazed at him, as if he were an enemy "Wait? Wait, by jumping hell! No!"

He set the control timer for transmission in five minutes and crept from his seat and down the ladder. Under the soiled tunic, he seemed all spidery arms and legs, and one yellow shock of hair.

Maclaren stood up again and stumbled toward him. "No," he croaked. "Listen, I realize how you feel, but I realize it's space lunacy too, and I forbid you, I forbid—"

Ryerson smiled. "How do you propose to stop me?" he asked.

"I—but can't you wait, wait and see and—"

"Look here," said Ryerson, "let's assume there is a freak in the signal. A test transmission comes through. At best, the standard object is merely distorted...at worst, it won't be recreated at all, and we'll get an explosion. The second case will destroy us. In the first case, we haven't time to do much more work. I doubt if I could climb around on the web outside any more. I know damn well you couldn't, my friend! We've no choice but to go through. Now!"

"If it's a ship at the other end, and you cause an explosion," whispered Maclaren, "you've murdered one more man."

Drearily, and as if from far away, he recognized the hardness which congealed the other face. Hope had made David Ryerson young again. "It won't blow up," said the boy, and was wholly unable to imagine such a happening.

"Well...probably not...but there's still the chance of molecular distortion or—" Maclaren sighed. Almost experimentally, he pushed at Ryerson's chest. Nothing happened; he was so much more starved that he could not move the lank body before him.

"All right," said Maclaren. "You win. I'll go through."

Ryerson shook his head. "No, you don't," he answered. "I changed my mind." With a lilt of laughter: "I stand behind my own work, Terangi!"

"No, wait! Let me—I mean—think of your wife, at least—please—"

"I'll see you there," cried Ryerson. The blue glance which he threw over his shoulder was warm. He opened the transmitter room door, went through, it clashed shut upon him. Maclaren wrestled weakly with the knob. No use, it had an automatic lock.

Which of us is the fool? I will never be certain, whatever may come of this. The chances are all for him, of course…in human terms, reckoned from what we know…but could he not learn with me how big this universe is, and how full of darkness?

Maclaren stumbled back toward the ladder to the chair. He would gain wrath, but a few more minutes, by climbing up and turning off the controls. And in those minutes, the strangely, terrifyingly negligent operator at the other end might read the teletype message and send a test object. And then Ryerson would know. Both of them would know. Maclaren put his feet on the rungs. He had only two meters to climb. But his hands would not lift him. His legs began to shake. He was halfway to the panel when its main switch clicked down and the transmitting engine skirled.

He crept on up. *Now I know what it means to be old,* he thought.

His heart fluttered feebly and wildly as he got into the chair. For a while he could not see the vision screens, through the night that spumed in his head. Then his universe steadied a little. The transmitter room was quite empty. The red light still showed contact. So at least there had been no destruction wrought in the receiving place. Except maybe on Dave; it didn't take much molecular warping to kill a man. *But I am being timid in my weakness. I should not be afraid to die. Least of all to die. So let me also go on through and be done.*

He reached for the timer. His watch caught his eye. Half an hour since Dave left? Already? Had it taken half an hour for him to creep this far and think a few sentences? But surely Dave would have roused even the sleepiest operator. They should have sent a teletype to the *Cross:* "Come on, Terangi. Come on home with me." What was wrong?

Maclaren stared at the blank walls enclosing him. Here he could not see the stars, but he knew how they crowded the outside sky, and he had begun to understand, really understand what an illusion that was and how hideously lonely each of those suns dwelt.

*One thing more I have learned, in this last moment,* he thought. *I know what it is to need mercy.*

Decision came. He set the timer for ten minutes—his progress to the transmitter room would be very slow—and started down the ladder.

A bell buzzed.

His heart sprang. He crawled back, feeling dimly that there were tears on his own face now, and stared into the screen.

A being stood in the receiving chamber. It wore some kind of armor, so he could not make out the shape very well, but though it stood on two legs the shape was not a man's. Through a transparent bubble of a helmet, where the air within bore a yellowish tinge, Maclaren saw its face. Not fish or frog or mammal, it was so other a face that his mind would not wholly register it. Afterward he recalled only blurred features, there were tendrils and great red eyes.

Strangely, beyond reason, even in that first look he read compassion on the face.

The creature bore David Ryerson's body in its arms.

# 17

Where Sunda Straits lay beneath rain (but sunlight came through to walk upon the water) the land fell steep. It was altogether green, in a million subtle hues, jungle and plantation and rice paddy, it burned with green leaves. White mists wreathed the peak of a volcano, and was it thunder across wind or did the mountain talk in sleep?

Terangi Maclaren set his aircar down on brown-and-silver water and taxied toward the Sumatra shore. Each day he regained flesh and strength, but the effort of dodging praus and pontoon houses and submarines still tired him. When his guide pointed: "There, *tuan*," he cut the engines and glided in with a sigh.

"Are you certain?" he asked, for there were many such huts of thatch and salvaged plastic along this coast. It was a wet world here, crowding brown folk who spent half their cheerful existences in the water, divers, deckhands, contracting their labor to the sea ranches but always returning home, poverty, illiteracy, and somehow more life and hope than the Citadel bore.

"Yes, *tuan*. Everyone knows of her. She is not like the rest, and she holds herself apart. It marks her out."

Maclaren decided the Malay was probably right. Tamara Suwito Ryerson could not have vanished completely into the anonymous proletariat of Earth. If she still planned to emigrate, she must at least leave a mailing address with the Authority. Maclaren had come to Indonesia quickly enough, but there his search widened, for a hundred people used the same P.O. in New Djakarta and their homes lay outside the cosmos of house numbers and phone directories. He had needed time and money to find this dwelling.

He drove up onto the shore. "Stay here," he ordered his guide, and stepped out. The quick tropic rain poured over his tunic and his skin. It was the first rain he had felt since...how long? It tasted of morning.

She came to the door and waited for him. He would have known her from the pictures, but not the grace with which she carried herself. She wore a plain sarong and blouse. The rain filled her crow's-wing hair with small drops and the light struck them and shattered.

"You are Technic Maclaren," she said. He could scarcely hear her voice, so low did it fall, but her eyes were steady on his. "Welcome."

"You have seen me on some newscast?" he inquired, banally, for lack of anything else.

"No. I have only heard. Old Prabang down in the village has a nonvisual set. But who else could you be? Please come in, sir."

Only later did he realize how she broke propriety. But then, she had declared herself free of Protectorate ways months ago. He found that out when he first tried to contact her at her father-in-law's. The hut, within, was clean, austerely furnished, but a vase of early mutation-roses stood by David's picture.

Maclaren went over to the cradle and looked down at the sleeping infant. "A son, isn't it?" he asked.

"Yes. He has his father's name."

Maclaren brushed the baby's cheek. He had never felt anything so soft. "Hello, Dave," he said.

Tamara squatted at a tiny brazier and blew up its glow. Maclaren sat down on the floor.

"I would have come sooner," he said, "but there was so much else, and they kept me in the hospital—"

"I understand. You are very kind."

"I...have his effects...just a few things. And I will arrange the funeral in any way you desire and—" His voice trailed off. The rain laughed on the thatch.

She dipped water from a jar into a teakettle. "I gather, then," she said, "there was no letter that he wrote?"

"No. Somehow...I don't know. For some reason none of us wrote any such thing. Either we would all perish out there, and no one else would come for fifty or a hundred years, or we would get back. We never thought it might be like this, a single man." Maclaren sighed. "It's no use trying to foresee the future. It's too big."

She didn't answer him with her voice.

"But almost the last thing Dave said," he finished awkwardly, "was your name. He went in there thinking he would soon be home with you." Maclaren stared down at his knees. "He must have—have died quickly. Very quickly."

"I have not really understood what happened," she said, kneeling in the graceful Australian style to set out cups. Her tone was flattened by the effort of self-control. "I mean, the 'cast reports are always so superficial and confused, and the printed journals so technical. There isn't any middle ground any more. That was one reason we were going to leave Earth, you know. Why I still am going to, when our baby has grown just a little bit."

"I know how you feel," said Maclaren. "I feel that way myself."

She glanced up with a startled flirt of her head that was beautiful to see. "But you are a technic!" she exclaimed.

"I'm a human being too, my lady. But go on, ask me your question, whatever you were leading up to. I've a favor of my own to ask, but you first."

"No, what do you want? Please."

"Nothing very important. I've no claim on you, except the fact that your husband was my friend. I'm thinking of what you might do for his sake. But it will wait. What did you wonder about?"

"Oh. Yes. I know you tuned in the aliens' transceiver and didn't realize it. But—" Her fists clenched together. She stared through the open door, into the rain and the light, and cried forth: "It was such a tiny chance! Such a meaningless accident that killed him!"

Maclaren paused until he had all his words chosen. Then he said, as gently as might be: "It wasn't so wildly improbable. All this time we've known that we couldn't be the only race reaching for the stars. It was absurd to think so; that would have been the senseless unlikelihood. Well, the *Cross* was farther out than men had ever gone before, and the alien spaceship was near the aliens' own limit of expansion. It was also bound for Alpha Crucis. Odd what a sense of kinship that gives me, my brother mariner, with chlorine in his lungs and silicon in his bones, steering by the same lodestar. Contact was certain eventually, as they and we came into range of each other's signals. Your David was the man who first closed the ring. We were trying to call patterns we could not measure, running through combinations of variables. Statistically, we were as likely to strike one of their patterns as one of ours."

The water began to boil. She busied herself with the kettle. The long tresses falling past her face hid whether she was crying or not. Maclaren added for her, "Do you know, my lady, I think we must have called hundreds of other space-traveling races. We were out of their range, of course, but I'm sure we called them."

Her voice was muffled: "What did the aliens think of it?"

"I don't know. In ten years we may begin to talk to them. In a hundred years, perhaps we will understand them. And they us, I hope. Of course, the moment David...appeared...they realized what had happened. One of them came through to me. Can you imagine what courage that must have taken? How fine a people your man has given us to know? There was little they could do for me, except test the *Cross*'s web and rule out all the call patterns which they use. I kept on trying, after that. In a week I finally raised a human. I went through to his receiver and that's all. Our technicians are now building a new relay station on the black star planet. But they'll leave the *Cross* as she is, and David Ryerson's name will be on her."

"I thought," she whispered, still hiding her face, "that you...I mean, the quarantine rules—"

"Oh, yes, the Protectorate tried to invoke them. Anything to delay what is going to happen. But it was useless. Nothing from the aliens' planet could possibly feed on Terrestrial life. That's been established

POUL ANDERSON

557

already, by the joint scientific commission; we may not be able to get the idea behind each other's languages yet, but we can measure the same realities! And of course, the aliens know about us. Man just can't hide from the universe. So I was released." Maclaren accepted the cup she offered him and added wryly: "To be sure, I'm not exactly welcome at the Citadel any more."

She raised large eyes to him. He saw how they glimmered. "Why not?" she asked. "You must be a hero to—"

"To spacemen, scientists, some colonials, and a few Earthmen glad of an end to stagnation. Not that I deserve their gratitude. There are three dead men who really did all this. But at any rate, my lady, you can foresee what an upheaval is coming. We are suddenly confronted with—Well, see here, the aliens must be spread through at least as large a volume of space as man. And the two races don't use the same kind of planets. By pooling transceiver networks, we've doubled both our territories! No government can impose its will on as many worlds as that.

"But more. There are sciences, technologies, philosophies, religions, arts, insights they have which we never imagined. It cannot be otherwise. And we can offer them ours, of course. How long do you think this narrow little Protectorate and its narrow little minds can survive such an explosion of new thought?" Maclaren leaned forward. He felt it as an upsurge in himself. "My lady, if you want to live on a frontier world, and give your child a place where it's hard and dangerous and challenging—and everything will be possible for him, if he's big enough—stay on Earth. The next civilization will begin here on Earth herself."

Tamara set down her cup. She bent her face into her hands and he saw, helpless, how she wept. "It may be," she said to him, "it may be, I don't know. But why did it have to be David who bought us free? Why did it have to be him? He didn't mean to. He wouldn't have, if he'd known. I'm not a sentimental fool, Maclaren-san, I know he only wanted to come back here. And he died! There's no meaning in it!"

# 18

The North Atlantic rolled in from the west, gray and green and full of thunder. A wind blew white manes up on the waves. Low to the south gleamed the last autumnal daylight, and clouds massed iron-colored in the north, brewing sleet.

"There," pointed Tamara. "That is the place."

Maclaren slanted his aircar earthward. The sky whistled around him. So Dave had come from here. The island was a grim enough rock, harshly ridged. But Dave had spoken of gorse in summer and heather in fall and lichen of many hues.

The girl caught Maclaren's arm. "I'm afraid, Terangi," she whispered. "I wish you hadn't made me come."

"It's all we can do for David," he told her. "The last thing we'll ever be able to do for him."

"No." In the twilight, he saw how her head lifted. "There's never an end. Not really. His child and mine, waiting, and—at least *we* can put a little sense into life."

"I don't know whether we do or whether we find what was always there," he replied. "Nor do I care greatly. To me, the important thing is that the purpose—order, beauty, spirit, whatever you want to call it—does exist."

"Here on Earth, yes," she sighed. "A flower or a baby. But then three men die beyond the sun, and it so happens the race benefits a little from it, but I keep thinking about all those people who simply die out there. Or come back blind, crippled, broken like dry sticks, with no living soul the better for it. Why? I've asked it and asked it, and there isn't ever an answer, and finally I think that's because there isn't any why to it in the first place."

Maclaren set the car down on the beach. He was still on the same search, along a different road. He had not come here simply to offer David's father whatever he could: reconciliation, at least, and a chance to see David's child now and then in the years left him. Maclaren had some obscure feeling that an enlightenment might be found on Skula.

Truly enough, he thought, men went to space, as they had gone to sea, and space destroyed them, and still their sons came back. The lure of gain was only a partial answer; spacemen didn't get any richer than sailors had. Love of adventure...well, in part, in some men, and yet by and large the conquerors of distance had never been romantics, they were workaday folk who lived and died among sober realities. When you asked a man what took him out to the black star, he would say he had gone under orders, or that he was getting paid, or that he was curious about it, or any of a hundred reasons. Which might all be true. And yet was any of them the truth?

And why, Maclaren wondered, did man, the race, spend youth and blood and treasure and all high hopes upon the sea and the stars? Was it only the outcome of meaningless forces—economics, social pressure, maladjustment, myth, whatever you labeled it—a set of chance-created vectors with the sardonic resultant that man broke himself trying to satisfy needs which could have been more easily and sanely filled at home?

*If I could get a better answer than that,* thought Maclaren, *I could give it to Tamara. And to myself. And then we could bury our dead.*

He helped her out of the car and they walked up a path toward the ancient-looking cottage. Light spilled from its windows into a dusk heavy with surf. But they had not quite reached it when the door opened and a man's big form was outlined.

"Is that you, Technic Maclaren?" he called.

"Yes. Captain Magnus Ryerson?" Maclaren stepped ahead of Tamara and bowed. "I took the liberty, sir, of bringing a guest with me whom I did not mention when I called."

"I can guess," said the tall man. "It's all right, lass. Come in and welcome."

As she passed over the uneven floor to a chair, Tamara brushed Maclaren and took the opportunity to whisper: "How old he's grown, all at once!"

Magnus Ryerson shut the door again. His hands, ropy with veins, shook a little. He leaned heavily on a cane as he crossed the room and poked up the fire. "Be seated," he said to Maclaren. "When I knew you were coming, I ordered some whisky from the mainland. I hope it's a good make. I drink not, you see, but be free to do so yourself."

Maclaren looked at the bottle. He didn't recognize the brand. "Thank you," he said, "that's a special favorite of mine."

"You've eaten?" asked the old man anxiously.

"Yes, thank you, sir." Maclaren accepted a glass. Ryerson limped over the floor to give Tamara one.

"Can you stay the night? I've some extra beds in the garret, from when the fisher lads would come by. They come no more, there's no reason for it now, but I've kept the beds."

Maclaren traded a look with Tamara. "We would be honored," he said.

Magnus Ryerson shuffled to the hob, took the teakettle, poured himself a cup and raised it. "Your health." He sat down in a worn chair by the fire. His hands touched a leather-bound book lying on its arm.

There was silence for a while, except that they could all hear the waves boom down on the strand.

Maclaren said finally: "I…we, I mean…we came to—to offer our sympathy. And if there was anything I could tell you…I was there, you know."

"Aye. You're kind." Ryerson groped after a pipe. "It is my understanding he conducted himself well."

"Yes. Of course he did."

"Then that's what matters. I'll think of a few questions later, if you give me time. But that was the only important one."

Maclaren looked around the room. Through its shadows he saw pilot's manuals on the shelves, stones and skins and gods brought from beyond the sky; he saw the Sirian binary like twin hells upon darkness, but they were very beautiful. He offered: "Your son was in your own tradition."

"Better, I hope," said the old man. "There would be little sense to existence, did boys have no chance to be more than their fathers."

Tamara stood up. "But that's what there isn't!" she cried all at once. "There's no sense! There's just dying and dying and dying—what for?—so that we can walk on still another planet, learn still another fact—what have we gained? What have we really done? And why? In your own God's name, what did we do once that He sends our men out there now?"

She clamped her hands together. They heard how the breath rasped in her. She said at last, "I'm sorry," and sat back down. Her fingers twisted blind until Maclaren took them.

Magnus Ryerson looked up. And his eyes were not old. He let the surf snarl on the rocks of his home for a while. And then he answered her: "'*For that is our doom and our pride.*'"

"What?" She started. "Oh. In English. Terangi, he means—" She said it in Interhuman.

Maclaren sat quite still.

Ryerson opened his book. "They have forgotten Kipling now," he said. "One day they will remember. For no people live long, who offer their young men naught but fatness and security. Tamara, lass, let your son hear this one day. It is his song too, he is human."

The words were unknown to Maclaren, but he listened and thought that in some dark way he understood.

"We have fed our sea for a thousand years
And she calls us, still unfed,
Though there's never a wave of all her waves
But marks our English dead:

We have strewed our best to the weed's unrest,
To the shark and the sheering gull.
If blood be the price of admiralty,
Lord God, we ha' paid in full!'"

When Ryerson had finished, Maclaren stood up, folded his hands and bowed. *"Sensei,"* he said, "give me your blessing."

"What?" The other man leaned back into shadows, and now he was again entirely old. You could scarcely hear him under the waves outside. "You've naught to thank me for, lad."

"No, you gave me much," said Maclaren. "You have told me why men go, and it isn't for nothing. It is because they are men."

## THE END

# ABOUT THE AUTHORS

## A. E. VAN VOGT

has been described as "the wellspring of wonder" by Harlan Ellison. Born in Canada in 1912, he settled in Los Angeles during the Forties. At the height of his career, in the Forties and Fifties, he was justly regarded, along with Isaac Asimov and Robert A. Heinlein, as one of the most important writers of science fiction, and soon won himself a permanent place in science fiction's pantheon. His novels, among them such classics as *The Weapon Shops of Isher* and *Slan*, were among the first science fiction to be published in hardcover by major publishers. He now lives in California with his wife, Lydia Brayman van Vogt. In 1996, he was honored with a Grand Master Nebula Award for a lifetime of achievement in science fiction.

## BARRY N. MALZBERG

was born in New York City in 1939 and was educated at Syracuse University, where he was a Schubert Fellowship Foundation Playwriting Fellow in 1964; he was awarded, but declined, the Cornelia Ward Graduate Creative Writing Fellowship in 1965. He worked for the New York City Department of Welfare and the New York City Department of Mental Hygiene before becoming a free-lance writer in 1968. An "unaccomplished" violinist with an extensive knowledge of music, he now lives in Teaneck, New Jersey with his wife, the former Joyce Zelnick. He is one of science fiction's most prolific, literate, and controversial writers; his honors include the John W. Campbell Award and the Locus Award.

## POUL ANDERSON

is one of science fiction's most popular authors, whose "enduring explosion" of works has continued without pause since 1947. He was born in Pennsylvania in 1926 and earned a degree in physics from the University of Minnesota. A multiple Hugo and Nebula Award-winning author, and the recipient of the Tolkien Memorial Award, Anderson has produced a body of work that is unequalled for its variety and quality, and which includes countless works of short fiction and over seventy novels. He is married to poet and writer Karen Anderson; they have one daughter and two "incomparable" grandchildren.

# ABOUT THE EDITORS

## JACK DANN

is the author of the highly praised novels *Starhiker, Junction, The Man Who Melted,* and *The Memory Cathedral.* He has won the Nebula Award and is the editor of *Nebula Award Short Stories 32.* His short fiction includes many Nebula Award finalists; he has also been a finalist for the World Fantasy Award. He is the editor or coeditor of over thirty-five anthologies, among them the critically acclaimed *Wandering Stars,* a collection of Jewish science fiction and fantasy, and *In the Field of Fire,* a collection of fantasy fiction about the Vietnam war that was hailed by the *New York Times Book Review.*

## PAMELA SARGENT

is the editor of several anthologies, among them the *Women of Wonder* series, *Afterlives* (edited with Ian Watson), *Bio-Futures,* and three volumes of *Nebula Award Stories.* She has won a Nebula Award, a Locus Award, and been a finalist for the Hugo Award; her *Women of Wonder* series was shortlisted for the Retrospective James Tiptree, Jr. Award. Her novels include *Cloned Lives, Watchstar, The Golden Space, Earthseed, The Alien Upstairs, Venus of Dreams, The Shore of Women, Venus of Shadows,* and a historical novel about Genghis Khan, *Ruler of the Sky.*

## GEORGE ZEBROWSKI

is the author of *Macrolife, The Omega Point Trilogy,* and *Stranger Suns,* which was a New York Times Notable Book of the Year for 1991; his book *The Sunspacers Trilogy* was published by White Wolf. With scientist/author Charles Pellegrino, he is also the author of *The Killing Star.* He has also edited several anthologies, including *Faster Than Light* (with Jack Dann), the *Synergy* series of original anthologies, and *Skylife: Habitats In Space* (with Gregory Benford). His short stories have been nominated for the Nebula Award and the Theodore Sturgeon Memorial Award.